Crazy Tales
of Combat Psychiatry

A Paul Marzeky Mystery

Stefan J. Malecek, Ph. D

DEDICATION

This book is dedicated to my very good brother Topher Allan, who believed in a starving artist, and without whose support in North Beach in 1984, this book would have died abornin'.

And to my very good brother, Harold Dick, Jr., who, since 1994, has consistently believed in this book; and helped me gain a perspective on the gap between my beliefs in the value of myself and my experiences, and the actuality of them by someone who shared many of them, and far, far more.

I love you, brothers.

This book is further dedicated to every man and woman who served, in any capacity, in the green and living hell of Southeast Asia. Welcome Home!

AUTHOR'S NOTE

This is a work of fiction. Everyone who served in Vietnam has a story, and each of them is completely unique. I have not attempted to portray the "bigger picture." I have striven to keep the historical facts and references as accurate, and true-to-life as I could. As far as I have been able, this books represents "the way it was" through my eyes and memories. I most especially want to thank Harold Dick Jr. for his frequent reading of early drafts of this book, and feedback on a wide variety of topics. Any and all errors or mistakes are my responsibility.

ACKNOWLEDGEMENTS

No writer lives in a total vacuum, though he or she might wish it were so sometimes.

I have been deeply blessed to have true friends who have supported me in a variety of ways all along the sometimes-torturous journey of my path.

I have also been graced with the presence of superb literary and editorial assistance.

I salute you all, especially all of my brother and sister vets of all times. Only we know the true cost of war.

"All this new talk of brotherhood! Does no one remember
Cain and Abel? There are good brothers and evil brothers.
The man I call my brother is the one who guards my back."
Jean Le Malchanceux   (in the 12th Century)

We few, we happy few, we band of brothers,

For he today that sheds his blood with me

Shall be my brother. Be he ne'er so vile

This day shall gentle his condition

And gentlemen in England now abed

Shall think themselves accursed that they were not here

And hold their manhoods cheap while any speaks

That fought with us upon St. Crispin's Day.

William Shakespeare
Henry V

The reason that all stories about the Nam involve hyperbole is because it was so alien a universe that no one who was not there at that time will ever grasp the experience, the smell of it, the feel, the taste, the terror, the moral outrage, the pure out-of-this- universeness of it. It is simply beyond art, language, and translation. It is ineffable. It is incommunicable. In our desperation to tell our fellow humans about what happened in the republic, in order to communicate the truth of the emotional, psychological, factual, and spiritual impact, our stories must dwell on the most intense, the most bizarre, the most horrific—and in pursuit of the reality of it, we are forced to utilize the power of hyperbole, myth, fantasy, and the blackest of black, black humor.

The Nam (1994) Michael Andrews *In Country* Michael Andrews & David Widup Hermosa Beach CA: Bombshelter Press (p. 37)

CHAPTER 1

Wake Up Call

June 1966 St. Louis, Missouri

Paul's grin split his face in an arc that ached his face so strongly from ear-to-ear that he feared his face might fall off!

His draft notice had arrived! He was jubilant with the demand that he report for duty on September 6, 1966. He had long-imagined the savory taste of his desire to escape the concentration camp of his childhood, albeit one in which he had not been allowed to hate his captors. It was a fantasy that had long simmered in him like a rich pot of cassoulet.

His mother sobbed, pitifully punctuating his father's staccato ranting. Paul stood watching, skewered like a passive chunk of meat in the sandwich of their opinions, as if he didn't exist. He rejoiced in knowing that neither of them had the ability nor the personal power and willingness to keep the United States Government out of its hungry grasp.

He had long burned to go as far away as possible, hopefully another planet. That piece of paper was the key to a new adventure-filled life! He always felt surrounded by the razor-wire of his parents' draconian attitudes and expectations, unable to move in any direction without injuring himself, as if he were a brain-damaged genius child who had no event horizon for his own dreams and visions.

He knew he was extremely intelligent, but his deep and sometimes unfortunate empathy for the needs of others led him to circumstances far afield of his desires. In his isolation and loneliness, he sought conversations about obscure topics and philosophies. He believed that he carried the seeds of greatness buried in his chest, but sincerely believed that he had absolutely no way to liberate them, to make his life shine the ways that he wished, in the face of their trenchant resistance.

Fort Leonard Wood, Missouri
October 1966

"Hey Jell-O butt, fall out and give me twenty!"

He knew that the constant harassment was designed to mold him into an automaton without a brain or will, turn him into an intricate part of the fighting machine. So, he simply smiled into the faces of his tormentors, because he had a secret agenda of his own. He had decided to use what the Army considered "motivation" to get himself there faster. He did more PT, and ran extra miles to get in top shape. He was going to be a sex magnet for women! They weren't going to break him, no matter how many times they threatened to recycle him for another round of Basic Training.

He had dumped fifty-six pounds in eight weeks, and managed to graduate with his class. When he went to his parents' house for Christmas leave, he gained back twenty-one pounds! It seemed that he couldn't really stand being successful for very long!

––––––––––––––

Fort Riley Kansas
March 1967

From Fort "Lost in the Woods," he went to then to Fort Sam Houston, Texas for Combat Medic/Hospital Corpsman Training. He had purposely selected California, Japan, and Germany as choices as duty stations in order to be as far away from the Middle West as possible. The Department of the Army, in its infinitely dubious wisdom, sent him "as close to home as possible," and assigned him to Fort Riley, Kansas.

Paul was granted the opportunity to train on the job (OJT) to earn the title of Social Work/Clinical Psychology Specialist. He was told he would have to pass a series of interviews to finalize the job after ninety days. He absorbed a tremendous amount of new information from trainings and in-house seminars, but also read extensively of the works of Freud, Jung, and Adler; of Maxwell Maltz, Otto Rank, and Wilhelm Reich, among many others.

It felt really natural, as if he were renewing his acquaintance with an old profession.

He quickly assimilated the rudiments of interviewing and counseling, and built a caseload of individual clients—military and civilian dependents both. With the growth in skill, came an equivalent expansion of self-worth and personal valuing— his duty truly contributing to an emerging sense of actually having and owning his own place in the world.

In very short order he became a semi-professional master of paperwork, this being the key area in which he was expected to excel. Being the lowliest member of the team, he became skilled at doing the scut work required of any enlisted man working for officers. He was a flunky, though a necessary one for the grinding wheels of the Great Green Machine. He became such an outstanding functionary, and gradually acquired the rudiments of intermediate counseling skills, that, by the time he was in the Army only fourteen months, he earned him both a regular caseload and the Specialist rank equivalent to Sergeant.

In the pursuit of even greater efficiency, he and two of the other enlisted guys created a form with blanks to fill in, as so many of their referrals were for men being "eliminated for the good of the service," and they almost universally had similar backgrounds—disrupted childhoods, prior criminal records, dropped out of school early, and judicial difficulties both before and in the Army. To expedite their removal for conditions that "existed prior to service," they devised a form that saved them twenty minutes every time they interviewed such an individual. Since these vets were considered untreatable, the military was able to disown responsibility, including disallowing any future veterans' benefits.

Paul's own form of self-therapy revolved around smoking the dreaded marijuana with a bunch of guys from California who'd also been marooned in Kansas. It was as natural for them as alcohol was for the lifers. It definitely assuaged his growing ennui with ever-stultifying military life. Smoking the sacred herb unleashed his mind to develop new possibilities other than that of having to return to St. Louis untested, and being required to endure its molasses-like mentality and strait-jacketed structure, the equivalent of a slow suicide.

Interviewing returned Viet Nam vets eventually added the final straw to his plan to release himself from Ft. Riley. As the days and weeks dragged along same-same, he owned the fear that lay underneath those he could easily name. He believed that, if he failed to participate in "his generation's war," did not risk dying, it would be as if he had never lived at all. He was haunted by visions of the many legends like Julius Caesar, Stephen Crane, Walt Whitman, Ernest Hemmingway, T.E. Lawrence, E.E. Cummings, J.R.R. Tolkien, James Jones, Arthur C. Clarke, William Golding, Robert Heinlein, Norman Mailer, Kurt Vonnegut, and J.D. Salinger all of whom used their war time experiences directly or indirectly to become famous authors. The intensity of war and the raw stuff of life informed all their words. He burned to be a world-class novelist. Viet Nam was such an absolutely necessary key.

He'd repeatedly been denied a transfer because he had a critical Military Occupational Specialty (MOS). Finally, after his third try, after eleven months in Kansas, the clinic's Non-Commissioned Officer in Charge (NOIC) entered his office without knocking, and took the client's chair across from Paul's desk.

"What's up, Sarge?"

"I guess you're finally getting what you want. But personally, I think you just stepped in the shit!" he said, and handed Paul his orders for the 'Nam.

CHAPTER 2
Moving Along Smartly

March 1968
Saigon, Republic of Viet Nam

The instant he stepped off the Flying Tigers flight at Ton Son Nhut, via Anchorage, and Okinawa, was one of the single most disorienting moments of his life. Besides an atmosphere that reminded him more of breathing water, Paul was assaulted by a mind-blowing redolence of tangy, exotic foods cooking, fermenting fish, diesel fuel and jet exhaust, compounded by the ever-present smell of human waste, while beyond the massive artificial barbed-wire enclosure, the verdant jungle ruled supreme.

Within minutes of landing, Paul came to understand that he was having a profound peripeteia, though it would be decades yet before he defined this experience as a sudden realization that everything in which he had ever believed, everything he had been told, taught, invested in, was a total and unadulterated lie. It was as if his brain had been invaded by an alien virus that instantly began colonizing him. It was as if he had been walking along on a bright and sunny day, and was suddenly enveloped in a fog bank, or a rainsquall descending.

What convinced him of this was not something that would ever be recoded in newspapers or history books. What tumbled his sacred belief in the domino theory and all that the government had promoted around it, as he stood there gaping, goggle-eyed, was a disheveled street urchin who walked boldly up to him, and sold him his very first bag of Vietnamese buds he materialized from a scuffed shoeshine box.

This seemingly insignificant experience started a process of deconstruction, an instant shift in Paul's awareness that the multi-billion, trillion even, dollar effort being staged in Southeast Asia was a scam, a purposely produced spectacle designed to convince the American people that there existed a real threat of Communist domination; and that young men (and women) were dying here to promote the lie of global democracy—a massive disinformation campaign induced by manufacturing the consent of the populace—in spite of glaring evidence to the contrary such as the CIA-backed assassination that put the puppet Diem government in place. Paul felt as if he were a visitor from another planet who had assumed human form. This tiny shift, that he could very openly buy his favorite sacrament in one of the busiest government facilities on the planet, was the first crack that opened the proverbial floodgates of all that was to follow, of all that was to shape the entire rest of his life.

———————

The ultra-safety of the Support Command Compound in coastal Qui Nhon was at first edgy and frightening. He was, after all, in a combat zone!

Within the Army, Air Force, and Vietnamese Army compound, helicopter companies and all manner of support troops, including the 14th General Dispensary where he would be assigned Temporary DutY (TDY). Dotted around the compound were Korean marine Black Horse Brigade detachments who did night patrols every night returning with heads they put on stakes as a warning; elements of the Marine Corps; 173rd Airborne; 101st Airborne; 1st Cavalry Division, and of course, the ubiquitous Special Forces. There were even tank farms in close proximity. The Tactical Area of Operations (TAO) extended from An Khe, to Phu Cat, Bong Son, and all the way to the Cha Rang Valley.

MPs tracked the number of trucks in and out; how many mama-sans and papa-sans in and out to perform any and all the menial tasks the occupying force refused to do—primarily cleaning and laundry, though they staffed the clubs and the PX too—keeping the compound free of the acrid smells, sights and sounds that were in some ways the essence of our war of attrition, far from the televised gore of war people in The World were told was the war. We were surrounded by the ville itself, offering up the pungent smells of *nouc mam,* water buffalo dung, open cooking fires and the excrement of tens of thousands of unwashed bodies using the open trenches on both sides of the unpaved dusty roads as convenient bathrooms.

"Old timers" who had been combat wounded but not badly enough to be evacuated to The World, often found themselves completing their tours in backwaters like Qui Nhon as supply clerks and armorers.

They were often the most vociferous about the bureaucratic irrelevance of Army rules and regs. They looked different, walked and talked differently. They tended to stay to the corners of rooms and the edges of open spaces—and never sat with a back to a door or a room. They were reserved, even gaunt, and laughed less—and sought each other's company, Black or White, acknowledging their common bond without a word, as if a smell or invisible sign marked them. The rest of us only recognized the right shoulder patches of the First Cav, or Fourth or Ninth Infantry; or the CIB (Combat Infantry Badge) or CMB (Combat Medical Badge) sewn above the left fatigue jacket pockets. They called us "REMFs" (Rear Echelon Motherfuckers) and we envied them, yet were also far too grateful not to have earned their decorations. We were in Viet Nam, and that was enough. We just all wanted to go home.

Yet these combat-tested vets always seemed to be the targets of the starched and stodgy senior NCOs, who harassed them for pitiful minor infractions like un-shined belt buckles or shoes, even for not having their sleeves rolled in the "regulation" manner. The lifers had no interest in anyone's combat experience. They were just marking off a "combat tour" to get the accompanying promotion and seemed staunchly committed on keeping "their Army" as unchanged as possible. For the most part, they had no idea of the amount of flexibility and adaptation, the field expediency, it took to survive in the real adversity of combat. All of the young heroes ignored all of their attempts at shaming them into compliance. They had no respect for the lifers who had not earned it. They were young men grown old far too quickly, who frequently took sanctuary in drugs and alcohol. Many even volunteered to return to "the bush" where every moment was precious, and everybody's blood is green.

They called the lifers "juiceheads," drowning their broken dreams nightly at the NCO Clubs. They called themselves "heads." There even some who managed a quiet heroin habit. They were constantly harassed as if they were in a stateside assignment, with demands for polished boots and brass, white sidewall haircuts and other military bullshit. The Army attempted to enforce blind obedience by using the "minor punishment" of an Article 15 or the more serious punishment of a Court Martial, for "disrespect," or "failing to obey lawful orders." This led, too, to occasional "fragging" where certain Non-Commissioned Officers (NCOs) were sent a warning with an unloaded grenade rolled into their hooch—or sometimes a live one, though Paul never really saw that first hand.

Some men just decided to stop communicating, worn down, completely exhausted by the superficiality of their trying to impose a false world on the true reality they had experienced. Many of the troopers were referred to him, some to start the process of acquiring the psychiatric imprimatur necessary for the Army to send them home without benefits.

Captain Richard Rydell was the only psychiatrist for the Support Command. The staff used to give him cheap shit all the time by calling him "Chief!" He, in turn, would give them his best Perry White imitation, scowling "Don't call me Chief!"

He'd entered the Doctor's Draft after his psychiatric residency at Benjamin Rush Memorial Medical Center in Chicago, and teaching for two years at Jefferson Medical College in Philadelphia. He had been unceremoniously dumped in the Central Highlands with little meaty clinical work to do. Whenever Paul complained about paperwork, Dr. Ryder would respond that he was the "real functionary," signing off dozens of evaluations every week, including those requested by other units. I remember very vividly a trooper from the 173rd Airborne ("Third Herd") who was so strung out on morphine that he had to detox in the hospital before being processed for his Undesirable Discharge.

Of course, the good doctor did a lot more than paperwork, often schmoozing with senior officers and smoothing ruffled feathers of those who sincerely believed Paul should stand to attention when they entered the clinic, or that Dr. Ryder should ignore his medical ethics to discuss his clients' confidential materials. Because each Division had its own complement of doctors and psychiatrists, they did not deal with the Cav, 4th Division or the elements of the 101st Airborne too often—though they occasionally got Merchant Marines and other civilian employees with drug-seeking or anxiety complaints.

What had at first been exotic and threatening quickly became boring and ordinary for Paul, even going into the ville to eat dinner and sexually consort with the local women. Naturally he sought new outlets for his hungry mind. Even smoking both of his hemispheres to the max every night with the finest buds soon became ordinary. He journaled nightly, writing many scenes and much dialogue gleaned from the different individuals in the many" sets" in which he sat and absorbed crazy tales along with high octane smoke.

Playing chess with "Da Chief" was one of his antidotes for boredom. If things were quiet, they might get two games in during the late afternoon. The doctor was a superior player who beat him regularly—once even five times in a row using the same "Fool's Mate!"

Of course, this inevitably led to Paul taking advantage of the easy access to broach addressing another topic that was dear to his heart. He had tossed and turned for weeks attempting to make a very significant decision. And when he had, he said to himself, "Fuck it! I just want to go home!"

He decided that an Undesirable Discharge was the lesser of the evil possibilities with which he was being presented. He knew he was giving up all hope of ever finding that deep river of gold that flowed in him. (It was not until much later that he would realize that as he was, in fact, making his Descent into the Underworld, the first critical element of his Hero's Journey. He had not yet encountered the depths of depravity needed to experience the Ordeal, and thus to arise again in the Ascent).

It should have been easy. He knew the proper clinical terminology, and he could eloquently and legitimately plead his own case—which turned out to be the crux of the problem.

"The Chief" sat behind his large wooden desk, managing to look tweedy and academic with his stubby reddish-brown moustache and smoldering pipe.

"I've actually been expecting this."

Paul stuttered and stammered, vainly trying to formulate a comeback as the doctor took his measure through thick eyeglasses.

"Every single Psychology Specialist I've ever had has tried this."

That's probably so Paul's tongue was glued to the roof of his mouth, before he got indignant.

"But everything I told you is true!"

"Probably for the majority of troops in this country. Besides, you know too much."

"But sir..."

"You have no significant history of dysfunction, either before or in the service. You don't fit the profile? Do you seriously think we could get away with it?"

Paul bowed his head and tears of bitter rage ran down his cheeks, band filled his voice.

"I hate this fucking place."

Doctor Ryder told him they could talk whenever he wanted— and, oh, by the way, did he want some anti-depressants?

Paul knew in that instant that he had to do something radically different, to experience everything in a new way. If his path were obstructed, he would have to find a way that did work, even though he had no idea what that might be. Then, as if the Universe were listening, John Thomas Halliburton III walked into his office, another hot and soggy morning in late September of 1968.

"JT" entered silently, radiating hostility. He stopped just inside the inner wall of Paul's tent office, and seemed to blend right in with it. Then he glared at Paul and scanned the area by quadrants. JT pulled out a cake-cutter and started touching up his Afro before he tugged on his scraggly moustache. He scowled again when Paul pointed to the metal folding chair across from his desk.

"What the fuck am I here for?" he snarled.

His entire presentation was so non-regulation that Paul didn't know where to begin—sun bleached fatigues, sleeves rolled below the elbows, boots scarred and bleached pale yellow with a "Big Red One" patch on his right shoulder.

"I hear people call you 'Doc,'" he said, sneering, "But to me, you just another honkey white guy pretending—until you got one of these," he pointed to the CMB just above his heart. It was clear that Paul was just another pretender with second-hand stories.

Paul was stunned, speechless. His small authority completely eroded.

His professional composure completely abandoned him. Paul leaned back in his swivel chair, frantically gathering what little clinical expertise he had that might apply to the situation. The world slipped away in tiny whirlpools beneath the wheels of his chair as he attempted to gather his swiftly disappearing courage. He thanked God that this guy wasn't pretending to hallucinate, like so many had when coming from sick call. JT simply glared at him, eyes red and burning. JT turned the chair around with his back to the wall, and an eye on the door to the tent, radiating "Kiss my Black ass."

"The First Shirt gave me a direct order to come here. I'm 62 and a wake up (last day). No way I'm going to Long Bien Jail (LBJ). And I don't need no honkey bullshit from you!"

Paul fumbled and sputtered like a rookie quarterback in a game against the World Champs.

"Well I, that is, the First Sergeant wanted..."

JT mocked him. "Do you understand why you've been asked to come talk to me, PFC?" he asked with just the faintest crack of a smile, as he made air quotes with his fingers.

"Well do you?" Paul spit out angrily.

"I told him I want to go back to the bush to get away from all this chickenshit!"

"What 'chickenshit?'"

"This here is still Viet fucking 'Nam! And I get an Article 15 for not shinin' my motherfucking boots?!"

Paul's brain was reeling, and he couldn't speak.

"Punk ass E-6 tells me I gotta be strack when his punk ass ain't never been there! Motherfucker! Wouldn't have lasted ten minutes in my old unit!"

Paul felt as if he were aphasic or brain damaged as perspiration soaked his fatigues. The angrier JT looked, the more Paul felt like laughing—some from pure anxiety, some from genuine amusement. And then he burst out in laughter as JT stood with his hands clenched into fists, glaring at him.

"What are you laughing at, motherfucker?"

Paul continued laughing, doubling over as tears rolled down his cheeks.

JT scowled again, and said, "You're fucking crazy, man."

When Paul finally caught his breath, he spoke through a partially closed throat.

"I... you're funny, man! You're just too fucking real."

Now JT looked more puzzled than angry.

"What the fuck?"

Paul was still gasping for breath, but still tried to speak.

"So many jive people come through my office!"

"Is that why you laughing at me!?"

"No! No! I'm sorry!"

"What the fuck's that mean?"

"I thought you'd be just another jive-ass! The First Sergeant thinks you're crazy!"

"I think you're crazy, man."

I looked him straight in the eye and said, "Let's go smoke a joint."

He jumped back as if he'd just triggered a trip wire.

"Are you Criminal Investigation Division (CID)? Trying to trap me because I'm political?"

"I'm not CID—and I don't care what your politics are."

"Weed's illegal", he said, still glaring.

"You gotta trust me."

"Sheeet! You're just a jive honkey!"

"Yeah, but maybe this honkey can get the lifers off your butt!"

"You have to tell me straight up if you're CID!"

"Yeah, right. I'm CID!" I said, and gave him back a withering look.

He relaxed then, and offered me a dap, slapping hands. Paul had seen some Black guys do elaborate displays that involved hips, elbows, and shoulders. As we talked, he told me that there was "so much jive racist shit going down in the boonies," even though it was a hell of a lot less than in the rear.

"Eldridge Cleaver says, 'You're either part of the problem or part of the solution.' When they killed Dr. King, I decided I had to become part of the solution."

"Is that how you got busted?"

"I never really had any problems until I got to this fucking compound!"

Paul spread my hands palms up, and said "So...?"

"I'm not sure I want to talk about it."

"Why not?"

Again, the glare. "You wouldn't understand."

"Try me, man. Square business."

His face imploded. His eyes glazed and a shudder passed through him. He started to speak, then stopped, choking on his feelings. Then he looked at me with a strange intensity, as if what he was attempting to speak lived in a dimension not of this world.

Beads of perspiration broke on JT's forehead, despite the air conditioning. His eyes remained glazed, and his words fell out of his mouth in a monotone, as if he were alone in a room filled only with his memories. His voice was hypnotic. The tenor and timbre of it instantly transported Paul to the deepest, most dank jungle as JT"s words echoed through Paul with a clarity and lucidity that inserted him immediately into JT's movie.

"My platoon followed this game trail into a small clearing, and a couple of grenades rolled out of the tree line just as a gook popped up out of a spider hole. Flash, the point guy, white cat, emptied his sawed-off (shotgun) into the zip's face, just as he fell down with two rounds in his gut."

JT sighed and met Paul's eyes.

"Then J-Man fired up this mama-san. She just materialized like out of the thin air, and started spraying her AK on full auto. J-Man saw her and stitched her up, like a whole set of navels from her crotch to her forehead."

He paused, shook his head, and then lit a Kool.

"I knew Flash was gone. I went after him, and started dragging this dead cherry out too. I heard this blast from just behind me and J-Man blew up this gook with Flash's cut down. Then they started dropping in pre-zeroed mortar rounds all around us. I dropped when I took a piece of shrapnel in the calf, and tied it off with a bootlace. Then the Radio Telephone Operator (RTO) took a round through his 'Prick 25' that exited out his chest. I stuck cellophane on both ends, and wrapped them before I grabbed him and Flash in one hand and the dead cherry in the other. That's when I took a round in the leg," he said gesturing with the cane he was using.

"God! Then what?"

"LT called in the fast movers. We all ate dirt when they came in and laid a load of napalm right on top of our position! Then this gook came out the tree line on fire and we all lit him up! Crispy critter motherfucker!"

JT looked as if he'd been soaked by his own personal monsoon. He swallowed hard, smacked his lips and reached for his canteen. He took a long drink, sat back in his chair, and lowered his eyelids.

"So," he continued after a brief interlude, "we had this Combat Photographer with us. He took a bunch of snaps of me pulling those three guys out. No big. My job. It turns out our RTO was some congressman's son. When a snap of me pulling him out of the jungle hit the front page of the Stars and Stripes, AP and all of the major news agencies picked it up. Next thing you know, I'm in for a Silver Star, and Stars-And-Stripes did a feature story on me."

"Wow!"

He laughed. "Don't mean nothing, man."

"That's in-fucking-tense."

"Ain't no thing!"

"I don't know if I can take any more!"

"Check it out. When I got back to base camp, I started hearing a lot of Black Power talk about Black men killing Yellow men for the White man!"

Suddenly Paul's own racist family history came vomiting up in his face, even though Paul had never personally bought into it.

"And?"

"The CG (Commanding General) personally presented me with a Silver Star and Distinguished Service Medal, at a big photo-op ceremony in front of the whole brigade." Then JT snapped his fingers, "Oh yeah, Purple Heart with an oak leaf cluster too. They gave me five days 'recuperation leave,'" he said, shaking his head side-to-side, grimacing. "The day I got back, I had fucking orders to come here. They had all my shit packed. I guess they thought I was telling too much of the truth, just too political. They rousted me the fuck out of the company before I could even tell the brothers what was happening. Motherfuckers!"

"Then what?"

"The second fucking day, the second fucking day I was here, some punk ass Sergeant who's flying a desk tells me I gotta shine my fucking boots! Ten months in the bush, and I ain't never shined my boots! So, I asked him 'what was he gonna do—send me back to the boonies?' And he told me 'Shine 'em up. That's the way it is.' I told him he 'could kiss my Black ass.'"

Paul laughed. "And they busted you."

"Yeah."

"'Disrespecting an NCO' my ass! Fuck him! Honkies wanted to put me in the stockade. I went to Judge Advocate, so all I lost was one stripe. Motherfuckers!"

"So, listen. I think I can help take the heat off you, but you have to tell me what you want."

"Whaddya mean?"

"If you really want to go back to the boonies, I could write you up that way," Paul said, and JT looked at him like he had just sprouted another head. "Or I could set you up with an appointment with the psychiatrist."

"Why?"

"He can give you a P-3 profile. That would keep the lifer assholes off your back, because it would state that you have a psychological injury, and, for medical reasons, they can't harass or threaten you."

"Are you shitting me?"

"Not for a moment."

"Why you doing this?"

"I told you, man. You're real and I'm bored. If you want, I can arrange for you to come see me once a week."

"And?

"Do you play chess?"

"Hell yes!"

"OK. We can play chess and talk."

"But what about your boss?"

"Show up and tell the truth. Captain Ryder is a square shooter."

"OK. OK. Fuck it!"

Paul wrote him up, and for the very first time, he appended another sheet, telling Captain Ryder that there was more to this man's story than met the eye; and requesting the opportunity to carry JT as an ongoing client. He suggested that the good doctor consider a Psychiatric Profile based on his traumatic experiences in the field, and failure to adapt to the subsequent change in duty status.

"Go see the psychiatrist at 1300 hours tomorrow at the 67th Evac compound." I handed him an appointment reminder.

"If anybody gives you any shit, tell them to call me."

He held out his hand and we dapped.

"I still think you're crazy. But thanks, man" he said, rising and turning in one motion.

Paul sat for a long time, pondering the strength and courage of guys like him—and wondered, not for the first time, if he could hack it in a combat unit. Paul had to admit he admired JT. He understood why they were out to get him. The guy was a definite threat to the Green Machine.

CHAPTER 3
Toad (Part I)

Toad was the Dispensary's clerk. He had dark, brooding looks, with a square nose and huge Zapata-style moustache. His hair was parted down the middle and stuck up in little horns. He'd earned the sobriquet of Toad one night in the Mess Hall when he let loose the most extraordinary, ululating belch, like a massive frog fart love song. It stopped every single conversation, and provoked someone to shout: "God! What a fucking toad!"—and the name stuck.

He made drawings every day, what he called "extra-dimensional spatial extensions" —wild, psychedelic, multi-colored twisting kind of pseudo-Cubist works. He also wrote every day, and got Paul in the habit of exchanging notes with him that eventually built into quite a portfolio. They got in the habit of writing back and forth after my clients and his daily reports. We would send communiques back and forth, expounding on all manner of things, from existentialism to zoology, and many of the "osophies" along the way.

Paul 's self-judgments about his value as a person compounded his concerns about his value as an artist and writer. He always compared himself to the Toad, the local maestro. At first, Paul tried to imitate Toad's style and phrasing, wanting to absorb some of what he considered to

35

be Toad's greater talent. What he really wanted was to be someone other than himself. He always exulted in praise from Toad whenever he found a word or a phrase of note in Paul's writing, sprinkled like an opal in a mound of oxen dung. Toad's usual response was that Paul was "mentally masturbating."

Since Paul was only TDY, he didn't have to pull any work details (like KP), but he had to pull guard duty. The senior NCOs made a big deal out of "mounting a vigorous guard," to reinforce our presence in a combat zone, albeit in the safest area in the Central Highlands. Even during Tet, a total of one mortar round had fallen innocuously inside the massive compound!

Toad and Paul had been paired one night on guard duty, Paul as Sergeant of the Guard. They became fast friends, standing two hours on, two hours off all night long—and playing chess in between.

Paul closed the client's file, put it into the locked drawer in the bottom of his desk and headed out of the Dispensary.

"Where the fuck you going, troop?" The voice was an unmistakable blend of snide and insinuating, underlain with laughter.

"Din-din is served, troop!" Paul retorted. "You ready?"

"I was born ready. How 'bout a quick game or three?"

"Naw, I need time to recover. After the way you tromped on me this morning!"

They had averaged around ten games a day for the past six months—and Paul hadn't won a game yet. Paul's father had taught him the rudiments of the game when he was ten. By age twelve, Paul had intensely studied chess books from the library, and his father refused to play him any longer, claiming he was "too busy" or had "chores to do." It only increased his embarrassment and insulted his dignity when Paul had innocently offered to spot him a knight and play the Black pieces.

Playing with Toad was in a vastly different Universe, simultaneously more interesting and frustrating. The post-game *tristesse* often left Paul feeling as if he wanted to torture small animals. Toad was a former Northern California Junior Champion who had played in tournaments, and he regularly beat Paul while he was doing crossword puzzles.

"You only teach by defeating, man" was Toad's most frequent riposte to Paul whenever he had the temerity to refuse to play after a stinging defeat.

Paul had recently swept the pieces off the board after a particularly humiliating defeat. Toad glared at him and silently picked up the precious pieces. But Paul hungered to learn, and it eclipsed his rage when he settled down. He knew he would shortly be begging to be forgiven, and groveling for another game. It was the only real attention Paul ever got. None of Toad's friends liked him at all.

Toad gave him a look of mingled disgust and disrespect.

"Fuck you, man! You chipped my White Knight!"

"I just get so fucking frustrated. Fuck! I'm really sorry about the knight."

Toad sat in his office chair puffing his pipe behind the cleared center of his desk, He had regulation manuals stacked battlement-like around the entire perimeter of his desk, and he sat as if he were in the center of an arcane castle warding off hordes of voracious invaders. He surveyed Paul for a moment longer before a gap-toothed grin split his face.

"Don't mean nothing, man. Not this fucking war or the fucking politicians! Don't mean nothing." He stood, extended his hand, and they shook. Toad had always refused to dap. Being native-born Californian, he considered it to belong exclusively to the realm of the "Bloods."

Toad accosted him as he was crossing the compound.

"So where in the fuck <u>are</u> you going?"

"Have a smoke. I've had a hell of a day."

Then Toad laughed. "What'd you think of PFC John Thomas, Combat Medic?"

"Cat was intense, man. Blew me away, talking about the boonies and shit."

He sidled closer, and spoke mock-confidentially.

"Watch out for that guy! He's 'Black Power.' He fucking told Ham we're all 'racist honkey mothas.'"

"Ham" was Staff Sergeant Ralph Hammons. He looked ordinary and bland, but he had a twisted heart. He schmoozed officers and senior NCOs like a total sycophant; and persecuted anyone of lesser rank. The hooch girls and bar maids all hated him because he always hustled them for a free "short time." Toad was able to manipulate him at will. Ham was convinced that Toad agreed with everything he said, even listening to his recurring re-up lectures. Ham had despised Paul at first sight. Some part of it was likely due to Paul's assignment, though he knew Paul could read his energy and did not like it one bit.

"Ham wants to send him back to a combat unit. He's really pissed, said he feels 'disrespected.'"

Toad was always impressed with draftees who made rank, indifferent though he was about anything else military. He always did just enough to survive but very carefully articulated his private thoughts.

"You gonna smoke him up?"

"Naw, man. He said it was 'illegal.'"

Toad was always friendly with Black guys, but wouldn't share with them. Even though he'd grown up in San

Francisco, he had kind of an uptight midwestern attitude about Bloods.

"You smoke way too much of that shit."

"Yeah, right. Like you never touch the shit!"

"Not like you do, man."

"I do it just to release the 'Muse', so I can turn out better art."

Paul felt his anger rising when he answered.

"But you've been getting loaded for years before we met."

Paul's fear of returning to the world unchanged grew stronger every single day, enriched by his encounters with Toad, and the larger life the man seemed to have lived. Every day Paul felt more of the residue of his earlier life started falling from him like the molted skin of a reptile. He did not want any reruns of his old life. He wanted something far larger and wilder, more real. He in Viet Nam he felt more alive than ever in his life, despite the noxious air and the stagnant water.

"I'm warning you. Nothing good is going to come from knowing him."

"Yes, mother," Paul answered, reflecting on one of his favorite topics. He hated being patronized, treated as if he were the lesser mortal he actually was. His rage was surfacing more and more, and he wanted to belong to what he saw as a rising movement of young people out to change the world. He wanted to be a part of the coming revolution. He believed he already did, being with his brothers, breaking the laws and subverting the stale military regulations. They carried it in their bloodshot eyeballs, and smoking their sacred weed.

Paul was walking aimlessly across the compound smoking a "Winstone" when a harsh, almost disembodied voice spoke.

"Don't turn around, troop! Hand me that cigarette."

Something hard and cold pressed into the small of my back.

Oh shit! He'd been busted!

CHAPTER 4

It Gets Stranger in a Strange Land

Eons passed as Paul's worst nightmare manifested!

A deep sniff, then silence.

"Smells like marijuana!"

Fuck! His shit was in the wind!

Then a long cackle of stoned laughter split the air.

JT was holding my joint in one hand and a Model 1911 in the other.

"Busted your ass!"

"Man, you scared the fucking shit out of me!"

He took another hit, smiled, and handed Paul the joint.

"Righteous weed!"

"I thought you said you didn't smoke!"

"No, I said it was 'illegal.'"

"And?"

"I had to decide how racist you were!"

"What?"

"Everybody's racist. Can't help it. I think we kind of inherit it...but not genetically."

"What?" His brain was stuck.

"Some people are grey."

"What?" This shit was getting old.

JT looked at Paul and smiled.

"You know? Not black or white. Grey."

"OOOOK!"

"And I decided you were a grey dude."

JT offered and Paul dapped in the accepted neo-tribal recognition signal.

They both laughed and Paul finally managed something more intelligent than one syllable.

"Now what?"

"Wanna slide over ta my crib? Smoke a number?"

"Amen" Paul said and they dapped again.

It looked like a standard hooch from the outside, with a corrugated aluminum roof and sandbags half way up all the walls. Inside, it was as if they'd been transported to a very hip living room back in the world. All of the internal walls had been removed, creating a large central space filled with a collection of chairs and ammo crates for seating with a wooden spool table in the center. Individual sleeping spaces had been fashioned around the edges, and an old parachute covered the entire ceiling. Jimi Hendrix, Malcolm X, James Brown, and Martin Luther King flashed from posters splashed on the walls. Smokey Robinson blasted from eight powerful stereo speakers aligned around the edges of the room and pointing to the center.

When Paul entered one step behind JT, the room went totally silent, the stereo died mid-note, and the temperature turned icy, despite it being eighty-five degrees outside.

Paul felt as if he were a leper at a garden party, or as if he had shit in the punch bowl. A sea of angry eyes glared at him with malice, and Paul felt an ugly violence crackle the air. JT smiled and allowed Paul to suffer an intense moment of discomfort as Paul watched the entire angry congregation stand as one man. Then he spoke.

"Brothers!" JT said, holding his hands up with palms out.

"Brothers! This man here is the psych guy I told you about," he said, cackling. One or two of the gathering nodded their heads, but most of them continued scowling. Only one came forward to dap with him.

"Paul! Paul Marzeky," I stammered. He threw a flurry of hands, feet and elbows in greeting, and smiled at Paul's discomfort. He felt like he had suddenly become the evening's entertainment, and he wanted to run or disappear, like a Nautilus into its shell.

He felt split between feeling extremely uncomfortable and ashamed, and observing that self from some vantage near the ceiling, simply watching this extraordinary peek into an unknown world.

Then, one after another, the brothers came and greeted him. Soon thereafter raucous conversation continued, as did an interrupted game of Bid Whist. The record changed to *The Jimi Hendrix Experience,* and the occasional curses and sounds accompanying cards being slapped on the table.

JT was a King Kong, a guru. Everyone seemed to agree with his positions on politics, racism, Black Power, even the war. Every time JT spoke, everyone else listened. Paul realized that they all felt the same magnetism he had felt. The man was so real that it was impossible not to listen.

Paul took hits off joints and bowls as they circulated. At one point, a big Black dude named Otis pulled up an ammo crate, and sat down next to him on the wall where he had been attempting to be invisible.

"Why you sitting there by yourself, man?"

"Don't know how to act, man. Don't know nobody here, but JT."

He shot Paul a dark look and said, "If this was a room full of white people, you'd know everybody in the room."

As Paul started to get up to sidle out, Otis put a hand on my arm and handed him a cold Budweiser. Then they dapped.

"Ho Dude."

"Yo. Thanks."

Someone attempted to press some thick white tablets into his hand.

"What the fuck?"

"Binoctal, man. Make you mellow," said the tall skinny man who wavered as he spoke in a slurred voice.

JT stepped up and pushed the man away.

"That shit dulls your mind! Just what The Man wants!"

The man slunk off like a wounded dog and JT turned to Paul.

"The First Shirt didn't give me no shit about the letter. Thanks, man."

He laughed again, like echoes of goose farts cascading.

"What are you trippin' on, man?"

"Uppers, man! Used to take 'em in the bush on night patrols!" he said, and handed Paul two small pale tablets.

Paul was already more loaded than he had ever been, and felt as if he were lost in a vast cartoon show. He wanted so much to be in control and have real authority. To be more like Toad or JT. He observed JT working a huge wad of bubble gum like a jackhammer on steroids.

Thinking about his altered state, Paul asked, "Will this shit make me like you?"

JT laughed and passed him power with a dap.

"You may be a gray dude, but you ain't never gonna be no Brother, brother!"

He hooted then turned, and did an elaborate dap with one of the other brothers. Paul put the innocuous-looking tablets into his mouth with the reverence of a First Communion. He almost made a sign of the Cross as he swallowed, savoring the bitter taste and having absolutely no idea what to expect.

The party roared on around him as he sat back and closed his eyes, waiting for a visitation from the space brothers or some manifestation of dramatic change. He soon fell asleep, lulled into a trance. And awakened to a room full of lurid greasy colors, and kaleidoscopic spirals, each carrying an unnamed dread. He heard his father's voice screaming "You must be a real man!"

Paul felt a titanic anger roaring in his belly, as if he were twisting like a marlin on a big hook. What brought him more fully awake was the cacophonic sounds issuing from gigantic tentacled mother figures all asking rapid-fire questions of him. He thought he was awake but kept seeing himself aging rapidly from the effects of ancient wounds. Then a massive crevasse opened beneath him, and he stepped into the welcoming embrace of its pale still waters.

JT's voice shocked him back from oblivion like 200 joules through cardiac paddles.

"Wake up, motherfucker!"

"Ain't this a bitch? Motherfucker's sleeping on uppers!" said Ho Dude.

Paul found out later that JT had inadvertently dosed him with Binoctal. He knew there was no valid reason he should have felt as immensely ashamed as he did. But in that moment, he only wanted to climb back into the languorous dream, in a deep stupor between the freshly starched sheets of his bed carefully made by mama-san that very morning.

CHAPTER 5
Awakening—Part I

When Paul awoke, his mouth tasted like he had eaten ten thousand cigarette butts for a bedtime snack. His brain was frantically scrambling to make sense of what little he could remember of the night before. He felt like a wet-brained alcoholic with Korsakoff's. Toad gave him a totally disgusted look when he shuffled into the Dispensary.

"What the fuck? It's only twenty minutes."

Toad continued to glare at him as Paul's guilt morphed into rage.

"Fuck Sarge and his white horse! What's he going to do—send me to Viet Nam?"

Sick call was particularity light and boring that day, routine stuff with no referrals. Captain Curtis Solomon, the draftee CO of the Medical Company, woke up pissed off every morning, hating the military and despising Viet Nam for separating him from his lucrative private practice and loving wife. The clinic staff always seemed to find new and innovative ways to create delightfully evil surprises for him.

There was a young and not very bright "frequent flyer" who invariably showed up on a Monday morning complaining of a "drippy dick." The very sight of him was guaranteed to raise

Dr. Solomon's blood pressure by thirty points. Some members of the clinic staff found it perversely humorous to, as one wag had it, "watch the steam come out of Doc Solomon's ears."

The young man had a fourth-grade education and been drafted from some backwoods town in West Virginia. He seemed to have the worst judgment of any human Paul had ever met. He just couldn't stay away from the massage parlors in the ville.

"You fucking pig! Not again!" Solomon shouted, the volume of his voice as loud as if he were in a Primal Therapy session.

The clinic staff had saved him for last, and everyone erupted in laughter. Titters to convulsions rippled through the clinic as people scurried like harried spiders to get a better opportunity to observe our "Commander-in-Chief," whose demeanor had shifted from intensity to fervor flavored with vendetta.

"You're barely human! What did I tell you I was going to do the next time I saw you in here with the clap? What? Tell me!" Dr. Solomon was practically apoplectic, maybe even epileptic, as he stood over the quaking young man demanding answers. His fury was at full gale force, his eyes boring into the young man like twin laser beams.

"Shut the fuck up, you bunch of assholes!" the good doctor screamed. He was in rare form. He almost never cursed.

As perspiration gushed out of the EM's face, he kept backing up until he hit the corner—sputtering and protesting, and then he started to cry. Paul thought the young repeater might go into shock. His urine-stained pants were down around his ankles, and his overlarge Adam's apple bobbed like a Halloween favor. His whole appearance was lax and uncared for; his fatigues were saggy and unwashed, boots scruffy. He had a wart and two huge yellow zits on his chin. He was blinking like a rapid-fire machine gun; his voice screeched and broke like a Victrola playing a damaged record. He finally stammered out a question.

"Sir! Sir! You're not really gonna cut it off, are you sir?"

Paul was laughing so hard he fell on the floor, and waves of laughter inundated the clinic, gouts and guffaws echoing off the walls and down the hallways.

Even Doc Solomon had to fight not to laugh, as he tried to assume the mien of his legendary namesake and maintain a straight face, but then he too failed, and started sputtering with suppressed glee.

"No, son, I'm not. But I'm going to tell you again that you can become sterile if you keep this up. And I'm going to have to report this to your Company Commander. You're a public health hazard. Do you know how many times I've treated you for this?"

"I dunno, sir. Quite a few."

"'Quite a few! Quite a few!' Twenty-eight times! And you've only been here five months! That must be some kind of record."

"Fat Doug" Emptor was the 91C at the clinic, the equivalent of a Physician's Assistant, that had cost him added an extra year to his service commitment. He was arrogant by anyone's standards, attempting to lord it over everyone in the clinic who he considered to be of lesser rank than himself. Conversely, he was extremely sycophantic with all officers and especially the doctors, who were the gods of the local Universe. In his mind he was just one small step below the doctors—and one big step above everyone else. His attitude made him made him practically *persona non grata* with the rest of the staff.

Emptor was infamous for harassing the hooch maids and waitresses at the EM Club where he was the manager. He always promised to "souvenir" them at the PX in exchange for "boom-boom." Neither harassment nor browbeating had any effect. When his false promises failed to work, he preached to them about Jesus.

He always carried a New Testament in the right cargo pocket of his fatigue pants, ready to quote the "holy book," always pretending to use it to reinforce his shady schemes. Toad always battered him with brilliant repartee and reduced him to a "babbling bag of shit." Despite his self-assumed authority, Emptor was not very intelligent and, in fact, rather dull-witted.

"Shoot him, Emptor. And use the special needle!" said Doc Solomon.

"Yes, sir. I will, sir."

Emptor smiled as he brought out the eight-inch long cardiac needle attached to a 50-milligram syringe. It was a small psychodrama the staff sometimes enacted with patients who had recurrent venereal disease.

"No! No! Please! I won't ever go back to that place again!" he said, pulling up his pants and scrambling for the door.

Solomon smiled and waved his hand.

"OK, Emptor. You may use the regular needle."

"Oh, thank you, sir" cried the man, lowering his pants somewhat cautiously to half-mast. "I promise. I'll go across the street next time," he said, quite proud of himself.

"Jesus, you're hopeless!" Solomon said, as he stormed out to "shoot some hoops" on the clinic's half-court. Paul was still laughing when he left, and immediately ran into Ho Dude. We dapped.

"What's hap-pen-ning?"

"Ain't nothing shaking but the bacon."

"There it is, brother."

There it is. These three simple seemingly self-explanatory words were used to express everything from rage to joy, from crotch rot to stepping on a land mine. It was applicable to every situation. The Zen of things in the 'Nam. There it is.

Paul asked him, "Wanna blow a number?"

"Nah, I got some pills to get high on!"

"What? Them fucking Binoctals?"

"No, man! JT had the real thing in his other pocket! I'm gonna get good and jacked on some Ritalin!"

"What the fuck is that?"

"Uppers! Ain't you never been high before?"

"I never did pills until the other night."

"You never get high back in the world?"

"No, man. I used to be a juice head!"

"Come on, man," he said, extending his hand to Paul with a glance over his shoulder. "Take this trip with Ho Dude, and get hip!"

An intuitive warning bell clanged in Paul's head, after which he immediately began to lash himself with the scourge of self-criticism. It was all related to the crippling ancient chains that bound him to the past. Paul felt angry for allowing himself to be held captive when a new life beckoned. What the fuck was the big deal anyway?

"Best you start with just one. See if you like it."

Ho Dude laid the pale green tablet in Paul's palm like a Catholic priest delivering a host. There was a reverence about the gesture that Paul remembered to this day, as if Ho Dude were aware of the initiation into which he was ushering him. He felt a moment of prescience that foreshadowed a richer future, though one still clouded in the present and demanding many trials of him to achieve. Paul closed his eyes, tossed the pill into his mouth, and swigged it down with a hit of beer.

He looked over to see Ho Dude was laughing.

"What the fuck is so funny, man?"

"You acting so serious, man! You white cats sure got funny ideas."

Paul glared at him, slabs of belly fat pushing his jungle fatigues out like a sausage skin.

"Fuck you, man!" was his most brilliant reply.

"You just getting high, man! Ain't no thing!" Ho Dude said and swung a clenched fist down onto that of another brother who was passing by, and then he walked away.

Paul mulled his fear of being alone versus his being willing to risk to entering a new life for a few minutes as he finished his beer. He had an acute awareness of a chemical shift in his body when a molten, volcanic wave swept up his back and through his neck like the Mekong River emptying into the South China Sea. He felt hatred and envy for everyone who was hip and aware—and badly wanted to be one of them. He believed he was a perennial outlier, a stranger even to himself. He wanted to be smug, arrogant, and contented with himself. He wanted to be welcomed and celebrated everywhere he went by all of the "cool" people. A small electric chill ran through his body as the first rush passed through.

The bond that young Black soldiers must have struck him poignantly. They seemed to possess a sense of solidarity with their brothers in the face of the rampant racism in the military. The Civil Rights movement had not even begun to penetrate the armor of the Army. Paul had heard stories about race riots promulgated by the Military Injustice System, both in and out of stockades and at LBJ. He empathized strongly with these young men and their rage at fighting the White man's war against Yellow people. They wore their collective brotherhood like a veneer of chain mail over their chronic fears and bitterness, eschewing the confusion and the isolation they worked so hard not to feel, much less display. He had not yet come to experience the immensity of his own isolation and cupidity, innocent of the peaks of his ordeal yet to come.

Paul gagged when the next rush hit, and an acidic wave reached up from his belly and grabbed him by the neck. Fresh bile blasted him, and then swiftly released a wave of loud laughter that took him a moment to realize was his own. He started shaking as if a high voltage turbine generator had switched on in his brain and ignited his neural circuits. A tongue of pure white light shot up the conduit of his spine, up, up, up through the vaulted ceiling of his skull— and out on an infinite journey to far distant star systems. Paul had met God face-to-face.

Ho Dude returned, and gave him a nasty look.

"Hey man! Stick your smile in your belly. You're a bust!"

His admonition only made Paul laugh harder, as he stumbled around, holding his sides.

"Oh, oh my God, man! You...look so...fucking funny!"

Ho Dude looked as if he wanted to hit him, but instead shook his head and walked away, mumbling something under his breath about "stupid fucking white guys."

As his sense of dislocation stabilized, it became clear that something really profound was happening. Paul was flying through the sky watching images of himself going through the motions of Earth life, laughing at his other self, as if in a room full of mirrors. But who was laughing at whom? He felt a moment of doubt and pain. He wanted to quickly pull back into himself as if nothing of note had happened—but it was far too late.

"Piss on that! Things are gonna change right fucking NOW!"

He spoke aloud his feelings of shame and redress. He

Stefan J. Malecek, Ph. D.

suddenly felt stronger and more confident as the mantle of being an architect of great change settled around him. A hundred dynamos wired in series ignited an almost overwhelming sense of invincibility that surged through his body in a quicksilver flash, and he knew, just knew, that this was the key to a new life, to shedding any excess weight and any of the emotional garbage he had carried for decades.

"Fuck that shit!" Paul laughed to himself. "Just because I'm fat don't mean I can't have fun."

He dashed after the retreating Ho Dude and threw an arm around his neck.

"What are you doing, man? You queer or something?"

"Fuck no, man! I'm high as a motherfucker! Just wanted to say thanks, and buy you a beer. I also got some monster weed too, man! MONSTER!"

"Cool your shit, Jack."

"Aw man, I'm so fucking high! How long does this shit work?"

"You're just rushing, man! You be high for another three hours. Want some gum?"

My mouth said "Yes," while my head said, "No." I normally did not like chewing gum. It always stuck to my teeth, though as I started chewing, the tension in my jaws gave way.

60

"Goddamn man, why the fuck didn't somebody tell me about this shit before?"

Ho Dude glared at him again. "You gotta keep your shit together. The Man is always ready to fuck with you."

The hours passed as if a minute. The pot smokers drifted off to bed, and the "juicers" passed out in their hooches, in ditches, or puking in the shitters. By the eerie early hours of the morning, Paul and the tweakers were the only ones left "sneaking and peeping" around the compound, the ever-vigilant guardians of the night. Paul and his confreres drifted and hid to not be noticed; crept and crawled and smoked a thousandth cigarette just as dawn began to break; reluctantly made the last shuffle of the Heart's deck; or put away the cribbage board for the boring routine of another day in Support Command Compound. Paul and his fellows ate another handful of the little sweethearts just to keep us going through another day saturated with the ordinariness and petty details of lifers and bureaucrats who wandered the compound, and controlled the day as they, the night watchers, had come to love and cherish the night with the infinite quicksilver of their minds, as they soared beyond the mundane, ordinary concreteness of military life, and transported themselves, illusion or not, into realms unknown and as yet unperceived by the "normals" who surrounded them.

CHAPTER 6
Flying

The lack of sleep did not seem to affect Paul at all. He felt as if the illicit substance were something that had always been missing from his body, like an arcane vitamin overlooked and neglected previously. The fact that he had actually shown up early for sick call for the first time ever did not escape Toad's notice.

"You been speeding, bat breath?"

"Nah. I just smoked a couple of numbers this morning." The lie came easily, instinctively, a protection from intrusion.

"Don't lie to me, asshole!"

Toad's eyes were liquid fire and his horned-rim glasses slid down his nose as he peered at Paul, who felt as if he had been skewered on a stick, and was being served as an appetizer in a sleazy Chinese restaurant.

Remembering his resolve from last night, he said "Fuck it!" to himself.

"I did a little last night. Shit is great!"

"You're speeding right now, you damn liar!"

Paul danced nervously from foot to foot like an electric rabbit, palms sweating, eyes twitching.

"Just a little. I was up so late, I had to take a little more to get through the day. I'll sleep tonight."

"That's what they all say. You've never seen the speed freaks in San Francisco. Those cats go for weeks at a time without sleeping because the comedown is so hard! The fucking headaches are a bitch! You're fucking with some bad shit!"

"Man, you act like you're my goddamn father! This is only the second time!" Paul wanted to get him off his back, even as he questioned why he even gave a fuck!

Then, suddenly, Paul changed tacks.

"Wanna get in a couple of games tonight after chow?"

"How about before chow? Then we can go and catch the movie afterward."

"What's the flick?"

"Ham ordered it."

"Groan! Not some dumbshit World War II film again, with the heroes all dying, and the survivors re-upping to avenge them, to protect Mom and apple pie?"

"Not quite that bad. But almost."

"OK. I give up. What's the flick?"

"John Wayne," then Toad paused for dramatic emphasis, "in *The Green Berets*!"

"No! You're shitting me!"

"No, man, you're my favorite turd!"

"Naw. Come on."

"Serioso."

"Jesus! The guy's taste is in his asshole."

"He's a fucking lifer, man. What do you expect?"

"Well that pretty much knocks me out of the movie market tonight."

"Why don't you come and catch it with me and Phil and Baldy? It'll be OK. Have a few yucks."

Phil and Baldy were two of Toad's roommates. They had knocked down a wall between their assigned pair of two-person rooms, and built a paneled carpeted hideaway with a bar and bunk-bedded sleeping quarters. Then they ordered an air conditioner that made their living quarters the envy of the compound.

"Yeah, but then everybody'll be sitting around drinking beer with Ham telling fake war stories and making racist jokes. I can't handle it tonight."

"Come on, man. It'll be all right."

"That fuckhead Ham doesn't like me."

"It'll be better than hanging out with the Bloods and eating speed!" he said, blood rushing to his face.

"Motherfuck that! I've only done it twice! Besides," he said, drawing myself up as tall as the scared-fat-kid inside would allow, sneering and trying to act dignified, "What the fuck business is it of yours?"

"You are fucking hopeless, man. You come out of the Mid-fucking-west, smoke a little Kansas weed, and all of a sudden you think you're hip! You are so full of shit, man!"

"Just because you fucking grew up in California doesn't make you the king of the fucking Universe!"

"I've seen plenty of burnt out people who couldn't remember their own names!"

"Oh man! Get over yourself! It's just a little speed!"

"People are starting to notice you being high!"

"Mostly been smoking weed. And what do you mean 'people?'"

"Ham for one. You coming to work late loaded all the time. And every fucking night, they sit around the Lifer's Club and talk about JT and that bunch of Bloods you been hanging around with! I heard Ham say they were 'gonna sweep that whole mess clean!'"

"Bunch of goddamn hypocrites! They sit around and drink their holy fucking alcohol and have the balls to condemn us!"

"Doesn't matter if they're a bunch of hypocrites! Remember The Doors, man? 'They got the guns, but we got the numbers.' Over here, they got the power to Court-Martial your ass, or send you to the fucking Demilitarized Zone (DMZ)! Besides," he said, and glanced down for a moment in an attempt to cover his embarrassment, "I kinda like having you around here. You're a lot more intelligent than Emptor, even if you can't play chess for shit!"

Paul realized that there was a hook to Toad's tendered offer, despite the good feeling Paul had about it. He was being asked symbolically to come back into the fold; to stop following the path that he had chosen to tread; and especially stop associating with JT and the Bloods. Paul felt that his life had amplifies tremendously in just a short period of time, and how much he had learned. He realized too that he had come to admire and respect JT for his honesty and forthrightness. There was no way he could simply trade the man as if he were a commodity. Paul felt like he was awakening from a lifelong sleep, and if he turned back, he would lose any possibility of ever becoming the man that he wanted to be.

Paul certainly felt both distress and elation. He felt that he was emerging like a butterfly from its chrysalis. His feelings were so much stronger, more violent and demanding, as if he were molten lava exploding from a long extinct caldera, as if he were being challenged by the Universe to birth himself, pull his new self out of the depths of his own gut, and leave behind the ragged husk of all that he had ever been, all that he had always despised about himself being for being simpering and sycophantic, for being willing to endure pain to please others. Now he was willing to endure the outrage of others, to shed his helplessness, his emotional paralysis, to change it.

An enormous montage of denigrated images cascaded through his head: of him castigated, rejected and ostracized; barely borne except when others saw the opportunity of exploiting him; tolerated like sidewalk cracks and traffic lights; bearing the demeaning self-flagellation with which he had been afflicted most of his life. He saw that he was becoming capable of managing his true needs and desires, that he could now stand for himself, by himself, for his real self—and finally be the one who cared about him, the one whom he had for such a long time longed, his own best lover and very best friend.

Paul had no idea where he was going, or what lay beyond this unfolding transformation—and did not care! In his heart of hearts, he knew he had to honor his own felt needs. If he did not have himself, he had nothing!

He was alive with thought, bursting with it. The keys to the kingdom—more a looking glass, a smoked lens—lay twisted in a cigarette cellophane in the bottom of his left-hand fatigue jacket pocket. Better living through chemistry. Two little pills—so innocuous, so innocent looking—yet of such potency as to transform him into a superhero version of himself with the confidence and ability to laugh in the depreciating face of adversity. Two little pills and he could be transmuted for six hours; freed from the frustrations of a regressed and bitter boy who had eaten insults, and run from fights, who still lived in his heart and threatened to take over with the least opportunity. He wanted to liberate that monster that lived in him, and suffer whatever trials and vicissitudes might await him so that he could be able to roam, to walk and talk and breathe freely in a brave new world of his own making. He wanted to pursue his own naked visions, his dreams and desires, to climb the heights of celestial mountains, and breathe the rare atmospheres of his inner eye. These prizes of consciousness would be his alone at long last. There would be no one interfering with his triumphs and tragedies—or claiming praise or blame for them. He would no longer grant anyone the right to intrude on the privacy of his divine thoughts and ideas.

Yet to embark on this Hero's Journey, it seemed he must needs betray one of the most intelligent and best friends he had ever had. For eight solid months, Toad had assisted him in plumbing his inner depths, but always with the guidance he himself had acquired through making the kinds of mistakes and suffering the ignominious pains Toad now did not want Paul to experientially have. It was a true conundrum.

Paul knew that this was his time of initiation. Toad was preordained to fail in his well-meaning attempts; doomed to fall beneath the onrushing tide of Paul's liberation; the onslaught of Paul's desire to grow beyond his old fears and pains. Paul hungered to disappear in the rush of speed and pure power; to be freed from the crippling encumbrances of all that he had ever known and carried. He knew this was the treasure beyond any price, even the destruction of the finest friendship he had ever known. This initiation was being demanded of him by Life Itself. It was the price of his liberation.

This entire encyclopedia of thoughts, this massive inventory of self-evaluation, had flashed condensed through his mind in the few moments it took to clarify his fleeting feelings and his ability to answer coherently.

"I don't know, brother man. I just don't think I can handle Ham's rap tonight."

Toad's eyes cut him like a scalpel blade, and he felt the full weight of what Toad perceived to be Paul's betrayal, but he refused to carry the baggage. He walked off feeling an irreparable gulf had widened between them with each step. Though he felt the Judas-pain in his heart and the cupric taste of treachery in his mouth, he knew he had to do what he had to do—come what may, come what must.

Paul had just settled into his favorite bunker to burn some herb to clear his head when JT appeared. He leaned back against the sandbags and wriggled his butt until he was comfortable. Only then did the man offer his hand in greeting.

"What's the word, Mr. Bird?"

"You the word."

"I don't know about that. But I could sure tell what was smoking!"

"I really need it. My head's all fucked up over how fucked up this place is!"

"Speak it, Zeus!"

"I'm just fucking sick of this fucking place, JT. All these motherfucking assholes running around pretending they're really in the war. That asshole Ham getting a Purple Heart for tripping on his way to a bunker, especially when there's cats like you who have really been in the shit and get no respect!"

Paul paused for a moment, took a deep hit on the joint and passed it on.

"I'm real raggedy right now! Real raggedy!" he continued.

JT hit the joint and passed it back to Paul, quietly watching as Paul continued.

"This might sound strange, but I'm thinking of asking for a transfer—out of this chickenshit into some real action."

JT was not surprised as he answered, "Not strange, but I think you're full of shit! Charlie's stuff is deep out there."

"I almost don't give a shit. I feel more awake, more alive!"

"Just because you woke up your head, you could still get yourself very fucking dead out there!"

JT held out his hand and we dapped.

"I heard you been kicking some ass lately" JT continued.

"Ti-ti boo-coo, man. I'm just starting to percolate!"

"Tell me something, man. Is there mental illness in your family?"

Paul laughed, coughing on the resinous smoke in his lungs.

"You are one crazy mother! You know that?" said Paul, meaning it as a compliment.

He was still laughing and choking with the very smallest end of the joint in his right hand when he spotted a shadow flicker across the mouth of our hideout. He ate the roach as they stood up and beat a quick retreat out of the other end of the bunker.

"Hey you two! Hold it right there!"

It was just a lifer, one of those who haunted the compound like the disembodied spirits in a mausoleum.

"What were you men doing in there?"

"Just shooting the shit, sergeant."

"Aren't you men supposed to be on duty?"

We answered in tandem.

"No, sergeant."

"Were you smoking marijuana in there?"

Again. "No, sergeant."

"Well, it smells like it to me. Maybe I better get your names and report you to the Duty NCO."

JT stepped forward as he began to pull out a small notebook.

"Lookie here, Sarge. We be off duty here. Can you dig that?" Paul reached under his fatigue jacket and unsnapped the cover of his unauthorized-to-wear-in-Support-Command leather holster containing his Colt .45.

The NCO suddenly seemed to have second thoughts as he shuffled his feet and said, "Uh, look here, you men, I, uh, really think you men should return to your duty stations, be a good example for the others." He turned, stumbling, and then abruptly on his heel, executed a perfect about face, and muttered. "Carry on, men," as he retreated.

JT turned to me laughing, as we dapped again.

"That doufuss motherfucker! Jesus! Did you see his face? He didn't know whether to shit or go blind!"

"I'm hip! Where's the joint?"

"I ate it!"

"Amen, brother!" he said, and we knocked fists again.

Paul wandered off to satisfy a pervasive need for solitude, unable to categorize or analyze it—and did not try. Everything seemed clearer and brighter when he was alone, and yet he was phobic about being in his own presence too much because his oldest fears kept reappearing and he grew deeply concerned about fucking up, or maybe getting killed.

Paul's increasing intolerance of other people's bullshit was growing. He was having occasional berserk machete fantasies, and the idea of carrying at least one automatic weapon gave rise to a host of other thoughts about revenge on those who had stolen parts and pieces of his past. Being high was his only real desire. The tyranny of his personal antiquity was completely unfolding now for him to re-claim. The dual nature of his earliest years had seemed so "natural" to him then—getting good grades, and being a "good boy" while he was dying inside, full of lust and desire for a life he was afraid he would never get to have unless he escaped. Paul felt cursed, isolated, and just so fucking lonely. His potential always seemed out of reach, a periodic table with no god to call him into manifestation; as if he were a moral cripple, or at best emotionally retarded.

It was only in moments of ear-ringing, eye singeing rage that his potential seemed available, when storms of fiery energy would flash up from the base of his spine—like the first time he drank alcohol, and his first attempt at murder.

FLASHBACK #37,812
St. Louis
December 1960

`Paul so badly wanted to feel as if he really belonged, just for once. Toward that end, Paul made the huge mistake of inviting all of the guys in the group of which he was a peripheral member, probably about ten in total, to his parent's house one day during the Christmas holidays. They, in typical fashion, decided to use the occasion to royally fuck with him.

Paul showed them where his father's liquor stash was located, feeling powerful and magnanimous. They raided it, randomly mixing whiskeys, gin, wine, vodka, and schnapps. This, in turn, only heightened the excitement, their finding ever greater enjoyment in tormenting him, mocking, harassing, and belittling him. Though they all seemed to take a turn, Paul was the one who chugged most frequently, and hence, became the drunkest and most quickly out of control.

The amount of alcohol consumed certainly fueled the malignant spirit of his teenaged nemesis, Peff, whom Paul caught plundering his sister's underwear drawer, and later putting tinsel in the Christmas tree light sockets that *subsequently plunged the entire house into darkness after they convinced a thoroughly besotted Paul to plug in the tree!*

They told him he had "gone nuts" attempting several times to stab Peff for his misdeeds as Paul chased him around the house, and managed to catch him hiding under the bed, and buried a steak knife in the bottom of his foot. At that point the hyenas finally stopped laughing, and saw that he was serious about killing Peff. They dragged away his limping enemy and restrained Paul before dumping him in the bath tub—his initiation into his teen-aged years.

Paul woke up face down in a bathtub full of ice cubes, unceremoniously dumped there by his so-called friends. They had gotten scared he might die because he'd barfed so much. Besides, they had to sober him up quickly so he could to clean up the house they'd so barbarously ransacked.

"Your parents will be here in half an hour!"

CHAPTER 6
Toad (Part II)

It had just been a month since Paul had found his new drug. He had vacillated between fearing he was strung out and knowing he was, to the point where he stopped caring. He couldn't remember when the change had begun. Staying high had become the new norm. He couldn't consider living without the accentuated mental states and endless Hearts games.

Being high obliterated all time and memory, and sharply inserted him into the present, into the living vibrant moment where he created who he was becoming or at least the illusion thereof—a risk-taker, adventurer, ass kicker—a feeling more potent, more alluring, than visiting any of the little sluts in the "ville," having previously mistaken his hunger and loneliness as a desire for sex, rather than a will to power.

The more stimulants he took, the more prominent his "Fuck the Army" attitude became. Although anyone with more training and clinical experience would have pointed out to him the error of believing in his own pretensions, he became increasingly arrogant and irritable. He began to believe that he was living a real, fully embodied life, the kind of life his father could never have imagined. It was, in fact, one of the driving motivations for him. He was channeling his enormous anger and disrespect for his father into living the kind of life NOW that his father would have warned him against; would have attempted to prohibit him from living; would have cautioned him against, that of feeling too much alive and vociferous. Paul sometimes felt like Emile Zola when asked why he had come here. He had replied, "I came here to live out loud."

Of course, Zola was not in the U.S. Army stationed in a combat zone surround by the lifers and military brass whom he considered to be the hostile forces arrayed against him, not just the North Vietnamese Army (NVA) or the Viet Cong (VC).

His hunger was to be bigger, more spectacular and larger-than-life. He wanted to be a hero, admired for his valor, bravery and courage. He had resolved not to end up waiting, waiting, waiting for some other person, some circumstance, some lightning bolt from the sky to bring revelations and enlightenment into his life as his father had done, his father who was still awaiting gratification and fulfillment to make him whole and set him free from the tyranny of the drunken, humdrum everyday life he had created.

Toward that very end, Paul visited the ville every chance he got, drunk, stoned and uninhibited. He considered that he was becoming a real "man of the world" (vis a vis James Bond), even though he sometimes longed with every cell of his being to get back to the state of relative ignorance he had lived in most of his life.

"Fuck a bunch of later!" Paul muttered to himself.

He was storming angrily through the compound, wanting to beat the shit out of somebody other than himself, someone or something upon whom to unload the burdens of his awakening from quasi-child to would-be man.

He wished so much he were jaded, a hard guy, "heavy duty." Even though he wanted to spew angrily most of time, his phobic fear of going to prison kept his edge somewhat in check. The predatory rats in Long Bien Jail were legendary—and how ironic, since LBJ the President and the Root brothers were profiting immensely from the war.

It seemed like eons since he had chosen to pass up the lifer's film. It was part of his commitment to wild abandon.

His rude and disrespectful behavior was a minor chord in the crescendo that was building compared to his relatively innocent association with the chopper crews of the 227th Assault Helicopter Company. How could Paul have known such an innocuous acquaintanceship would lead to his tragi-comedic denouement? Everyone in that august company sported huge bushy moustaches with waxed handlebars that curled beyond the planes of their faces. They were essentially a completely autonomous unit, so there were very few, if any, who could countermand anything they decided to do.

They used the 14th for their medical needs, and Paul got to know some of them when they dropped in for sick call. He always "massaged" the waiting list to get them preferential treatment. Paul really identified with the glamor he saw in their jobs. Plus, they admired each other's moustaches.

"What do you use to wax yours?"

"We usually use Pinaud's. We get it from the local pharmacy, or sometimes in Saigon."

"Why don't some of you guys come by my set one of these nights? One of the guys works in the OR and he can probably fix you up with a good supply of bone wax. It's what I use on mine."

He shook hands and dapped with the Crew Chief. Very soon thereafter the 227th became part of the extended family of the 14th General Dispensary underground. Shortly after that, Paul became the "go to" guy for placing orders with their crews to secure "trade goods" in Saigon—anything that wasn't nailed down from boxes of steaks and cases of Scotch to replacement military equipment for which they did not want to wait through regular channels. The clinic staff, in turn, provided the very best weed and stimulants, and, of course, the best in medical care.

Paul felt as if he had aged a thousand years. He had embraced those he called the "Mole People" because they were the most "underground" individuals on the compound. Of course, they were all heads and embraced the position that they were to be an active part of changing the world, even here in Viet Nam. Or perhaps especially so. As a group, they collectively acknowledged that the world was filled with cupidity and hypocrisy, and they had dedicated themselves to subverting the Army in as many ways as possible. (Of course, for some it was just an added layer of rationalization for their drug dependency).

Paul believed he had become a better soldier, though in a strictly non-military sense. He was handling all of his referrals more efficiently (usually within the first 24); his paperwork was strack; his provisional diagnoses were usually right on the mark and Captain Ryder had complimented him for his excellent work. He was diligent, actually better than before—and had the neatest, cleanest office in the Dispensary.

He had absorbed untold pages of psychiatric theory in order to validate his opinions (clinical or political) with citations and references. He had really begun to see most people as shallow and pedestrian. In spite of his circumstances, he had come to believe he was one of the new wave of human beings destined to rule the Earth, when all the less-evolved died by some kind of cosmic fiat leaving the planet for those who could better utilize its resources for higher ends than war and fascist business. Paul had come to believe that all of Freud's discontents had been related to not living fully. It was, therefore, imperative to be completely honest and to fully live his dreams and fantasies. Unbridled expression of emotion was the true and only path to sanity.

The strictly military side of soldiering for him definitely left something to be desired. Essentially his state of mind was completely illegal 24/7, and he would be considered a criminal if he were busted. That, in turn, compelled him to lie almost all the time, believing that he owed no one the absolute truth, especially not those who claimed authority over him. He did not respect them. They had not earned it. This latter position interfered with his desire to both be free and honest, setting up a conundrum for which he did not yet have an answer.

Paul had also become something of a Social Darwinist as he adopted the attitude that he could have anything he wanted; and by definition, if he had it, it was absolutely right, no matter what he did to obtain it. He decided that what they had called "situational ethics" in high school was nothing more than what he now called "field expediency." Paul had come to believe that everything was ultimately situational, and whatever worked to keep you alive was absolutely proper—including deflecting Toad's sanctimonious rap.

"Hey man" he said, scowling when they encountered each other, paths crossing in the night.

"Hey."

"Haven't seen much of you lately."

"Yeah. Been busy."

Toad's gaze was laser sharp, loaded with disdain and resentment. Even though he was a genuine California sex, drugs, and rock-and-roller, he now seemed as rigid and dogmatic as a fundamentalist Southern preacher.

"You don't know what you're doing to yourself. You're not the first person who's gotten strung out," he said, eyebrows knitting together like a dark caterpillar.

"I'm not strung out, man."

"You're just using every day. Right?"

"I don't need to listen to this shit!"

Toad stepped closer, and laid a hand on Paul's shoulder.

"Brother, I feel kinda responsible for you. I was strung out on speed when I was younger, so I know what you're going through."

"No, you don't, man. The whole scene here is completely different."

"Yeah, it is. But using is just the same."

Paul shrugged my shoulders. "Maybe."

"It is, man. And your attitude sucks too!"

Hot anger slashed through Paul like a razor-honed blade.

"Fuck you too!"

Paul gathered his hands into fists, spread his feet and prepared to fight.

"See what I mean? You're all ready to fight over my suggestion that maybe you should just cool out a little. People have noticed how much you have changed. Doc Solomon. Ham. Me."

"What's Ham gonna do? Send me to Viet Nam?"

"There are worse places than being here."

Survival sirens screamed in my head.

"Like where?"

"Some people think you might be better off somewhere else."

"Thank God he doesn't have the power to transfer me."

"No, but 67th Evac does. You're only TDY here."

"Is Ham getting ready to fuck me over?"

"I don't know nothing, man. It would help if you softened up your attitude a little."

I felt a momentary flash of our old camaraderie.

"Hey thanks, man."

"You're not going to like this, but you've gotten nasty lately. Everybody's noticed. And how much weight you've lost. You ought to lay off the shit for a while."

Another red fiery bolt streaked through me. Toad noticed and stepped back.

"Just take it a little easy. OK?"

"Yeah. Sure, man. Stay frosty."

Paul walked away muttering to himself, "Take it easy, take it easy." Same same fucked up shit people had been trying to sell him all of his life. And who were they to fucking judge him? As if they were all so fucking successful! Jive jealous assholes! He was making a break from all the culturally-imposed societal cages, from being controlled by the fucking government from first breath to last.

A lot of former combat vets had been reassigned to Qui Nhon to wait out their tours, and many of them thought life there was a Number One duty assignment. Paul had heard so many boonie stories that he felt as if he had spent the last eight months out there. But none of the conversations could ever hope to fill his aching notebook with tales to tell, real life stories *a/ a* Stephen Crane, Ernest Hemingway or James Jones.

He had written, "Yea, though I walk through the valley of death I will fear no evil because I'm the baddest motherfucker in the valley" on his helmet cover, but it was total wanna-be bullshit. Looking back, he realized how dangerously delusional he had become—though his actions would very soon teach him the power of thought when, against all odds, he manifested a set of circumstances that helped him escape what he had, to that point, called "the bullshit."

CHAPTER 8

Arrogance and Ignorance

For months Paul had been like a starving man allowed into the banquet hall unsupervised, gobbling down stimulants and acting without any restraint or discrimination. In his drug-fueled haze, he had made the classic error of conflating momentary awareness and temporary power with real and significant self-care and confidence. The other crucial crack in the foundation of his Universe was believing in his own press releases, while ignoring the well-meant advice of those far wiser.

It was the dangerous, potentially deadly, combination of arrogance and ignorance that had driven Paul to request a Mental Hygiene job when he had no solid experience or education. The same onerous twins had led him to volunteer for Viet Nam. Now he had fallen into a decidedly non-regulation manner of acting and dressing that guaranteed to set off a nuclear reaction in any King Kong lifer's brain.

Paul wore sun-bleached fatigues with sleeves rolled non-regulation below the elbows, and shined his boots shined with a chocolate bar. His totally unauthorized boonie hat barely covered his shaggy almost-shoulder length hair.

Declining to shave for a week at a time added to his appearance as being a Skid Row junkie transported to Viet Nam. And being loaded on speed, weed, and alcohol—the Minimum Daily Requirement for him? Oh my God!

In keeping with the perfect timing of the Universe, it was then that Paul had the bad fortune (some might say the inevitable karmic encounter), with the newly arrived Sergeant Major Ronald Kosciusko Jackowski.

The man was the textbook example of what a "strack" stateside soldier should be. He wore brand new, highly starched and tailored jungle fatigues; his belt buckle was bright and shiny; jungle boots perfectly spit-shined and glossy; and his head shaved so clean you could use it for a mirror. He was striding confidently across the compound, believing he owned all he saw, when he stopped like a hunting dog on point rendered aphasic. Jackowski was so affronted by the vision of Paul that he believed he might have been hallucinating, while Paul remained blissfully unaware of the older man's his presence. Paul invariably skulked around the edges of the compound, sticking to the shadows, preoccupied with his own thoughts, and singing along with the idiosyncratic music in his head.

"Soldier!"

Since Paul had long before resigned from the U.S. Army in his mind, the man's address was the equivalent to a mosquito buzzing his ear. When he noticed a beet-red pinhead cherry sergeant standing in close proximity and shouting, he kept walking.

"You there, troop!"

Paul continued scuttling along, ruminating about pain and glory, completely preoccupied with his own process.

"You there, Specialist!" said the Fucking New Guy (FNG) as he rushed toward his target of interest like a guided missile.

The two of them came together like a pair of locomotives running full speed headlong into each other on the same track. The older man came into Paul's peripheral vision and raised an angry finger at him like an arthritic old woman, like God about to kick Adam and Eve out of Paradise!

Paul stopped in his tracks, and innocently pointed at his chest.

"Me?" he asked, incredulous at such a strange encounter.

"Yes. You. What's your name? And your unit? Who's your NCOIC?"

"I'm the Psychiatric Consultant at the 14th General Dispensary. And I don't know who my NCOIC is, Sergeant."

Jackowski's face seemed to explode as his capillaries and corpuscles leaked blood from under the surface of his skin. Then he pushed his crimsoned face so close to Paul's that Paul was forced to inhale the Aqua Velva wafting in steam clouds from the folds of the older man's neck.

"Stand at attention, soldier! My name is Sergeant Major Jackowski. I'm the new Support Command top-kick. And I ORDER you to shave that moustache off! NOW."

A white-hot shot of rage blinded Paul as he fumbled for his wallet. When the haze cleared, Paul realized that the punk-ass lifer reminded him of every man who had ever fucked with him, starting with his father. In spite of realizing he had been severely triggered, in the next billionth of a second, he sorted through options of how to kill the man: strangle him; dismember him; cut off his head; disembowel him; and/or shoot off his balls. Instead Paul ripped out his wallet, and pulled loose the entire contents seeking his ID card. Then he took a step forward, and jammed the laminated card into Jackowski's flushed face.

"You cannot ORDER me to do that, Sergeant Major! My moustache is legal! It's on my ID Card, Sergeant Major!" he snarled, spittle flecking the older man's face and uniform.

The troops had been warned he was coming, and everyone got brand new IDs with hair and moustaches intact. If it was on your ID, they could not force you to change.

Jackowski was apoplectic, eyes bulging, cheeks puffed. He looked as if he might stroke out. He peeled Paul's ID off his face and silently noted the information in a small notebook.

After he wordlessly handed Paul back his ID, he drew himself up to his full five feet six inches, squared his shoulders, and smiled maliciously.

"We will meet again, Specialist! You can count on that!"

Paul continued his internal monologue. What a fucking arrogant little prick! Fuck him and fuck his regulations. He still wanted to kill him!

By nightfall, the story had made the rounds. Paul heard differently embellished versions of it as he made the rounds of various sets, smoking weed and drinking enough Scotch whiskey to destroy gravity. At some point, he passed out in somebody's hooch, sitting in a chair, neck askew, elbows akimbo.

He woke up with an artillery barrage in his head, a thousand-gun batteries firing simultaneously. His mouth was filled with metallic cotton, eyes stuck shut with Super Glue, ears stuffed with excelsior, and brain turned into overcooked oatmeal. Both his short term and immediate memories were completely erased.

Then, with a start, he looked at his watch.

"Oh, fucking shit! I'm already forty-five minutes late!"

As he straggled, bedraggled, in through the back door of the clinic, Paul saw that the place was packed. He dashed down the hallway, nabbed a cup of extra-strong coffee passing through the Preventive Medicine Section and opened his office door—to find Toad sitting in his chair, doing a crossword.

"Hey man."

"Hey yourself."

"Looks busy."

"It was. It's slow now. Doc Solomon was looking for you earlier. He had a referral. Doc Smith did too."

"I guess I'm in the shitter now."

Toad raised his eyebrows and said, "I don't know, man. They sent them over to the 67th."

"Oh, fucking shit! I'm really gonna hear about this!"

"Uhmm, I don't know, man. Ham is in my office waiting for you. Heard all about you and the new Sergeant Major. They were both here earlier looking for you."

"Oh, motherfucking shit!"

He shook his head.

"I'm sorry, man. I tried to warn you."

"Yeah, I know. Thanks man. Guess it won't hurt if I finish my coffee first," Paul said, taking another sip.

"Let me know if there's anything I can do to help."

"OK, brother. And thanks."

Paul looked deeply into Toad's eyes and they shook hands.

"I'm sorry I been such an asshole lately. But," Paul said, shrugging his shoulders, "you know how it is."

"I surely do, man. Get back to me when you're done. We'll smoke a joint."

"Cool, brother."

Ham was sitting behind Toad's desk (which was better quality than his own), sipping from a large mug of coffee, reading the *Stars and Stripes*. He looked more porcine than usual this morning. The instant he turned his flat, baleful eyes on Paul, he knew there would be no reprieve.

"Hi, Ham. Toad said you wanted to see me."

"My name is Staff Sergeant Hammons. And these" he said, shaking a sheaf of paperwork in his left hand, "are the orders rescinding your TDY here at this Dispensary. Here's your travel orders and a reassignment to the Ninth Infantry Division."

"I, I, I don't...understand."

"It's really simple. You're outta here. ASAP. Forthwith. Today. Get your shit and git. If you don't leave today, you're to sleep in the Transient Barracks tonight. By order of the Colonel. At the 67th."

"Fuuuck!"

"You done fucked with the wrong man this time, troop."

"Thanks, a fuck of a lot."

"He could have had your ass in the stockade for insubordination and refusing a direct order."

"I'm going to the Inspector General (IG)!"

"NG, troop. The Colonel already talked to him about your inconsistent attendance and poor military attitude."

Paul staggered out of the office, feeling like the target of a scatological air strike.

Paul's thoughts ratcheted around his head like a berserk pin ball. Fucking Ninth Infantry Division! Jesus! Shit! What if they're sending him as a combat medic? Holy fuck! With an infantry platoon? He'll get fucking killed! Jesus H. Fucking Christmas Tree! Those fuckers!

Leaning against the outside wall of the Dispensary, Paul hastily checked his orders. He checked all of the details. Everything seemed to be in order. 94G20. Social Work/Clinical Psychology Specialist. Thank fucking God! Thank fucking God!

It wasn't nearly as bad as he figured. He'd probably be assigned to Headquarters Headquarters Company (HHC) to a clinic down in the Delta. He was still tripping in his own head and could not deny his desire to blow the old lifer bastard up! At least he was getting the fuck out of Qui Nhon! He might even get to spend a day or two in transit in Saigon! And again, thanked whatever gods there were that he was not going to the boonies. He was scared shitless actually, now that he had had a too-close encounter.

"Did you hear about this shit?" Paul said, shaking the paperwork in Toad's face as the other man approached.

"Just now. I was looking for you."

"My head is fucking killing me. I gotta go find something stronger than aspirins."

"Here," he said, "Take these."

He opened his hand and a half dozen Darvons fell into Paul's outstretched palm.

"I nabbed them from the Pharmacy."

"Thanks, brother man. I really appreciate it. You know," he started, but tears welling up in his eyes. "You been a real friend to me, in spite of all the shit I've laid on you. I'll never forget it, man." Tears were rolling down his cheeks now, but he didn't even try to hide them.

Toad looked embarrassed and turned away. "Forget it, man. I'd do the same thing for a white man." He laughed. "I'll see you at chow. Don't take any more of that shit."

"OK" was all Paul could manage.

Paul then spent the day gathering his belongings, checking out of his TDY assignment, moving his few belongings to the Transient Barracks, and ducking official looking people at the 67th. Fuck 'em! He was leaving. They could shit in their hat! He was on the manifest for an 0630 flight for Bear Cat, Ninth Division Headquarters.

He sat on his bunk, feeling ripped off and depressed, yet unable to avoid assigning responsibility to himself. When JT sauntered in, "picking" the back of his modest Afro, he stopped and they dapped.

"Hey! I heard what happened, man. Hope they don't send you out to the bush. Shit's nasty down there."

"They can't—unless there's a classification for 'Combat Social Worker.'"

"The Man can do anything he wants. Look what's just happened to you."

"I'm glad to be getting the fuck out of here. That new Sergeant Major is an asshole."

"He'll soon get his ass fragged!"

"I'm glad you came by. I sky up at 0630 tomorrow."

"Wanna get good and loaded tonight? Are you taking any stash with you?"

"Just some buds."

"I'm hip."

His craving had grown so much more intense, especially since the remedy for his crushing headache was sitting in his duffel bag. He had packed a large stash of speed, but then decided to donate it to JT's educational fund. He had eaten the six Darvons and was feeling half past human, as the tight steel band cutting into his aching head was finally lightening up. He reached into his duffel bag and handed JT the bottle.

"Eight-skate-donate! Thanks man!" he said.

"No problemo. I'm swearing off the shit."

"That's cool, man."

I raised my right fist and said "Power to the people."

He laughed and they passed power.

"There it is."

Paul had what was for him a totally strange impulse to go to the chapel. He feeling disgusted about his past, concerned about his present and scared about his future. His life was a fucking mess. He had nowhere else to turn.

He sat in the chapel for an hour, alternately crying and cursing what had befallen him. Eventually, he fell asleep. When he awoke, felt better, filled with a sense that somehow everything was going to be all right.

Part of this confidence was related to a dream he had had of a new America, one in which all people would be free to pursue the lives and lifestyles that suited them; be free to have or not have any job or profession for which they were mentally and physically qualified; and free to live and be in whatever ways they chose to as long as they didn't injure others. It reinforced his belief that he would survive the 'Nam to see his dreams and visions come true; that he would walk the haunted, vaunted streets of her heart, and cry aloud in protest and shame deeds done in her holy name. He ached to breathe deeply this mysterious freedom that America so profoundly represented. He walked out of the chapel with a powerful aura of peace that overrode his confusion, and whatever potential horror awaited him.

He ran smack into Toad.

"Been looking for you, man."

"Just sorting out some shit."

"Wanna smoke some mary-jew-wanny?"

"Does the Pope shit in the woods?"

They went to a rarely used bunker, in this sleepy compound in the capital of Quang Nhai Province. Paul was so grateful to have a true friend in his world that had suddenly been turned upside down.

Toad pulled a joint out of his pocket, lit it, and took a deep hit, then passed it.

"Good shit, man. Damn good shit."

Paul broached another topic that was on his mind. " I wanna come live in California when I get back to the world. Can I look you up? "

"Everybody does" said Toad, and smiled wistfully, perhaps thinking of all the changes the Golden State had been through already, and how much more it would change with the influx of other pilgrims like Paul seeking the illusionary freedom it promised. Then Toad said, "OK, brother. You've always got a place with me."

"That's righteous, man."

"I've always been your friend. I tried to warn you about that shit!"

"Yeah, you did. But you always came across like my father lecturing me."

"You'll probably write about it some day."

"Thanks to you. I learned a lot hanging around with you."

"You were always willing to learn—and you pick up on stuff really quick too."

Paul was getting embarrassed so he asked Toad if he'd ever heard of the one-two snake.

"No. What is it?"

"This guy gets bit right on the head of the dick by this snake. The medic tells his buddy 'You gotta suck the poison out right away, or he'll die!' So, he turns to his friend, and says, 'Doc says you're gonna die, motherfucker!'"

They both fell back against the wall of the bunker laughing and choking on the smoke.

"That's some great shit!"

"The 'Nam has some of the best I've ever had!"

Toad's mood shifted then, and he said "I've got something for you."

Then he handed Paul a huge manila folder containing all of the messages, poems, and other scribblings they had written back and forth during the previous eight months.

"If you want to be a writer, you gotta see everything as grist for the mill. It's all good shit to write about."

"You're the only person I know who could say that to me right now—and get me to believe it."

They smoked the joint to the end. Paul's fear and depression had gotten worse by the end of the smoke. He declined to have another.

"I gotta go, man. 0630 comes mighty early."

"Where you gonna sleep?"

"I don't know. I suppose the fucking Transient Barracks. Ham was pretty insistent about that."

"Fuck him! Go get your shit. You can sleep on the floor in my hooch tonight. I'll get you to the airfield in the morning."

"Dynamite, brother. Simply fucking dynamite."

CHAPTER 9
Interview Techniques

It was raining so hard that it was impossible to tell the difference between Nature's torrential revenge and his own sweat. He cursed the rain, the wrath from the skies that soaked his boots, his fatigues, even his food. It rotted his crotch and ruined his mood. It rotted his feet, his face, his fingers. It turned his dick into a prune, got in his eyes, his ears, his nose, his butthole. It beat at him like an infernal, eternal drum, the heartbeat of an uncaring giant, throbbing with the ancient rhythm of the curse that kept him living in the damp, the cold, and the mold while self-righteous rear area assholes sat warm and comfortable in their aluminum sided hooches, smoking dope, and writing letters home complaining about the rain. It beat him relentlessly into submission until he finally came to understand the inspiration for the infamous Chinese torture—the rain, the rain, the eternal fucking rain. It made him wonder if God had taken a day off when rain was invented. It eventually numbed him, washed away all thought, all fear, all pain, even his thoughts until all he could think about was the rain, the rain, the eternal fucking rain.

It was pouring down in horizontal sheets when Paul landed at Bear Cat, Ninth Infantry Headquarters in the Mekong

Delta. He was there less than a day before they shipped him out without consultation.

"What the fuck are you doing here?" was the only thing he was asked.

Not having known that he was coming or having a copy of his orders other than the ones he gave them, their elemental wisdom had been to send him on when they found out he was not a genuine combat medic. The very same thing happened with the First Infantry Division at Lai Khe when he landed there. There he had had to argue that he would likely kill more people than not, if they intended to send him to the field. They cut him temporary orders on the spot, and dispatched him forthwith. "The Hundred and First always needs warm bodies."

He'd arrived red-eyed, disoriented, dazed and confused at the 101st In-Country Orientation School, completely unprepared for "The Eagle's Nest," Division Headquarters in Biên Hòa. There was a huge wooden "Screaming Eagle" demarcating the Division Headquarters building. He had to assume that airborne qualified troops were exempt from incoming mortar and rocket rounds, since the "powers that be" had seen fit to have this perfect target constructed and installed.

A Staff Sergeant in starched fatigues called the troops to attention as they assembled themselves in the blowing red clay dust, then gave them "Parade rest" and introduced himself.

"My name is Staff Sergeant Williams. I am NCOIC of Repo Depot, where all of y'all are currently assigned. While a member of my command, you will be expected to fall out for all formations, including reveille, and police call."

This elicited groans and catcalls of derision, especially from those who had been in country for a while.

"A-ten-shun," Williams commanded.

As they snapped to, the sergeant's face took on a scarlet shade of fury.

"You cockroaches are in this country to fight for the honor of the United States of America, and as representatives of the U.S. Army. A lot of people think that military discipline should be slack because this is 'Vit Nam'; that troops shouldn't have to get haircuts or shine their boots. That, gentlemen, is not the case as long as you are a member of Repo Depot. You will be expected to maintain military discipline. Do you understand me?"

"Yes, sergeant." A unanimous reply escaped the lips of the assembled crew of about fifteen replacements, most of them fresh out of jump school and new in country. The NCOs who had been on Paul's flight had been separated out when they arrived, and shepherded away elsewhere by another lifer.

The replacements were then turned over to the care of a very young buck sergeant wearing camouflage Jump Wings and a CIB above the left pocket of his tiger-striped fatigues. His eyes swiveled like a pair of marbles in his head as he walked slowly to the edge of a low wooden platform and faced them. His presence commanded total respect and attention. As the silence unrolled, the few, the fortunate few, stood rooted to the ground. As his icy eyes surveilled them, his eyes spoke volumes into the silence.

Then he roared, "GENTLEMEN!"

The intense force of his voice caused the Universe to momentarily blink, and all of those gathered fell into a cone of almost unnatural silence. Paul felt his skin stretch hard against muscle and bone, and he narrowed his concentration on the man.

"There are only two kinds of people in this outfit."

He basked in the moment like a consummate actor in his very best role.

"The quick and the dead."

No one spoke. No one dared.

"I want you to listen up. I'm only going to say this once."

His face took on an ancient patina and his energy seemed infinitely older, harder, and crueler. His eyes had sunk into his skull, as if seeing visions of a secret, sacred terrain to which only he could go, and none of the rest of them ever would.

"Something I say today may save your life."

Paul was scared shitless. He had wished for a deeper slice of life, and he was getting it big time—only this time it was the real thing. His bullshit bravado could only get him in a hurt locker. Immediately after the formation was dismissed, he started counting the days to his Date of Estimated Rotation from OverSeas (DEROS), even if it meant having time to serve in the world.

Later that same afternoon, while Paul was hanging out in the Transient Barracks, his name was called. When he reported, he was hustled aboard a C-47 heading north to Phu Bai. He was glad he'd made out his will. In that moment, he understood "living one day at a time, as if it were your last."

Paul had expected a dusty, fly-blown outpost in the middle of a reinforced, triple concertina-wired, land-mined fortress where everyone was walking around in flak jackets and steel pots, with automatic weapons loaded with clips taped end-to-end. Conversely, Phu Bai was an up-to-date base with the best equipment and facilities modern military-industrial technology could provide for a "forward area" —sitting in the midst of some of the most disputed territory in the entire country.

Once upon a time, the lifers had tried to reinforce a lot of jive military discipline jive there—formations and other military nonsense—but after a few "fragging incidents" convinced the hierarchy that they were now too close to the real war for that to wash.

Paul's MOS was in great demand, especially by the 101st, so he was spared some measure of the usual same-o same-o. He spent his first night in the Transient NCO Barracks, lying awake half the night anticipating the siren and the sounds of incoming rockets and mortars. In the morning, he had barely choked down coffee, powdered eggs, bacon and toast, when a young Specialist from HQ tracked him down carrying a thick wad of orders in his hand. The greater wisdom had decided that he should be assigned right there "temporarily."

"Then what's the fucking urgency?"

"There's somebody for you to see right now!"

"Right now? I just got here!"

"Workie, workie, troop!"

"Fuck off!"

"Don't shoot me, man! I'm just the messenger!"

They were glad to have him, even as a non-Airborne "leg." Counting Paul, there was only four of them to cover the entire Division (approximately 11,000 men at that point). The 101st was inundated with requests from units for evaluations of men who were combat fatigued yet expected to ruck up, and go back into the fray. There had been a continuing wave of men who'd decided they'd had enough of combat or the 'Nam or both, and demonstrated their lack of verve by getting Article 15s and Courts Martial. All of them needed a Psychiatric Evaluation as a part of their required package of paperwork to go home.

The day Paul arrived, he replaced an E-6 who jumped on the same chopper off of which he had gotten. The man had been skating for weeks and left Paul a backlog of cases to resolve. He set up appointments, did the social history and made a provisional diagnosis for his boss, the Division Psychiatrist, who would fly in on a chopper, and see thirty or forty guys in a day. He would always review Paul's work, make a few comments, and then add his own signature.

The war had changed so dramatically after Tet of 1968, when the NVA and the VC overran many installations, even attacked the Imperial Palace in Hue and the U.S. Embassy in Saigon. Though U.S. forces had re-captured all of it, the fighting had been intense and garnered worldwide media attention, many of whose pundits speculated that it was a real turning point that did not bode well for the continued U.S. presence in Southeast Asia. Many of Paul's clients expressed a sense of futility at risking their lives and losing their friends. It was clear that, combined with poor command responsibility and leadership, the NVA and VC (backed by both China and the Soviets) were going to win.

He was told that Dr. William ("Wild Bill," of course) McKenzie had been there yesterday. He had evaluated thirty-two guys, and would be returning "in a few days." So, without any further ado, Paul checked in with as many of the battalion medics as were available for him to apprise them of his presence, and then started making appointments, going through the files of those who had requested to be seen by Mental Hygiene. There were two others with his job were at locations in I-Corps at different fire support bases (FSB), as well as a lifer Spec 6, who ran the show in Biên Hòa.

The quality and tone of those wanting psych services were similar to those he had seen at Fort Riley or Qui Nhon, though with the added stressor of having been exposed to active combat. Many were from broken homes, had problems with authorities, and/or simply hated the service, or the 'Nam, or both. Even when Paul explained to them about the consequences of an "Undesirable Discharge," it made no difference. Invariably they all had "good reasons" for wanting to leave, and, equally well-fabricated fantasies about how wonderful everything would be when they got home. Then there were those with legitimate psychiatric complaints who should have been ruled out prior to service, and those who had been affected as a direct result of severe traumatic experiences.

RTO Todd Wilkins of Elko, Nevada was such a one.

He came in grimy, sweating, complaining of many injustices, and reeking of cigarettes. The platoon medic had referred him to the battalion medic, who referred him to one of their docs, who sent him to "see the shrink." The more he listened, the more he realized that the man had a substantive complaint.

He was "just a grunt," he said, another college drop out who'd lost his deferment, and been sent greetings from Uncle Sam. He sat in the chair next to Paul's desk, twisting the ends of his red moustache, and chain-smoking cigarettes from a pack he'd opened from the bottom to keep the filters dry. Paul had an actual desk there, but sometimes he used a jeep or a tent, anywhere he could get a little bit of privacy. He and everything in his office was lightly sprinkled with red clay dust, ubiquitous in I-Corps, settling on anything moving or stationary.

After quitting stimulants, Paul had resolved to straighten up and attempt to be a more functional soldier. He vowed to make a difference, do some real counseling, and bring real assistance to the men who were actually fighting the war!

Soon thereafter Paul realized that he had tried to fool himself again, having created a fantasy to insulate him from being truly true to himself. Even those who professed to believe in the spurious claims promoted by the media about the "domino theory" despised all the political wrangling involved when what they wanted was to "win the war." The military and the government were renowned for very effectively promoting the kind of "reality" they wanted so that men would blindly obey the mandates handed down from on high.

"Hey man! You awake over there?"

Paul had been spacing out, and had been busted. He covered as best he could, ashamed and waving his hand in the air, as he said, "No man, just trying to absorb what you're telling me. I'm the FNG here."

"Cherry boy?"

"I did eight and a half months in Qui Nhon before this."

Old timers sometimes called it the "Hundred and Worst," or even the "Thunder Chickens." Paul couldn't help myself. He was proud to be with this legendary outfit, where the war was a daily reality, in spite of how really dysfunctional the Army was.

"So, you fucked up!"

"What'd ya mean?"

"Must have to get sent to this shithole!"

Paul was suddenly aware of how completely naïve he must appear to the men who were daily living the war.

"We're actually here to talk about you."

Wilkins laughed and choked on the smoke pouring out of his lungs. He sighed deeply, and took up his narrative.

"I been here five months now. I'm getting freakier all the time. I might frag the CO. I don't want to go back out there. Can't you help me, man?"

"What do you want me to do?"

"I don't know. Can't you get me a psych profile or something?"

"For what?"

"How about I tell you something really weird I did?"

"Like what?"

"I shot this gook, see, then I ran up to him and emptied a whole extra clip into him just to make sure he was dead."

"Makes sense. And?"

Paul too had gotten freaky in just a few days. His sleep was lighter, and disturbed by weird dreams. He had learned to sleep in his fatigues, and could already distinguish between in-coming and out-going in his sleep. He was smoking almost two packs a day now, but at a dollar a carton, that was easy to manage. He was drinking twenty or thirty cups of coffee every day, desperately trying to fend off the lingering effects of his abuse of stimulants. He wanted to wake up in some way he was currently unable to fathom. He was smoking as much weed as often as he could.

"What the fuck do you want, man—war stories?" Wilkins asked, then slammed his fist down onto the top of my desk.

Paul came up with a good line of psychobabble to help move the situation forward—and to not appear intimidated. He still believed he had to look as if he knew what he was doing.

"I don't want anything from you. I'm just here to listen."

"OK, man. I'll tell you a story about what happened to me my very first week. It's still bothering me. It's why I want to get out of this fucking place."

"If that's what you want."

"I was one of two FNGs in the platoon. The old timers treated us like we had leprosy. They told us we were bad luck. I got baptized by fire that very first week."

Paul sat impassively, absorbing as much of the other man's raggedy emotions as he could. He believed that emotional release was the key to any client's predicament, no matter how otherwise horrendous the experience.

"We were working our way down this game trail. There were Ho Chi Minh sandal prints everywhere. We knew the VC owned the ville, still about two klicks (kilometers) away."

His gaze turned inward and his voice softened.

"Sometimes it's so beautiful out there. I was walking along, scared shitless and bored at the same time. I started tripping out, checking out the jungle and watching all the incredible colors. I should have been paying attention. Fuck! Then BAM!" he said, slashing the air with the knife-edge of his hand.

"'BAM?'"

"Somebody pushed me face first into the mud. I jumped up ready to fight."

"And?"

"It was Happy Jack. He was the assistant squad leader, even though he's only an E-4. He's in his second tour, so he's real hard. He always smiled when he was serious, —and he was smiling at me."

He coughed again, and chain-lit another cigarette.

"He said 'Pay attention, cherry. You're a long way from home,' then turned back to start scanning the trail. I didn't even see him come up on me."

"Then what?"

"I mumbled 'Goddamn motherfucker,' and he heard me! He was like ten feet away, and I barely whispered!"

Paul nodded his head, to keep Wilkins moving forward.

"Then he was standing in front of me, still grinnin', but with his Bowie knife stuck under my chin. 'This time I'll pretend you didn't say that.' Then he just turned and disappeared like a wisp of smoke."

"He scared the shit out of me! But he was the best in the boonies. All I did was hump—up and down the hills, and through the valleys, sweating my ass off. My brand-new uniform irritated the shit out of me. And I was bored fucking shitless. I started counting trees, bees, water buffalo turds, like a little kid on a long trip. I started thinking about home, about women, and food. God, I was missing women more than anything. Fuck! I missed sex! I used to fantasize about getting' a quick blow job from a "round-eyed donut dolly." If I didn't beat off two or three times a day, I'd have wet dreams."

Paul laughed even though he was not intending to do so.

"Why are you telling me all of this?"

"I was tripping because I felt like my life was disappearing! R-and-R was a thousand years away! And I couldn't stop thinking about dying! All the old timers always made jokes about killing each other!"

The guy was a trip, and a poet at that! Paul was going to write down his story as soon as he left.

"What the fuck am I telling you this shit for? You're just another REMF!'

Paul didn't know what to say. He stared at him, hoping a magical notion would roll out of his mouth.

His client started to leave, but Paul motioned him back down.

"You're right. I am a pogie, but a very well trained one. I can help you, but you have to tell me what's really going on, or I can't do squat."

He sighed and made an appraisal of me from under his beetled brows.

"Some old ass Christian lifer Chaplin tried to 'inspire' my platoon one time. He read us some shit from Joyce Kilmer, the WWI poet. He somehow thought it would make our lives easier to consider Jesus's suffering."

"What do you mean?" asked Paul.

"You know. You must have read it in grade school. It was supposed to have been written by some infantryman in the trenches, comparing his suffering with that of Jesus. 'Lie easier cross upon his back?'"

"Oh. OK. I do kind of remember that."

"A bunch of my guys just started cursing him. I said 'Fuck that, Padre. Let him hump an M-16 and a Prick-25 for a while!'"

Paul laughed at the picture of an old White Chaplin talked to battle-seasoned troops that way. Then he took a breath, and attempted to bring his client back to his presenting complaint.

"So, what's happening right now?"

"I have bad dreams all the time. Sometimes I feel like I'm not real, like somebody else is living my life, like everything is happening to somebody else."

"Like what?"

"I don't know if I want to talk to you any more, man. This shit's eating at me, but when I talked to our doc, he told me to 'forget about it, don't mean nothing,' but I can't. I keep remembering."

"What? What do you keep remembering?"

"Another guy in my platoon, that fucking Franklin. Me and him got to be friends, probably because we were the only cherries in the platoon."

"What happened?"

"We just took a break to nab something to eat. And I was complaining about having ham and motherfuckers (lima beans) again. Franklin was sitting on the other side of this tree, right next to me. I asked him if he wanted to trade. He'd been bored too, complaining about how he would like something to happen, even if we got hit."

Wilkins was sweating profusely, twisting his boonie hat in his hands, cigarette hanging out of the corner of his mouth.

"Aww fuck, I can't talk about it, man!"

"We did pretty good for today. We can talk again."

"No, man. I can't take any more fucking bad dreams about this. Doc says maybe you can help me, but I don't see what good it does to talk about it."

"I can refer you to the Division Psychiatrist."

"Think he'll give me a profile? I can't go out to the fucking bush like this."

"Let's talk some more next week. Just go on sick call and tell them you have an appointment."

"We're supposed to be going back to the bush again tomorrow."

Wilkins got up and started pacing in circles, smoking frantically.

Paul kept talking to him. "Listen, I think the Army sucks, too. But you can't just get out because you don't wanna go back to the boonies."

"So, what do I have to do? Kill the First Shirt?"

"That'll only get you sent to LBJ. I hear they got rats down there bigger than dogs!"

"Yeah, and the guards kill them with their M-16s!"

We laughed, breaking the tension.

Paul knew from the moment he walked in that he was a head, so he thought he'd smoke a joint with him. Paul knew it was "wrong" clinically, that it violated all the rules. He just really wanted to get high!

"Let's smoke a joint!"

"What?"

"FTA! Let's smoke a joint!"

They did a short dap and headed outside. They walked up the hill behind the Battalion Aid Station, upwind from the shitters. The smell of burning kerosene and human feces would cover any smell of the buds, and from the hillside they had a vantage point from which to see anyone approaching.

"This is a trip, man! You do this all the time?"

"First time actually!"

"Why me?"

"I knew you were a head as soon as you walked in."

He laughed. "I knew you were, too."

"I was sitting there wanting to get high. And decided 'Fuck it!'"

"Right on, brother!" he said as we dapped again.

Paul asked, "Wanna go back in, and rap a little more?"

"I like it better out here. Feels safer. I can see what's coming."

"I'm hip."

He turned very abruptly and put his face close to mine.

"So. Franklin bought it, right then, right next to me. We were just sitting there eating—and BAM! His whole face just blew up! Sniper. One round right through the C-rat (ration) can. Blew up his whole head, man. I had his fucking brains all over me! I keep waking up in the middle of the night screamin' with his brains all over me! I can't eat. I can't sleep."

Paul felt as though someone had scooped out his insides with a dull spoon. He was paralyzed with the vison that had just been painted as Wilkins turned away sobbing, shoulders shaking.

"I feel like I'm dead unless I'm drunk, or when doc gives us uppers to stay awake in the bush. But I'm getting afraid to even do that. Every time I get loaded, I get freaky. All I want is to kill a bunch of people."

"You didn't seem particularly freaky until just a minute ago. Maybe you ought to just stick to weed."

"I know, man, I know. But every once in a while, I <u>need</u> to do some speed, or get really drunk. Otherwise I feel like I'm going to explode!"

"I'll talk to my boss. See what we can do. Tell your doc to call me."

"Thanks, man. Maybe you ought to smoke dope with all your clients!"

"Maybe I will."

We shook hands and then dapped.

"Gotta sky, brother," he said, right fist in the air, thumb extended.

CHAPTER 10
Wake Up Call—Part II

"Wild Bill" McKenzie ran bent over, pushed by the prop wash of the helicopter blades into the Medical Battalion HQ tent, and then quickly brushed himself free of some of the ubiquitous red clay dust. He was tall and rangy with coal black hair worn almost to the collar and a moustache that was a close match to Paul's. He'd been in country almost ten months, and he and Paul recognized each other immediately, like brothers from different mothers.

"How you doing, Marzeky? I'm Bill McKenzie," he said, slapping a floppy boonie hat against his right thigh.

"Yes, sir. I know, sir."

"Nice moustache" he said, fingers straying to tighten the twist of his own.

"Thanks. You too, sir," Paul replied, a little off guard by his less than military approach.

"I'm short. Why don't we dispense with the 'sir' shit, OK?" he said, with a lopsided grin that totally belied the incredible sharpness of his mind. He obviously used it to great effect to get to the heart of matters with clients. "Call me doctor, unless the brass is around, and Bill when we're alone. OK?"

"Fine with me, Doctor McKenzie, er, Bill. I've been with the Hundred and Worst almost a week now. I was wondering when I was gonna meet you."

He stiffened, bristling and then pursed his lips and spoke tersely.

"Let's get one thing straight. Never, understand, <u>never,</u> call it the 'Hundred and Worst' in my presence. I'm 'Airborne all the way.'"

"I thought you were a draftee."

"I am the only Airborne Qualified Board-Certified Psychiatrist in the Army."

"Wow, sir."

"Good. Just so we're clear. I've been reading your case files. You've been doing some good work here!"

"Thank you, doctor."

"Your referral, Todd Wilkins. He's the first one you sent me who wasn't a '212.' I'll see him when he's on stand down. Set it up. I'll give him some meds, but I want you to carry him, see if we can keep him with his unit."

"But he's freaking out, having flashbacks, maybe hallucinations. He probably needs a psych profile."

"Does he have any Courts Martial? Article 15s?"

"Negatory."

"Then he's not a 212."

"No. The cat's been on line since he got here. Now he's having major anxiety symptoms. He meets the criterion for Combat Stress Neurosis, especially the depressive and anxiety symptoms. The guy's legitimate."

"Most of the Division's up in the A Shau."

"'A Shau?'"

"About 75 klicks from here, on the border with Laos. The Ho Chi Minh Trail is supposed to be five thousand miles of roads and trails."

"What?" Paul was shocked.

"The NVA move five tons of material every month through there by hand and on bicycles."

"What?" He was incredulous.

"The Marines been there and the First Cav before us. They both got pretty fucked up."

"Why don't we just bomb the shit out of it?"

"We do, but they've got concrete reinforced bunkers and a whole city underground. I heard that the Second of the Oh Deuce (2/502 Infantry) has been getting their collective ass kicked up there. They found a whole highway system buried three or four stories down. They captured tanks and trucks, all kinds of food and weapons, even some crew-served 85 mm arty."

"No shit?" My brilliant repartee was showing.

"And an entire surgical hospital, with a series of recovery wards hidden five stories down."

"How do you know all this?"

"The guys just really like to talk to me. Must be my healing presence!" he said with a smirk.

Paul looked around carefully before he addressed his next question.

"Sir, Bill, are you always this loose? With enlisted men?"

"Marzeky, I've been here a long time, and I basically do not give a shit! I am short! But don't tell the brass. They want me to re-up!"

"Jesus!"

"We have really important work to do here. I don't just mean the '212' shit. Some units been hit really hard." He leaned toward me, and pseudo-conspiratorially whispered, "This next piece has to remain completely confidential, OK?"

He looked around too. The HQ building seemed relatively deserted.

"Some units have had 30% KIA (Killed in Action), and as much as 50% WIA (Wounded in Action). Of course, the NVA are losing far more than we are. It's this goddamn war of attrition we're pursuing!"

"What's that, Bill?"

"If we kill more of them than they kill of us, we win!"

"What the fuck kind of thinking is that?"

"There's two very erroneous aspects to that kind of thinking."

"Please tell me."

"First, they've got approximately two million men and women under arms. They can throw a lot of force at us, absorb those kinds of losses and keep coming."

"OK, I get that. And?"

"The NVA don't have film crews broadcasting into the homes of Mr. and Mrs. America every night!"

The pro-war defenders had a great deal of difficulty with the war being broadcast from battlefields. In print and media, the dead were always noble, painted as having given their lives in "valiant and essential encounters to preserve the American way of life." Paul had heard a rumor that someone's mother had actually seen her son killed via live feed from an embedded film crew. (The Tri-lateral Commission would, after the war, effectively shut down live coverage of wars, and totally control the media-spin that led to the gigantic popular "uprising" that put an end to the extremely profitable Vietnam War, stating that Americans had had access to "too much democracy.")

Paul's poor little Midwestern mind had never heard anything like this. He had mainly heard the sanitized version promoted by the government and its lackey media.

"Jesus Fuck!"

Bill took a deep breath and then switched tacks.

"I'll give Wilkins a Temporary Profile. That'll keep him out of the boonies for a while. But I want you to keep good case notes, and see him every week. Plus, we'll meet for supervision once a week."

Paul was both excited and scared at the same time. It was a lot of responsibility he was being given as well as his first real case to carry.

"Fine by me. I, uh, actually carried maybe a dozen clients, total, during the time I was at Fort Riley. Nothing like this, of course."

"Good. Good. You need anything? Having any major problems?"

"Well, sir, er, Bill, sometimes I get scared shitless. I love flying. I really get off on the adrenaline rush, especially when there's an emergency, like that guy up at Nancy." Paul had received an urgent call to go to LZ Nancy (north and east of Sally) to talk to a trooper immediately.

Paul had asked them to transport him down ASAP.

"You don't understand, doc. He's locked up in a Conex container. He tried to kill the First Shirt. You gotta come up and talk to him. He's under guard."

In due course, Paul did just that. The man remained in chains when they spoke, and his initial provisional assessment was that there seemed to be no significant psychiatric condition. (He did, of course, have some degree of what would become known as Posttraumatic Stress Disorder [PTSD], but then almost everyone in-country did.) Of course, since Paul was not a Qualified Mental Health Professional, Bill had had him transferred under guard to the prison ward at LBJ for further evaluation.

After this reflection, Paul picked up the train of his narrative.

"I get really freaked out sometimes. I am just so afraid I'm gonna die."

"Wild Bill" grinned his trademark grin, and twisted the ends of his moustache—then slapped me on the shoulder.

"We all gotta die sometime, Marzeky!"

"Thanks a fuck of a lot! I never really had much of a life before the Army. I want to get back to the world and have a real one."

He laughed again. "Just keep your shit together. You'll do all right."

"Yeah, right."

Just then, Paul heard an arriving chopper and the prop wash swept into the building like a virulent storm.

I shouted to be heard. "And if I don't? Sin loi (sorry) motherfucker, huh?"

He laughed and raised a thumb into the air.

Paul felt immediately better knowing that Wilkins was going to get a profile. He had to acknowledge that his "clinical objectivity" had slipped. Strictly speaking, what he had done was unethical and unprofessional. He had seen his client as a human, a brother, even a potential friend, not just a client. He didn't feel he had the right to "stand apart in clinical judgment" of him. Fuck that! He felt more bonded with him than to the fucking Army! Paul was getting really sick of having to defend the position of "military psychiatry," which was really an oxymoron. He saw it as the military's way of using psychobabble to justify releasing without benefits anyone who did not fit its arbitrary guidelines—or returning them "to duty" without ever questioning the rightness or propriety of exactly what the fuck they were doing there in the first place! It really royally pissed him off!

All Paul really wanted to do was to go home! He longed to claim all that he felt was due him, paid in full and guaranteed by his survival. He knew intuitively that he was being hammered on a large anvil, as if he were part of a great molten river being purified in this urgent crucible for purposes as yet unknown and unconceived in the Great Beyond. He was absolutely powerless to change or defend his relationship with the Great Green Machine. He was part of a totally impersonal juggernaut that could, would, and did use everybody and everything.

Except the gooks. They were regularly kicking our collective ass.

They were the fucking Americans! The best equipped, best trained fighting men in the world! And no scrawny little yellow rice-eating motherfuckers in black pajamas carrying second hand weapons and home-made explosives were ever gonna beat them!

Except they were.

Paul believed they were perhaps the most effective guerrilla fighting forces ever assembled. They were committed and determined. They would do anything to defeat the U.S. They had been practicing the arts of war for a very long time before Americans came along to occupy their homeland.

Viet Nam had been taken over by the Imperial Chinese Empire from 111 BCE to 938 CE before achieving liberation. Successive Vietnamese royal dynasties flourished and the nation expanded geographically and politically into Southeast Asia—until the "Indochina Peninsula" was colonized by the French in the mid-19th century secondary to The Opium Wars (1839-1842, and 1856-1860). This determined the political and economic life of the country from that point forward. Following the Japanese occupation in the 1940s, the Vietnamese fought the French in the First Indochina War, eventually expelling the French in 1954 at Dien Bien Phu. Then the Americans arrived—ostensibly to stanch the spread of Communism—but actually to assume the French partnership with the Thai Mafia in the worldwide heroin trade, processing and distribution via the CIA.

Being an occupied nation for over a thousand years gave the Vietnamese plenty of practice at being resourceful. Almost everything U.S. troops discarded was recycled, often with fatal results. Brass artillery and cartridge shells were often reused, as were unexploded ordinance. Old runway mats were turned into housing shells. Soda cans were made into hats. Discarded tires became "Ho Chi Minh sandals." They showed extraordinary dexterity in their efforts to rid their country of the "American parasite."

The NVA co-opted the VC for political purposes and in the field, often using them as a mass force against the U.S. forces, and to keep alive the idea of a "popular revolution," even though the VC regularly "taxed" the peasant population for rice, guns and other materiel. (The Viet Minh were the original "People's Army" after the French War).

In spite of the tremendous bravery and honor of the men in the field; in spite of the best equipment ever made for battle; in spite of more bombs being dropped than in the whole of World War Two and Korea; in spite of creations like "Puff the Magic Dragon" (a highly modified C-130) spitting out 6000 rounds a minute from electric Gatling guns; in spite of incredibly advanced helicopter usage, both offensively and for medical evacuation—the U.S. and their allied forces were hampered by self-serving politicians and handicapped by desk-bound generals and all their minions who were often only interested in getting promoted as a result of their "combat exposure." Most of the command structure was composed of men who had fought in WW II using the now antiquated strategies, against an enemy who had perfected guerilla warfare. The most effective fighting force that ever generated against them were the special ops (or "black ops") teams who infiltrated into areas that were ostensibly "off limits" to wreak death and destruction or to call it in to the fire teams, naval gunfire, or even the "fast movers" (A-4 or F-6 jets).

Paul had heard countless stories about the brave and foolish exploits of the VC. During Tet of 1968 in Biên Hòa, when the sky was filled with star clusters and illumination rounds, and all kinds of automatic weapons, including quad-50s, were sending thousands of rounds (every fourth one a tracer) through the air like electric hyphens, like phosphorous fireflies. A sapper squad used bangalore torpedoes to breach the wire, and turned the claymores around ("Front toward enemy") so that they'd kill or injure us when we detonated them, as they snaked through the triple tangled concertina and razor wire. They had entered the compound with satchel charges of plastic explosives and kept coming. Later it was found that many of the men who had been severely wounded—shot five, six, or eight times, limbs missing—were found with opium balls taped in their nostrils and multiple tourniquets tied on their arms and legs so they could keep coming. They had died *en masse*, indomitable, driven by the fervent desire to take back their homeland.

None of the "imperialist forces" ever considered them to be human. They were gooks or dinks or zips, or slopes—utilizing the old psychological propaganda trick to dehumanize the enemy. "The invaders" didn't feel anything for them, or their culture that it was ten times older, and a thousand times subtler than that of the U.S. None of the troops cared that they had wives and children, friends and lovers, brothers and sisters, who were fighting and dying just as savagely, just as painfully, as they themselves were.

The more Paul thought about these things, the closer he got to the abyssal edge of complete burn out, with three and a half months still to go before having to hack Stateside service.

Paul wanted to get altered to the max! He felt completely tilted by his first meeting with The Boss and didn't know why. He was struggling to fit all the pieces of his intricate puzzle together. How could people who were opposed to fascism and who rejected authoritarianism, still support a corrupt, denigrating system like the military? All he wanted to do was help people. He knew he had to do what he had to do. Otherwise he would just go crazy like a clerk he'd heard about.

No one seemed to know the man's real name. Everyone just called him "Specialist Wilson." He had always wanted to be an infantryman, so when they made him a clerk-typist, he went Airborne, and sent him to Viet Nam to fly a desk. He became increasingly angrier and more isolated.

He typed up the morning reports, and all the official correspondence. He knew who was coming in and who was going home (either in an airplane seat or in a body bag). He knew where and when and why— and even typed the letters for the Captain to the families of the dead. In effect, he ran the company from his desk in the orderly room. When he finally got overwhelmed, he started using heroin— cheap, pure and plentiful. He became even more reclusive and disgruntled, but never said a word to anyone. Instead, he took to scribbling short terse verses in a black notebook, trying to assuage the immensity of his shame and pain. He continued to file requests to go to a combat unit, all of which were denied. He was "too valuable," they "needed" him.

One morning, totally out of character, he did not show up for work.

His NCOIC found the day's reports neatly typed and ready for signature, squared up in the middle of his freshly polished desk. He also found Specialist Wilson, syringe still in his arm, skin and lips blue and cyanotic. As the massive overdose hit, he had slumped forward into the rush, and fell onto the mat rug—candle burning, and his notebook open to his very last poem:

False faces hide the truth.

Who are the true warriors?

Brave in death am I.

CHAPTER 11
Flying—Part II

Paul loved the dinky dau (crazy) weed. He bought it whenever and wherever he could. In Qui Nhon he had souvenired mama-san two cartons of Winstons or Newports for one carton of "Winstones" or "Newpots." He bought bulging one-ounce bags of flower tops for ten bucks. He smoked opium-soaked buds, and triple-long Esmerelda joints sealed in cellophane, ten for two dollars, with a flying purple dragon on the cover.

He scurried up the hill beyond the shitters, and had just lit a bomber when he saw Todd. He flashed him the peace sign, and he flashed it back. Many people have believed it was a "V for Victory" vis a vis WWII, but it was taken as the logo for the British Campaign for Nuclear Disarmament in the 1950's. The peace symbol was drawn on flak vests and helmet covers, often with a wry comment like "Kill a Commie for Christ."

Todd Wilkins took a deep hit of the joint, held it for a minute, and blew out only empty air.

"So, is the shrink going to be here when we're on stand down, man? I can't sleep. I can't eat. Always have one eye open, and one ear half cocked."

"I understand. Want another hit?"

"Nah, it would just make me worse right now."

"This is the only thing that helps me."

"I'm hip. People tell me they're gonna quit when they get back to the world, but I don't believe them. Even when I have long gray hair down to my ankles and a beard to my knees, I'm gonna be getting high!"

"A-fucking-men!" Paul said, and they dapped.

Todd spoke to his desire. "I wish that big old motherfucking Freedom Bird was gonna scoop me up and take me home tomorrow!"

Paul answered enthusiastically. "I hear that! And you know what pisses me off the most? The thousands of fucking protesters who don't know shit about what's going on over here calling us 'baby killers', and 'mother rapers!' If any of them spent even one day over here, they'd never talk shit again!"

"Fuck yeah!"

"Are you sure you don't want another hit, man?"

"Yeah, what the fuck? Over," he said, making a microphone out of the air.

He took a long hit and held it, freezing his diaphragm to keep the smoke in.

"I been reading this book, reminds me of you. It's called *Been Down so Long it Looks like Up to Me* by Richard Farina.

There's this cat Gnossus Popandoupolus—he's always trying to hold his smoke for a whole minute."

Todd exhaled with a mighty gust. "See? No smoke!"

"I'm hip. That was well over a minute, man. I been trying for two. Of course, old Gnossus was back in the Fifties. But their weed wasn't as good as this!"

"Fuck no! This is the killer shit of the whole universe!"

"Before I space on it, Captain McKenzie said he'll see you tomorrow at 1000."

"Is he going to help me?"

"He said he could give you a temporary P-3 profile. He wants you to see me for a while, once a week. If only you didn't have such a good record..." Paul mused. There's a line from this song, 'Handful of gimme and a mouthful of much oblige.'"

"Who said that? I mean about 'handful of gimme'?"

"Fred Neil. Great blues singer."

"Well" he said, and stuck out his hand to shake, "I appreciate all your help. And thanks for the smoke."

That night Paul watched the fireworks. The artillery batteries were sending out harassment and interdictment (H&I) rounds to keep the gooks from getting too comfortable. Watching the muzzle flashes really messed up night vision, though most troopers could adjust within seconds. For others it almost instantaneous, but they had had greater need, self-preservation and the greatest of teachers, fear.

By the next day, Paul had completely forgotten about Wilkins. He was spacing out on his way back from LZ Nancy, a windblown FSB northeast of Phu Bai. He was nicely toasted, and the terrain unfolded beneath the skids of the chopper like the insides of a kaleidoscope as he landed. The crew chief pointed to his ear, and he clicked on his headphones.

"HQ ASAP" was all Paul heard.

He raised a very stoned eyebrow and simply nodded his head, giving the pilot thumbs up. What the fuck did they want with him now?

CHAPTER 12
Party—Part I

"Wild Bill" was waiting at the edge of the landing pad. He was about to catch the same bird out. He held onto his boonie hat with his left hand, leaned close, and shouted in Paul's ear.

"That guy you sent me? Wilkins?"

Paul's brain was momentarily blank.

"You know—the profile?"

"Oh yeah. Hell yes! Wilkins. Spec 4."

"I had to send him back to duty."

"I thought you told me to carry him for a while. Give him some meds."

"His record was too good," said "Wild Bill." "Good referral though!" and he raised his thumb in the air.

When Paul got back to his hooch, he fell onto the bunk, suddenly exhausted.

He couldn't believe it! Wilkins was the sickest puppy he'd yet seen, and he gets sent back to duty!

Paul just wanted to get high, fly free of gravity. He felt so constrained, paranoid, as if there were actually something working to keep him down, as if there were actually a "God" who was personally fucking with him!

He was at least casually acquainted with most of the line medics at LZ Sally in his capacity as the "mental health advisor." He always had a standing invitation to attend their outrageous parties when they were in base camp on stand down. By the time he arrived that night, the entire perimeter of the chopper pad was armed and extremely dangerous, everybody locked and loaded. Electricity was crackling as more and more men arrived with a constant influx of yet more drugs and alcohol. There was very little possibility of the lifers interfering with them that night.

Someone offered him a baggie full of multicolored pills he had called "fruit salad," but Paul just passed it along, as he did with to the heroin, barbiturates, a sticky wad of opium, and even the LSD sent from the world on the back of postage stamps by somebody's sister. Paul was smoking weed and drinking a beer when someone handed him a bag of large orange tablets.

"What the fuck? Malaria tablets?"

"No, man. Preludin" said one of the battalion docs, "diet pills. Guaranteed to speed up your mind!"

Paul took two of the bitter tabs with a swallow of beer.

They shook hands and dapped.

"Paul. Paul Marzeky."

"Doc Roach."

"I've never seen this many people getting loaded at once."

"I'm hip. We got some Cav guys, a bunch of Marines, and even some Seabees from Phu Bai."

"What's the latest poop?"

"Second of the O-Deuce captured four tons of rice hidden in a whole new bunker complex. First of the O-Deuce lost a bunch of guys in the A Shau. 'Course they only found three dead gooks, but they claimed twenty from the blood trails."

Body counts were ludicrous. It all started after the debacle of the Battle of Ia Drang Valley in 1965, where the outnumbered First Cavalry (200 men) ran into three battalions of NVA (1600), that body count got established as a viable way of claiming victories. Dogs, water buffaloes and blood trails got added into the count.

The estimated kill ratio that day was 12:1, and led the U.S. high command to declare a war of attrition. Those foolish officers embraced and promoted the prospect of killing so many of the enemy that the other side would just quit. The seemingly insignificant problem they ignored was that the North had two hundred million men and women they could throw at expelling the invaders. This, in turn, led to the inflation of the official statistics that by late 1969, the equivalent of the population of both North and South Viet Nam had been destroyed—yet the "little yellow people" were still kicking the collective ass of the U.S. might.

As Paul sat quietly contemplating the incredible spectacle all around him, the first blast of the diet pills exploded in his brain like a billion electric splinters. Any memory of the experience pain ever in his life was obliterated. The exhilaration was so immense, so intense, that he forgot who he was, where he was, or even that he was. He felt like a newborn Star Child. When he took off his glasses, he could see perfectly, though what he was witnessing seemed surreal. His brain was a film projector gone berserk. A timeless time later, the initial rush passed, leaving crimson flames of scathing paranoia flashing. It was as if he had just awakened having been magically transported to the chopper pad. He felt totally sensitive to the fact that he was immersed in the intimate acquaintance of fifty seriously loaded folks.

He wondered how could so many stony folks, all so totally trashed, have gathered without some lifer causing a ruckus? He had been gnawing the insides of his cheeks along with a giant wad of chewing gum. His anxiety was streaming through him like molten lava. His paranoia grew until he was convinced the lifers were coming! They were gonna bust them! He had to tell Roach!

"Roach! Roach! They're coming, man! They're coming to get us!"

Roach grabbed him, and forcibly pushed down him to sit. Every cell in Paul's body was straining to run as he clawed at Roach's sleeve. They're coming!

"You're tweaking, man. It's just the rush." Roach handed him a bottle of vodka, and said, "Have a hit of this."

He didn't want any, but he had to trust somebody. As the liquid fire burned down his throat, another rush shook him like a grand mal seizure. It felt like his skin was splitting open, light and heat bursting out of every cell.

"WOOO-EEE!! This shit is a motherfucker!"

He extended his hand, and they slapped palms.

"This place is getting a little too freaky. Wanna play some Hearts?"

"Abso-fucking-lutely!"

Gathering two other like-minded troopers, they drew the shades, and prepared two separate decks for play. Paul couldn't sit still with his stomach jumping, cheeks raw from being chewed on. He kept feeling someone behind him, even though he had his back firmly against a wall. He kept whipping his head around just to be sure.

"Come on, man. Play fucking cards. I got your back. You got mine, dig? We're cool. Besides, we got a man inside," said Roach, and dapped Big Dog, one of the K-9 handlers.

"What do you mean?"

"One of our guys is the Sergeant of the Guard tonight. The lifers are partying too."

Bopper, one of the chopper mechanics, wailed, "Oh man! He broke fucking hearts on the first trick! Shit! There goes my motherfucking run! Now I'm gonna eat it big!"

Rowdy laughter, shouts, and occasional harsh words punctuated the night. As a thin slice of dawn began to crack the sky, Paul was lighting another huge bomber, and Sonny burst in and almost got shot for his efforts.

"Hey! Did you hear what happened to Monster last night?"

"Monster" stood six foot five inches tall. His massive frame was all muscle. He rarely touched anyone, but his presence was severely intimidating.

Roach asked, "Oh shit! Who'd he kill?"

Sonny was jumping from foot to foot like an epileptic rabbit, running his hand through his hair, almost unable to contain himself, waiting to tell his story.

"You know how weird Monster gets when he drinks tequila! So, when Wade came by..."

They all knew Wade Harbison Jr. He hated the Army, though when he was Sergeant of the Guard, he was determined to do the duty the best he could. He was only five foot six inches tall, but carried himself like a much larger man. When the lifers had summoned him to complain to him about the rowdy bunch of heads at the helicopter pad, he went forthwith, if for no other reason than to stop a pre-emptive firefight that might easily erupt otherwise.

Wade approached the chopper pad and requested, not unkindly, "Dudes, you gotta cool it a little! The lifers are complaining!"

"Fuck them!" shouted an anonymous voice.

"Fuck you!" shouted another.

In a much sterner voice, Wade asked, "Who said that?"

As Monster stepped up, all six foot five inches of human steel, he stuck out his chin.

"I did. What the fuck are you gonna do about it?"

A thick silence enveloped the pad like a pall and reigned supreme. Several people jumped up to calm the behemoth, but he pushed them away, and turned, snarling.

"Shut the fuck up!"

Then he looked at Wade, and smiled.

"Well, you skinny motherfucker, what are you going to do about it?"

The circle around them parted like the Red Sea, as Wade stepped forward, then in a single smooth and silent move, brutally smashed his .45 across Monster's face—with his arm pointing directly at Monster's nose.

"And there it is, brother!"

Monster was bleeding profusely, with Wade's gun unwaveringly pointing at his nose. The big man shook his head and pushed a huge paw toward his face, wiping blood from his eyes. Then, unbelievably, he started laughing, then bending over, moaning, holding his belly and gagging as if he were going to puke. He fell to his knees and looked up with tears in his eyes before flashing a genuine smile.

Wade stood still as if hewn of stone, and Monster got up from the ground unassisted.

"You're the first person who's stood up to me since I was twelve, including my bastard father!"

Wade nodded and closed the hammer on his weapon. Monster stood up straight, held out his catcher's mitt of a hand to the diminutive Sergeant of the Guard who only then tentatively holstered his weapon.

The larger man asked, "What's your name, brother?"

"Wade. Wade Harbison Jr" the other man said still shaking off the adrenaline rush.

"They call me 'Monster,' but my real name is Herbert."

Several people snickered incredulously. "Herbert?"

Monster turned and shouted, "Anybody calls me that eats his tongue! Got it?" When silence reigned again he said, "And anybody fucks with this man, fucks with me!"

Still laughing, Sonny said, "And then they went off arm in arm to the Aid Station for doc to sew him up. Monster actually seemed happy! He finally found somebody he couldn't bully!"

Paul laughed and said, "Un-fucking-believable!"

"Unreal, man!" spoke Roach agreeing.

"You're jiving us!" shouted Bopper.

"No, man, I swear! Can you believe that shit? 'Herbert!'"

When he stopped laughing, Paul said "I'm so totally fucking wasted. I'm glad I've got a ghost day today."

"Call in sick, man!"

"Yeah right!" Paul said, then pulled a mock falsetto, he said, 'Hello Sergeant? This is Mrs. Marzeky. Paul's been up all-night partying! He won't be coming to the war today!'"

After another round of laughter, Paul said, "I gotta go get some coffee!"

"Take some more of these" said Roach, handing him the large brown glass bottle of diet pills. "You won't need to sleep for a week!"

"No, man. I don't want to get strung out on those fucking things. But" he said, extending his hand to dap, "it was a fucking gas!"

"No fucking sweat, GI!"

He headed for the Mess Hall, shot to shit. He thought he was a little bit weird because he actually like the washed-out adrenal rushes of coming down. There was just enough flash to keep him moving. He probably should have listened to Roach, but if he started staying up just because he had shit to do, he'd never, ever stop.

Then suddenly, Paul had an enormous appetite. He drank four cups of pretty decent Army coffee, and ate four sausages, toast and scrambled eggs. He went to the showers, and steam-cleaned his brain. For once, the water was hot enough to pucker his skin like a prune. It almost restored him to his senses.

He changed into a fresh set of fatigues and socks, and headed for the Aid Station to check in before crashing out— and ran smack into the ever-mysterious "Wild Bill" McKenzie.

CHAPTER 13

Into the Fray

McKenzie was wearing tailored and pressed khakis. His gold caducei and silver Captain's bars were shined.

"Jesus, Sir. Do I have to salute you now that you're so fucking strack?"

He laughed and said, "The day I leave this shithole is the day you can salute me."

"So, what's up, Doc? TDY to Sydney?"

"After almost a year, they got me a replacement! I'm going to Hong Kong!"

"Excellent! Most fucking excellent!"

"My replacement will be arriving tomorrow. His name is Martin Browne. He's a cherry, but I think he'll do fine. He did his residency at UC San Francisco."

"I'll get to talk to him about my favorite city."

"I didn't know you'd been to The City."

"I even spent my leave there before I came over."

"Last time I was there was '66."

"I was there in '67. The City is just such a beautiful place! The most beautiful women in the world live there!"

Then *apropos* of nothing else, he said, "I'm sending you to Sally."

"What? Why? Did I do something wrong?"

"I need somebody with experience up there. McCorkin decided to go home instead of extending."

"Shit! Sir!"

"You'll do well. Trust me. I know."

We only shook hands because he was an officer, then he raised his right thumb in the air, and dashed out where his flight was waiting.

"Gotta sky," he said. "See ya!"

Paul was instantly bummed, and went to crash. He fell into an extremely deep sleep—his mind whirling, swirling, spinning like a Technicolor vortex filled with dreams that took him to other planets where he interacted with beings far more advanced than those on Earth. He felt like he was entering the next phase, of what he knew not. Apparently, he had done a good job, and was being "promoted." He awakened abruptly from the zone of oblivion to find the First Shirt standing over him. His fatigues were clean, but his boots eternally bore the scars of the boonies and he glowered at Paul through slitted eyes.

"Wake the fuck up, troop!"

"Wha? What the fuck? Who the fuck is it?"

"Get your ass up, troop! Chopper's waiting for you."

"I got people to see today!"

"You got five minutes."

"What do you mean? Five minutes?!"

"You got people waiting for you."

His head was pounding, and his eyeballs felt as if he'd had an industrial accident with a tube of Super Glue. His mouth was stuffed with cotton batting, and he had "five minutes?!"

"Wait a minute. Wait a minute. I shouldn't have anybody until tomorrow!"

"It is tomorrow, troop!"

"What?"

"You been fucking sleeping for eighteen hours! We got hit last night. Your buddies hauled your sorry ass under the bunk and put mattresses over you! Now get your ass up and get moving! And", he paused, and smiled for the first and only time since Paul had known him, "see ya!"

Holy shit! He had slept the clock around and hadn't even known it! Damn! That fucking Preludin was some kick ass shit! He grabbed his shit and didi'd to the flight line.

He loved flying, rotors slapping, blades whirling, all the sights and sounds and smells related to getting the beautiful bird off the ground—and the thousands of intricate parts cooperating to do just that, much like the human body (and, same same the failure of even one small part could crash the entire bird!) He had even come to love the smell of burnt kerosene in the morning. Cruising along sixty feet off the ground watching the world disappear in verdant shades of green was such a trip, unless Mr. Charles was shooting at you. Paul always sat on my hard hat! He'd heard all the stories! That's why he always preferred a gun ship when he could hitch a ride on one. God bless door gunners!

Rice paddies and hamlets looked like tropical vacation snapshot images in the triple canopy, except that bomb craters, burnt out villes, and the aftermath of napalm strikes took the quaintness away. Then, of course, any time he took fire, all the sweat and toxins in his entire body pushed their way out of every single orifice at once, and a bitter cupric dryness suffused his mouth, and he couldn't swallow to save his life; he clutched his flack vest tight around him in spite of what he knew (he'd heard all those stories too) as the door gunner poured out hundreds of rounds from behind his smoked glass visor; Paul worried sometimes about mid-air stalls and autorotation, but he had to trust the chopper jocks and crew; he shared his "lurp rats" (Long Range Reconnaissance Patrol special freeze-dried rations) with them, way better than the Mess Hall; jive and joke and have a smoke (on the ground usually); get his clothes stained with blood and shit and gun oil, sometimes his own; haul ammo, food, cigarettes, beer, soda, and bodies with equal aplomb as he tagged along (it was a courtesy ride); calculating his air time figuring out how many Air Medals he was going to earn; hear about but never witness "hundred foot interrogations" as a way of getting vital information from uncooperative gooks (one example was usually enough for them); ducking and scrambling under the blades; scared shitless the time a load of fifty-calibers tears up the floor just inches from his toes and he swore he'd never fly again; and then he was out there on the flight line cursing the fact that he couldn't catch the supply chopper to Bastogne until half an hour later.

Paul was scared and elated at the same time. Hue was the ancient provincial capital sitting on the Perfume River, containing the old Walled Citadel. He had heard it had been incredibly beautiful before the U.S. started bombing the shit out of it—and before the Marines made a stand at the South Wall for twenty-two days during Tet when the city had endured the most intense house-to-house fighting since WW II.

Sally looked like nothing other than a bleached and barren patch gouged out of the jungle. He landed slightly disoriented on a chopper pad near HHC. The crew chief gave him a thumbs-up, and immediately didi'd (departed). If he'd been expecting someone to meet and greet him, he would have been in a pile of hurt. He grabbed his shit (duffel bag, camera, canvas bag holding his civilian stuff), and headed toward the nearest building to ask directions, and then hitched a ride to Bravo Company, 326 Medical Battalion, his new workspace. In the distance, he noted a PSP runway, surrounded by some trees and brush, with several small hangers incapable of holding more than a single engine plane. On the ride, he noted different unit areas—notably the 501st and 502 Infantry, and the 1/327 Recon as well as arty emplacements. The clerk who first met him was decidedly non-military, with his hair almost to his collar, fatigue shirt hanging open, dog tags taped, a huge moustache, and a cigarette dangling from his mouth. He told Paul they could "do the paperwork later."

LZ Sally was located eight klicks northwest of Hue. Compared to some of the deep shit the grunts were encountering, this was easy duty. But compared to Phu Bai, he was in the fucking boonies. It was half tents, half Quonset huts. Fortunately, the Medical Company was situated in a good area not too far from the Mess Hall, and he'd have a private room of his own—RHIP (Rank Has Its Privileges), and all that.

"Specialist Marzeky reporting as ordered, sir!"

The Medical Company Office screen door creaked, there was red clay dust everywhere, and the CO was another draftee Captain.

He had a thick red moustache that wriggled when he spoke (which was little) or smiled (which was a lot); eyes that were red and bloodshot already at 0830, but Paul wasn't passing judgement. Fuck, he couldn't wait to fire one up himself.

"Miller Swanson, Specialist. I'm in charge of the Medical Company here. You probably already met Master Sergeant Moder. He's our acting First Sergeant," he said, pointing across his body to the left.

Paul nodded. "Not yet sir."

Master Sergeant Moder was the biggest, Blackest man I had ever seen—and huge, in every way. He stood six foot three, weighed at least two twenty-five. There wasn't an ounce of fat on his body, except maybe in his brain—since he had twenty-four years in the Army.

"So, you're our new bac si?"

"Sir?"

"Bac si. Medic."

Paul produced a sheaf of orders and handed him a set.

"As you must know, sir, I'm a Social Work/Clinical Psychology Specialist. Not really a medic."

"Everybody in this company is a bac si."

"Thank you, sir."

"I don't have anything else for you right now. First Sergeant?"

"You might want to check in for the end of sick call. You've got your work assignment already. Captain Browne will be here tomorrow morning. Once he gets here, you'll want to show him around." He turned, drew a deep breath and let out a mighty bellow. "Specialist Porter! Front and center!"

It turned out that this was the stoned-out clerk I'd first met. Jed Porter came on the run, and stuck his head through the doorway. Their eyes met, and Paul knew he was a head, his eyeballs so red he needed a quart of Murine.

"Yes, First Sergeant?"

"Show Specialist Marzeky around, make sure he gets some chow—and make personally sure he's at 1700 formation. Do we understand each other?"

"Yes, First Sergeant."

With just a twitch of his head, he motioned me out of the office.

"Jumping Jed Porter, your Number One Airborne Company Clerk."

"Paul. Paul Marzeky. Wow! Is the fucking Captain a stoner, or what?"

"Everybody in this company is except the First Shirt! And even he's cool."

"And I fucking thought I was going to be in the fucking boonies!"

"You're pretty fucking close, brother. We been getting boo-coo casualties from all over I Corps. Victor is getting thicker than fuck out there."

He offered his hand, and we dapped.

"So. What's the weed situation?"

"Wanna smoke a joint?"

"Damn straight! But the CO said something about catching the end of sick call!"

"Fuck that! You're not even official until I sign you in. And," he smiled, as we walked, "I can't sign you in until I'm officially on duty—which I ain't until I get my head right. So, your first official duty in this unit is to get high!"

"Amen, brother!"

He assumed the mien of a tour guide as we passed through the company area, showing me points of interest, and giving a raised airborne thumb to various stoners.

"On your left is the Mess Hall, which is best left alone except for special occasions, such as Sundays. Over yonder is the 1/502 and beyond that is the 2/502. Most of them are up in the A Shau right now. Lot of heads in both those Battalions. Right up there is the 217th Assault Helicopter Battalion. And there's the 2/11 Cav—they're just detached here to us from the First Cav. That's 'B' Troop."

"When are we gonna smoke that joint, home?"

"I spaced!" he said, then produced a huge Bomber. "Here, man. Fire it up."

"Where? Here?"

"Where else? Oh, that's right. You're new here. Everybody here smokes."

"At this hour of the morning?"

"Fuck yeah, man. It's cool."

Paul put the number in his mouth, and snuck a surreptitious look around. When the hot smoke roared into his lungs, a white flash of heat lightning streaked through his brain pan, searing his lungs as the Delta-9 tetrahydrocannabinol started danced with his neurons—and he started coughing like a fucking cherry virgin! Him, who had previously thought himself to be a purveyor of the finest weeds of Southeast Asia!

"Gotcha'!" Jed said, then grabbed the joint. He took a long hit, rolled his eyeballs, and then exhaled in short bursts before handing it back.

"Killer weed, huh man?"

Paul croaked like a bullfrog with laryngitis.

"Fuck yes!"

"Wanna buy some?"

"Fuck yes!"

"I can get you a real nice ten-dollar bag."

"Damn straight!"

"You've obviously never smoked weed like this before."

Paul held out my hand palm up, and he slapped it.

"Amen brother! Where in the <u>fuck</u> did you get this?"

"Local product, man."

"Jesus! I've never smoked anything better!"

Electric tingles were running through him, like the silver songs of dolphins. Paul thought he might be developing Parkinson's.

"Is this shit soaked in speed?"

"Nada, brother. Just pure Number One Hue City flower tops."

"Jesus H. Christmas Tree!"

Paul took another hit, and again his lungs exploded in an intense rush. He kept the smoke in for at least a second before he coughed, and got another almost-paralyzing rush.

Jed laughed and took the joint from him.

"That's enough for you. You can't look <u>too</u> stoned right now."

Paul was unable to remember where we were going or what he was supposed to be doing! Jesus fuck! Two hits, and coughing like a motherfucker! It had to be brain damage.

"Where in the fuck are we going?"

"I think we're both stoned enough. You wanna get something to eat?"

"Are you shitting me? I couldn't eat right now if my life depended on it."

"I've got the munchies, so I'm gonna go to the Messed-Up Hall."

Paul really didn't, but he was too stoned to care.

"Sure. Why not?"

It was just another Quonset hut tenement. A Spec 5 was working the door, holding a little hand-held counter that he clicked twice as we passed in. He nodded to Jed, who shoved his thumb over his shoulder and said, "He's with me. I'll get him a card later." Then, to me, "You'll get a meal card to show at every meal—at least until the door dudes get to know you."

He took bacon strips, scrambled eggs and toast. Paul could barely manage a cup of coffee.

The room was fifty feet long and half as wide, filled with wooden tables and benches. There were a few stoned looking people scattered about, most lingering over a last cup of coffee. Jed nodded to one here and there, exchanged a jive or jest with others. Paul worked his way through a pretty decent cup of coffee. It helped level him out.

"Man, are you <u>sure</u> you don't want some grub before it's too late? I'm gonna go get some more!"

"No, man. I'm <u>so</u> fucking stoned. I can't believe that weed. When you gonna get me some?"

"Be patient, my man."

CHAPTER 14
Awakening—Part II

Paul's routine at Sally gave him even greater opportunities to get stoned, and become increasingly less military. There were dozens of guys pouring in to see him, referred by platoon and battalion medics; from infantry and artillery outfits; by chaplains and rabbis; from First Sergeants and Commanding Officers with complaints of "goldbricking" to unfit for duty; from Judge Advocate attorneys wanting a Psych Eval to use in defense for Courts Martial for everything from AWOL to attempted murder. The men who referred themselves complained of everything from Combat Stress to general malaise and hatred of the military—and they all just wanted out of the crazy fucked up Army, or at least the crazy fucking war. Many were just out of the boonies. They poured in like a human wave assault, like the torrential, unstoppable monsoon rains.

Even if none of the major schools of psychology would have approved, the new twist Paul had added to his interview method stood him in good stead.

"Wanna smoke a joint?" opened doors that even years of psychoanalysis could not have. The men knew they were co-conspirators. Paul considered the cost of the weed as a necessary "business expense," though one for which he would never be reimbursed.

He was sitting at his desk, completing an eval on a man who had been accused of trying to frag his First Sergeant with a White Phosphorous grenade.

"I was watching the First Shirt's Quonset hut, waiting for the asshole to come back from the Lifer's Club. I was sitting tight. Me and Willie Peter. Just when I saw him staggering down the path, Luke the Gook started lobbing mortar rounds! I tossed the egg at him just as he stumbled over a sandbag. He jumps up screaming 'They got me!'"

They had both laughed at the vivid picture the man had painted of the old, drunken lifer flopping around in the middle of a mortar attack—and never knowing how close he had really come to dying!

His report to Paul, frank and honest, left him on the horns of a moral and ethical dilemma. Theoretically, he was supposed to report him, but he couldn't ethically divulge his revelations in the context of his confidential consult. CYA was Paul's prime directive.

Just as Paul was considering how much information to put in his case notes, a tall urbane-looking Black man walked in unannounced. He looked awkward in his brand-new jungle fatigues. Paul started to get pissed, then noticed the man's Captain's bars. He rose from his seat, thinking the man might be a Company Commander come to make a personal referral.

"May I help you, sir?"

"You're Specialist Marzeky"

"Yes sir." Most people came asking for the "psych consultant" or "the shrink." How'd this obvious cherry get his name?

He offered his hand.

"I'm Captain Martin Browne, Bill McKenzie's replacement."

Paul was stunned. And must have shown it. He'd never met a Black psychiatrist before.

Captain Browne laughed, more an easy modulated chuckle, as he took in Paul's incredulity.

"I asked Bob not to tell anyone. I wanted to gauge prejudice for myself."

"It's not prejudice, sir. I've met very few Black doctors, and never a Black shrink."

"Most people expect me to be a witch doctor or vodun priest."

Paul raised his eyebrows, and simply nodded.

He sat, at ease and casual in what had recently been brand new territory. Paul felt like a laboratory animal under close scrutiny. Martin Browne took his measure in a glance—sun-bleached fatigues and battered boots; dark brown hair far too long by military standards; wire frame glasses; beads around his neck; and red-rimmed eyeballs, his contribution to the revolution.

"Uh, what can I do for you, sir? Need any help with anything?"

He held my gaze for a moment longer, then smiled.

"I understand you've been to San Francisco."

"My favorite topic, next to women." Paul didn't say anything about his other favorite topic—dope. He feared his attitude would put him at odds with his new "boss," who had no sooner completed his residency than he got his "greetings" from our dear esteemed Uncle—and practically came straight to the 'Nam.

"Yes, sir. I'm moving there...soon as I get out of this place! I am short!"

"Don't feel too short, Marzeky. Anything could happen. This is still Viet Nam."

"Yes, sir. Victor Charlie's definitely got his shit together here."

"I've read some of your evals. You're good. Are you going back to school when you get out?" he asked. The doctor became more and more composed, even though he was twisting his wedding band around with his right thumb and first finger.

He seemed to like Paul's "office", a medium sized canvas tent for which he had traded a bag of weed.

"I want to have a real life when I get back to the world. There's just so much happening in San Francisco."

"Don't lose your momentum."

"Yes sir. I understand sir", came out slurred and sounding more like "Yezzir, I ownerstanzir."

What Paul really wanted was to get to San Francisco, and party his ass off. All the incredible women, the music, and the revolution! What a potent stew! He didn't want a straight gig. He wanted to be an outlaw, live in the underground world. But he could certainly use the GI Bill for a while.

Paul had actually heard Janis Joplin with and Big Brother and the Holding Company in a little club on Haight Street for fifty cents! The room was lit with only four strobe lights, and filled with half-naked ladies dancing without getting hassled by the guys! It was holy, much more so than any church to which I had ever been! God! Forty-four and a wake up! But right then and there, he decided to extend his tour so he wouldn't have any time to serve when he got home. And, he was going to put in for R-and-R forthwith!

Paul must have been spaced out into his fantasy. The next thing he remembered was looking up to see Captain Browne smiling at him.

"Sorry sir. I was just thinking about San Francisco."

"I understand. It's a wonderful place."

"I'm hot to see something other than Asian women."

"I understand. But some of them surely are fine."

Paul found out later that he was married to a Chinese-American woman who was a ballet dancer and a native San Franciscan.

"Absolutely. But I never get a chance to meet any nice round eyes here, sir."

Paul had been slaking his lifelong fantasy for Asian women since Qui Nhon, but it was never anything more than sexual release.

"I'd love to get to Sydney. I hear the honeys are <u>very</u> friendly!"

He rolled his head in a manner suggesting whimsy, but said nothing—and Paul's anxiety increased again.

"Have you met any of the other 91Gs, sir?"

"Yes, I've been getting around. They've given me a hooch at Eagle."

I laughed.

"I understand, sir."

He rose as if to leave, then said "I've enjoyed talking to you, Marzeky."

Paul said, "Thank you very much, sir," holding out his hand to shake. "You're all right."

And was surprised as hell when he slapped my hand and grinned.

"Wow! You do learn fast!"

"I feel like you've been pretty real with me. I appreciate it."

"Thank you, sir."

"I understand you've developed unique interview technique."

Paul looked into his broad smiling face, and hesitated.

"What's that, sir?"

"Oh, I've heard that you have ways of getting the truth out of men, no matter how angry or strange they might be."

"Yes sir. I tell them right up front that they aren't going to get anywhere lying to me; but if they tell the truth, I'll help them any way I can."

"That's all?"

"What else might you be referring to, sir?" No way was Paul going to tell him!

"Oh, nothing, nothing at all, Marzeky. I've got to go."

"Thanks again sir."

Paul hoped he wasn't one of those officers who tried to be a "friend" with his men. It never, ever worked.

Paul went to look up Jed posthaste. He couldn't wait to get loaded. It seems that his friend was of the same mind.

"Motherfuck, man! Could not wait to get my ass out of there! I literally could not breathe. The First Shirt had a hair up his ass all day today. Absolutely nothing was right! Somebody dumped a purple smoke into the supply sergeant's tent last night. He like to shit in his pants. I thought it was funny as hell. But Top didn't think so. He asked me three times if I knew anything about it."

"But, of course, you didn't!"

"Fuck no, man. I was asleep last night at 2100 hours."

"Yeah. Right!"

"No really!"

"OK. OK. I believe you. Hey check this out! I just met Bill McKenzie's temporary replacement. He's a Black cat, ultra-smooth; super educated; and very, very cool."

"Yeah? Does he smoke?"

"I don't know, man. He might. He's hard to read."

"What do you mean?"

"I just cannot read him. Maybe I was too stoned when I met him."

"Where's he from?"

"Back east somewhere, New York, Boston."

"Is he US, or did he enlist?"

"You ever heard of a <u>doctor</u> enlisting, except a serious lifer?" Paul lit a number, took a deep hit, and handed it to Jed. We were each sitting on sandbags. Jed leaned back, hit the joint, then scowled, and took another.

"Hey Mr. Bogart! Like that joint, do you?"

"Oh, sorry man! I was just thinking about the First Shirt. Now I understand why dudes come to you wanting to off people, especially senior sergeants."

"I'm hip, man. That sumbitch is a real stickler for this Army shit! "

"The CO likes him. He keeps the military shit in order so the CO can stay high."

We laughed, and then dapped.

"Do you think there's any chance of you getting me on a manifest outta here?"

"You going AWOL?"

"On R-and-R, asshole! Preferably somewhere like Sydney."

"Yeah sure. Come see me in about four months. That's the wait is for Sydney."

"No!"

"It's fucking worse for Hawaii. All the married dudes want to go there and screw their old ladies."

"I can dig that. What about Hong Kong?"

"I'll see what I can do. But you only been in the Division a short time."

"But I been in country almost eleven months and never had an R-and-R!"

"Sin loi, motherfucker!"

"Fuck you too, Porter!"

"I didn't say I wouldn't try, man. But there are guidelines."

"Fuck a bunch of guidelines. I gotta get out of this motherfucker for a while."

"I'll get you on the waiting list. You might get lucky."

"Thanks, man" Paul said. They dapped and went separate ways.

Paul felt incredibly much better the next morning. Getting a full night's sleep once in a while was good for the heart and soul, though a rare thing for him. Most times he averaged about four hours.

He ate a large breakfast of scrambled eggs, sausages, sweet rolls, and coffee. Then he kicked back, and then drank three cups of decent coffee, lingering over a pair of cigarettes. He was feeling substantial when he left, and was strolling along casually, rolling his head, and surveying the kingdom.

And ran smack into Sergeant Moder, standing tall, Black, and strack. He had on his no-nonsense face, but wasn't the angry. The difference was subtle enough that Paul didn't pick it up right away. He went into what he called "mental health mode," that he used for dealing with juiceheads and lifers—hidden disdain and mind games.

"Good morning, First Sergeant" he said in a mocking tone that couldn't have been construed as anything less than respectful.

"Marzeky, I don't have time to deal with you this morning. That damn Porter is having a bad influence on you. Coming here an E-5, I thought maybe there was a small hope of getting some real soldiering out of you. But I guess not."

"No, First Sergeant, I guess not. Forty-three and a wake up!"

"All that shit's irrelevant right now. Go see the CO, forthwith."

"What's up, First Sergeant?"

"Just didi your butt to the CO's office. NOW!"

He wasn't gonna let the asshole spoil his day. Fuck him! He muttered as he left.

Jed was obviously loaded, but avoided eye contact when he saw him. The CO himself opened the door, and motioned him in.

Paul's paranoia started running rampant. What the fuck was going on?

I came to attention. "Specialist Marzeky reporting as ordered, sir."

He threw me a halfhearted salute, and said, "Sit down, Marzeky. I've got some bad news."

Oh fuck! Who died? Oh my God!

"Marzeky, I'm not very good at this sort of shit, so I'm gonna tell you straight up."

They were sending him to the boonies as a medic! Somebody in his family had died! Fuck! He did not want to go home! Shit!

The Captain was clearly uncomfortable with whatever news he had to impart. It had clearly ruined his high.

Oh fuck! Here it comes. Not his mother! Please! Not his mother!

"This morning, on a military flight leaving Camp Eagle, Captain William McKenzie was killed in action."

The Captain's words stunned him, as a palpable vacuum filling the room. He couldn't breathe. He felt paralyzed. He stared at him in disbelief. Tears rolled down Paul's cheeks.

"It can't be! He's supposed to be on R-and-R!"

"I'm sorry, Marzeky. It is true. He got delayed, and was on a MAC flight out."

Paul jumped up and screamed at him. "Don't fuck with me! He's alive! This is some kind of bad fucking joke!"

"Sit down, Marzeky. I'm sorry, but it is true."

Paul kept seeing Bill's face in his mind, his smile, and his stoned red eyes, his pride in being Airborne. Then he whispered, "But how?"

"The pilot reported that they were taking fire as they were turning to gain altitude, and an RPG round blew them out of the sky."

"Oh, my fucking God!"

"I'm sorry, Marzeky. He was a good man, and my friend too."

"May I be excused, sir?"

"Yes, of course. Captain Browne will be taking Captain McKenzie's place. He'll be here later to talk with you privately. Why don't you take a few hours personal time?"

"Thank you, sir."

He got up and left without saluting. He just needed something to deaden the pain.

CHAPTER 15

On the Road Again

Jed followed Paul out of the office, shaking his head in disbelief, tears streaming from his eyes. Paul was too embarrassed. He sped up.

"Leave me alone. OK?"

"I just want to help, man."

Paul was moved by his unexpected empathy. Even more tears burst out of him and he covered his face in shame and rage. Jed kept watch as a witness to his humanity.

He cried not only for Bill McKenzie, but for all the others who had died in this country fighting this impossible-to-win war; all the good and honorable men who had shed their lifeblood furthering the U.S. military myth of superiority. He cried for the death of 100 million Indians, upon whom his beloved country was founded. He cried for those who suffered because the demonic Empire-builders who had put the ruling junta here into power through the CIA, a move that violated the civil rights of thousands every day. He cried out of frustration for the idiocy of the so called "leadership" of the land of his birthright for pursuing this war, this fucking war, and promoting inexcusable genocide. He cried in frustration of his own helplessness, out of the total fear that he might, at any moment, be called upon, no matter how inadvertently, to surrender his life or body parts to the struggle to "free" South Viet Nam from the grip of a liberation movement that would reunite her after over a thousand years. He cried out of anger, rage and a creeping madness, for the utter senselessness of it all. He cried because he needed to go away from feeling it all, even if just for a little while.

"The first time is the worst time."

"What do you mean?"

"Same thing's happened to me. Cat name of Stan Smith. Crazy motherfucker. Smoked more dope than any human I ever knew. From Florida" he said and laughed, eyes glazed in memory. "Told me he rode the Trans-Siberian Railroad form Vladivostok to Moscow in 1963! Crazy, crazy dude! He was clerk over at Headquarters Company 1/503. One Sunday, he "borrowed" the CO's jeep to score some weed in Hue City. He was late for curfew, driving too fast, not paying attention—and ran over a mine."

"That's pretty fucked, man."

"And he asked me to go with him. Maybe if I'd been there, he wouldn't have died."

Paul's psychiatric mind clicked in. All of a sudden, our roles were reversed.

"Or you might have died too."

A single tear coursed down Jed's cheek.

"Sometimes I wish I had. I feel so fucking guilty sometimes."

"I understand," Paul said, then we laughed and dapped.

"Every time somebody dies, it reminds me of that crazy red-headed motherfucker."

Then Paul continued. "I just cannot believe fucking Bill is gone! Man! That fucker was just here just a few days ago—laughing, acting like a crazy man, not like a shrink at all."

He nodded his head.

"Let's get loaded in his honor—and Stan Smith's."

Everything Paul had ever believed in had been undermined by his experiences here in I Corps. All the myths and fables of his earlier life had been brutally exposed as lies of the highest order, the military and the government behind it showing themselves to be totally duplicitous and corrupt. His fear of becoming outcast had been greatly ameliorated by the genuine connection he felt with other young soldiers of every stripe, and the malicious campaign waged, ultimately, against the bulk of humanity's arising out of the collective brainwashing of the sclerotic binding of past ideologies. He was beginning to feel that he belonged; beginning to see that the lies he had incorporated and internalized, the violence to which he had been subjected, and the utter depravity of his teenage years were all a major illusion, one that was so strongly implanted as to deserve the title of delusion, and had created in him, and all of his generation, a sense of worthlessness and damaged that belied recovery. He was seeing first-hand the dark underbelly of lies and deceit that held together the treachery of the so called "war effort." (He wouldn't find out until years later it was called peripeteia, or as Grace Slick sang, "When the truth is found to be lies, you know the joy within you dies.")

The media distortions about these same brave warriors who, whether true believers or not, daily tested their mettle and risked their lives, often paying the ultimate price in defense of their brothers in boonieland. It was all so purposely distorted to promote the salacious stereotype of vets as drug-crazed mother-rapers and baby killers. There were, of course, always those who had lived too long with the lid off of cultural restrictions and became psychopathic murderers. Paul met one such shadow warrior when he arrived late one afternoon at an obscure FSB east of Quang Tri.

Nobody knew the man's real name. They just called him "Cherokee."

Cherokee was dressed in tiger stripes and a black cotton VC shirt, and wore his hair cut in a Mohawk. He stood six three, and weighed at least 250. He was almost a hallucination, dark and leathery, with feral yellow eyes. When Paul jumped off the chopper, he had half a dozen guys hanging off of him, attempting to keep him from continuing his "work" on a papa-san laying on the ground with a bashed-in face gushing blood.

"God damn slope had LRP rations. Musta' stole 'em!"

Farmers and villagers always got caught in the middle. Those who favored the North hid weapons and food—and stayed silent, while those who favored the South were taxed, scared and intimidated—and stayed silent.

"Who the fuck is that?"

"It's just that crazy fucking Cherokee, man. You don't want to know."

"Is he assigned here?"

"You ask him," he sneered. "I think he's a spook!"

One story said he had come as an advisor in 1962; another that he had been a Green Beret. No one really knew. He had found life in-country to his liking and decided just to stay on his own terms. Word had it that he had worked for all of the CIA cover agencies and then gone rogue. Apparently there had once been a bounty on his head, but the Agency kept losing the teams it had sent to "retrieve" him. Another rumor was that he did the sort of freelance work that gave them "plausible deniability." In return, they allowed him to drift freely with no immediate superiors. Sometimes he claimed allegiance to Material and Assistance Command Viet Nam (MACV), sometimes Special Operations Group (SOG). Some claimed he worked for Air America, others the United States

Aid for International Development (USAID). It didn't really make a lot of difference ultimately. They were all covers for clandestine activities.

It seemed that "Cherokee" thrived on violence, like nutrients for his black soul. Killing was a second pulse, akin to breathing for him. He lived with trusted hill tribes, running counterinsurgency operations, and not accountable to anyone but himself. His SOG card gave him almost total immunity no matter what he did or did not do. It authorized him to wear any uniform, carry any weapon, travel anywhere by whatever means available; and that he was not to be arrested or detained without prior authorization by the U.S. Embassy in Saigon. Paul later heard he had once gotten into a firefight with a bunch of MPs at a cathouse in Saigon.

They went their way to smoke a joint. The acrid smell instantly soothed Paul. By the time they had had two hits, his brain seemed to separate from his body and he drifted away in a kind of dreamy rhapsody. Next thing he remembered was Jed shaking him. He was completely disoriented, like he had been in the bunker for hours.

"Hey man! You asleep or something?"

"Give me a hit!"

"Pretty good shit, huh?"

"What the fuck is it?"

"Just some wacky weed, man."

"No way. This shit is kick-ass!"

"Just striped with some liquid opium."

Paul momentarily had a horror-story flash about heroin and Jed laughed.

"Like that shit, do you?"

"Damn straight!"

"Most of what you hear about opium is bullshit. You can get strung out on it, but there's just some times when it's just medicine. Then he screwed up his face and did a terrible Dicky Peterson imitation from the Blue Cheer days. "I need some real painkiller, doctor—or I believe that I'll be dead!"

Paul started laughing, then said, "I can't remember what happened without feeling pain."

"Sounds like some of that psychology shit."

"Sometimes psychology is a bunch of shit. But when I think about my childhood, it makes a whole lot of sense."

"Yeah? You and Sigmund Freud!"

"Some of his stuff is pretty damn good. But there's more to psychology than that."

"Like what?"

"I haven't really read enough yet to understand it all, but when Jung talks about the 'collective unconscious' as a kind of pool out of which we all come, he makes a lot of sense. We all have more in common than not—under the skin."

"So, the gooks are our 'little yellow brothers,' huh? That kind of shit?"

"Well, think about it, man."

"I've heard all those arguments before. All I know is they're here trying to kill us, and we're trying to kill them." Then grinning, he said, "But they sure have good fucking drugs!"

The rest of the day passed in a haze, punctuated with occasional hits of another opium-striped joint that Jed turned him onto. Paul had no appetite and simply wandered around the compound, finally deciding to schedule some new referrals that he had deferred.

He was just finishing up his paperwork when Jed burst in.

"Man, I'm sorry, but I got some more bad news for you!"

"They didn't cancel the war for lack of interest?"

"No. Serioso."

"What? What? Tell me!"

"You're R-and-R request got turned down!"

"What? You're shitting me!"

"No, man. I'm sorry."

"What the fuck, over? Especially after I extended to get the fuck out early."

At least now he was within striking distance of getting the fuck out of the Army totally! Halle-fucking-lujah!

Paul wasn't quite sure what form it would take, but he <u>knew</u> he would be living in California before too long. He had been getting letters from Toad. He had hit his ETS and was living part time in Berkeley, and part time in the Sierras building his parent's retirement home there. He had repeated his invitation to visit him, though he had carefully avoided couching it in terms of "staying as long as he wanted." Paul knew that after this experience, he would be capable of surviving wild and free in any circumstances. Fuck a bunch of laws! He was gonna be an outlaw! Smoke dope and drink, take speed and LSD; stay awake for weeks fucking and partying non-stop, until he dropped!

"That's part of the problem," said Jed, shaking him out of my reverie.

"What do you mean?"

"Since your extension went through, you got boo-coo time left in country."

"What do you mean? I only extended thirty-three days!"

"Yeah. And that leaves you with like a sixty something days."

"Sixty-one and a wake up!'

"Whatever. The brass musta figured you for a lifer or something."

"Why's that?" he asked with a building sense of dread.

"You also just got orders for Camp Evans."

CHAPTER 16
Incoming!

We were rebuilding the latest iteration of Camp Evans, twenty-four clicks northwest of Hue City off Highway One. From the air, it looked like a shattered moonscape ant pile that had been disturbed by a malicious giant with a big stick—pitted and cratered, with amorphous piles of detritus everywhere: broken sand bags, shattered wooden posts, and the remnants of piss tubes sticking out of the ground; clusters of tents like mushroom pods; empty ammo crates, and artillery shell casings; discarded tires, sheets of corrugated aluminum, empty spools of concertina wire; C-Rat cans, and everywhere sandbags; even the remains of the Marine Corps ammo dump that had burned for twelve hours after being blown up the previous year by an NVA rocket attack. Men everywhere scurried and hustled under the broiling fucking sun, sweating and slaving like an army of mindless robots reinforcing the berm, and the gun emplacements; filling sandbags, stringing razor wire and concertina, digging emplacements for mortars, and arty; building bunkers; filling sandbags, leveling ground, Chinook traffic dropping pallets of materiel, food, ammo, medical supplies; digging shithouse holes, filling sand bags;

rebuilding guard towers; food being cooked in the "field mess;" setting up a fuel depot and an ammo dump; building bunkers; filling sand bags, constantly filling fan endless number of sandbags. Paul was nominally in charge of his detail, but he worked as fast and furiously as everyone else.

Eventually the 3/187th Infantry Regiment, the 2/94 Artillery Regiment, the 63rd Signal Battalion, and the 18th Surgical Hospital were relocated there. The 20th Tactical Air Support Squadron moved in to use it as a forward operating base. Unless a visiting General decided to visit, clean uniforms, formations and inspections were all deleted from the program.

All of which gave the NVA many opportunities to reconnoiter us, and drop in shitloads of rockets and mortars on us night and day. Paul had been hit many times before, but never with the intensity, frequency, or duration as he experienced there.

"INCOMING!"

The incoming baggage came like heaven's freight train slamming full speed into the earth—his belly, his brain, even his intestines shook. It was always a Fucking New Guy who shit his pants. "INCOMING!" He always heard a round long before it hit, telegraphing its menace as he just didi'd for the nearest bunker—grateful as a motherfucker just to get safe. "INCOMING!" Even in his deepest sleep, he woke up running even before he had his eyes open. He only made the cherry mistake of taking off his clothes once, lessons learned. "INCOMING!" The call would shatter the night or bust up a card game. If he got moving, he likely wouldn't die—though Paul once saw a bunker that took a direct hit from a 122 mike-mike rocket that killed everyone inside. "INCOMING!" The whole world turned into a giant cocktail shaker. California dudes always said it was same same as a major quake, but it was far worse. It was definitely pucker factor zero or less. "INCOMING!" Sometimes Charlie would drop in a single harassment round at 0-Dark-Thirty just to fuck with them. Usually by the time they located the mortar tube, and sent some outgoing, the gooks were long gone. Mission accomplished. Other times the shit would rain down in a steady, but intermittent stream, night or day, like living a nightmare with his eyes open. "INCOMING!" He learned to ignore the noise and the shock and the smells. Just another inconvenience, part of the daily shit—There it is! — of a reality to be endured, better ignored than too deeply explored, on his journey through hell. "INCOMING!"

Stefan J. Malecek, Ph. D.

CHAPTER 17
Brother Arrow

"I think I need some help, doc."

"What can I do for you?"

He was a tall, gangly trooper with the shock of wheat-straw colored hair and two missing front teeth. Paul brushed the omnipresent red clay dust off his fatigue pants as they walked toward his office/tent. This was well into a sandbag afternoon, and so Paul welcomed the break.

"I hate this fucking Army, and I especially hate the 'Nam. I want to go home."

"And?"

"I figured, if I told you some crazy shit from out in the bush, you'd know I was fucking nuts, and they'd send me home."

"I've heard all the stories. None of them make you 'crazy' by Army standards."

"But my girlfriend's pregnant. I gotta get home."

"Sounds like Red Cross territory to me. Maybe they can get you a compassionate leave to go home and marry her."

"'Marry her?' I want to kill the bitch for screwing around on me!"

Paul laughed and shook his head. "It's still not grounds for a discharge."

"What if I told you I was hearing voices, and thought I was Jesus Christ?"

"Sin loi, brother. I've heard that before too."

"You're a hard motherfucker, man. I thought you were here to help people."

"I am, man. But I'm <u>still</u> in the fucking Army, and they won't let <u>me</u> out."

"Well, thanks anyway, man."

Then it was back to sandbags with plenty time for smoke breaks.

"OK, Mr. Bogart, pass the fucking number!"

"Oh. I spaced out."

"Good weed, huh?"

"Damn straight."

"Can you get me some?"

"Sure. How much?"

"How much is it?"

He reached over to his nearby fatigue jacket and pulled out a bulging bag.

"This one's got a couple of numbers out of it. I paid ten bucks."

"Good fucking deal. At least inflation hasn't hit Dong Ha yet."

"Amen!" he said and they dapped.

"Let's finish the fucking joint, and call it a day."

There was always a mad scramble to get to the makeshift shower, even though it was always cold water—it just made the hot chow served from Olive Drab-colored insulated containers taste a little better.

Even with his extension, Paul was down to thirty-seven and a wake up. "Short!" was the first word out of his mouth each and every morning, a prayer that went out to the Land of the Big PX. His dream was always of a brighter, better future than the malignant past from which he had been in retreat all of his life. Paul just couldn't shake it. It was like a parasite buried deep in his brain, constantly poisoning his present, never allowing him to forget. He sometimes thought he might be mentally ill —believing that he had permanently changed his life, erased all of the too-well remembered traumas. simply by being away from his being away from his parents' pernicious influence, though he knew that would be the equivalent of chopping off his little toe and cursing after stubbing it in the middle of the night. It really sucked, always living for the future, a yet-to-be-born life, and simply enduring the present, but in many ways, it was far better than cold food, wet boots and people trying to kill him.

The more the camp shaped up, the more the lifers seemed to think they should embrace the stateside notions of "military discipline." The more the lifers pushed for inappropriate shit like shined boots and brass, and regular haircuts, the higher the incidents of fragging and Mental Hygiene referrals. Most of the troops had no idea what he did or what they hoped to accomplish in coming to him. Paul had had to start triaging the enormous number of referrals that came in every day. The one major exception to his new rule drifted in one day while he was in the midst of writing up a stack of completed evals.

He was a small, unobtrusive-looking trooper wearing tiger-stripes. He had gaunt, sallow cheeks that defined the planes of his weather-beaten face. His blond hair was crew cut, and he wore Screaming Eagle patches on both shoulders of his sun-bleached, uniform jacket, with an "LRRP" tab on the left. I was surprised. Usually the "Lurps" were an extremely tight bunch and kept themselves to themselves. They had to be, spending days, even weeks, in small bands ranging from three to eleven men out in the most isolated locations with only each other to depend on. The man at the entrance to his office had a banana clip in his AK-47, an old K-Bar worn handle down on the left side of his chest, an SAS boot knife in his left boot, and a 45 caliber auto on his right hip. Most of my clients disarmed themselves first, but I figured, this guy is LRRP, he deserves to be a little freaky. He'd rather give up a body part than a weapon.

Paul kept thinking he was really young, but he looked far older than his years. He had the "thousand-yard stare" that those who had seen too much trauma wore, and lost contact with the reality to which most of them usually subscribe. Paul thought for a moment that he might have been loaded. The stealth trooper stood just to the inside of the tent, scanning left-to-right, front-to-back, eyeballs swiveling like marbles in olive oil.

"How can I help you?"

"You can't, man. Nobody can."

"Then why are you here?"

He shook his head, looking genuinely confused. "I don't know, man. I really don't."

Paul squirmed deeper into his seat, all senses suddenly alert.

"Do you want to have a seat, talk about it?"

He did another quick scan, then pulled the chair against the side of the desk with the tent flap doorway in his sight. He draped his weapon casually across his spread knees, keeping his finger on the trigger guard. He began to speak, as if to the very air, as if conversing with others only he could see.

Paul felt completely intimidated, transported to another reality where nothing he had previously known applied. He stuttered and stammered, trying to form coherent words. His intuitive alarm bells were all going off in sequence and series, and his nerve endings were working at hypersonic speed. A montage of psychiatric nosology and diagnoses poured into his inner television screen, and his sweat almost inundated his respirations.

The recon man sat stone still, watching and listening. Paul had a paranoid flash that the as-yet-identified man was reading the wild thumping of his heart, and analyzing his body fluids by smell. He knew he was freaking freely. He sent out innumerable prayers to gods unknown, for the tools to handle what was transpiring.

"So, uh, what's going on?"

His new client's focus suddenly deepened, eyes blazing with a rabid fire, and the palpable sense of danger increasing exponentially.

"We're all gonna die, man. No one here gets out alive."

It was the last as part of a Doors' tune, but he'd spoken it so flatly that Paul quickly decided that the man was not hearing rock-and-roll in his head. Paul knew he was in deep shit, and sinking fast.

"What do you mean?"

"Shorty and Roscoe," he said, followed by a long pause. "Fucking McNeer. Hurdley and Santos—they're all dead, man. The LT, and the cherry. They're dead too—and so am I."

Paul momentarily considered attempting a "reality orientation," but swiftly changed gears. The process was far too shallow and vapid. He desperately needed some fucking help, but anyone who walked in was likely to get shot. Then Brother X (as he had started calling him) might decide to make him dead too! Paul wished myself far away on a beach in the arms of a loving woman where they had never heard of war. Instead he made a critical error.

He asked who all of those men were.

Brother X stopped breathing, then he took a very slow and measured breath through his nostrils. Paul thought that if he smoked dope, this cat could hold a hit for <u>three</u> minutes! Then he breathed out, "Bllaaaahh!" all in a rush that startled Paul, who twitched out of pure reflex, and made a little screech as goose pimples raced up and down his arms and the hair on the back of his neck stood straight up. Brother X scrunched his head down further into his fatigue jacket like a fossilized turtle, and flicked a steely-eyed hawk look at Paul before freezing again.

"You know who they were, man."

Oh shit! Now Paul was being written into the man's fantasy, or delusion, or whatever he was experiencing. And he straight up didn't like it. He felt paralyzed, totally unable to do anything sane, like get the fuck out of there. He felt hypnotized, as if by a snake in the eyes of a bird of prey. Paul froze too, feeling the acuity of danger. For the thousandth time he experienced a vagrant impulse to leave, but he knew he couldn't move fast or slow enough. Brother X would definitely shoot him.

Then Paul made an even bigger blunder.

"I've never heard of them before."

His head swiveled toward Paul as if mounted by a disused set of gears in an ancient monastery. And then, again, "the look."

"Come on, Doc—they were in our platoon."

Jesus fuck! What next? Paul pondered how he would get out of this alive. He was having a war within himself about being therapeutic versus just being human, or even humane. His quandary was exacerbated by the fact that he had to piss like a motherfucker. He didn't think Brother X would be affirmative about him going out to the piss tube!

"I really wasn't in your platoon, but why don't you tell me about it?"

"They're all dead, man. And so am I." His mantra.

Clearly traumatic dissociation; probably delusional. Combat Fatigue. Shock. Possible fugue state. Fuck, he didn't know— maybe Multiple Personality! This felt like a kind of bizarre psychotic reaction, but he had no experience with anything like it. He swore he would never again complain about writing up 212 Discharges! He listened and decided to trust the intuitive directions that were coming to him.

"How do you know you're dead, brother?"

Brother X answered in the same flat voice devoid of emotion, seemingly pulling the words from a deep and painful place he could barely stand to touch.

"Dead people don't feel things."

Paul leapt intuitively into thin air without a parachute.

"It looks like you're feeling pretty sad."

His neck almost creaked as he answered.

"I'm scared, Doc."

He was talking to Paul now, not the platoon medic. Paul had to keep going.

"What are you scared of?"

A single tear ran out of the corner of his right eye, and dripped down the front of his fatigue jacket. Paul really didn't know what to say.

"Something with your team?"

"No! Yes! I don't know."

Paul was momentarily tempted to offer to smoke a joint with him, but that was contraindicated. He was the one who needed the smoke! But suddenly, he realized that he no longer had to pee.

"What can I do to help?"

"Nothin', man. I'm dead."

"I'm sitting here talking to you. I know you're alive."

Fiery liquid tears filled his eyes, and he replied "I'm dead...inside."

"Inside?"

"I can't feel anything."

"Like what?"

"Nothing."

"Isn't there anything you like doing?"

"Killing gooks."

Great. What next?

"When I get pissed off, I'd just as soon kill people as look at them."

This is progress? Paul thought to himself.

"But don't you feel something then?" Wrong question.

His eyes shot fire at me as he jumped up, weapon at port arms.

"Pure hatred."

Oh, Jesus fuck! In the sudden silence, he sat again.

"And now?"

He quieted quickly, and sat again, rifle across his lap.

"Now I'm dead."

Paul debated, then decided to take another risk.

"Would you to please put the safety on, brother? Just in case."

He looked at Paul for the longest time, his empty stare suddenly focused entirely on him. Paul was filled with dread. Then Brother X blinked and looked away before putting the safety on.

"Thanks."

Now what the fuck? Where was Captain Martin Browne, wonder psychiatrist now when he really needed him? Paul had no idea. Brother X obviously needed hospitalization, probably even to be shipped back to the world for long-term treatment. Paul had no idea how to get from here to there!

"Look man, I think you're really suffering. I think we should walk to the Battalion Aid Station. You need some rest."

"I just need to go back to my team. Then I'll feel better."

"And feeling dead inside must be really scary for you."

"Yeah it is," he said quietly. Then he jumped up, put a hand to his head and screamed.

"They're here! They won't leave me alone!"

"Is there anything that helps?"

"Only when I'm smacked out!"

That was not going to happen!

"Will you come with me to the Aid Station?"

"I don't wanna die! Please Doc, don't let me die!"

"I won't. I promise."

Just as suddenly the storm passed. Brother X turned angry and suspicious. Obviously, this was a relapsing and remitting illness, Paul thought to himself.

Brother X dropped his rifle barrel until it pointed directly at my belly.

"That's what you said to Shorty! And he died!"

Paul didn't want to die either! Help me Lord Jesus! A warm trickle of long-suppressed urine ran down his pants leg as his intuition fed him further words.

"He was going to die anyway. It would have been worse to tell him!"

Stifling a sob, Brother X dropped back into his chair and said, "You're right, Doc. I'm sorry."

Paul took three deep breaths before he felt he could speak without squeaking.

"Look. Let's get to Battalion Aid. I want to talk to the doctor."

Momentarily surrendering, X simply nodded his head. Paul very carefully came out from behind his desk, staying immediately in front of his client, who suddenly seemed completely done in, depleted, as if he had gone as far as he could under his own power. Now Paul would have to take over, even with his fatigues soaked with sweat and piss, and his brain operating on a wavelength that he hadn't even known existed. He was so strongly reminded of Nietzsche: "That which does not destroy me makes me stronger." Paul knew he was would be a strong motherfucker after today!

Paul parted the tent flap, and we walked out slowly, taking tiny shuffling steps. X carried his weapon in his left hand with a finger in the trigger guard. Paul walked beside him, talking to him in low, soothing terms.

"Don't worry about anything now. Just walk with me. OK?"

He nodded his head again, shuffling his feet, eyes downcast. And then, out of the periphery of his eye, Paul saw Rush coming. Motherfucking shit! Not now!

They all called him Rush because he would drink, shoot or smoke anything for the rush. I had seen him shoot speed, heroin, and whiskey, even water. He was the only person Paul had ever seen put a cubic centimeter of air into a vein to get high.

Lately Rush had been walking around babbling in a rambling monologue spouting garbled poetry. Nobody seemed to know what he was doing at Sally, except maybe that maybe he worked permanent night watch in Battalion Supply (S-4). The man always knew when to keep a low profile, but he could be extremely intrusive too. This coming encounter was freaking Paul out! It could get totally dangerous if Rush acted like a wrong-o right now!

Paul tried to steer the pair of them away from Rush, but he had locked on like a heat-seeking missile.

"I am the chalice of the mendicant...lost in the great and gravid graveyard of old dreams and schemes..."

Oh, fucking Christ! Now what?

"...I am ages of medieval penury and deprivation...with no vision or purpose..."

The monomaniacal mush of his words preceded him like the droning intonations of a mad monk. Paul could see an otherworldly light burning in the man's eyes. Oh, Jesus God protect me!

Brother X must have sensed Rush's alien energy because he tensed up, standing tall. Though Brother X's eyes were still glazed, his weapon slipped naturally into his hands. He motioned Paul behind him and whispered, "Don't worry, Doc. I got it!"

Paul felt like he might fragment into a thousand shards of broken crystal.

"...the hangman is shadowing my dreams, but I am again denied..."

Click!

The sound of his safety switching off broke Paul's reverie. His brain was in high gear trying to concoct a miracle crisis intervention as various scenarios ran through nanosecond speed from conception to rejection. Rush and Brother X halted facing each other, peering deeply into each other's eyes—and then they both smiled!

What the fuck? Over.

Rush made a peace symbol with his right hand, and then moved on as if he'd just had another chance meeting with an old friend.

Brother X's face looked slightly less ashen and he slipped the safety back on. His smile was as eerie as a rictus and he slouched along at Paul's side

"Some people just shouldn't take drugs!" was all he said.

Paul laughed, feeling massive pressure easing off his chest.

"Amen, brother!"

Then Paul asked, in his most soothing voice, "What your name, brother?"

"Arrow."

"Great name!"

Arrow smiled his secret smile, though his eyes were far, far away, deep in his own dream.

As they neared Battalion Aid, Paul spoke soothingly again.

"OK, Arrow. We're gonna be talking to the doc here. You're gonna have to check your weapons. I'll make sure I get a receipt for them."

He stiffened at the mention of having to give his best friends to a stranger, so I spoke harshly into his ear to get his attention.

"Listen man. I'm on your side. You have to trust me. Dig?"

Paul guessed he had hit just the right tone because Arrow nodded weakly.

"I'll trust <u>you</u> with my weapons."

"Roger that."

Arrow tensed as a Spec Four corpsman stuck his head out.

"I gotta see the doctor right away. It's Paul Marzeky, the Psych Consultant."

Paul turned to Arrow. "OK, brother. I am not going to desert you—no matter what these folks want. They're good people, but they are REMFs."

Doctor Jacob Miescowitz was tall, handsome, and heavily fleshed, with thick bushy eyebrows and black hair above a very Semitic nose. He came through the tent flap accompanied by a corpsman, and an E-6 Clinical Specialist. Fortunately, it was one of the doctors with whom Paul had some previous acquaintance from one his rare visits.

"I NEED SOME HELP! NOW!" Paul spoke with total urgency in a quiet intense voice.

Arrow very reluctantly pulled the clip out of the breech, dropped it on the ground; then pulled back the bolt, and ejected the round from the chamber and caught it in his other hand. Then he snapped the safety on, and handed it to Paul with a look of sadness. As if on automatic pilot, he went through the same procedure with his 45, implying that no matter how bad things otherwise were, there was still a proper way of managing weapons. Then he unstrapped his K-Bar rig as if it were a bodily organ, and handed his boot knife to Paul too before he allowed himself to be assisted onto a gurney, insisting that Paul stay close.

"I'm the only one he trusts at the moment, sir," Paul told the doctor, setting Arrow's personal armory a safe distance away. He and the doctor shifted positions slightly so as to speak privately, and still keep an eye on Brother Arrow.

After a quick glance at Arrow, he met Paul's eyes and said, "What's up?"

"Sir, I believe this man is having some kind of psychotic reaction. He does not appear to be on drugs. His entire team was wiped out. I have no details about that. He believes he is dead. He initially thought I was his team medic. He's dissociated, completely stressed out, certainly delusional. He's very suspicious, easily startled, and has razor sharp reflexes. Don't move too quickly around him, and please speak softly."

"Why do you say 'psychotic'?"

"I believe he is delusional. He told me that he's dead." (Paul found out much later that this is a rare symptom called Cotard's delusion, named after the man who discovered it in 1880).

"Well, clearly he is alive!"

"Yes, sir."

"What do you want us to do?"

"See if you can raise Captain Browne on the net. He's most qualified to deal with this. In the meantime, keep him in the quietest place possible. I'll talk to him, see if he'll take some meds, maybe a Valium. Could be he hasn't slept. This may all be transitory, but it surely looks like Combat Stress Syndrome to me."

The doctor conferred with the Clinical Specialist, who then disappeared deeper into the tent. Then he did a very uncharacteristic thing— He agreed with me without asserting his authority!

Paul stayed by Arrow's side as the orderly took his vital signs, and the Clinical Specialist got a line running with normal saline with 5% glucose. Though he seemed comatose, Paul stood by, whispering quietly, reassuring him. The doctor ordered some Stat (immediate) labs— electrolytes, complete blood count, serum toxicology screen, liver function tests, and a couple of other panels—and then, at length, spoke to me.

"Do you think he'll answer a few questions?"

"The basic bullshit will probably agitate him. I just spent the last two hours getting him to trust me enough to get him here."

Arrow started screaming in his comatose/fugue state "I'm dead! I'm fucking dead! They're all fucking dead!" The doctor ordered five milligrams of Valium through the IV lock just as Arrow shouted, "It's all my fault!", and started sobbing, pulling at the IV line, attempting to get off the stretcher. We had to use leather restraints to secure him.

"Captain Browne will certainly establish his own diagnosis, but my provisional one is exhaustion; acute psychotic state with delusions, secondary to Combat Stress Syndrome with severe dissociation, auditory hallucinations, paranoid ideation, depression and flat affect."

Doctor M looked at him for a long moment, and then asked him if he had worked in a hospital before he was in the service.

"No sir."

"You've got a very good sense of protocol and patient care. I am going to write a letter of recommendation for your 201 File."

"Wow! Thank you, sir. I really appreciate that," said Paul, genuinely moved.

"You handled a very difficult patient very, very well. He could have gone over the edge very easily."

"I didn't have time to think too much about that, sir. I just knew he needed help right away. I wasn't sure I was up to it, honestly. Sir." I suddenly felt washed out, and extremely faint.

"I think I...I'm gonna pass out", Paul said, gripping the edge of the desk for support as his entire body quickly slipped out of his control.

"Bring me some orange juice! Stat!"

"Drink up now. That's an order."

Paul immediately felt fresh energy course through his body—and then had a refill.

"What you're feeling is low blood sugar. It's called hypoglycemia. Any history of diabetes in your family?"

"Yes sir. My father and uncle. Maybe an aunt too."

"All on your father's side?"

"Yes sir."

"I want you to come and see me. I want to test you for diabetes."

"Yes sir. I will, sir. Is Arrow going to be all right?"

"Probably needs about two weeks sleep from the looks of him. Maybe then a reassignment to the States, some good meds, and lots of psychotherapy."

Even if Mr. Charles himself had danced into the camp right then, what I wanted more than anything in the world was a shower and ten hours sleep.

CHAPTER 18

Outta Here—For a While

Paul was inhaling as much dust as marijuana smoke, but he didn't give a big fuck. Victor Charles and his big brother, the NVA, were busy as fuck. They must have gotten a serious re-supply of mortars and rockets from the Ho Chi Minh Trail Store in Laos because they were dropping a shit load on us.

"You'd think that they'd get tired of this shit once in a while!"

"I wish they'd get fucking tired of this war and cancel it!"

"Dow Chemical wouldn't like that!"

"I'm hip! And Standard Oil!"

Hands dapped in the dark, and the joints passed.

"Hold on, dude! I'll fire up another one."

"Are you sure you're not CID?"

"Ha-ha! Very motherfucking funny!"

"Well. Are you?"

"If I was CID, I'd be busting Black Marketeers, and heroin smugglers, my man. Wouldn't have time for you!"

"Yeah, right" said the anonymous voice, followed by the rasp of a Zippo.

"I think anybody who can declare war should have to spend at least a month in a combat unit!"

"That means we could run for Congress when we get home!"

"None for me thanks!"

"Reminds me of that quote from General Sherman: 'It is only those who have never fired a shot nor heard the shrieks and groans of the wounded, who cry aloud for blood, more vengeance, more desolation. War is hell.'"

"Amen, brother!"

Paul went back to his bunk, nicely toasted. Even though his hooch was next to a 155 Howitzer battery (the stuff of bad dreams and broken eardrums), he had learned to distinguish between outgoing mail and incoming, even sleeping.

But he didn't care! His R-and-R had been approved! He was gonna be gone for five marvelous days! He was in shock as he prepared to leave—ears ringing, sinuses clogged, brain fried. The self that he called his own lay buried underneath so many layers of skin, and heart, ligament and muscle, and just so numbed out. He desperately needed to get away so that he could be sure he could feel again. He jumped onto an outbound chopper heading for Sally, and then caught a ride on a Cobra gunship to Phu Bai. He was still in his fatigues, caked with the dust of ages inside and out, carrying a canvas bag with one set of khakis and a set of civvies.

When he got to Eagle, he marveled at the relative comfort. He had forgotten how civilized it was compared to where he had been. He took a hot, hot shower until his skin puckered, more human finally than an inbred jungle animal. He wondered briefly if he could even feel normal again—then decided that he didn't want to be, but he was willing to settle for being reasonably clean, happy, well-fucked, and stoned to the bone for the rest of his life.

It being a Sunday, he headed for the Seabee's Mess Hall. He knew they put out one hell of a feed on Sundays. He took it as a good omen that he was in the right place at the right time.

"You're gonna have to check your weapon. The fucking cookie would shit biscuits."

He seemed like a good enough cat, so Paul went to the Armory, and got a receipt. He was back in three minutes.

"Welcome to the Seabee Mess, Specialist" he said, taking a copy of my orders since Paul was a transient. "Enjoy your meal."

He couldn't believe his eyes. There must have been a hundred guys sitting around at tables with tablecloths, real dinnerware and utensils. A half dozen white-coated men all wearing white toque hats stood behind a gleaming steam table serving thick, succulent steaks, baked potatoes, corn on the cob, and freshly baked bread with real butter! Paul went back for seconds, and then thirds! They didn't deny him. He forced himself to eat real apple pie and fresh ice cream with icy-cold milk out of refrigerated spouts! And the genuine thick strong coffee afterward! It was so cliché, but he genuinely believed he'd gone to heaven—or at least a suburb! He decided that all the deprivation had been good for him, now that he finally got to feel so good!

He had met a very shadowy fellow at Evans one day after sick call, and asked to talk to him privately. He was asking about a man who had been referred to Paul from sick call. Citing client confidentiality, he refused, and referred him to Captain Browne. Then the man slipped a leather-bound case out of his pocket, and produced what seemed to be a legitimate CID identification and badge, identifying him as Warrant Officer 3 Hamilton Burgess. He claimed he was investigating my client because the man was up for a Top-Secret security clearance, and he needed wanted Paul's evaluation of him.

"I'm only an enlisted man! I don't do evals!"

"Do you really want Captain Browne to know about your special interview technique?"

"Fuck you, Jack! Go tell him!"

"Maybe the Chief Medical Officer for the Division might like to know. Won't look good for either you or Captain Browne."

"How do you even know about that?"

He just looked at me ominously, then spoke again.

"Look, maybe we got off on the wrong foot here. All I need you to verify, in broad general terms, what you two talked about. Not his personal information."

Paul went silent, wanting to kill the asshole on the spot. He considered, on the other hand, that it might all be legitimate, but he didn't like being threatened or blackmailed.

Then he said to himself, "Fuck it!" He laughed and gave the guy a throwaway line, "He didn't reveal any nuclear secrets to me!"

The man went stone still, and threw a penetrating gaze at him.

"Don't bullshit around! Tell me what you talked about!"

He was both pissed and scared. He didn't want to get into with this asshole.

"Just the same same bullshit. He hates the Army, hates the 'Nam, and wants to go home. Nothing more. I swear!"

The ostensible CID man seemed to relax after that, and lit a cigarette—as if this were just another casual day at the office for hm. Then he told Paul that he knew Paul was heading to Taiwan, even though Paul himself had just that day been told. Hamilton told him he might be able to "make a connection for him there." He the produced a blank card with the name and number of a woman who, he was told,

Paul could trust to make my visit to Taipei "outstanding." Paul should call and use the Burgess's name. All Paul had to do was bring back a small package for him.

"Why else do you think I helped arrange your R-and-R there?"

Paul dismissed this last statement as some kind of self-serving bullshit, and Paul just got on with his process to unass myself out of fucking I Corps.

His flight to Biên Hòa was ear-splitting and boring. The C-47 Army workhorse, was essentially an uninsulated cargo plane. They were jammed, and tied in with cargo belts—despite which, Paul fell asleep almost immediately.

Paul had toyed with the idea of going to Saigon for the adventure, but when he finally got to Biên Hòa, the very thought of spending one more minute in-country was revolting. He went to the flight line, and talked with the man at the gate.

"Where are you headed, Specialist?"

Paul showed him his orders and the man checked his manifest.

"Your flight is in two hours. Have a good time" he said, and leered lasciviously.

CHAPTER 19

On My Way to Taipei

Paul decided he was going to debauch himself in the time-honored manner of servicemen on foreign soil through times immemorial—drinking, whoring, fighting, and carousing.

Since patience had never been his strong suit, waiting two hours seemed like an eternity., He stepped out into the eternal squalor, the surreal contrasts of Saigon, and went looking for a place to get high.

He met another couple of brothers who were similarly inclined. Over a bomber, they discussed the locations where we were headed. One of them was a blond, surfer-type with a 4th Infantry patch dangling from his pocket and a CIB above his left pocket.

"Are you married?"

"No, dude."

"Then why are you going to Hawaii?"

"It's the easiest place to catch a plane home."

"Home?"

"Yeah, man. The World!"

"Seriously?"

"Hell yeah! Manhattan Beach, California!"

"No shit!"

"It's all arranged. My girlfriend will pick me up in LA," he said, then gestured to his canvas travel bag, "After I change clothes in Honolulu!"

"Wow! That is far out!" and they dapped.

Paul had considered trying to bring some weed with him, but he had heard that the penalty for the first possession in Taiwan was an automatic five years in prison. He figured there were boo-coo vets there on R&R, so he shouldn't have a very hard time scoring. He'd heard that Customs used fluoroscopes. Officially, twenty three percent of all personnel in Viet Nam were using some kind of substances (though he knew it was much higher than that). He had heard that opium and heroin were really cheap and available in Taiwan because they were "traditional' there, not the "drugs of the white devils."

Paul floated back into the terminal with minutes to spare. He settled into his seat, hoping for some sleep, but he should have known better with a plane full of rowdy vets.

We were on a Flying Tiger flight. The stewardesses were some of the best-looking women he'd ever seen. They weren't shy about showing a little flash of stockinged thigh, even a tiny peek of a breast—but no fucking touching allowed!

The inevitable fly in the proverbial ointment was a drunken lifer sergeant who started ordering drinks before they were even off the ground, calling the stewardesses "Honey" and "Sweetheart." He was a fat and sloppy pig, with rolls of fat pouring over the top of his trousers, a MACV patch held in place with a safety pin on his shirt like an errant grade-schooler. Once we were airborne, he just got worse.

"Honey. Get me another double."

He was drinking Jack Daniels and soda, two little airline bottles at a time, and laying Greenbacks on the stew—eyeballing her, and telling her to keep the change "just cause you're so cute!"

Paul was slowly sipping a Johnny Walker Black on the rocks, contemplating what lay ahead—and nursing a swelling hard on. The young woman working his section of the plane was a super pretty brunette with dark eyes (my favorite, though he had been known to appreciate blondes and redheads on every possible occasion). Her every movement was titillating, stimulating him. She was lovely, and he was throbbing. God! He wished she'd initiate him into the Mile-High Club!

He noticed that the lavatories seemed unusually busy, with a lot of guys holding newspapers or magazines to cover their crotches getting there. He totally understood. He was working up the courage to go there myself when he saw his current fantasy woman slap the drunken lifer across the face.

"You are a pig!"

"But...OK, two hundred dollars!"

"You're an ugly drunken pig!"

"But I been in Vit Nam for five months without a woman," he slurred.

"I expect you to act like a gentleman" she replied

"Hey honey, I'm sorry. Can't blame a guy for trying!"

Almost immediately he fell into a stuporous sleep. Within moments, he was awakened by the co-pilot, the navigator, and the affronted stewardess—and a Sergeant Major none of us had noticed before. At the sight of the senior NCO, the doofus lifer started sweating buckets. A bunch of the other men were exchanging sideways glances and smirks while they collectively watched the tawdry drama unfold.

"No more alcohol for you!" the co-pilot said in a very loud voice. "If you cause any more trouble on this flight, any, I will have you arrested when we reach Taipei, and sent back with a military escort." The Sergeant Major beamed doom at the sloppy asshole, and promised that he would personally escort him to the brig when they landed, if he caused any more trouble.

The drunken lifer nodded and grumbled under his breath, still trying to plead his case. As soon as the little delegation left, he starting campaigning to those near him to get him some more alcohol.

"Back off, lifer" said a young grunt with a 25th Infantry patch on his left pocket, two rows of ribbons including a Silver Star and a Purple Heart with an oak leaf cluster over his left pocket, above which was his CIB. "We'll just say that you fell on the floor and broke your nose, you being so drunk and all."

The fat-assed pogie grumbled once again, and then fell asleep, slobbering on his uniform shirt. I fervently hoped that he'd get ripped off by some greedy bar girl in Taipei, and gutted by her boyfriend.

CHAPTER 20
Taipei

Taipei ran on a twenty-four-hour clock that did not stop for emergencies, natural disasters, or God. There were blocks and blocks lined with side-by-side bars, all featuring weak, expensive drinks, and women of every variety who could also be very expensive and potentially dangerous—all anticipating the next planeload of men from the 'Nam.

All of the women working the bars were contract players, needing to have their fees negotiated through the mama-san in charge, and paid for up front to her. Anything after that was between the man and his "date" for whatever period of time was contracted.

Paul watched as other men walked out of the airport where they were besieged by a phalanx of cab drivers. All of them babbled about having "the most beautiful women and the best hotels," each and every one of them touts that were the source of much of the bad reputation, injuries and losses Taipei had earned, from taking GIs on long meandering rides for extra cab fare to outright assaults orchestrated by them and their confederates.

As guys were hustled into cabs, Paul looked around for a pay phone, but couldn't find one. So, he asked at the information kiosk, and was rewarded with the use of a landline instead.

"Wei-wei."

He started to speak Pidgin English, and was quickly told that the woman on the other end of the line spoke "excellent English!"

Paul explained that he had been given her number by Hamilton Burgess, and was wondering if she were free to make an arrangement with him.

He knew he would pay more for the services of a higher-class working woman, but this woman started earning her money immediately by directing him to find a cab driver, and have him come to the phone. The first man objected strenuously, and Paul gave the second one in line an American dollar, and promised him another one after the call.

Papa-san argued vociferously, cursing, screaming, yelling, and finally capitulating as he handed me back the phone. Then she spoke to me again.

"Pay no more than two dollars Taiwan. You should be here in ten minutes."

It was so, even though papa-san acted like he'd just sacrificed his youngest son.

The building to which Paul was delivered appeared quite ordinary at first glance, even non-descript in a Chinese kind of way, on a little street in what seemed like a good neighborhood. He did not realize until much later that Madame Wo lived in a superb house in an extremely nice neighborhood—in a country where many people lived a subsistence existence, at or beyond the edge. There was no minimum wage, and it would take the average citizen fifty years to make what a U.S. citizen made in one year.

Once inside the door the house just kept expanding, room after room filled with exquisite furnishings, rare rugs, and delightful art of every sort.

Madame Wo was quite good looking though considerably older than him, but she was exquisitely turned out in a cheongsam intricately worked with gold threaded pictograms. She had jade green eyes, exquisite skin the color of old ivory, and a remarkable figure with quality gem stones in rings on every finger.

"Hamilton has told me," she said, referring to the man who was our common link, "that you are interested in exploring the intricate pleasures we have developed here."

Paul was awestruck, out of his depth, so overcome with awe that he could not speak.

She invited him into a lavish parlor located just off of what she called the "great central hall." There was a well-stocked bar there and she offered him a drink.

When she brought him a Johnnie Walker Black Label, he realized that there was an expectation that he would soon produce a considerable amount of cash, but when he fumbled for my wallet, she laid her hand on his arm, and shook her head slightly.

"We will settle on payment later. And I have a little package for you to give to Hamilton when you return. But we will talk about that...later."

By now, her smile had acquired an otherworldly glow. As she looked at him, he felt distinctly uncomfortable, and he turned from her piercing gaze feeling fear and shame. He was afraid that she could see him, really see him; that she was peeling away the careful façade he had constructed, and could see the undistinguished amorphous glob he really was; she could see through the disguise he had worked so hard to create of being powerful, worldly, and strong.

"We'll see, Paul Marzeky. We will see."

He then turned to matters that were, for him, of greater import.

Even considering what he had heard about all the penalties and consequent pains, he figured that Madame Wo's status in her society would allow her access to anything he might desire. He didn't know or care what she might want in return. He needed some buds!

"What you are suggesting is highly illegal."

"Madame, I appreciate your...graciousness and all, but your entire business here is illegal, isn't it?

"*Au contraire, ma cher!*" she said, switching to French.

"Pardon?"

"Perhaps some aspects of my business might be considered to be illegal, but overall, I am a licensed business owner; I pay taxes, a great deal of taxes as a matter of fact."

"All I want is a bag of buds!"

"You do not understand why marijuana is suppressed in this country."

"No, quite honestly, I don't. And it really sucks when I could just go down to the pharmacy and buy heroin over the counter."

"You Americans clearly have no real idea of what it means to be oppressed."

"What does oppression have to do with weed?"

"Marijuana is considered to be a Western drug, even though it grows readily in Asia, as I am sure you know."

"Damn straight!"

"But the government here suppresses its use quite stringently to," and she made air quotes with her fingers, 'Suppress the growth of the White Devils.'"

"What?!"

"Marijuana is a cultural artifact. Using it is part of Western culture. By suppressing it, the government hopes to help keep Western culture from overwhelming Taiwan."

"But why?"

"Western culture is...hungry, greedy. Westerners have vast appetites. They want to own the world. Taiwanese people do not wish to be owned or swallowed up, like your Indian people were."

"Well, I understand that the Han Dynasty in the 1800s drove away or killed many of the aboriginal peoples who lived here for thousands of years!"

"It's not the same situation! Indigenous people here today are being recognized; their cultures are reviving. But that has nothing to do with suppressing marijuana!"

"Why suppress weed? Opium is far more addicting!"

Now mildly irritated with me and my naiveté, she made a small moue, and then continued.

"Opium was used here very sparingly for many centuries as a pain killer, long before any European ever set foot on our shores. It was the British East India Corporation that brought widespread opium use to Mainland China, forcing the Emperor to import large quantities in the 1800s after they had seized a portion of southern China. With their superior navy and armaments, they threatened to invade the rest of China. So, the deal was struck."

Paul was getting very impatient with the history lesson.

"What does this have to do with me get some weed?"

"This started what we call 'The Century of Humiliation,' when we were essentially under the imperialistic heel of the British Empire!"

"And?"

"You have to understand, opium had only ever been used medicinally before that! Within ten years, there were twenty million addicts in China! The British were exploiting us, and making enormous profits off our suffering!"

"But marijuana's not addicting!"

"It's still considered to be a Western drug! We do not want to be enslaved to the U.S.!"

"You don't seem to mind taking the GI's money when we come here!"

"Ah, you begin to see. We have bars where our women are made readily available to you. You may buy our 'cheap copies,' as you say, of your manufactured goods, records, books, furniture. But, at the end of the day, we retain our autonomy—no matter how tarnished you may think it is! We retain our pride!"

Paul was really taken aback by this woman who had seemed so restrained, almost demure, and was now reading him the riot act about deep historical references.

"Wow! I never thought of it that way before!"

"You Americans are so naïve. Our culture was ancient when yours was not yet even born!"

"OK. So, I guess that means I have to go out and get my own weed."

"You're not listening! It is highly dangerous and highly illegal! You'd be arrested, and sent back to Viet Nam, if you are lucky!"

"'Lucky?'"

"You could end up being kept here, and being sent to prison. They are not at all like American prisons."

"But I am an American soldier!"

"Just don't try any smuggling drugs! The fine points of the law sometimes get blurred when it comes to smuggling drugs!"

"What do you mean?"

"You might just disappear."

"All I want is a little weed!"

"You're a fool! Hamilton told me he thought you were smart!"

"What?"

"Opium, heroin, morphine—they are treated as acceptable, even normal. Marijuana...is totally unacceptable here, no matter how it may be elsewhere in Asia."

"Wow! Seriously?"

"Absolutely! You must most solemnly swear that you will not continue this pursuit! If you want this 'weed,' you will have to leave my house! Immediately!"

Holy shit! He understood that what he had heard about weed was not a myth. Jesus! Was he ever wrong!

"But what about this 'little package' I am supposed to bring to Mr. Burgess?"

"Ah, we will discuss it at another time. It is not drugs, and it will be very carefully hidden. Bribes will be paid. Do not fear."

Paul muttered a weak agreement. As the beautiful madam walked away, he felt genuinely torn. He really wanted some weed, but, God, what a cost!

By the time I managed a scintilla of composure, a small, lithe young woman had descended the spiral staircase that descended into the center of an ornate living room. She walked up to him, smiled, and without a word, took his hand before leading him down a sumptuous hallway to a well-appointed bedroom. His dick was throbbing and he immediately started trying to take off her clothes. but she would not allow it.

"Madame says 'Not yet'."

She undressed him without a word, completely ignoring his aching penis, and led him across a green-and-white tiled chess board floor and seated him in a deep sunken tub. His whole body liquefied instantly, and he could make no more than a token resistance as he sat neck deep in the steaming water.

"Oh my God," Paul moaned, as she applied incredibly strong, nimble fingers to his entire body (with the exception of my still aching dick). She rubbed and scrubbed him and dried him with a thick, white Turkish towel—and then, finally, led him to the adjoining room.

No sooner had she dropped her one-piece wraparound than he thought he had lost his mind. She was exquisite! She looked as if she had been sculpted from the most exquisite spun glass. And, fantasy fulfilled, she had carefully shaven her pubic area.

"Madame said you would like that."

She pushed him back onto a thick, downy duvet atop a large bed in a mahogany frame. As she put a small, delicate hand on his penis, he started coming in great white gouts. But she had been prepared and took the streams of jism into yet another fluffy white towel.

Paul felt so ashamed. He wanted to disappear. He started to turn away, but she stopped him.

"You have been too long without a woman, neh?"

His head was spinning, so overwhelmed by her casual and yet compassionate way of managing his shame. He was totally out of his depth. He had never experienced such a thing. He was helpless. He would do whatever she wanted. He even forgot about his penis for a moment.

He deigned he was "in love." In his mind, he attributed all manner of qualities and virtues to her simply because of her beauty and kindness. He fell asleep filled with her fragrance, her essence, and slept deeply dreaming of her.

He awoke. Alone. He could not remember anything other than dissolving into her incredible eyes. Maybe he had been dosed, and this was some kind of weird plan to blackmail him. But for what? It didn't make any kind of sense. He felt disoriented, dissociated, almost disembodied, floating, maybe still dreaming. Despite all this, he felt lighter and less substantial, almost ethereal yet empowered. Mi had put him to sleep, after utterly exhausting him with a guided tour of the joy and wonders of her wondrous, muscular body, having shared with him a seemingly limitless encyclopedia of sexual pleasure.

He was acutely aware of the incredible soreness in his loins, and was grateful for the woman who had helped produce it. It was then that he realized—that despite all of his work, all of his dedication to creating and absorbing new and abundant life experience—that he was full of shit. All his posturing, and the worldliness he had attempted to adopt were crude and superficial. He knew the man he wanted to be wanted to be, but had no idea how to achieve it.

This realization so filled him with sadness that he burst into tears that deepened into chest-heaving sobs. He felt as if all of the detritus of his life, all the shame, the rage and depression, was flushing out of him, signaled by the premier sexual encounter of his life.

It was all flooding out of him, as if it were an end-of-life review, a compendium of all that he had experienced, shown to him in the moment before he died. Flash-bulb pictures of his life popped, flickered for an instant, and were gone—only to be replaced by yet others equally intense and brilliant, whole montages of emotion-filled balloons like jelly doughnuts. He could not stop crying. Deep memories of a hidden past assaulted him, his most shitty childhood thrown up in his face, along with all of the rage and hatred that he had harbored festering like a poisonous abscess.

The variegated pastiche of what he could only call his karmic history—blaming the Universe rather than owning himself—smashed into him as if by the blows of a gang of thugs intent upon great bodily harm. Paul moaned and thrashed, tearing up the sheets until he ended up in a heap on the floor.

It was only then that he really awakened and realized that he had been in a dream within the dream. Still there lingered a taint of the purging that had filled him in the dream, and he felt deeply moved within himself to make it happen in his waking life; to be deserving of the power he had always given to others as being more worthy than he, buttressed by the accumulated contents of the ancient mantle of unworthiness he had so long worn. The sumptuous comfort, the beauty of his surroundings brought to mind the suffering of others. He could not completely enjoy such awesome wonders when he knew that thousands of his brothers were suffering and dying from the gravid consequences of war. It was as if the floodgates of a dam had opened onto a dry lake bed that could not stanch the waters. His small acquaintance with Nietzsche's extreme existentialism—that he had created himself, and his fate—were of absolutely no comfort. There was a burning ache in his gut. It was excruciating, like a white-hot poker up his butt, his entire body screaming for release, for drugs, for some good medicine to ease his agony!

He got up from the floor, collapsed onto the bed, and...

...fell into an extremely troubled sleep populated by dark, slippery figures with no faces who spoke unintelligibly to each other in a language filled with glottal stops. They turned their blank faces toward him as if peering eyeless into his heart. He awoke, completely sweated through—and filled with an even greater desire to get blasted. Fuck the consequences!

Paul slipped into his only set of civilian clothes, and crept down the long hallway. He felt a little guilty for abandoning his delightful hostess and her gifts, but he knew he had to go. He had no idea where. The garish, lurid lights of the downtown area beckoned him with the lure of trashier pleasures than the sophisticated palace where he had, by dint of tremendous good fortune, landed.

CHAPTER 21
Taipei—Part II

The house sounded asleep, creaking and groaning occasionally as if an elder citizen were thrashing about. He crept out, feeling guilty about breaking his word, but determined to smoke some magic weed. He needed it to straighten out his head, but he had every intention of returning before dawn after his screaming brain had been somewhat palliated.

Paul set out for the Shilin District, the most famous of the night markets. Ever since heavy foreign investments in the early '60s assisted Taipei in developing a high technology force, many of the night workers flocked to the markets that had been flourishing there for over a century.

He had heard that everything from food to black market vinyl records was available in the raucous party atmosphere where loudspeakers blared music and propaganda until dawn. He hoped he would encounter some crazed GIs roaming around. The simplified versions of banquet dishes called *xiaochi,* snack foods, named after regional towns, were supposed to be locally famous.

He had been walking for approximately fifteen minutes, and had already refused three very aggressive papa-san cab drivers who tried to troll him with offers of "Numbah One bar in Taipei," and "Numbah One girl cheap, GI!" When yet another cab rolled past him and stopped, he was prepared for more of the same bullshit, when a raggedy looking GI stepped out of the back, holding a beer bottle—and called his name.

"Marzeky? What the fuck are you doing here?"

Paul had to look twice, and even then, couldn't believe his eyes. It was Alan Allan, an X-Ray Tech from the 18th Surgical Hospital, a medium-tall guy with a droopy moustache who hailed from Jupiter, Florida. He had told Paul he had chosen three years in the Army rather than three years in jail for stealing a car, and possession of marijuana. They had partied together a few times. He didn't know him all that well, but knew him to be stoned-to-the-bone! If there was weed to be had, he'd know about it.

They shook hands, then dapped. Alan was drunker than hell, and they just stood there laughing like a couple of loonies newly released from the bin.

"Jesus fuck! Man am I glad to see you!"

"Me too! Where you staying?"

Paul started to launch into his story, but Alan held up his hand like a traffic cop, and stopped him.

"So. Nowhere, right?"

"Yeah."

Alan drew himself up, hitched his pants, rearranged his crumpled looking Hawaiian print shirt, and said, "It just so fucking happens that I have a two-bedroom suite at the Royal Mandarin. They fucked up my reservation, so they comped me a suite!"

"No shit?"

"No shit!"

"And?"

"Wanna share with me?"

"Goddamn man! Does the Pope shit in the woods?"

We dapped again, and Paul asked about the weed situation. AA told me pretty much what he'd already heard. Then he sniggered, reached into his pocket, and pulled out a half-smoked, hand-rolled joint.

"Except for this little beauty. It's the only one I brought."

"Let's smoke that motherfucker!"

"Gotta be cool, troop! Not here, and not now. Besides I got another little treat to turn you onto. I got two beautiful local women in the back seat. You're buying dinner! Let's go!"

They were *en route* to the Grand Hotel for dinner, the most opulent and expensive venue in all of Taiwan, and it was certainly grand. A huge circular driveway three lanes wide led to a soaring, elegant *porte cochére*. We walked up the marble front steps, through the colonnaded portico, where a liveried doorman opened the door into the main foyer with its vaulted ceilings. As we strolled through the lobby, Paul felt distinctly underdressed. They were checked out by many of mostly older Chinese couples—the men in tuxedos and the women in evening gowns. The young women who were accompanying us had had some idea about the cultural requirements, and fit right in. Alan and he were viewed as just another couple of crazed GIs, and hence were forgiven our relative lack of decorum, being very casually dressed.

The lounge was discretely lit, and filled with deep-upholstered booths that offered maximum privacy. The main dining room was lushly appointed with linen-covered tables set well apart from each other. There were well-tended potted palms and other greenery scattered throughout. The wait staff all wore tuxedos with stiffly starched shirts and black bow ties. Even the very youngest bus-boy-in-training had a pressed uniform, crisp shirt and tie. They were all obsequious in their attentions to the diners without being intrusive.

They went through to the lounge to await our table. He still felt disoriented, though less so. Jane (as she called herself) was small-breasted and petite. She told me she was a college student who "worked" part-time to supplement her scholarship. Her friend Theresa was tall and thin (Alan's favorite). He felt very lucky that Alan had chosen her because he was very turned on by Jane.

They were summoned by a very respectful looking older gentleman who bowed low, and led them into the formal dining room. He seated them at a table for four with a view of a semi-tropical garden.

Jane and Theresa had ordered the meal ahead of time. Apparently, our meal needed to be ordered twenty-four hours in advance, and the women had divined that there would be four for dinner.

Alan said, "We're supposed to be having a meal that we could not get anywhere else in the world!"

"I'm looking forward to that! Paul said, then lowered my voice and said to him, "I am very fucking grateful to you, brother! I was fucking freaking out when you found me. I won't forget this."

"Don't mean nothing" he said, trying to dismiss his largesse.

"No, I really mean it!"

The entire dining experience quickly became the most amazing of his life. When he dropped his linen napkin, a bus boy whisked it away while another replaced it with a fresh one. Water glasses were always filled, and small plates of fresh lemon wedges had been strategically placed for cleaning the fingers between courses.

And the food!

It seemed like it would never stop coming! First it was small dishes of asparagus with black bean sauce and tofu, followed by tiger prawns in ginger and garlic with thinly sliced scallions, and then chicken with black mushrooms, snow peas and bamboo shoots served with brown rice. Then there were roasted eels, cut into rectangular cubes seasoned with sesame oil and exotic herbs. Absolutely delicious! One of the women commented on Alan and Paul's gusto.

"We will be having nine courses. Don't get too full."

As one set of bus boys cleared away the detritus, another veritable army of young boys arrived with small plates for each of us, and an array of serving dishes filled with black bean paste, hot peppers, finely chopped scallions, and steaming hot rice flour tortillas. After they left, a young man about his age appeared, bowed, pulled out a carving knife and sharpening steel, ran the blade twice down each side, and stepped back as a teenaged boy delivered a whole cooked Peking duck. The waiter swiftly cut off the wings, legs and thighs. Then dismembered it, slicing off most of the available meat, split the keel bone and separated the breast. He arrayed the duck on a large platter in such a way that it resembled an uncut duckling, allowed himself a small smile of satisfaction, bowed and departed, while yet another younger boy took away the carving platter and bones.

The meat was incredibly tender and succulent. The ladies instructed us to roll it with bean paste, bean sprouts, scallions, and pepper paste like a Chinese burrito. Just as we thought the meal was over, a huge steaming cauldron of duck soup arrived in an iron kettle.

"They keep the fires burning twenty-four hours a day. It is their specialty. The bones from our duck are already cooking to make a pot of soup for someone else's meal."

It was absolutely the finest meal he had ever eaten. By the time they were served blood orange wedges and small almond cookies with a pot of green tea, he was practically unable to move.

Paul started to leave a tip twice the size of the bill in to cover everyone involved in the production of the vast repast, but Jane cautioned me against it.

"They are all one family—fathers, uncles, brothers, cousins. They will all share whatever you leave."

I put an extra twenty dollars on the table—four times what the incredible meal had cost for all four of them!

"Don't mean nothing. It was absolutely the meal of a lifetime."

CHAPTER 21

The Next Level

Paul was fucking dying to smoke some of that awesome large roach that Alan had in his pocket; even more than he was craving sex. When they got to the hotel and Alan pulled out the nefarious cigarette, both the young women freaked out.

"No, throw that away!" From Theresa.

"Flush it in the toilet!" From Jane.

"It'll be gone in a minute. Open the window, Paul!" From Alan.

"Ab-so-fucking-lutely," he said.

By the time he got the window open, both the women had fled, fearful and in high dudgeon.

"Fuck them! There's plenty more where they came from."

"I agree, but there ain't any more of this fucking smoke!"

"Amen, brother!"

They locked the door, and put a chair under the door knob. Then Alan pulled back the curtains and Paul opened all of the windows before giving him the singular honor of the first hit.

The smoke was thick, rich, and resinous. It barreled into his lungs like a freight train on steroids, and he earned a Bronze

Star with a "V" device for dope smoking that night, and managed to keep every bit of it in. At first, he thought it was some kind of bogus weed; or that Alan had gotten ripped off, because nothing happened for a long time. The second hit was also deep and rich, and tasted more like hash oil than marijuana. But still no rush. Weird, he thought.

Just as he emptied his lungs from that second hit, the walls started to shimmy, as if made of Jell-O. He thought it might be an earthquake, but when he looked up, Alan was looking at him the same way, and experiencing the same same thing!

Paul raised his right eyebrow in a question, and Alan just smiled. There was something so mischievous in his eyes that Paul burst out laughing.

Alan grabbed his nose to keep from snorting out the smoke, and then gasped as his breath exploded from both his nose and lungs. Seeing this, Paul fell out of the chair in which he was sitting, and his outburst redoubled.

Then Alan went over the edge, grabbing his sides and cackling in a high-pitched voice that sounded a little like a Volkswagen exhaust in winter. He promptly fell on the floor too, holding his sides, snot running out of his nose. The sight of him, the sound of him, was all too much for Paul. He grasped his sides and started snorting, trying to get a breath. His lungs finally gave out and his face turned bright crimson. This set Alan off again as he weakly tried pointing his finger at him, hiccupping giggles as he did so. When Paul started seeing purple moons and whirling planets floating in front of my eyes, he took what he thought might be his last breath.

"Call a medic! I'm leaving my body!"

This started Paul honking and snorting, flipping back and forth like a trick dolphin angling for a treat. He rolled over and over, until he inhaled a mouthful of loose carpeting—which, of course, was the funniest thing Alan had ever seen, and his glee became completely unrestrained as he rocked back and forth like an autistic kid doing a ritual.

Paul managed to choke out, "Shut up! Shut the fuck up! I'm dying!"

He laughed and laughed, as if he had never laughed before, tears rolling down his face, belly cramping from the exertion, and bursts of colored light detonated against the dark landscape of his eyelids. He tried desperately to pull in a full breath, and failed miserably, succeeding only in laughing even more as he gagged and dry heaved in hysterical glee.

Then he fell back onto the couch, and tried not to look at Alan. He knew he was fucked if he did.

Of course, Paul looked. And promptly started to vomit, but then held extremely still, and managed to get his belly to stop spasming, even as his whole body broke out in an acidic sweat. Alan looked at him and gave a weak chuckle as if in apology.

This, of course, had exactly the opposite effect—and Paul started up again, until his belly decided it had just had enough. And the wonderful meal he had had, started to come up.

Alan saw his face turn white, and then green. He scurried over with a towel, then threw it at him and choked out a feeble laugh with his right index finger shaking at him as if he had developed Parkinson's disease.

Paul wiped profuse perspiration from my face, and yelled at him, "Fuck you, asshole!"

He turned his back, still shaking, arms akimbo and trembling.

Then, with a glint in his eyes, he looked at me and said, "Pretty good fuckin' weed, huh?"

I started choking, and then hacked up a glob of phlegm. I ran to the bathroom to get rid of it, and then took a giant piss.

"Damn you, man! You are a true motherfucker!"

"Thanks, man."

"So now what? Want to go hustle some chicks?"

"In a while. Meantime I got something else you might like."

"Better than pussy?"

"Maybe."

"Ain't no such thing!"

"Maybe not better, but it might be a lot of yucks!"

"What is it?"

"Romilar AC," he said, producing a vial from his pocket that was filled with little orange BBs. "I got them from a Chinese pharmacy."

"What the fuck is Romilar?"

"They're cough pills with codeine."

"Cough pills?"

"Yeah, you know, like if you're coughing."

"And these are supposed to be almost as good as pussy?"

"I've had them before. If you take like twenty of them, you'll be trippin' hard!"

"What the fuck does that mean?"

"You never tripped? Like LSD?"

"No, man."

"Oh. Whoa, man. Maybe you ought to just take like five."

"What the fuck? Why?"

"You might not be able to handle it!"

"What the fuck you mean by that?"

"It's different...than weed."

"So?"

"I just don't want you to flip out or anything."

"Fuck you, man! If you can handle it, so can I!"

"OK. OK. But just take five."

"Those fuckers are so tiny!"

"Yeah, but they kick ass!"

"How many you gonna take?"

"I don't know. Maybe fifteen."

"Then I will too!"

"Fuck you, man! You're fucking crazy!"

"Come on, man!"

"No! I don't want to have to babysit your ass! When the rush wears off, I want to go out and get some chicks!"

"Me too!"

"Grab us a couple of fresh beers to wash these fuckers down."

"All right!"

His sense of adventure was really piqued. He was going to take a totally unknown drug, in a foreign country where he did not speak the language, with a guy he barely knew! But it felt right! What the fuck? His arrogance coupled with his innocence was a powerful force that easily overcame whatever misgivings he might have had, giving rise to him ignoring the strong and frantic signals of his intuition.

As Paul stepped back into the room, holding two Taiwan Gold Medal beers, Alan was shaking a handful of the tiny orange bullets into the palm of his hand.

"How many you gonna do?"

"I think I can handle twenty!'

"Twenty? Sheeee-it! And I'm supposed to take five, and babysit you? Sin loi, motherfucker!"

Paul watched as Alan shuffled the small pile in his hand, corralling exactly twenty, and returning the rest.

"How many're left?"

"Plenty, man, plenty," he said.

He put the pills in his mouth, took a deep draught of beer, and started to walk away.

"Gotta piss."

"The pills," I said, and gestured with my hand. He tossed them to me.

"Don't take any until I get back."

"OK."

I carefully counted out twenty of the little atom bombs, and waited, holding them in the palm of my left hand.

As he entered the room, I said "Hey Alan!"

As he looked up, I tossed the pills into my mouth, and quickly emptied the entire bottle of beer.

"You crazy motherfucker! How many did you take?'

"Twenty."

"What? Oh, my fucking God! I'm tripping with a cherry! Jesus!"

Paul just stood there with an idiotic grin, as if he had just played a practical joke on his older brother, only he had no way of gauging the effect of this one.

Alan was pacing in circles, muttering to himself.

"Oh, my fucking God! What the fuck?"

"Oh, don't fucking worry about it, man. I'll be fine!"

"You stupid motherfucker! You have no idea what you've done! None!"

"Fuck you, man! I can handle it!"

"You have absolute no fucking idea what you're talking about!"

Within a minute, Paul had the first inkling that he was right. He noticed what seemed to be small creatures swimming in his peripheral vision through the suddenly gelid air.

Alan noticed it too.

"Better get your ass ready, motherfucker! It's coming on already!"

Still filled with false bravado, he pretended to ignore the sensory distortions, and stood tall, as if nothing untoward were happening.

"Hey man, I'm telling you—sit the fuck down! This shit is comin' on like a motherfucker! It may even be too strong for me!"

As Alan sat on one of a pair of facing couches divided by a coffee table, Paul felt the atmospheric pressure in the room shift suddenly, as if he were standing in extremely close proximity to a hurricane's gathering strength that created a tremendous negative ion flow as it sucked in all of the available oxygen. Paul felt sick to my stomach and turned pale—first white, then green, feeling like a rainbow.

"Can we stop this shit, man?"

"It's already being absorbed, probably on its way to the liver or the small intestine. Just sit back, motherfucker! The rush hasn't even started yet!"

Paul had absolutely no fucking idea what he was talking about. He had had tremendous rushes with weed and speed, but this portended to be of a completely different dimension. It would be unfair to say the room exploded, because, in effect, the exact opposite seemed to occur. There was this huge SPLOOOSHING sound and the room seemed to turn inside out, as if we were being digested in the belly of some great beast. Paul fell prone onto the couch, and attempted to breathe deeply—which was, of course, impossible when all of the vital energy in his body was being drained out of him by a gigantic magnet. He groaned, whimpered, cried—hell, he might have screamed. Paul had no way of knowing because the tiny part of his brain that managed to remain conscious until that moment surrendered to a primal rush of white wind whirlpools in every cell that simultaneously shook him as if he were at the epicenter of an earthquake so immeasurable that Richter Scale quit trying. He started shaking madly, even thought for a moment he was having a grand mal seizure; and then worried he might shit his pants or piss on himself; and finally surrendered to the Great Void enveloping everything including him. Or what may have been him. He was no longer sure there even was a "him." Whatever was left swiftly disappeared into this immaculate sound that swept away all fear, all consciousness, all thought, as he undulated, twisted, and spun, helpless and hapless in the grip of a cosmic creature foreign to anything he had ever known, or even conceived.

Eons later, he managed to pry open his eyelids that felt welded shut. He tried to speak, though no words emerged. In his head, he knew he had formed words, but none had managed to emerge. He tried again, just Alan's name, to see if he had such a thing as a voice any more.

"Aaaaaaaaaaaaaaalllllllllllaaaaaaaaannnnnnnnnn!" came out as if recorded on super, super slow speed, thousands of times slower than regular, and played back at normal speed.

He tried again, hoping he had had just a slight lapse, from which he would assuredly emerge soon.

If it is possible to be wrong about how wrong one actually is, then he defined it, as what rose out of the great Dismal Nitch of his consciousness, from the tangled and disrupted neurons and dendrites made his first attempt sound like the London philharmonic by comparison.

"Aaaaaaaaaoooooooouuuuuulllllllaaaaannnnnn!"

Alan, for his part, had been lying quietly, seemingly untouched by the immense chaos that had been created in his brain. Alan turned his head slightly, and whispered with the intensity of a Force Ten gale.

"Happy now, motherfucker?"

He tried to laugh, but his belly and voice box fell out of his body, sundered by an unseen force with the precision of a surgeon. He was altered forever, would never, could never live in an ordered world with neat and tidy categories of right and wrong, good and bad. He felt utterly emptied out, as if all of his internal organs, every thought and memory, had been flushed down a cosmic toilet bowl.

Seeing the utter panic and dissolution on my face, Alan exercised a small moment of compassion, or maybe he didn't want me to puke on the carpet.

"It'll pass, man. That was just the rush. It'll settle down in a few minutes, but we still got some stony hours ahead of us."

CHAPTER 22

What's Next?

Paul was convinced that he had suffered brain damage that night. To this day, there is a great deal he simply cannot remember—and if it were to be recounted to him by a reliable witness, he would not believe it.

Somewhere in the night Paul had gotten a wild hair to go the lounge and find a woman. It was a measure of how badly Alan's brain was working that he had agreed to come with him. Of course, he was a veteran tripper, and soon smoothed into a mellow steady groove from which he could navigate that great big old world out there. Paul, on the other hand, was a total basket case. His mood was swinging from one end of the Universe to the other, vacillating so wildly as to not be adequately described.

It seemed so cliché to say, but he really did not remember much until he found myself standing on the wrought iron circular staircase, attempting to negotiate walking with feet that were now under the control of the Great Puppet Master. They were certainly not his, especially since he was moving at about six or eight thousand frames per second, so infinitesimally slow that entire sections of the history of the Universe could have been written during the time it took him to make one step. Yet he felt as if everything were totally wonderful! He was laughing and giggling, especially when Alan scolded him to "Take your fucking smile and put it in your belly! You are a walking bust, man!"

How they ever got to the middle of the staircase was beyond him. Alan had given up on their going anywhere. He seemed relatively normal (for him), albeit much more fluid-seeming than usual. He would ascend two or three steps, talking to Paul as if he were beside him, and turn around to find Paul had moved his left foot approximately three inches, somehow believing that he had made an enormous stride toward their destination. Of course, standing there wrapped in a bath towel, with psychedelic spirals twirling in his eyes did not make him the poster boy for Mental Health Week.

Alan alternated between being hugely pissed off at him, and freaking out that the Taiwan National Police were going to show up, called by some nice old couple in from their homestead two hundred miles away to celebrate their fiftieth wedding anniversary—and were confronting the stereotypical drug-crazed Viet Nam vets in the hallway!

In the midst of all the chaos, Paul was blissfully unconcerned. Looking back on the experience now, he had to admit that he was completely unanchored from "consensus reality." He was not relating at all. Everything seemed completely symbolic, as if he were starring in an avant-garde art film, produced by an obscure director from another planet. He laughed uproariously and repeatedly at Alan's fears and concerns. He could not take anything too seriously until Alan threatened to leave him on the staircase to fend for himself.

"What do you want me to do?" Paul asked, though it came out sounding like one word run through a milk shake machine.

"Come back to the room so I can trip a little too, asshole!"

He was clearly stoned, but in a way that was completely different than Paul, as if they had taken different drugs together. With him leaning heavily on Alan's shoulder, he left the towel in the hallway, and made it back to the room without incident. Paul was having brief moments of being ashamed for his behavior, but it passed swiftly as laughter and tears interspersed with moments of lucidity. Mostly he felt like a giant human vegetable swimming in a gelid, pale-yellow liquid sea, and still able to breathe. Every time he tried to speak, it came out mangled as if his forebrain were disconnected from his speech center, and then run through a high-speed blender.

"Wha...in...the...fu...is...goi...on?" made sense if the listener were able to translate it into English, or had the brain speed of a one-celled organism speaking Albanian.

By the time he got to the couch (many hours later in his estimation), and once his body believed he was safe, the next phase of the drug kicked in. It could have been called the maintenance phase. But the effects were so amplified by the massive amount he had taken, that his overdose symptoms: profuse sweating, cold and clammy skin, dizziness and confusion, nausea, weak pulse, drowsiness and weak muscles—became amplified, joined by a new set of hallucinations—lurid purple dragons with enormous fangs cavorting with deadly intent through the air, menacing him—and he started screaming, and Alan quickly mashed a towel across his mouth.

"Shut the fuck up man! You are such a bust!"

On the screen of his eyelids, he had images of ten thousand Chinese policemen chasing him, an image William Burroughs once used to describe his paranoia ("I got the fear! I got the fear!) during an overdose with cocaine.

"Open your eyes! Open your eyes!"

Paul didn't even know they had closed. He was cold, huddling in on myself, seeking a non-existent warmth and comfort.

"Your fucking eyeballs are so pinned! No way Jose you're going out of this room!"

He threw a blanket over him after Paul assured him he would stop screaming. Wave after wave of disinhibition swept through him, urging him to go down, down, down into the sleepy depths, and join the fabulous creatures of the Underworld.

"Keep your eyes open! You ain't gonna die on me!"

He remembered making attempts to comply, but mostly he desired only to sink deeper and deeper into the foggy haze. Every time he tried to speak, it came out in such an ultra-slow-motion manner that he believed his tongue had been removed, and believed he would never speak again.

Alan kept checking his lips and fingernails, and watching his chest rise and fall. The fact that he was still breathing, getting oxygen to his extremities seemed an occasion for some relief. He determined that his pulse was slow and steady, and grateful in the extremis that Paul was not vomiting, fainting, or having seizures.

"I'm sorry, man!" must have been coherent enough that Paul got the gist of it.

"You are! You're a sorry motherfucker!"

"No! No! Really!"

With a gesture of disgust, he brushed aside this *mea culpa*, went to the refrigerator, and pulled out a cold beer.

As he sat in one of the armchairs, Alan said, "I'm gonna sit here and have this beer. And I don't want you fucking screaming, or I will personally kill you! Cong bick?" he asked in pidgin Vietnamese to see if I understood what he was saying.

Paul nodded his head slightly, and drooled.

"You are one fucked up motherfucker!"

Those words only echoed the personal derision he was feeling. Flashbacks of childhood scenes ran full-speed through his brain, that was now functioning at a level slightly higher than a paramecium. When he started sobbing, Alan ignored him. At least he wasn't having grand mal seizures!

Eventually he succumbed to the lure of losing consciousness, as Alan drank several beers before he took a shower, and changed clothes. He went over me very carefully, a pseudo-clinical assessment that would have made Hippocrates proud.

"Listen up, troop! I'm goin' out for a little while. You just lay the fuck here! If you think you're gonna puke, use this trashcan there," he said indicating the one he had put by the side of the couch.

"And, I'm bringing back a girl for me, seein' as this is my fucking hotel room!"

Paul could only nod his head weakly before drifting down again.

"And don't you fucking die on me!" he said, and left the room.

The next indeterminate period of time was filled with long stretches of weird, multicolored, and often violent dreams, sometimes including material from the many hundreds of horror stories he had heard from his clients, many of them fresh from the bush, wearing leeches and centipedes, or the blood and brains of dead comrades.

The other vivid memories Paul had of the ensuing hours were of Alan cavorting madly with an exquisite Asian woman, having sex in the living room, on the coffee table, in the bathroom, and, at one point, literally waking him up to ask if Paul were interested in "having some." He made the invitation as she sat there on her haunches, totally naked and alluring. His only response was to groan in pain and frustration, and pass back out again.

He awoke totally disoriented, feeling extremely ashamed and full of self-punishment. He lay awake for a long time, ruminating on all the shit that had happened in his life in the last year, and started crying silently—ashamed to cry, ashamed to shed water for the dead, ashamed of his lack of "character," ashamed that he couldn't live up to his father's toxic injunction never to cry, and hating him at the same time, ashamed of his government's not giving a fuck for all his brothers who died in her name, ashamed for his confusion, feeling that he shouldn't be feeling what he was feeling, ashamed of his fear of returning to the 'Nam, ashamed...

Sometime much later he woke up again—he assumed it was the next day, whatever the fuck that was, because there was sunlight coming through the windows. He was alone, naked, and feeling completely disgusted with himself. His self-loathing had reached new heights as he lay there repeatedly assessing the situation. One of the things that kept nagging at him was that he owed an apology and money to Madame Wo and the delightful Mi. When he thought of her, he immediately started getting aroused, so he had to assume he was not yet totally dead.

And a giant apology, and a thank you to Alan, no matter what an asshole he was, he had clearly saved his life. Of course, that allowed him not to hassle with his dead body, the fucking TNP, and the bloody MPs!

Sometime much later, a timeless time later, he awoke clearheaded and hungry. He was still alone, figuring Alan had abandoned him for the tender mercies of a beautiful young woman. He had no idea where he was, and didn't care. He went to the bathroom and pissed for what seemed half an hour. He felt grubby, and badly wanted a shower, but then realized he had completely fucked up his only set of civilian clothes.

When he wandered out into the kitchen to get a drink of water, he spied a note on the dining table. It was unsigned, but clearly from Alan.

"If you're reading this, you're not dead! Qi Mary (last name first in Chinese, remember!) and I have gone to check out a few places she wanted to show me. There's food in the 'fridge and a new set of clothes on the chair. Your old shit was too fucked up to save. Sin loi motherfucker! See you soon."

He had then appended "Don't go out, man. Your eyes are such a fucking bust! Take a fucking look!"

I stumbled into the bathroom again, and braced my hands on the edge of the sink—and looked up.

His pupils were extremely pinpointed. Anybody looking at him would immediately suspect that he had been using narcotics! Fuck! He was fucked! (Little did he know then that this would become a permanent feature).

"Fuck! Fuck! Fuck, fuck, fuck!"

Paul started to panic, trying to figure out what the fuck he was supposed to do next. He managed to take a deep breath, and quell his rising panic. First things fucking first! Coffee!

His legs did not yet seem to be functioning properly. He felt like he was still moving in slow motion through a viscous liquid, but his mind seemed relatively unimpaired, or so he hoped. He shuffled into the kitchen on legs that seemed far too large and primitive for his body.

He saw the coffee pot and filters sitting on the countertop where Alan had obviously left them. He cleaned and rinsed the pot, filled it with fresh water, and enough coffee for six cups, but water for only making three. He badly needed to clear out the mental remains of the night before!

Then: Let's eat! He opened the refrigerator to find an absolute bounty of goodies! Alan had obviously been to the PX!

There was bacon and sausages, fresh eggs, bread, real butter, and two kinds of jam! A large container of fresh milk, what looked like a package of pastries, and a pot partially filled with cooked oatmeal that he would ignore. There were fresh oranges and apples too! Wow! No matter what else he had thought of Alan, the son of a bitch had really scored!

Paul started cooking a sumptuous breakfast. He was suddenly ravenous.

He started bacon cooking, then split and threw in a couple of sausages. He put two slices of bread in the toaster, and started cracking eggs, figuring four would be a good start.

He set one place at the table, put out both flavors of jam (apricot and fig), took a whole stick of butter and put it on a small saucer, and placed it in close proximity of the table setting, finally putting out a knife, fork, and two spoons.

When he sat down at the table, fully prepared to devour his meal with great gusto, but after only two or three bites, he found his stomach revolting, absolutely refusing to allow in anything other than coffee.

He pondered this as he drank the pot dry, and considered making another.

Despite the caffeine induction, he felt extremely sleepy and overwhelmed, and started to nod off right there at the table, but forced myself to push off toward the couch, at which he launched myself before dropping his eyelids and passing out again. The dreams were still lurid and greasy, though much less intense. He managed to sleep this time without having to wake up to pee. The very next thing he remembered clearly was the sound of a key in the lock, and the sight of Alan and Mary walking into the room, holding hands, and looking very engaged with each other, almost as if they were truly a couple.

"Hey troop, welcome back to the world!" said Alan in a conversational tone that was still too loud for my sensitive ears. Paul cringed when he spoke, and this only elicited laughter.

"We kind of thought you might be awake by now."

"What time is it?"

"Getting on to be 7:30 in the PM, that's 1930 for you lifer types!"

"Shit! I must have slept all day!"

Aland and Mary looked at each other, and laughed again.

"You did better than that, man! This is Thursday night!"

"Oh bullshit!"

"I jive you not, motherfucker!"

"No! It can't be!"

"It is! Square business!"

"No! It just can't be!"

"It is, man. You've slept away most of your R-and-R!"

"No! It can't be!"

"Yeah, man, it is! You're due to fly back tomorrow!"

"No!"

"Yes!"

"No!"

"You better have some more coffee!" he said, surveying the congealed grease on the food, and other damage I had left on the dining table.

"Fuck! Fuck, fuck, and fuck!"

"That's better!"

Paul started to get up, then blushed because of his nakedness in the presence of the young woman in the room.

"Don't be shy, man! She's the one who undressed you the other night!"

"What the fuck?!"

"For fucking sure!" Alan said, as he smiled at me, and she nodded her head.

"That other offer you made me the other night still stand?" I asked as I exposed a rigid hard on.

His expression changed rapidly as she blushed.

"Don't be insulting to her, man" he said, and looked at Mary, smiling. "We've gotten involved."

"Involved?'"

"I'm...thinking of staying!"

"What? Are you fucking shitting me?"

"Not in the least."

"What do you mean 'staying?'"

"Staying here. Not going back."

"What? Are you fucking nuts? You could never go home! You'd be a deserter!"

"I'm sick of the military bullshit! And the fucking war is a fucking joke!"

"Look, man. We gotta have a serious talk!"

"We don't have much time, man. Your plane leaves at 1000 tomorrow."

"Shit! I can't go back and leave you here!"

"Too fucking late, brother! My plane left this afternoon!"

"What?"

"Yeah! No shit!"

"Oh my God! What have you done?"

"I just did a big FTA!"

I sank my head in my hands and started crying.

"What the fuck am I gonna do?"

They both approached and gently laid their hands on my shoulders. Alan spoke.

"You're gonna take a shower, and get dressed. Then Mary and I are gonna take you out for a good dinner at one of the noodle stands. Then you're gonna come back here and get a good night's sleep. Tomorrow morning we're gonna take you to the airport, and you're going back to the 'Nam."

"But what about you, man?"

"I got less than nothing waiting for me in the world, man. I'm staying here."

"How? What the fuck are you going to do for money?"

Mary smiled, and spoke for the first time. She had a sweet, mellifluous voice that aroused his penis, though he knew my brain was not its equivalent.

"He will do well here. I can help him get papers. My family is, how do you say, 'well connected.'"

"I thought you people didn't like *hiong-sin ok-soah?*"

She looked genuinely shocked to hear me say the words. Alan looked perplexed.

"What did you just say?" he asked, hands gathering into fists.

"It means 'devils' in Taiwanese. It's what the locals call us guys."

"How do you know?"

"Somebody called me that when I first got here."

Mary quickly resumed her composure.

"I love him. I will make it right."

"How?'

"We will get papers. Maybe move to Singapore. Maybe the U.S."

"Jesus, brother! Are you shitting me?" he asked, looking directly at Alan.

"Hey, brother! What can I say? Sometime everything is just perfect."

Paul looked at him for a long time, saw the resolution in his eyes, and shrugged my shoulders.

"Well then. *Ālea iacta est.*"

"What the fuck is that?

"Latin. It's what Caesar said when he crossed the Rubicon, defying the Roman Senate's orders. It means 'The die is cast.'"

"I just fucking guess it is!"

"Thanks, man, for everything," he said, and went to hug him. He held up both of his hands palms out toward me in the universal gesture of repulsion.

"Whoa, dude! First of all, you fucking stink! And second, you're fucking naked!"

CHAPTER 23

Landing, or Taking Off?

Paul was both angry and sad as he boarded his flight, pondering so many imponderables that it gave him a headache. Contemplating having to jump back into the shit completely freaked him out! Any noise above a whisper was torment. "Normal" conversational was like a fucking grinding wheel working on a diamond, screeching away at a million decibels. Paul felt brutally overamped, as if he had taken a massive hit of speed while buried in a blanket of fog. The air itched with tension, his skin crawled, every smell an assault on his nostrils—attracted and repelled moment-to-moment as he broke out in a profuse cold sweat with his neurons still scrambled.

He asked for earplugs and a blanket, and slept almost all the way back, and awoke from a shattering dream. He'd been in a pitch-black bunker filled with GIs. Incoming was raining down all around him. He kept making bad jokes, his black humor an attempt to sweeten the grim situation. But there was no laughter, no response at all, even though he knew the bunker was filled with others. When he went to light a joint with his Zippo, the stench noticed the stench of decay, and screamed when he recognized he was with a bunch of dead guys all wearing fatigue jackets whose name tags he recognized—Monston, Eppler, Davis, Washburn, Smith— endless ranks of them crammed into the bunker with him. When he looked at the hand holding the lighter, he saw that he was a skeleton too!

The rapid deceleration of the landing approach jolted him awake, just in time to hear that they were touching down at Ton Son Nhut.

Fuck!

He had absolutely no idea what he was going to do. He momentarily considered turning myself in to Captain Browne and pleading for mercy. But he realized that that course of action had one of two immediate consequences: either he would buy it at face value, but want to know all of the dirty details, especially Alan's name and unit; or he wouldn't buy it at all, maybe accuse him of malingering. Either way he was fucked!

He felt boo-coo fucked up, more confused than he ever had in my life. He felt overwhelmed with shame. He wanted so badly to perform at a higher level. He was massively disappointed with himself, mightily castigating himself when the voice of one of the stewardesses shook him out of his reverie, reminding him that he was the last remaining passenger and he needed to deplane immediately. Paul must have looked seriously fucked up because he could see the concerned look in her eyes while conversely, her body language screamed, "Get the fuck off my airplane.

He wiped the sheen of perspiration off his face, and shook his uniform shirt to aerate it. He was soaked through from head to toe, and his mental state would not pass any exam ever devised. She stepped back as he got out of his seat. She had her hands extended palms out toward him in a warding gesture that would have been more appropriate for a leper from another planet. His hearing was still doing that funny in-and-out warped Doppler effect flowing in from everywhere. His head was filled with sounds and echoes—even though he seemed to have developed the ability to distinctly hear multiple conversations at the same time, as if he had been elevated to a weird kind of superhero status.

"Thank you for your kindness," was all Paul could manage before lurching down the length of the aircraft. Standing at the top of the movable staircase and looked out at all of the frantic activity spreading like a multicolored stain froze him. There were so many people, and he was seeing visual trails from each of them! He had to concentrate really hard just to see the objects versus their energy signatures! Jesus! And he was expected to function? To just get on a plane headed north, and "go back to duty?" Fuck, not a chance!

He self-diagnosed a hundred times, always arriving at some kind of drug-induced altered state leading to a transient psychotic state. But, he argued with myself, if he were able to make such a judgment, he must not be that fucked up after all—and hence should be perfectly capable of resuming his duties unimpeded.

Shit! There was no way that someone experiencing a psychotic condition could function as well as he—but he came to the very startling conclusion that he was planning not to go back at all! He was going to go AWOL in Saigon!

CHAPTER 24
AWOL in Saigon

The first problem was the uniform. He had traveled in Class-A khakis. He would be a bust pretty much anywhere he went wearing it, even though some of the pogies in Saigon did apparently wear them every day. But then their ID cards would stand up to their being in proper uniform—and his would not. His orders were to return to his duty station forthwith. And as he stood there at the top of the platform, surveying the hurrying, scurrying humanity spreading out self-importantly as far as his eye could see—fuel trucks refilling all manner of aircraft, choppers coming and going; military people of every branch scurrying, filled with focus and direction like a bunch of harried spiders in a rainstorm; thousands of gooks wearing their authorization badges that didn't prevent them from gathering intel for their VC friends and relatives; even mangy dogs hoping to scrounge a meal before they themselves ended up in the cook pot of some poor displaced farmer come to the big city, lured by the prospect of better wages and better living conditions. The longer he stood there, the stronger became his certainty that he was <u>not</u> going back.

He felt like he was starring in a rerun of a very bad movie, like a gyroscope with no center, assaulted by thousands of disconnected sense impressions, and assailed by billions and trillions, of bits of information that his hyperactive brain refused to process coherently. It was like looking at a pointillist painting and trying to read each pixel individually. He felt overwhelmed by the total insanity of it all, and having his eyes open only made it worse.

Paul reached up a hand and absentmindedly pushed his hair back with his right hand. It was reaching collar length now, far exceeding acceptable military length. Many of the civilian employees affected this style to distinguish themselves from those in the military. His attitude was civilian, his thoughts were civilian, his bearing, and demeanor were civilian. It was only the presence of the uniform he wore that gave away his deepest secret.

He had absolutely no idea what the fuck he was going to do, or how he was going to do it. His body was going through about a hundred thousand changes every second, and he felt torn apart in many directions. He felt as if he had been splayed on a rack in a dank dungeon after being transported to the Middle Ages. He had a vague notion that he could score what he needed from the thriving Black Market in Saigon. With the profuse American presence in the country, everything from frying pans to artillery shells ended up on display at some erstwhile vendor's space on a dusty, cluttered pathway somewhere. Securing a uniform from a gook sidewalk sale would be easier than getting a new re-issue from the Army. Getting weapons might be more difficult, but it would be only a matter of seeing the right people.

The same stewardess, accompanied by the Captain and two other members of the crew appeared behind him with their black leather cases, and an aura of great impatience.

"Can we help you, Specialist?"

Paul shook myself, and worked his way down the stairs unsteadily, gripping both rails since he had no luggage. He did not want any of them getting a better look at his name tag. He was a total fucking bust!

He decided to go to one of the bars at Tan Son Nhut, have a few drinks, and sort out his head a little. No matter how fucked up he was, he had to make the right moves in the right order if he ever wanted to get home to the Land of the Big PX. Every nerve ending in his body was screaming for him to just get the fuck back to the flight line and catch an outgoing flight to Phu Bai. But in the supreme wisdom of his admittedly still lingering altered state, and a bizarre sense of adventure, he decided that he at least owed it to himself to see what opportunities Saigon had to offer him.

Just like the British Raj in India, the U.S. decided to allow locals onto our compounds to do all the scut work like laundry, housekeeping, and other menial chores. The fat cats sitting in their well-upholstered chairs in their well-appointed (taxpayer-financed) offices never had a thought or care for the fact that most of those so employed were connected to the VC or NVA, and they were constantly gathering intel while ostensibly working for the troops on the ground.

No sooner had he sat down for a beer than he was accosted by a street urchin (with an authorization badge, of course) wearing cut off military fatigue shorts several sizes too large and a sun-bleached boonie hat. He was carrying a shoe shine box. He walked right up to Paul bold as hell, squatted down, and spit furiously on his highly polished right shoe, and then began rubbing it off with a filthy rag.

"Numbah One shine, GI! You pay me one dollah MPC!"

"Fuck off, asshole! You just fucked up my shine! 'You pay me two dollah MPC!'"

MPC were the *lingua franca,* initially instituted to keep hard currency out of the hands of the NVA and the Cong who would use Greenbacks to buy war materiel on the international market. The colors and styles of paper were often changed to stop the inevitable hoarding. Every once in a while, bases all over the country would shut down for currency exchange, after which the old paper was rendered worthless.

"Civilian employees" were kept off the compounds during these times. I'd heard of a papa-san in Nha Trang who opened up his belly hara-kiri style when he got caught short with $12 million in unredeemable paper.

The kid looked up and smiled.

"Numbah One pot, GI! Make you boo-coo dinky dau!"

Paul looked around hypervigilantly and slid my eyes to his battered box. No one was paying the least attention as he lifted the lid and revealed his bags of hidden treasure, bulging with bright lime green flower tops. Everything seemed casual.

"How much?" Paul whispered. He seemed to be savoring my fear, tasting it with his tongue like a Gila monster, rolling it around his mouth like a fine wine.

"Numbah One, GI! Make you boo coo dinky dau! Ten dollah!"

Paul still had Greenbacks in my pocket, but he knew he could get five times face value for them on the black market. They were a strong international currency, while the piaster was always being devalued globally. But he was dying for some smoke. If anything could smooth out my head, it was a bomber of some of Southeast Asia's best. He flashed the edge of a five-dollar Greenback, and saw the intense greed in the street boy's eyes. He licked his lips, and tried again.

"Ten dollah, GI! Make you boo-coo dinky dau!"

"Fuck off! You Numbah Ten Thousand! I'm not a cherry boy," I said.

"OK. Five dollah!" he said, his hand out.

"No fucking way, Jose! Give me the fucking weed!"

Hand down, he handed me the bag under the table, and Paul tucked it into his canvas bag. He substituted an MPC bill for the illicit Greenback, and the boy snatched it, disappearing seamlessly as if he had never existed.

Paul quickly finished his beer, and went in search of a way to get supremely toasted. He could not possibly make any further decisions until he did.

He wanted to run away and hide, somewhere where there were no OD uniforms, but there was nowhere to go other than out into the wild world of underground Saigon. There he could disappear into the confusion, where a profusion of weapons was *de rigueur*; where exotic, quixotic sights and sounds were replete; where a polyglot of dozen of languages clashed; where cars, jeeps, trucks and tanks clanking; where pedi-cabs and palanquins, bartering and bargaining, bars and whorehouses, elegant glassware clinked in elite restaurants, taxi horns blared, jets and choppers and transports landed and left, whistles and bells and chimes, schoolgirls' songs, Buddhists' prayers unfolded—all the raw stuff of everyday life burst forth, an oracle's harvest, while in ancient Annamese temples, Mandarin palaces, French Colonial mansions and churches, ramshackle houses with dank hallways filled peopled from rafter to roof, corrugated tin and flattened beer can houses, cardboard shacks, even the gutters teemed with people, thousands upon thousands of people, in every shape, size, and race, wearing straw hats, boonie hats, discarded rags, helmet liners and steel pots, all intent on their own businesses; artillery casings to oxen dung recycled until it returned to dust; the smell of foods from a thousand cultures permeated the air, rich and redolent—Chinese, Indian, Malay, Viet, Annam, Thai, Cambodian, Burmese and French, even hamburgers and French fries.

Tan Son Nhut had been built by the French in the 1920's, taken over by the Japanese during WWII, and finally became a joint-use base for USAF and the SVAF. Nearby Biên Hòa Air Base (11 klicks away) was where most of the tactical aircraft were stationed. As soon as Paul stepped onto the teeming streets of Saigon, he would be putting himself at great risk of either getting busted by the military, or killed by their so-called allies, many of whom were ARVN by day and VC by night.

Everywhere there were Americans. Many were clearly heads, wandering around blatantly stoned already by mid-morning. As Paul made his way through the masses in the terminal, he made brief eye contact with at least a dozen guys whose casual indifference to military standards, blood-shot eyeballs, and very sardonic smiles blatantly gave themselves away. Some were pogie types in their Class As, while others were obviously working stoned-to-the-bone. He felt better knowing there were so many stoned folks around. It seemed to ease his nausea too. He was still having flashbacks from the overdose, though he had thought they would have stopped by now.

Then, out of the corner of my eye, he caught a flash of a Screaming Eagles patch. For me, seeing it seemed like home. There really was something to unit camaraderie and identification. When he caught up with the guy and made eye contact, Paul knew he was the right person. He was a double eagle—101st patch on both shoulders, signifying both a previous and a current tour—and he looked seriously blasted!

A smile spread across his face as Paul approached from his periphery. He turned, shifted his weight, and stood facing him as he approached.

"Hey, brother!" Paul said as he got close.

He didn't say a word, simply offered his right fist for a dap.

"Hey, I understand that the 101st has a hospitality suite hereabouts for visiting troopers."

"Could be. Who are you?"

"Paul Marzeky. Charlie Company, 326 Med. Evans."

"And you're on vacation here in Saigon, huh?"

I raised an eyebrow.

"Not exactly. Just looking to get loaded."

His grin deepened, and he said "Hereabouts we kind of hope that visitors bring a little gift to the party."

"No sweat, GI! Locked and loaded!"

He held out his hand and we shook Roman-soldier style.

"Harold Sykes. Arlington, Texas. Go Cowboys!"

"Paul Marzeky. I'm more of a Raiders fan myself!"

"We always have classic battles with you guys!"

"Ain't that the truth?!"

"So, you're looking for a little in-country R-and-R?"

"Just for today."

"When you due back?"

"Today. But I could probably wrangle an extra day or so. What's going on around here?"

"As they used to say, ain't nothing shakin' but the bacon!"

"Well I got a brand-new bag of flower tops that's just aching to be opened!"

"Well let's get to it then. You mind a little company? They're all brothers."

"Lead on!"

We left the terminal, and headed for a jeep parked in a No Parking Zone. There was an MP Sergeant eying the unit specifications as we approached. I became immediately paranoid until he looked up and smiled.

"Oh, it's you again," he said, standing tall and proud in his shiny helmet, and brassard designating him as Military Police. He smiled at Paul's new-found friend and they dapped. Jesus! It was really loose-o around here!

They chatted for a moment more, and then the MP departed with a small mock salute.

"Just exactly what do you do around here? And how is it that the MPs leave you alone?

"Oh, that guy? He's a head. We've smoked together."

Just like that, casual as hell. Then he got to thinking about how all over the country, from the Delta to the DMZ, at any given moment, guys of every age, rank and race were gathering with pipes and bowls, with joints and chillums, smoking the sacred weed in their form of divine communion, uniting in ritual intake; sharing beyond the specious rigors of military expediency, partaking of a substance that was shifting them, even momentarily, to a different, more elevated state, one that took them far away from whatever violence or banality they might have seen. In hooches and houses, in smoky, sleazy bars and upscale private rooms, in huts and hotels, on river craft and aircraft, in bunkers and even the boonies—men were smoking weed and creating newly minted life experiences. In the shabbiest of hovels to air-conditioned custom-made hooches with artillery shell crate chairs and the music of revolution blasting; in tanks and trucks and APCs; on berms and flight lines; on ships and boats and sampans; from the lowliest private to the General Officers Quarters, even, it was rumored, in Long Bien Jail, men were gathered, smoking sacrament—and blowing their minds together!

"Hey man! You spaced out on me!"

"Just tripping on you and the MP smoking together."

"Don't mean nothing, man! In another life, we might not have even spoken to each other. Here it's all same-same."

"I can dig that. But why were you at Tan Son Nhut?"

"I'm kind of the general factotum for HQ!"

Paul laughed and said, "What the fuck is that?"

"Mostly I ghost. I'm not short enough to go home yet!"

"How short?"

"I could parachute off the edge of a dime, I'm so short!

"How short is that?"

"Eleven and a wake up!"

"Fuck! That makes me seem like a lifer!"

"How long?"

"Twenty-six!"

"Boo coo long time, GI!"

"But I'm getting totally out. No Stateside time for me!"

"Me either! Fuck that!"

"So, when we gonna smoke that joint? I really fucking need it!"

"I'm headed back up to Biên Hòa, so you can ride along and we'll get loaded on the way."

"Or?"

"Or right here, right now! Roll 'em—unless you're intent on goin' back north today."

So, there it was. In his face. What was he gonna do? His head was aching, and he needed a few hits of some Number One weed to cure that. But then what? It was so confusing! Paul had almost a month left, and just plain could not handle it any longer. So, he decided to take the day off, sky up to Biên Hòa and get loaded on the way. It would be easy to get a ride back—always lots of traffic both ways, a tank or track or truck.

"Let's sky up, brother!"

He handed me his locked-and-loaded M-16. I checked to make sure the safety was on, and we headed for the gate.

"Shouldn't be any problem, but you never know."

"Right on!"

There was another stoned-looking MP at the gate who smiled behind his sunglasses and waved them through. No sooner were they out of the gate than Harold pulled a huge bomber out of his pocket.

"Fire that up!"

It was instant relief. Paul's entire body just absorbed the smoke. It wasn't until the second hit that he really started unravelling, then he stopped worrying about what he was gonna do, and just enjoyed the ride.

They cut through the northeastern part of Saigon—a billion bicycles, with pedestrian traffic thick as a swarm of flies on a corpse, cooking smells from ten thousand food stalls, dentist and barber chairs right there on the streets, U.S. and Viet military vehicles everywhere, monks and nuns in saffron robes, and so many of the displaced peasants the war had created; beautiful women in *ao dais* riding in pedi-cabs, Citroëns and other old French cars; taxis and traffic jams, especially at the traffic circles; boats and bridges and riverine craft, even sampans and dilapidated houseboats; and then, just as they crossed the Song Sai Gon river, still heading north/northeast, he looked back over his shoulder to see a huge rectangular billboard: *Welcome to Sunny Saigon* with a photo of a Pan American Airlines Clipper landing. They hit Highway 316, the main and most traveled route to Biên Hòa (ostensibly the safest), but Paul kept a stoned eye on all of the traffic and especially dodgy looking jungle spots that dotted the route.

Paul totally spaced out on portions of the journey, simply enjoying the relative lack of mental anguish. He still could not remember whole parts of the "trip" he had taken in Taipei; and kept questioning his need/desire to be so excessive, but eventually this excruciating interrogatory also got lost in space the weed had brought.

At length, Harold looked over and said, "Guess there wasn't any weed where you were, huh?"

"How'd you guess?"

"You're like a cherry hitting his first toke!"

Paul laughed, and said, "Surely is good to be back home!"

He held out his right fist and they dapped.

"It seems like more than not having weed for a while."

I just looked at him, eyes wide behind my sunglasses.

"You're fucking spooky, man!"

"How's that, man?"

"It's almost like you're reading my mind!"

"I read people pretty well. I know something's bothering you."

So, Paul dumped it all, right then and there. All of his pain and fear and anger; the overdose and semi-recovery; all of his concerns about returning, and not wanting to return; all of his concerns about returning to the world and how was he gonna act—just everything.

Harold just sat there and listened as we crossed the Son Dong Mai river, inching ever closer to Biên Hòa, when the whole process would shift radically when we crossed the Newport Bridge. The rear area of the 101st was still the 101st. He had to make some decisions very quickly.

"Or not," Harold said, again acting like he had been surveilling my thought stream.

"Whaddya mean?"

"The joint helped calm you down. Come to my barracks—we're all NCOs, all heads. Have a good meal, smoke some more weed, and see how you feel in the morning."

"Ya think?"

"What the fuck, over? Another day shorter, and closer to home!"

We dapped again.

Harold was a bit of a history buff, and regaled Paul with the provenance of Biên Hòa. The city was captured in 1861, an important allied victory in the Cochinchina Campaign fought between the French and the Spanish allied against the Vietnamese. What had begun as a limited punitive expedition led to a French war of conquest, and nearly a century of French colonial dominance.

"Jesus! How do you know so much?"

"I been here almost two years. And the last six months or so, I've been spending a lot of time in the library, researching Viet Nam. Maybe I'm gonna write a book about this place."

"Wow! Yeah, man, me too!"

They talked a little about *The Quiet American.* They had both read Graham Greene's classic, set in Viet Nam during the time he was a war correspondent from 1951-1954 for *Le Figaro* and *The Times of London.* They laughed about the tremendous differences they had experienced from what he had written almost two decades earlier.

Paul decided he was a good brother and replied with a non-sequitur.

OK. I will."

"Huh?"

"Stay at your barracks until morning."

"Oh. Of course! That was a hell of a transition from talking about the book."

"Guess I'm pretty bombed!"

"Ya think?"

CHAPTER 25

Adventure or Self-Destruction?

That night was a fucking blast! All of the men in Harold's barracks were combat vets and definitely had jaundiced views of the Army and the 'Nam. Paul broke out his bag of weed as a party favor, and it was heartily welcomed. They stayed up late drinking, smoking, and playing Hearts.

When Harold roused me the next morning, Paul found a battered set of fatigues, two pairs of clean socks, a boonie hat, and a pair of slightly worn boonie boots that were just right for his feet, all laid out on the bunk next to mine.

"I just nabbed some of the extra stuff that was laying around. Depending what you want to do next, I imagine you'll want to fin d a weapon or two."

All the brothers had treated Paul like visiting royalty. He beat up a little on himself when he realized he had blabbed perhaps too much about his situation after drinking and smoking too much. Then he remembered part of a Technicolor nightmare that had assaulted him during the night. He was this invisible speck watching a panorama of war crimes being committed in his name, in the name of all that was holy and honorable, in the name of "national security," in the name of a war in which he no longer believed, for a government to which he no longer felt allegiance. He felt torn apart, drawn and quartered, intestines spilling out of his eviscerated abdomen, and could do no more than watch as hundreds of thousands of people died for the concept of liberty, the false promise of unification and free elections after living under the yoke of a thousand years of imperialism.

He realized that, once again, his dreams were serving as his guide. He now clearly knew he would not go back, could not go back—not now, not today!

He was short and decided he suddenly had to see old friends all over the country he might never see again. It was likely the continuing effects of the codeine, or perhaps just his own innate madness, that had been unlocked by the psychotic episode, or was a result of it, he was going to have an adventure. NOW!

Paul did not share any of this with Harold as it was flashing through his brain but some of it must have shown on his face.

"Got it. Get your ass up and moving! Let's get some chow before all the sausages are gone!"

He showered and dressed quickly, the fatigues an almost perfect fit. He was especially pleased to see that the sleeves had no rank insignia, and only camouflaged 101st patches on both shoulders. The left boot was perfect, but the right needed two socks to fit tightly enough. He was ready within minutes and Harold took him to the Mess Hall. They entered with a wink and a nod to the stoned-looking doorman, and just as easily grabbed a large plate of American breakfast each, with plenty of sausages!

The night before, someone had produced some Riz La rolling papers, and Paul had cleaned and rolled his entire bag. He was reduced to eight good-sized joints, and gave Harold two as they walked toward his appropriated jeep.

"Seems like I gotta make another run to Saigon today. You need a ride anywhere?"

"Damn man! You are one good brother!"

"Takes one to know one, man!"

The return journey was completed in stoned silence, with Paul contemplating what lay ahead. His major impetus was to go see some old friends in country—Doc Adams, a lab tech friend from Fort Riley who was in Cam Rahn Bay; an old homey Virgil, who was at some kind of secret installation in Dalat; and maybe hang out in Saigon just a little bit, so as to create a chapter entitled *AWOL in Saigon* for a future book. (It seems ridiculously juvenile in retrospect, but he was young and crazy, loose in Viet Nam, feeling the surge, no matter how misguided, of incipient independence, invincibility, and getting the fuck out of the Army. It all made perfect sense at the time. It all had an impeccable logic).

French colonial architecture was everywhere, of course, since they occupied the country for almost a hundred years. Some of it was really spectacular, like the Basilica of Our Lady of The Immaculate Conception, with its sweeping arches and beautiful lines, sometimes called "Saigon's Cathedral of Notre Dame." Paul could not help but reflect on the entire question of Catholic influence that had spread its brutal tentacles through manipulation, coercion, violence, and murder here as well as everywhere.

He tucked his hair under his boonie hat and pulled it down to sit directly above his stoned eyes, before putting on his prescription sunglasses and prepared to exit the jeep a few blocks from Tan Son Nhut. When we stopped, Harold silently handed me a Colt 45, three clips, and a holster rig.

"Found this laying around the armory. Didn't want you to be unarmed here in the big city—or anywhere else you might decide to go."

"Oh, and you might want this too" he said, reaching behind the seat to produce a battered M-16 and a cloth bandolier of magazines.

"Don't worry. It's officially 'lost!'"

Paul was genuinely touched, and tried to express it, though he was sure his face said it all.

Harold just dapped with him said, "Don't mean nothing, brother. Stay frosty," then drove away without looking back.

Paul decided to check out Saigon, at least in part for further literary veracity. He turned south toward the steamy, jumping-with-every-kind-of-life-you-could-imagine city, a place where he'd been told anyone could fulfill any fantasy if he had enough money—something that may have been true anywhere, but it was epitomized by Saigon in January of 1969.

The wild fury of the city swirled all around him as if he were at a berserk circus. Paul felt like a country bumpkin in the metropolis for the first time. There were so many bars with so many women willing to have sex on the street, and so much traffic—buses, cars, pedi-cabs, tanks, bicycles, and massive crowds of people everywhere—and all of them moving at a frenetic pace to get somewhere, anywhere, else. He had no choice but to plunge into the bone-jarring, mind-numbing maelstrom, awash with fear like a newborn denied oxygen, soiled and corrupted by the gasoline-fumed air, as if someone had poured sulfuric acid on anorchid.

He walked for what seemed like hours, and ended up in Cholon, where the Chinatown was located and a thriving center of black-market activities. He wandered streets that were ancient when America was "discovered," getting strange, often hostile, sideways looks as he walked the streets heavily armed, enticed by the sights and sounds and smells, baited by prostitutes, harangued by hawksters, and

Black Marketeers. His original intention for going into Saigon melted, and re-merged into a vague fantasy of simply "going underground," living adventures only hinted at by Hemingway in his tales of war.

Then he had a stroke of what he could only call unfortunate good fortune.

Unfortunate because the man calling out my name was sitting in the driver's seat of a Military Police jeep.

"Paul! Paul Marzeky!"

How could they had found him already? And how did they know his bloody <u>name</u>? Paul was totally perplexed.

The MP jumped out of the jeep, and ran toward him. He didn't have a loaded weapon in his hand, so that was a good thing.

The MP smiled, and Paul fell back against the wall. Fuck! He might as well just surrender. As he turned to confess his sins, the MP stopped in front of him, made eye contact and started wildly shaking his hand.

"Paul fucking Marzeky! What are you doing here?"

Fortunate because the MP's facial features slowly coalesced into that of a "home boy" from the world! who had dated his sister!

"This is unbelievable! Steve fucking Short! What are you doing here!?"

"Usual story. Got drafted, got shafted. First Infantry, Purple Heart then an oak leaf cluster. Now I'm the driver for the C.O. of the 716th MP Battalion."

"That's un-fucking-believable!"

"How about you? Are you under cover? CIA or something?"

"No, no. I just got promoted so I took off my stripes. I'm gonna be E-5 too" I said referring to his sergeant's stripes.

"What unit?"

"Oh. 101st."

"Where are you stationed? When's your DEROS? Are you short?"

His interrogatory had more the flavor of actual information-seeking than embodying an intention to bust me, so Paul decided to come semi-clean and see what would happen.

"Actually, I just got back from R-and-R in Taiwan. I'm twenty-five and a wake up."

"Wow! You <u>are</u> really short. I've got another five months."

"Hey man! It was really cool seeing you again. I've got to sky up."

"Why so soon? Don't you have time to smoke a joint with a home boy?"

"With an <u>MP</u> home boy?"

"Sheeeet! Everybody I know is a head! Don't tell me you're not!"

"Fire one up, brother!"

He tilted his head toward the jeep and said, "Let's roll. That way I can monitor the radio while we burn one."

"Dy-no-mite, brotha!" Paul said, and we passed the power in a dap.

"When did you get so fucking hip, man?"

"First day I got here. You?"

"Started at Fort Riley with a bunch of marooned California guys. We used to take over the day room after chow in the evenings. We'd open the windows, draw the shades, get loaded and blast out the psychedelic tunes."

"Far out!"

"It lasted until some lifer CQ turned us in. But nobody got busted."

"That's cool."

"I'm hip."

"This fucking weed is great, man!"

"Thanks. I get it from my papa-san. He's a serious business man."

"Sounds like a good man to know."

"Amen, brother. Can you imagine having a pile of this in South St. Louis? You'd get rich, and have all the best pussy for miles around!"

"You could make a fortune, and stay high forever!"

"There it is!" he said, and we dapped and then slapped palms and knuckles.

"Damn! Who'd have believed it? Steve Short a fucking MP?"

"Here the fuck I am, brother!"

"So, are you sending any of this home to St. Louis?"

"There's some very hip people there now, some hip neighborhoods, like up around Forest Park, in the Central West End (CWE). You remember Gaslight Square?"

"Most of them probably came from somewhere else. To go to Wash U."

Steve replied, "I might go there when I get out. But in the meantime, I am doing my best to invest in my future! I want to retire early!"

Paul responded, "I want to move to San Francisco. I can collect unemployment for a year, stay loaded, and see what happens next. Maybe use the GI Bill, see if my brain still works!"

"Wow! We never really ever knew each other before."

"Wow! I was just flashing on that too!"

"You're a pretty cool dude, man!"

"You too, man."

"I'm...not legal right now. Just a day overdue from R-and-R."

"Shit happens, man!"

"Since you're Mr. Saigon, can you turn me on to a hotel?"

"Shit! You can stay in my barracks! We're all heads!"

"A whole barracks full of MP heads!? Jesus!"

It was the natural transition for vets WIA to become MPs. The 716th MP Company was a prime example.

"No sweat, GI! I know a place where mama-san makes Number One burgers!"

"Drive on, brother!"

Steve played tour guide. He knew all the hot spots— restaurants, bars, whorehouses, and places that had been hit during Tet '68.

I pointed out all of the construction sites and the sawhorses that read "BRJ-RMK."

"Yeah LBJ is making millions on this war!"

"No! How?

"Royal Marine Korean-Brown, Root and Johnson."

"LBJ Johnson?"

"Damn straight. Him and his butthole buddies from Texas, George Brown and the Root brothers, have exclusive construction contracts with the Navy all over the country."

"What? That's got to be illegal!"

"It probably is, but these fuckers slicked it in. They're making millions!"

"What the fuck are they building that's worth so much?"

"Runways, the big ten thousand-footer here; Naval bases; hospitals; covered storage facilities; fuel depots; base camps. They even built all of the four major bridges around Saigon: Bình Phước; Bình Điền; Bến Lức; and Tân An.

They're big into concrete." (The estimated $2 billion dollars that they generated then is the equivalent of $15 billion in today's currency).

"Come on! He's a sitting President!"

"Don't mean nothing, man!"

"That's bullshit! Friends of ours are dying, and that son of a bitch is making a mint!"

"There it is, brother."

"Jesus! When did you get so fucking political?"

"Laying in the hospital the second time gave me plenty of time to think."

"You sound like this cat I knew in Qui Nhon."

"Getting shot takes away your innocence for-fucking-ever!"

"I fucking guess."

"That's why I'm building my retirement nest egg while I can! Fuck paying taxes to The Man when I get home!"

"Can I get in on it?"

"Maybe. Let's rap about it a little."

"I'm already a day late. Maybe I can invest a little while I'm here? Maybe just enough for me to get high on when I'm home?"

"We'll see," was all he'd say, then handed me another joint of that scary weed.

"Ah. Here we are," he said, pulling up in front of a nondescript building hidden away on a back street near the soccer stadium. Once he parked the jeep (illegally, of course), we walked through a thick, iron-reinforced wooden door, and into a gigantic single unit that had been cleverly transformed behind the facades of three houses. The adjoining walls had been removed to create a single huge space. The interior walls were covered with fine tapestries, the floors were hard wood, and covered with Persian rugs. The exposed woodwork glistened, exuding lemon oil. The front public part of the building had been decorated to accommodate Western tastes with antique furniture, and a long mahogany bar complete with brass foot rail. We drifted away from the busier portion to the more rarely used library. The floor-to-ceiling shelves were filled with volumes in Viet Namese, Chinese, Lao, French and English. Many were First Editions.

There were stunning young Vietnamese women everywhere, all smartly dressed though clearly not hustling like many bar girls elsewhere. We ordered drinks. Johnny Walker Black for me, while Steve had an icy cold Carlsberg.

"Jesus! Un-fucking-believable!"

"Like it, huh?"

"Never seen anything like it in my fucking life!"

"Yeah, I come here a lot."

"I thought we'd be hassled by all the officers. But they didn't say a word. They all fucking smiled at me!"

"This is a <u>very</u> private club. I'm pretty well known here."

Paul looked up and saw an elderly mama-san come waddling across the floor. She had a gold-toothed grin spread wide across her seamed and leathery face. He figured she must be the hooch maid or cleaning lady, since she was, in contrast to all the other women he had seen, dressed in baggy black pajama pants and an off-white wraparound blouse made of coarse material.

"Who in the <u>fuck</u> is this?" Paul asked, with a certain amount of derision in his voice.

Steve ignored him completely, and hugged the old woman warmly as she greeted him.

"Sergeant Steve!"

They spoke briefly in Vietnamese, then he hugged her again and turned to me.

"Paul, I want you to meet my very good friend Thahn Ahn. I told her you were a home boy from the world."

"Chao, co-ba" Paul said in the best of the local dialect.

She laughed and put a surprisingly dainty hand to her mouth.

"I am no longer a young girl, but thank you. You friend Sergeant Steve's, you friend me," she said in broken English, and sent one of the young women scurrying to bring us more drinks and put in a double order of Steve's usual order of cheeseburgers and fries.

"She <u>owns</u> the place. I'm her hero. I kicked a drunken Marine's ass who was hassling one of the girls!"

"I should fucking hope, Mr. Rope-a-Dope!"

"I am!"

"This place blows my mind!"

"You know what they say: A mind blown is a mind shown!"

"Maybe I'll write about it one day." He was glad that his little adventure in Saigon was already taking a nicely twisted turn.

"Maybe you'll will. One never knows."

Steve then pulled out a bulging bag of bright lime green flower tops, and a pack of Spanish Zig-Zag rolling papers. He broke a portion of a long, thick top into a small silver serving dish and carefully pulled out the seeds and set them aside in a cellophane from a cigarette pack. Next, he crushed the leaves into semi-fine mulch, deftly filled the crease in one paper almost to bulging. With two quick rolls to balance out the level, he rolled once more and licked it, turning it into a joint of beauty that he handed to me.

I was impressed, and told him so.

"Nothing to it, man."

I lit the finely rolled number, and started coughing like a cherry!

"Jesus! My lungs have collapsed!"

"Good shit, huh?"

"Damn fine."

He just laughed. And he started rolling another one.

"Wow! Are you some kind of superlungs or something?"

"I roll a bunch when I get a chance. Got to be ready."

"Amen."

"Got to stay high to survive. Remember what Freddie the Fabulous Furry Freak Brother always says."

I laughed and asked, "Who in the fuck is that?"

"Character in an underground comic book. My copy's making the rounds in the hooch. These three brothers, one of them is Freddy, says 'It's better to have dope in times of no money than to have money in times of no dope!'"

"Wow! That is righteous!"

"Amen, brother."

We dapped again.

He arranged through Steve to cash some Greenbacks he had stashed, mostly money his mother sent every once in a while. Steve agreed and Thahn delivered four MPC for every Greenback—quite a tidy sum.

"How do you manage to get your stuff home?"

"I'm an MP. Nobody hassles me. But I take precautions anyway. Pack it in two or three plastic bags, and then wrap it inside of socks or clothes. Then I sprinkle cinnamon or nutmeg around the packing materials, and triple-seal it. Don't make the packages too large."

"That's pretty cool. But you can't be getting too much home at that rate."

"I send two or three packages a month to different addresses. Got maybe twenty pounds waiting for me. My goal is a hundred before I leave!"

"Damn!"

"I know this one cat that's been sending back like twenty pounds a month. His brother sells half and stashes the other half."

"I'd be afraid of getting busted."

"Me too. The Customs guys can be tight. And the Post Office is supposed to be using x-ray machines now too."

"I guess it's like anything else, you just gotta be cool!"

"I heard about this other guy who walked through Customs with three quarters of his duffle bag full! Eighty-eight pounds!"

"A-fucking-mazing!"

"'Course he was coming from Korea."

"Wow!"

"Hold Baggage is good too—except there's a lot of heads working there who might just rip you off! And who you gonna complain to?"

"I'm hip."

Paul started laughing about the picture he was having in his head, of the two of them, home boys from St. Louis, sitting in Saigon smoking and drinking like a pair of cultured gentlemen, comparing notes on how to smuggle some dope home!

"I might be able to move a kilo tomorrow if the price is right? I know some hungry dudes in Biên Hòa?"

"Hell yes! No sweat, GI!"

Stefan J. Malecek, Ph. D.

CHAPTER 26
Free Enterprise

Hitchhiking a ride to Biên Hòa was as easy as breathing. There was so much stoned traffic on the highway that it would have been hard <u>not</u> to get a ride!

"Where you headed, man?"

"Biên Hòa."

"Me too."

"Dynamite!"

"Where in Biên Hòa?" he asked loudly, above the din of his portable radio, hung around the jeep's rear-view mirror, blasting hot tunes of revolution.

"101ˢᵗ."

"Cool. I'm going right by there."

"Wanna smoke a joint?"

"Hell yes." He held out his palm and we dapped.

"Wally. Wally Chester. Scranton P-A.

"They call me Jay," I decided on the spot to name myself after a joint. Why not? I was reinventing myself anyway, and I needed a *nom de dope*.

He had named his hometown up front, the second most frequently asked question in the 'Nam. Even the dinks did it, learning names of faraway places like some kind of mantra.

He was remined of Bob Dylan's line: "To live outside the law you must be honest," and decided again that it was good and true.

Paul took one hit of the man's mediocre weed, and snuffed it out in the ashtray.

He looked at me, angry and weirded out.

"No offense, brother. Try some of mine. OK?" Paul said, and lit one of his own hand rolled.

The younger man started coughing, and almost ran them off the road.

"Holy shit!"

"Pretty damn good, huh?"

"Wow! One fucking hit and I'm already blasted!"

"Put it out and save it for later. My head's right."

"Wow! Thank you, man! Jesus!"

Paul laughed when he remembered a time when the CID fucked up big time at an FSB he occasionally visited. Everybody in this particular company was a stoner, and they had become a sort of underground supply depot. They got hot because they were moving so much dope. The Army, in its infinite wisdom, decided they could send in some "undercover officers," who were supposed to "fit right in" because they had moustaches and slightly shaggy hair. But they couldn't fool the good brothers who had the word days before they arrived. They figured they'd have some fun and bait the doufuss assholes with a stash of cheap weed planted for them to find. When they did, the interlopers decided to make a big spectacle of their contributing to "eradicating the drug threat." The entire assembled and stood at attention while they laid the weed on the ground (maybe thirty pounds), slashed it with bayonets, doused it in kerosene, and set it afire, sneering at the assembled heads. Just then a huge wind blew in, and carried the smoke directly into their faces, and they stood rigidly at attention, breathing deeply as the lifers scurried around yelling at them to not inhale, but no one had bothered to dismiss them from attention!

Paul felt a little paranoid on his way to Harold's hooch, but everyone looked copacetic. Amazingly he found the man lying down in his bunk, snoring.

"Hey brotha'! What's burning?"

"I didn't really expect to ever see you again!"

We dapped, and I said "Wanna smoke some mary wanna?"

He started coughing on the first hit.

"Is this some kind of joke weed?"

"What do you mean?" Paul asked with mock innocence.

"You put some kind of shit in here, didn't you, to make me cough?

"I did the same thing first time I smoked it."

"Jesus H. Christmas Tree!"

"I hear that."

He took another hit, and managed to hold some of the smoke in.

"Fuck! That shit's outrageous!"

"I.M. Hip" Paul said, holding out my hand and they dapped.

There was a crunch of footsteps then, and two other faces appeared.

"What are you guys doing in there? Smoking 'mary-hoony'?"

"Gimme a hit, or you're busted!"

"Bunch of fucking cherries" Harold said, laughing while they coughed. "I guess you can't handle this smoke, huh?" he said, making as if to leave.

"Wait a minute, wait a minute. You got some more? You got a bag for sale?"

"Just one!"

"I'll take it! How much?"

Figuring my time and investment, and a cut for Steve, I hit on what seemed a fair price.

"Two hundred!" I'd paid one hundred.

"For a fucking bag of weed? You are dinky dau!"

"For this shit, you can charge fifteen dollars an ounce, and still double your money!"

"I'm quite sure I can find somebody who will want it," Paul said, revealing the treasure hidden in his canvas bag.

"Jesus! Look at that!'

"Wow! Where'd you fucking get that?"

"I'll take it," said Harold, immediately handing me the cash in MPC.

Harold turned to me, and said, "You must have a good friend in Saigon."

"A friend in need is a friend indeed."

"Righteous, man. Really righteous!"

He nodded at his two friends, who were still choking, whether from the weed or the quality of the kilo, Paul didn't know

"Wow, brother! This is really righteous!"

"Righteous is as righteous does!"

"Can you get any more like this?"

"Don't know why not. How much can you handle and how quickly?'

"Let me talk to the brothers. Go get some chow and I'll see you in an hour."

When he returned, Harold was grinning psychedelically.

"Look, I know you're running hard, so we got up as much cash as we could. Can you do us a one-time score of ten of those kilos? Today?"

"I... I don't know. Can you drive me?"

"Roger Willco!"

They drove back, leisurely smoking yet another joint. Paul had Harold drop him off near the PX, and walked the rest of the way.

When he found Dave, he explained that he had been intending to give him twenty dollars as his share of the sale, but that now he had a man waiting who wanted ten packages; and Paul had all the cash on his person.

As soon as Steve quickly recovered from the shock and rationalized his paranoia (he had known Paul boo-coo long time), he told Paul to go to the NCO Club and have a drink, and he would meet him there forthwith.

In a time much quicker than he could have imagined, Steve returned with a big grin.

"All fixed. And my end is already in. No extra charge."

"Wow! Righteous!"

They went to the back room of the club. Paul laid out the money in fans of one hundred dollars. Steve collected the money, and returned in just minutes with a large cardboard box in the back of his jeep.

"Jesus!"

Paul insisted on checking one bag, since "It isn't my money!" He rolled a joint out of a random package, and swiftly went to meet Harold, having assured the entire amount was awaiting them at the back of the NCO Club.

"What? Are you shitting me?"

"Square business, brother!"

In short order the deal was concluded with big grins all around.

When he next addressed Steve, he proposed using all of his earnings to make a purchase to be shipped home.

"Do you think I could employ your delivery service...for a price, of course?"

"Is the bear Catholic?"

"Man, you are one good brother! I'm really glad you dated my sister."

"Me too. She's a good chick."

"I think so too."

"Hey, do you think I can get one of those kilos to travel with? Personal stash?

"Yaah, shure, you betcha!"

Paul was really feeling the heat (literally and metaphorically) by the next day, and decided that he had to start his journey forthwith, or risk never getting out of Saigon, seductive as the prospect was.

They met over breakfast, the usual great fare of sausages, eggs, toast with real butter, and good coffee, but they kept their conversation very low key. Leaving the mess hall, Steve turned to him and said, "I have the proverbial good news/bad news for you. What do you want first?"

Paul sighed and said, "Fuck! Give me the bad!"

"The bad is that there's no more of the weed I sold you yesterday!"

Shit! He thought, thinking of the bright lime green flower tops being history.

"So, what's the 'good'?"

He grinned, and said, "A picture is worth a thousand words!"

"What the fuck does that mean?" Paul said, snarling.

"Come with me, troop!"

He followed, a bit confused and angry, though this was supposed to be the good.

He led me into his hooch, and revealed a perfectly constructed hidey-hole built into the floor. He pulled out a cellophane wrapped package, further covered in Vietnamese newsprint.

"Is that the shit?"

"Oh, is it ever!"

"Lemme see!"

"At ease, troop! All in good time."

"Close your eyes."

"What?"

"I said close your eyes!"

"OK."

Paul heard crinkling as the package was unwrapped and thrust under my nose, and almost fainted when the rich aroma hit me. Then he opened my eyes and saw a veritable forest of bright red buds! He could not believe his eyes!

"Oh wow! Jesus! Can I touch?" he said with the greatest reverence.

They looked like gnarled red hands with fingers outstretched. As Paul picked one up, he realized it was sticky with resin. He almost got high just holding it.

"Oh, my fucking wow!"

Paul broke off a fingertip, and rolled a small, thin joint. He already knew this was killer dynamite, so it didn't need to be too big. If we had to take two hits to get blasted, he'd be surprised!

They each had one decent hit, and the joint burned out on its own. There was so much resin that the rest of the paper was stained reddish-brown.

They just sat back, and zoned in a very comfortable silence, the sort of peace and quiet anyone can only get when they're in the presence of someone they really trust.

An indeterminate amount of time went by before either them us felt it necessary to move. When they did, Steve spoke first.

"Now, if you're really ready, I've got the better news!"

"What could possibly be better than this?"

"If you give me a mailing address, and a hundred twenty-five dollars each, I will see to it that you have as many of these as you want waiting when you get home!"

"Oh, super fucking wow!"

He wrote down the address of an old friend he had known since grade school. She had written me a letter asking if the "grass was really greener there," so he had decided to trust her with his homecoming stash. He turned over almost all of the money he had in MPC, amounting to the price of ten kilos.

He secured a large plastic bag full for the journey, and then carefully rewrapped his stash. Steve has some chores for the Captain, and told me to rack out for a while. Paul was trippin' so hard on the righteous smoke, he just laid down with his canvas satchel on one side and his weapon on the other; and drifted into a deep, easy sleep.

He was dreaming that a very large and persistent monkey was fucking around with his foot. He shook him off twice. When he came back a third time, Paul leveled his pistol at the little fucker to shoot him.

Steve laughed as he pushed the barrel of the gun down, and said "Don't be shooting yourself in the foot, troop!"

"You crazy fuck. What time is it?"

"1515. Time to sky. Airborne! I got another little treat for you."

"Really? What could be better?"

"I had one of the brothers cut you some new orders. Travel authorization AAA. You are authorized to go to Cam Rahn Bay, Nha Trang, and Dalat. And," he said, holding a sheaf of paperwork in his hand, "this is the only two sets! No one can trace you!"

"Holy fucking shit!"

"I just wanted to give you a good head start!"

"Man, brother, I'm going to make a point of seeing you back in the world, even if I have to come to St. Louis to do it!"

"Hey brother man. It's been totally fucking real," Paul said to Steve as they parted.

"Remember man, you've always got a place to crash with me."

"You too if you come to the coast with the most!"

They dapped and he headed for the chopper pad to go back to Tan Son Nhut.

Paul fantasized that he was a kind of mythic adventurer who appeared out of the mists, as Jack Bruce and Cream had sung, "With tales of brave Ulysses and how his naked ears were tortured by the sirens sweetly singing," and dropping in unannounced on friends the length of Viet Nam. Then he would sky back up to Evans, get his clearances, and be gone even before the lifers knew he'd been back. All they would feel is the vapor trail of his Freedom Bird leaving their sorry asses behind. Retrospectively, it was so totally naïve of him to believe that the Army would just forget about him, but Paul was immersed in the adrenaline of the moment, probably still a little psychotic, and living out a fantasy produced and sanctioned by his own neurons.

Fuck it! He <u>was</u> goin' home.

CHAPTER 27
Party

Paul had visions of living really living large, making his life count for something big and splashy! His experience had made him larger mentally, and hungrier emotionally. He absorbed information and insights very, very quickly, seeking only to know, and do, and be, more every day—and he was goin' home! Nothing could stop him now! He had been on hold since the day he was born, and now he finally was giving birth to myself in a kind of male parthenogenesis, his new self emerging from within himself. And he was goin' home!

He couldn't stop grinning!

"SHORT!" he called.

"SHORT!" he yelled.

"SHORT!" he cried.

"SHORT!" he shouted.

He was fucking goin' home! Jesus! He was teetering on the edge of total manic delusion as a tiny portion of my brain argued for sanity, and reminded him that he was officially AWOL. He reasoned with myself—as if he had had a commissurotomy, his brain split apart into bicameral hemispheres—he had over a year in-country, two and a half in the service, and nineteen months in grade as an E-5. What the fuck were they gonna do? Send him to Viet Nam? He would very soon be the highest rank of all. Civilian!

One of the guys from Paul's class at Fort Sam was in Cam Rahn Bay, working nights in the lab, and swimming and surfing every day! And that the drugs were in-fucking-credible! Paul decided he just <u>had</u> to go.

He saw himself as a legendary figure in the annals of the Viet Nam oral history, a living character like Monster or Cherokee. He wanted people to remember his deeds, to stop in wonder years later, and say to their friends, "Do you remember Doc Jay? And what that crazy motherfucker did when...?"

He went to the flight line, cocky as hell with his new travel orders, declaring him in transit, and legal as a motherfucker. He had a kilo of dope in his little canvas kick, more than a thousand dollars in cash left in a money belt, and an attitude that said "Lock all the doors, hide the women and children, a bad ass dude is coming home!"

He felt at a pinnacle of personal power. He felt that it was magnified in meaning because he represented all those who would never walk and talk in the world again; whose brave deeds and humor would be left untold except in the minds of those who survived and celebrated them, as L.M. Bailey would one day do, on a poster of a Field Cross he had drawn and lithographed:

"Because of the fate our comrades met,

We, the survivors, must <u>never</u> forget."

Walking out with all his arms and legs and balls seemed a terrific accomplishment, even though his brain might be impaired, perhaps for life. He had known many men who had suffered so much more than he had; had endured hardships and pain beyond his imagining; had endured traumas that most people could not even imagine. He felt as if he had been hammered on the anvil of Life here, tempered his personal mettle in ways that others might not have considered for fear of failure or smallness of spirit. He saw his experiences there as a gift to himself, and perhaps to many others with whom he had had contact; perhaps too, for many who would yet have contact with him, the new and improved him, who would shine as an even brighter light in years to come. It was a treasure of such great price as to not even be distinguishable, except to those who had endured it. And he was proud to be such a one. And he was SHORT!

Paul's timing was unusually good when it came to flying. Maybe it had to do with his astrology chart. He had caught so much well-meaning cheap shit for being a "straight leg" in an airborne outfit that he would have gone to jump school in-country if they'd offered him the opportunity. His timing held true this time and he touched down on the 10,000-foot cement runway (built by RMK-BRJ, of course) in Cam Rahn Bay in less than thirty minutes.

Miles of white sand beach defined the geography, though private and military contractors delineated the context of life. Money-controlled destiny was evidenced by the many fine French colonial villas along and above the elegant shores. By comparison, Saigon was jaded by real life danger and hustle, by violence and penury. But here was some of the best duty one could get. The atmosphere was exhilarating, and the primary MOS was Party Dude. Of course, it was the top in-country R&R spots for both U.S. and troops from the north. It was also a rear area rehabilitation center where everybody was stoned and unconcerned about the war. Tet of '68 was the only time they were <u>ever</u> on alert. They had otherwise never received so much as a mortar round.

Cam Rahn had grown from the sleepy little backwater port that Marco Polo had visited and reported on in the 14th Century, and became one of the best deep-water ports in the world (thanks to billions of Uncle Sugar's dollars, and multinational largesse). There was even a milk recombining plant built by Meadow Gold, churning out milk, butter and ice cream for all the rear area pogies and the Generals!

The 6th Convalescent Center (CC) compound was built within a hundred yards of the beach. It had always been considered sacrosanct and had never been attacked. Though the wards were filled with combat wounded, the staff—far less exposed to the rigors of war—allowed themselves to be lulled into an indolent lack of attention to the ordinary, and they cultivated altered states of consciousness.

As Paul walked into the compound, I met a guy called "Buzz" who embodied this attitude. He seemed extraordinarily ordinary. His standard military haircut, Army-issued Coke-bottle thick eyeglasses lent the appearance of his being pretty doufuss. As the man drew closer, Paul noticed that his Olive Drab baseball cap was sideways on his head. Though the man looked overweight, his fatigues were at least four sizes too large, giving the impression of an oversized inflatable balloon stuffed into human skin.

He could have been one of Rousseau's innocents naïvely expecting protection from the Universe. He had impeccable radar, seemingly able to instantly read people's energy. His whole demeanor shouted "What war?" When we made eye contact, we were standing completely exposed in the middle of one of the wooden sidewalks that connected various parts of the rambling medical facility. He handed me a joint without saying a word. I freaked out! What the fuck? I looked around in every direction, but there was no one in sight. I didn't know the ground rules here, and I certainly didn't know this cat. But his presentation drew me as if into a vacuum, then he launched into what I found out later was one of his patented verbal assaults.

"What's your name, brother? Are you a grunt? A medic? CIA? SOG? Don't be paranoid, man. My name's Buzz, man, because I'm always buzzing. Where you from? In the world I mean."

I couldn't read the cat, and refused the offer of the joint, having flashes of CID guys pouring out of all the tents with automatic weapons leveled at me. I glanced around nervously again, and accepted the joint the second time he offered. I decided the guy was well and truly nuts, and obviously speeding, though there had to be a primary psychiatric process at work too. I left him standing in the middle of the sidewalk talking to himself as if I were still there, and went in search of Doc Don Eden, the man from Paradise, as we had called him at Fort Riley.

Everybody Paul encountered was loaded to the max, and seemed unconcerned that anybody else knew it! He was used to being loaded on obscure Fire Bases and LZs, but this was a very major, very prominent hospital with thousands of patients and more than double that many staff with tons of brass hats around. Yet everybody was loaded in the middle of the day! He felt a bit paranoid, and jealous at the same time. He decided that, despite Zeno's aphorism, maybe there was something new under the sun.

He had no idea where he was going, but felt pulled toward the miles of pristine beach where he ran into another stony-looking cat wearing surgical greens and horned rim glasses that made him look like a schizophrenic lizard.

We looked at each other for a moment, eyeballs clicking like castanets, then simultaneously burst out laughing.

"You look funny as hell, man!" we both said, and laughed some more.

"Wanna smoke a joint, and talk about it?" Paul finally managed.

"Is the Pope a bear?"

We shook hands and dapped.

"Doctor Jay."

"Clark the Clerk" he said, like it was a title of nobility.

We waded into the three and four-foot-high dune grass fronting a deserted stretch of beach.

"This is our private beach, man."

"Who's us?"

"The Hospital Company."

"Hey man, would it be too much to ask where we're goin'?"

"We have arrived."

"Where?"

"Right here" he said, bending from the waist and disappearing from sight for a moment; and then stuck his head out of the grass and smiled.

"Secret entrance. Check it out."

If he hadn't been shown, he would never have been able to find it. The perfectly camouflaged hut had been built in the grass and completely concealed by it. There was a woven straw mat on the floor, with wooden IV crates for chairs, and corrugated aluminum walls covered with camouflage poncho liners. The roof was built of corrugated aluminum sheets covered in ponchos and covered with enough dirt

that the thick beach grass kept growing. Jefferson Airplane's first album was playing and nearby to the eight-track deck was a rack of tapes—The Doors, Santana, Big Brother and the Holding Company, Jimi Hendrix, and Bob Dylan among dozens of others.

Paul shook hands and dapped his way around a small circle that included an X-Ray Tech, an Operating Room Tech, and two orderlies. No one seemed at all surprised that he didn't remove his hat.

"Always trips people out the first time they see how the other half lives."

Paul took a hit of the joint that came, and awaited the inevitable interrogation.

"So, who're you with?"

Dwayne Adderly was a tall, thin, spindly Black cat who looked like a basketball center, and worked in the OR.

"I'm in the 101st. I came here to see an old friend, Don Eden."

"Oh yeah? You know Don then?"

"Yeah. We were stationed together at Fort Riley."

"Kinda tall, and blonde haired, surfer type guy?"

I suddenly felt claustrophobic, and I felt the circle tighten around me. I casually put my hand on my 45.

"The Doctor Don I knew was medium height, brown hair, wispy moustache."

"Works in Nuclear Medicine, right?"

"What the fuck's with you guys? He's a Lab Tech, and an old friend of mine from the world!"

"Are you a narc?"

"Are you fucking shitting me?"

"You gotta tell us if we ask you directly. Are you CID? Are you an undercover?"

Paul drew his .45 and raised his voice.

"Fuck you, man! You motherfuckers have been taking too much speed!" and prepared to didi when a familiar voice stopped him.

"I heard someone was asking for me! Marzeky? What the fuck are <u>you</u> doing here?"

Paul jumped up to hug him and dislodged his hat in the process.

There was a sudden quiet as the gathered group stared at me with their mouths agape like a bunch of baby birds at feeding time.

"I came to see you, asshole! But your home boys here been roastin' me about being CID!"

"Where did you get all that fucking HAIR?"

It was then that Paul realized that his hair had fallen down.

"Oh, I guess I forgot to get a military haircut this week!"

"You show up out of nowhere, and you've got this" Don said, touching his hair.

People gathered around us, some reaching out to touch his long locks.

"Yeah, it's real!

"Hair! God! He's got hair!"

"Hey brother! I know people in the world got less than you!"

Don apologized. Their set had heard that the CID was going to infiltrate a new undercover narc into the Medical Company. Their first concern was that Paul might have been him. Their paranoia had been amped out of control by the good amphetamines to which they had access, some of them far too readily it seemed.

"Then why did you invite me in?"

"Well dude, if you had been The Man, you would not have walked out. You would have simply disappeared!"

He recovered my composure, and asked the universal question, "Wanna smoke a joint?"

"Far out, man!"

We all sat, and somebody inserted a Country Joe and the Fish tape that I had not yet heard.

"Joe's a vet, man. Navy"

"Far out!"

"Hey! Hey! Turn it down a little. I can't hear!" someone called out.

Paul opened his canvas bag, pulled out a hairy, red bud and handed it to Don.

"Wow! Where'd you get that?"

"Right out of my little bag here! Watch. I'll do it again" I said, then reached in and pulled out another, handing it to Dwayne.

"Wow! This shit smells killer!"

"Somebody roll one, huh?"

"Why don't you, man? It's your weed. Wouldn't want to smoke too much."

"I guarantee you won't be able to smoke too much of this" Paul said. He quickly broke apart a small portion and set aside the seeds—somebody was always saving seeds—and then proceeded to roll a large party bomber.

"Fire it up, brother!'

"You've come a long way since Fort Riley!" said Don.

"We both have!"

More people arrived, and were spacing themselves around the perimeter of the circle. Paul felt like a celebrity and kept hearing the word "HAIR!" whispered in reverential tones. Don lit the joint—and started coughing as his friends jeered.

"Cherry!"

"Get some lungs!"

"Bogart!"

"Pass the joint! I won't cough!'

"This shit is strong!" Don said to me, the in hushed tones, "Got any for sale?"

"No, but I'll turn you onto some before I sky up."

"How long can you stay?"

"I don't know. Maybe a couple of days."

"Ex-o-lent! We really party hardy here!"

"I'm a little overdue...at Camp Evans."

"Weren't you in Qui Nhon? Are you a patient in the hospital here?"

Paul briefly related the story of his long journey, which garnered comments like "Fuck that motherfucker!" and "Right on, man!"

"That's right. You work in Mental Hygiene, right?"

"Close enough."

"So, what the fuck?"

"Just came for a little visit on the way back."

"Hey! I'm very glad, man."

"Me too. Good weed, huh?"

"<u>Great</u> shit!"

Just then he heard a metallic clanking sound coming from the little tunnel that led to this jungle hideout. Paul immediately flashed that they were being raided, and he drew his pistol, clicked off the safety, and pointed the barrel toward the doorway. Don laughed, and pushed the barrel down.

"No sweat, GI! It's just Buzz!"

Oh great! Just what I need! "You mean he's welcome here?"

"Of course. He's the man."

"For what?"

"Nitrous oxide."

"Laughing gas?"

"You betcha!"

"Never had any before. What's it do?"

"Don't worry, cherry boy" he said, "It's a gas" he said, laughing at his own bad joke.

Buzz wheeled in a dark blue painted metal canister, and settled it in the middle of the clearing. Then he very methodically and very professionally attached lengths of surgical tubing, with hemostats snugging closed their ends, to a large metal outlet tube. They looked like bizarre octopus tentacles.

"Woooooeeee!!"

"Let's party!"

"It's ruuuuussssh time!"

Paul asked again, "What's it do?"

"It's a rush! You'll dig it. Dwayne puts half empties outside, and Buzz wheels 'em over."

Don grabbed a tube, and said, "Watch."

He breathed out, emptying his lungs completely. Then he detached the hemostat, he put the tube into his mouth, and inhaled as though it were his last breath. Someone else quickly reattached the clamp before Don fell back against the wall holding his breath.

He watched as Don's eyes bulged, ears turn crimson, nose twitched, and neck muscles stretched as if he had torticollis—and then exhaled a huge gout of empty air.

"PPAAAUUUGH!!"

Don sat back stunned, eyes tearing and glazed, as if he'd just had a stroke.

"Are you OK?" Paul asked, now more skeptical than ever.

He nodded, eyes still unfocused, and far, far away.

"Shit looks pretty nasty."

He waved me away, matters of more moment occupying his attention.

Paul put a tube to his lips, loosened the clamp, and took a tentative puff.

It had a cool, almost sweet taste, but absolutely no effect on him.

"This stuff ain't shit!"

"Deeper" Don croaked, barely able to articulate. Everyone was sucking on the tubes like they were a connection to the Divine, as if the gas carried a new vision of the Messiah of the Age—or more, like a bunch of strung-out, brain-dead laboratory rats. He'd always heard that, given the choice between food and cocaine, lab rats would compulsively choose cocaine until they died.

He tried another breath. A little taste tickled the edges of his mind. He took a deeper hit that immediately tore through his head and blew off the top of his cranium in a temple-pounding, blood-shushing rush that raced through his veins and capillaries like an icy blizzard blast down a deserted freeway; and then, just when he thought he had peaked, ten billion electric splinters shot up his spine, and scattered throughout his body. He morphed into a primitive creature drawn up from the primeval ooze. First all of Asia, then the entire globe melted into a gigantic mélange of tiny bubbles filled with different lives and different lovers, all of them known intimately to him. Conversations in multiple languages occurred simultaneously and he understood every word. An extraordinary sensuality pervaded him, unlike any he had ever known, and he had a simultaneous orgasm in all of his cells.

He lay basking in the extraordinary power of his release—no more shame, no more fear, no more worry, no more war.

Then he breathed out. It all disappeared.

He was immediately catapulted back into the interior of a small hut built on the beach, ten thousand miles from home and a likely candidate for some serious punitive action when he finally reported back in. It all flooded in at once. Fuck! And then a headache slammed across both his hemispheres as silent voices demanded more!

He arose from the sodden heap into which he had collapsed and acted without volition. Shoving several men aside, he quickly hyperventilated twice, stuck a tube in his mouth and inhaled to the furthest extent of his lung capacity. As the magic gas infiltrated his alveoli, the little bubbles reappeared, filled with wondrous people living intricate lives—with pains, joys, and pleasures that grew and unfolded the longer he held the enchanted and enlivening vapors in. He grieved their deaths as he breathed out. Many were the many hands that tried to take away his connection to the tank. Many were the voices that shouted at him as if through an aquarium full of water. But he could not stop, would not stop. He was on a mission! Each and every one of those little lives depended on him. He was their God! He shared in their dramas and joys! He was alive in each and every one of them, shared a sentient existence with each of the men, women, and children, even the animals and plants. They owed their very existence to him! He stood apart from the "he" that was him, in a little window like a control booth in a recording studio—separate from all the drama and trauma, the picayune struggles, torture and torment of any form of singular existence, high above it all as if his frontal cortex had been surgically separated from the rest of his brain, a voyeur God in miniature. He clamped the tube in his mouth, breathing in and out as quickly as he could, fighting off the hands that tried to tear it away, desperately trying to salvage the many lives that existed within him, because of him. The precious gas was their life force. Herds of wild beasts tore at him, pummeled him, eviscerated him with their teeth as livid, vivid demi-gods plundered the temple of his demesne. He fought and tore and struggled until a primal scream erupted from him, the tube torn from his bleeding lips, leaving a jagged edge of rubber tubing flapping from his lips. There seemed to be hundreds of hands restraining him as entire Universes of worlds perished in an instant.

"NONONONONONONONONONONO!"

The previous headache was like a mild spring breeze compared to the agonizing migraine, like a giant piston smashing into my face over and over, driven by a massive turbine engine, a maddened, crazed, runaway machine with no mind and no operator, sending billions, trillions of shrieking bolts of pure incandescent pain through him until he lost his ability to scream and a radiant, turbulent silence emitted from his mouth.

They had killed them! All of his worlds had disappeared in a flash! A holocaust of unthinkable dimensions! All gone, evaporated in a nanosecond!

Then the whispering began, nibbling at the edges of his consciousness as he slowly slithered back into his body and the screams of the multitudes faded, echoing in the abysses of his brain.

"You breathed that shit too long, man! It'll cause brain damage!"

"I'll be fine. Just give me a tube" Paul croaked.

"You still don't get it, do you, man?"

"No more for this guy tonight!" Don announced to the circle.

There were uncounted billions, trillions, of demons wearing football spikes dancing gleefully in his lungs whose only assignment was to squeeze his air sacs repeatedly, and get him to confess that he was sorry he had ever learned to breathe. The tightly stretched antelope drum skin of his brain reverberated painfully with every movement, with every zephyr gusting. He felt like he had been in the hands of Inquisitors for eternities, and they had already extracted every confession they could, and were now simply torturing him for their own entertainment. He rued his obsessive lifeways as the proverbial jackhammer smashed white hot knitting needles into his cerebellum in partial payment for his continued existence, just to prove to him that he was still alive. He wanted to barf, but he was afraid that everything would come out—stomach, heart, lungs, liver, spleen, kidneys, intestines!

Don assisting him half-crawling/half-walking, shambling to his own barracks where he dumped him on a bunk. Paul mercifully and thankfully dove into a deep black hole pool of unconsciousness. And pulled it in after him.

CHAPTER 28

Short Timer Blues

The room was alternately spinning and whirling as he repented his sins, and the life he had lived, for surely he had died, and was stuck out on the far edge of a miserable bardo. He was assuredly the victim of a natural disaster, and it was him!

White-hot shrapnel shards lanced through every cell. When he tried to speak, nothing came out, like a cartoon character with a blank speech balloon. He knew what it was like to be both autistic and aphasic.

He tried again, and what emerged sounded like walrus farts on helium.

"Don?" he croaked. "Docta Don?"

It was as if he had spoken into a void. No one answered. He levered himself out of the bunk as spasms of purest, most distilled pain shot through nerve endings he didn't even know he had. He had slept with his weapons at his sides. He safed them and stretched, a motion that equivalent to having an avalanche the size of Greenland fall directly on him, sending further cascades of agony through him. Then he cracked his back cracked three times, and he instantly felt clear, bright, and hungry despite his body feeling minus zero on the funky scale. He felt like an overused cleaning rag saturated with gun oil that had been shoved down a barrel too many times. Looking over at the next bunk, he found a clean set of towels stashed at the end of it, and set out for the shower room. He had absolutely no idea, nor did he care, what time it was.

He stripped and jumped into the hard-pulsing needle spray. He luxuriated in the hot water until he was a bright pink prune, then put his funky fatigues back on.

Then he suddenly realized he was missing his canvas bag! Shit! He must have left it at the set last night. Fuck! He needed at least two good hits to clear my brain—and a gallon of strong, black coffee!

"You are one crazy motherfucker."

It was Don, wearing a white lab coat over his fatigues.

"You can't possibly mean me!"

"Don't mean nobody else!"

"Hey! Have you seen my little canvas bag? I don't remember much after Buzz showed up!"

"You were totally out of it, man!"

"Hey that shit should be illegal!"

"You kept talking about we were 'killing all your friends!'"

"There were all these people alive in the nitrous bubbles! I was like, their God!"

"You were acting more like a demon, brother!"

"I guess I just tripped out a little bit!"

"You've just become another legendary character of the 6th CC!"

"Hey! My bag!?"

"I came to talk to you about that."

Oh shit, here it comes.

"I found your bag."

"And?"

"Well..."

"You and the dudes smoked it all up!"

"No! Hell no!"

"Then what?"

"Turkey butt!"

"Come on, man!"

"We did have a couple or three joints out of it."

"'A couple or three joints?'"

"Yeah. That's all."

"I thought you were gonna tell me you'd smoked it all up!"

"Nevah hatchee, GI!"

He went to his wall locker and procured my bag. The kilo was just slightly dented. They really had just smoked a few joints!

"Hey man! You really are righteous!"

"Thanks, man!"

"Let me give you a handful of this! Get a bag or something."

"Cool!"

He returned with a copy of the *Stars and Stripes*.

"Will this work?"

"As long as you don't think it will get contaminated!"

"No way!"

Paul reached in, pulled out about a quarter of a pound and dropped the pile of thick, red, ropy tops onto the newspaper.

"Wow! Are you sure?"

"I could have lost it all!"

"That's dynamite!"

"Listen. I gotta sky up. SHORT!"

"How short are you?"

"Almost invisible! Nine and a wake up!"

"Naw?!"

"Absolutely! Aren't you getting close? We left Fort Riley about the same time, didn't we?'

"I took two extra weeks at home before I came, then I extended."

"So, did I."

"Mine was for two extra months. I'll be early out! I've got twenty-one now."

"That's cool."

"Let me get an ambulance. I'll take you to the airport."

Paul rolled two joints while he was waiting. He came back jingling a set of keys.

"I just made the dispatcher happy. Gave him a finger!"

We each had two good hits on the way to the airfield.

"I'll look you up when I get back to California!"

"Absolutely!" he said, handing me a paper with his parent's address and phone number. "They'll know where I am."

"I'll be in San Francisco as soon as I can manage it."

"Call me, man!"

"I will," I said and we dapped.

It seemed crucial for Paul to go back to Qui Nhon. He needed to see how much had really changed, to see if any of his personal changes were real, measured against the people who had known him before the crucible of war had melded him into something stronger and more durable. He desperately wanted to see if Ho Dude or Hemp were still around; or any of the others with whom shared the highs. He knew Toad and JT were long gone back to the world, and enjoying freedoms about which he could only fantasize. He had very mixed feelings about the Sergeant Major—on the one hand, he still wanted to blow his fucking balls off; on the other, he wanted to thank him, despite his dishonorable intentions.

Paul wandered around the Support Compound like a visitor from another planet. Most of the old places were still there, but they were filled with strangers. He kept having the feeling that he was being followed, but he didn't spot anyone. He felt alienated. Qui Nhon was very lame, very tame, even parochial for him now.

Even the heads he recognized seemed standoffish and suspicious, so he decided to get loaded alone. He had just settled in an old favorite bunker, and lit a joint with his pistol close at hand. When a strange young cat came walking in with a crab-like sideways motion, Paul leveled the weapon at him.

"Don't shoot, man! I'm cool," he said, flashing the peace sign.

"Glad to hear it! Wanna hit?" I said holding out the joint to him.

"Sure" he said, taking the joint, but didn't hit it.

"What's your problem, Mr. Bogart?"

"Oh. Nothing. It's just that...well we were wondering, I mean me and some of the guys, if you were CID? I mean you gotta tell us if you are and we ask you, right?"

"Give me my fucking joint back and get the fuck out of my bunker!"

"<u>Your</u> bunker?"

"That's right! I used to smoke in this fucker every day. I got enough hours logged in this here fucker to own it! And if you don't like it, you can fucking didi, brotha!"

"When were you here last?"

"About five months ago. Why?"

"You knew Hemp and Ho Dude?"

"Why?"

"They're all gone now, back to the world. They almost got busted by a bunch of CID dudes they infiltrated in!"

"No shit!?"

"The fucking Sergeant Major became a giant prick! Everybody started asking for transfers—even the fucking officers! Joker planted a claymore alongside his fucking 'Welcome' mat! Blew the motherfucker's legs off! Then the heat got really bad! In-fucking-tense! And they busted Joker! He's in Leavenworth. Dishonorable Discharge, and ten years hard labor. They couldn't prove it was him, but got him for conspiracy to commit murder!"

"I'm truly sorry about Joker! He was a good cat! And fuck that motherfucking Sergeant Major! I just wish I could have done it myself!"

"Wow, dude! Who are you?"

"Doc J. Paul. Paul Marzeky!

"Jesus! They still tell stories about how you got in the face of the Sergeant Major about your moustache!"

"Really? Cool!"

"So, we're still a little weird around the edges!"

"Jesus! No shit!"

"Larry Tannum," he said and we dapped.

"Doc Jay.'

"So. What <u>are</u> you doing here?"

"Just passin' through. What happened to everybody else?"

"Ho Dude and Tony James went back to the world. T-Bone is doing time in Long Bien Jail."

"What'd they get him for?"

"Caught him with twenty pounds of weed!"

"How fucked!"

We finished the joint, and I gave him a large finger of weed.

"Thanks, man. And good luck, brother."

"SHORT!"

Paul caught a quick ride in the back end of a deuce and a half truck, glad that fucking Joker had fixed that motherfucking Sergeant Major! He got on a flight for Dalat to see another old friend from back in the world. After all, he did have travel orders! He passed out with his rifle in his hand, and his canvas kick under his arm.

Built as a resort in the early 20th Century for aristocratic French administrators, the French endowed Dalat with opulent villas and broad, graceful boulevards. There originally was a health complex, golf course, parks, schools, and homes, but no industry. They built boarding schools where children from the whole of Indochina were indoctrinated by French priests and nuns in much the same manner as American missionaries—to indoctrinate the native population into a "Christian" orientation to counteract any indigenous beliefs they might harbor—and abjure any possibility of political tremors in future generations. The children were also taught "proper manners" and to speak only French so they could become good servants for the invading aristocracy. The brutal legacy finally died out in the '60s.

Paul had come to see Virgil Terwilliger, a friend since grade school. At thirteen, the two of them became drinking buddies, and by sixteen were cruising the streets of South St. Louis in his 1961 Pontiac Bonneville on Saturday nights, drinking and smoking cigarettes, talking incessantly about the nature of the Universe, and the availability of certain high school girls; about the nature of good and evil, and sex, about which neither of us had much first-hand experience at that time.

They'd drifted apart after high school, and eventually both ended up in the Army. They had exchanged a couple of letters in-country, so Paul knew his location but Virgil was very vague about what he was doing there. Paul knew he had ended up in some kind of electronic communications unit, and had seemed extremely uncomfortable when Paul broached the idea of a visit.

Paul wandered through the delightful pine-forested, European-flavored resort town. He had to ask several GIs where the obscure unit might be. At length, he was directed to a very secluded compound far up in the hills, bristling with hundreds of antennae of differing heights and thicknesses. He was not allowed to enter the chain-link-and-barbed-wire enclosed compound. Grim-faced guards with locked and loaded M-16s imply told him to wait.

Scowling, Virgil came out of one of the air-conditioned trailers, and walked toward him.

Paul smiled and waved his hand.

"Hey, man! Good to see you!"

He growled at me from the other side of the fence, and said "What the fuck are you doing here?"

"I just thought it might be a trip to visit you, since we're both here ten thousand miles from everything we've ever known!"

"Are you fucking nuts?"

"Fuck no! I just had the opportunity and took it!"

"You can't come in. I'll meet you later at the EM Club, around 1715. Just go down the road here, take the first left. See you in two hours," he said curtly, turned on his heel, and left.

Paul shook his head. They had once been the best of friends, and now Virgil seemed to have become a total asshole.

By the time Virgil showed up at the club, Paul had taken the time to toast his head thoroughly. Virgil immediately ordered two beers, and sat down scowling.

"What the fuck are you doing here?" he asked, no "Hello" or "How are you?"

"Wow, good to see you too!"

"No, I mean really, what the fuck are you doing here?"

"I told you—I was in Qui Nhon, and came up!"

"That's it? You got a wild hair and showed up?"

"That's about it."

"You almost got my ass in deep shit! My NCOIC was shitting bricks when they announced a 'nameless visitor' requesting to see me!"

"They had my name, my ID, and a copy of my travel orders!"

"They didn't tell me that!"

"Fuckers!"

"Part of why it took so long. They had to run a security clearance on you before they would even let me talk to you!"

"What the fuck?"

"And I'm not allowed to tell you why, what they found out, or what I'm doing here!"

"What?"

"As it stands, your clearance is only good until tomorrow morning, since it's so late in the day. Otherwise you'd have been on the next flight back to Qui Nhon!"

"Jesus, Virgil! What the fuck?"

"Told you—I can't talk about it?"

"Well, how 'bout you? How you doing?"

"You always were a crazy motherfucker!"

He finished his second beer, noticing that I was very much nursing my first. It had grown warm and somewhat stale. It was two hours old.

"Want another one?" he queried.

"No thanks. Actually, I was hoping we could smoke a joint!"

"That shit? You're fucked up in the head! I tried it once, and it didn't do anything for me!"

Paul explained to him that it was fairly typical for the first time; and asked him to smoke with him. He knew he'd get high if he tried his weed!

"No! Fuck that! I'd lose my security clearance! Want another beer?"

He again declined while Virgil drank another three or four cans before we went to the air-conditioned Mess Hall for chow—some of the best food I ever encountered anywhere in-country. That night it was roasted chicken, real mashed potatoes (no dehydrated, powdered crap for these folks!) with gravy, some kind of fresh green vegetable grown locally, and cherry pie with ice cream and real coffee.

"Jesus! You guys eat really good!

"Doin' our best for the war effort!" He said, and smirked, the first real show of the old Virgil I had known and loved for years.

When they made it back to the club, and Virgil was on what must have been his seventh beer, Paul made the huge mistake of using his comment to attempt to bridge the gap into a discussion of politics and the anti-war movement.

"All those motherfuckers should just cut their hair and get a job! Those low life assholes are what is wrong with this country!"

"Jesus, man! When did you become such a Republican?"

"I've worked my ass off to make money! And those assholes want is to be on welfare so they can protest the war and smoke marijuana!"

"Are you fucking shitting me?"

"No! Now that you're smoking dope, have you turned into some kind of Communist fruiter, anti-war protestor too?"

Typical of him to pejoratize war protestors as homosexual and anti-American!

"Wow, man! It's like I don't even know you anymore. What the fuck happened to you?"

"This fucking place!!" he said, again turning down my offer to smoke some weed, as I had turned down his offer of another beer.

Paul felt a great sadness that Virgil had seemingly not changed at all; that he had, in fact, gotten more deeply entrenched in the kind of thinking and attitudes that were so pervasive in South St. Louis, the ideology with which they had grown up. It was as if he had become just another cookie-cutter reproduction of his father, and his father's father, *ad nauseam*.

On the other hand, being around him gave Paul just cause to celebrate all that had changed in his life; how he had stepped up and accepted what had been presented to him, and used the best way he could. A niggling, wiggling worm of doubt nibbled at his heart in that moment about the wisdom of his current adventure, but he grandiosely dismissed it out of hand. Whenever else would he ever have such an opportunity? Besides he would have great stories to tell for years to come! Besides that, he was goin' home very, very soon. Fuck 'em! And fuck Virgil too! As much as the man had meant to him, all of the support and guidance he had lent him, Paul had moved on to a new and far better life, in his estimation.

"Listen, man, I'm moving to San Francisco as soon as I get out of this motherfucker! And I'm gonna keep smoking dope every day of my life! I been in some shit with the 101st—and I'm an anti-war protestor!"

Virgil took severe umbrage with this, and clumsily attempted to stand up, as if he intended to start a fight with him!

I walked around the table, and pushed him down into his chair. I threw a handful of MPCs on the table.

"Have another beer, man! We been friends too long for it to end this way! I'm skyin' up! See ya!"

Paul left without a backward glance, symbolically walking away from his earliest life. He had always hated the mid-West, could not wait to get away, and would be damned if he would go back! He was grateful for the twists and turns his life had taken!

When Paul got to the airport, he smoked a joint with a guy who'd put him up in his hooch the previous night, and beat feet for Da Nang, a major port for over a thousand years. During the war, its airport had officially become the busiest in the world. That status helped him remain anonymous as he slipped through a terminal filled with a massive mix of people of every ethnic origin, including lots of military and the ubiquitous "civilian contractors." There was also a vast array of chickens, ducks, dogs, and even pigs in wooden carriers being transported in passenger compartments. Dogs were often thought to be a delicacy in Viet kitchens (especially puppies), and most of them were both wary and quick, or not in evidence at all.

As I walked out of the terminal, I ran into a guy who had a moustache that was almost as big as mine—and styled in a similar manner, with huge handlebars curled at either end and waxed. Since I had learned the style from helicopter jocks, it seemed a safe assumption that the guy was a head. Besides his eyeballs were blazing.

"Hey brother, wanna smoke a joint?"

He laughed, and pulled a well-smoked pipe out of his pocket.

"Or we could smoke a bowl!"

He was assigned to the 236th Medical Detachment Helicopter Ambulance (MDHA) in Da Nang as a Dustoff medic. Medical helicopters' call sign was "Dustoff," yet another extremely dangerous job since they frequently landed in hot LZs to pick up wounded and dead. In the early days, the bright Red Cross painted on a white field made a perfect target for RPGs and deadly accurate 37mm NVA anti-aircraft fire.

In short order, we were both toasted, and went to his company area for a meal, followed by an afternoon hanging out in the Ready Room, where crews on-call congregated awaiting assignments. Though he was not on call, Tomkins often hung out there anyway. Four of us (including one guy who only drank beer, but did not smoke) sat around and played Hearts. After a pretty decent dinner, and in a particularly mellow frame of mind, I drifted off to deeply entertaining cartoon-like dreams laced with hot sexual flashes of naked dancing women, all with smaller-sized breasts and pink nipples. I was deeply immersed in this dream when I was jolted awake by the scream of the incoming siren as rockets started slamming in, punctuated by the more distant rumblings of multiple mortar rounds landing higher up in the Marble Mountains.

We spent the night on Red Alert, fully locked and loaded, mostly in the bunkers. At different times, NCOs would show up and grab guys for replacement guard duty on the berm. Mostly we sat and bullshitted, even played the occasional game of Hearts by candle light. It finally got quiet around 0500. A couple of guys managed to fall asleep in disturbed snatches until the sun light filtered through. Paul was struck by a sense of the surreal, as if he were disembodied, floating above it all; or even as if all of what he was experiencing were actually happening to someone else, and he would soon awaken from this strange, strange dream. His deepest fear was that he had become truly psychotic, yet the knowledge that he was thinking that gave him an odd comfort because he had been led to believe (perhaps delusionally) that having such thoughts was some measure of sanity.

Scuttlebutt had it that the gooks had hit the Marines up on Marble Mountain the previous evening, some of them carrying flame-throwers as they probed the cave complexes; and had also caused severe damage to the "communications facilities" most often used to track NVA and VC troop movement through electronic listening devices deployed by aircraft along suspected enemy trails. All outgoing flights were canceled, and we were put on Yellow Alert (steel pots and flak jackets; loaded weapons; but not on the berm or ready rooms). All of which played hob with Paul's getting back to Phu Bai that day. There was absolutely nothing moving on the flight line except helicopter gunships and resupply choppers. He really had intended to get back ASAP, now that his little adventure was winding down.

The tension quickly wound down when there was no "full scale frontal human wave attack" forthcoming, as predicted (and desired) by the lifers. It seemed that many of the older juicehead crowd wanted a small taste of what they considered the "glory of modern warfare"—in essence, they were a bunch of fucking "glory-hounds" driven by the desire to add another ribbon to their chests, or have another story to tell to their fellow lifers as they safely gathered at NCO Clubs in non-combat zones, and got to briefly be "one up" on their erstwhile buddies. For his part, Paul was bored shitless, and stayed stoned with the helicopter jocks—who also seemed to have an endless supply of the finest beer, whiskey, and other amenities (like coffee from San Francisco) not usually available. He just wanted to get on with things so he could go home. SHORT!!!

CHAPTER 29
Camp Evans Transient

After yet another night of revelry and reverie in the bunker, Paul slept a few hours before he finally awoke, immensely refreshed. Then he hopped a flight north with a whole load of cherries. The FNGs looked so literally green in their new fatigues, unloaded weapons, and dog tags clattering loudly. They were all anxious, sweating hard, and playing at bravado, as anyone who had been there could see at a glance. They chattered excitedly about the exigencies of the war, as if it were a philosophical notion, as if they had a fucking clue. They all looked so young, with their brand-new boots and overstuffed duffel bags, and shiny faces, all clustered together like newborn baby birds. They were all shouting to be heard above the din of the C-47's engines, trying desperately to assuage their fears while cutting sideways glances at me, but too afraid to speak to me directly.

"Do you think we'll be in the same platoon?"

"Wonder when we'll see some VC?"

"Hey! I'm short! Only 348 to go!"

"I wonder if everybody in the 101st is in the field?"

"Where you gonna go on R-and-R?"

"I'm writing my girlfriend so she'll know where to write me!" Paul could only shake his head in wonder, and keep a silence best reserved for such moments. This was a bittersweet flight because he knew that the end of a road for him was near, a path he had walked with as much boldness and brashness as he could muster, foolish though he may have been at times, living day by day awaiting his time to leave forever this land of shit and blood and brains. All in all, it seemed like it had been such a negative existence, having spent more than a year living only for the future day when he could leave. It had all boiled down to staying alive one day at a time, even though there were times when he had felt like a fake, a poseur, knowing that so many other good men had tasted so much more deeply, so much more harshly, than he the starkness and joy of bitter battle. Now that the time was close, he felt a sadness tinged by the memory of some he'd known who would never reach this golden moment; by a vague fear of the future whose destiny was not yet known, could never really be known even by the most prescient; and by knowing that he had changed here, grown, lived, and become forever a part of this other world; and that part of him had died here, as neatly and cleanly as if excised with a scalpel. He knew he would never be the same, even in deepest retrospection or reclamation, no matter what the vast unknown future might hold. The experiences he had had were indelibly etched into the very fabric of his heart and soul as if with the purest of reagents.

He passed through camp as quickly and surreptitiously as possible; and made his way to the chopper pad to catch anything going north. His luck held, and he soon landed in the eternal red clay dust of Camp Evans. He had gotten in just after a rocket attack, and he was almost drowning in the increased humidity that foretold another monsoon season. He got his clothing list signed off in exchange for some red buds; and then the company clerk stamped his papers, putting an indecipherable signature above it. He packed his duffel with everything he needed to turn in at Phu Bai, and his few remaining personal items, journals, the manuscript he and Toad had written; and was back at the chopper pad inside of two hours, bidding a fond farewell to Camp Evans forever, preparing to face his biggest hurdle yet at Eagle.

CHAPTER 30
Phu Bai Redux

Apparently, for good or ill, his reputation had grown. Word of the strange red weed had bounced back to Phu Bai. It had become a kind of *lingua franca.* He was easily able to trade for administrative favors. It only took one hit for the supply clerk to readily assent to make another indecipherable signature on his checkout list.

"Yo Tommy Gun! Sign this."

"Who in the fuck are you?"

"Paul Marzeky, the Psych Consultant."

"Holy fuck! The First Shirt's been looking for you!"

"I know, I know. Just sign this, will you please?"

"I wouldn't want to be in your boots when the First Sergeant gets a hold of you!"

"With a little help from you he never will!"

"What the fuck is it?"

"My check-out list."

"I can't sign that. The First Sergeant is supposed to sign that!"

"How long have you been in country, Private First Class?"

"Six months, Specialist Five."

"Then as ranking short timer NCO in this room at this time, I order you to sign this paper for me!"

"I don't know if I should."

"They won't check up on you. If they do, say you never saw me."

"I don't know, man."

"It's worth a handful of red buds to me!"

"Oh, fuck yeah!"

As he left, Paul very purposefully did not look back. He was afraid that, like Lot's wife, he might turn into a pillar of salt.

It all became much more difficult when he ran into Jed Porter.

"Paul! What the fuck are you doing here?"

We hugged each other, dancing around like a couple of peasant farmers with St. Vitus Dance.

"Woooee!"

"I heard you were either dead, AWOL, or back in the world!"

"Maybe all three!"

"Where in the fuck have you been?"

"Around."

"No! Come on! Where?"

"Like Mark Twain once said, 'Rumors of my demise are greatly exaggerated!'"

"Man! You are fucking incredible!"

"I just needed a little vacation.'

"Damn! Man, your shit must be made out of gold!"

"I'm SHORT!"

"No, you're not, man."

"Bullshit!"

"You're not!"

"What do you mean?"

"Anybody who sees you is supposed to turn you in!"

"WHAT?"

"That's right. You are AWOL!"

"I'm also SHORT! And I'm outta here—today!"

"How are you gonna manage that?"

Paul showed him his paperwork, lacking only Finance and Personnel Files that he would secure in Biên Hòa.

"Who signed for you at Company?

"The less you know, brother, the better."

"What the fuck are you doing?"

"I'm going home. What else?"

"You are a crazy mother!"

"Thanks, man. Let's go get loaded."

"Now?"

"Of course. I've got to sky up for Biên Hòa!"

"No way you're goin' home, brother! They're gonna fuck with you!"

"They can't! I got my shit together."

"Yeah. Right."

"I'm going home <u>tomorrow!</u> And I want to get high with you <u>today</u>!"

"You ought to turn yourself in, man!"

"Nevah hatchee, GI."

He sighed, then said "Why the fuck not? Let's party!"

Jed was depressed about what he knew about his situation, but tried to keep things upbeat.

"Come on, man. <u>I'm goin' home</u>! Lighten up!"

"If you say so, man!"

"It's gonna be cool. Believe me."

Paul caught a glimpse of the First Shirt as he didi'd out of the Company Area, but kept going. Fuck him! He <u>was</u> goin' home! Home. The bullshit was over.

Maybe it was a full moon, he didn't know, but the party mood became infectious. What started out with just a few of us going to go smoke some buds, quickly became the biggest set I have ever attended. Even before dark, people started arriving, in ones, and twos, and threes, from all over, to join our set. We finally had to move to one of the chopper pads when some Korean Marines, loaded with bags of weed, and cases of plum wine showed up. A whole load of Seabees showed up with two 55-gallon drums loaded with iced Carlsbergs. Of course, the Marine Corps brought its unique presence—a bunch of crazed jarheads with bottles of Jack Daniels, and weed of their own, planted themselves and claimed one corner of the pad. There were little pockets of speed users, chatting a million miles an hour, while on the other side of the gathering were those whose habits ran to the opioid peptide family. It was the most incredible experience with almost-total strangers he had ever had. No one was tripping out or being macho. It was as if everyone recognized a spiritual connection between the all of their being there, having a single focus and identity. That did not prevent the entire perimeter from being locked and loaded, totally ready, totally secure.

"How many fucking people did you tell about this party?" Paul asked. Oly looked wall-eyed and crazed from the combination of Tequila, buds and barbiturates.

"Everybody!" he slurred and slumped back.

Smoke hung over the pad like a bittersweet ghost, people shifting positions like segments of a stoned caterpillar gyrating. Bowls and joints were passed, even a chillum from Afghanistan—hand to hand, spinning round and round the circle, an intoxicating carousel, even the most loaded somehow aware of the beauty of the ceremony.

Jed said, "Unbelievable!"

Paul agreed, "Nobody in the real world would ever believe this!"

"I am hip!"

"So, which world is more real?"

"I don't know, man, but why's nobody hassling us?"

"I don't know, man. I don't care. I'm SHORT!"

My voice echoed around the pad, and reports started coming in.

"One oh six!"

"Lifer!"

"Seventy-four!"

"Re-up!"

"Thirty-six!"

"SHORTER!"

"Nine and a wake up!"

"A WAKE UP!"

"Oooooeeee!"

"Damn! Now that is short!"

"Goin' home, brothers!"

"Hallelujah!"

The Corporal and the Sergeant of the Guard passed by, and got loaded with us. We heard singing coming from the NCO Club, and got word that some lifer was leaving in the morning, so they were all juicing it up.

POP!

Dozens of safeties clicked off simultaneously, as we collectively hit the dirt, feet inward, facing out, and hypervigilantly scanned our perimeter.

"Some juicehead lifer probably!"

"Somebody's just clearing a round!"

POP! POP!

The adrenaline wave swept through us as if we had but one spinal column. No one had reported a muzzle flash or heard a round.

Sniper!

POP! POP! POP!

The short burst punctuated the night, and then star clusters lit the berm with phosphorous parachutes beyond the triple tangled concertina, claymores, and minefields. Suddenly mortars started thumping, and more and more illumination rounds filled the sky. Buttholes puckered, mouths went dry from an influx of atropine, and bladders emptied in preparation for a human wave assault—fingers tightening and hypervigilant eyeballs searched every quadrant. Then somebody, he'd never really know who, lit the fuse that ignited them with two little words.

"MAD MINUTE!"

A fierce, blistering surge, a massive incendiary barrage, erupted—quad 50s from the watchtowers, then more mortars and even arty lobbing short rounds into the jungle; then somebody blew all of the claymores, and finally even the drunk juicehead lifers joined in blasting away everything they had from what was their collective six (back). Even the red clay dust died that night in a cathartic purging of emotion that swept through them as if moved by a gigantic hand. It was a release of hydrochloric bile and molten joy, of massive unspent rage celebrating the holy communion of war—firing bursts and slamming in clips, firing again and again, an ecstatic release like a gigantic ejaculation shared by the one mind that ruled them all, exaltation in the smell of cordite, sweat, blood, and tears.

Then, just as suddenly, a massive, pillowing silence enveloped them. With glazed expressions, they looked at one another, and said "What the fuck?"

Shortly thereafter, like sleepy lovers after great sex, they all silently acknowledged that the party was over. They drifted off, if not necessarily to sleep, but for a certainty, to reflect on the wondrous nature of God and man—or at least on the marvels they had each that night experienced.

CHAPTER 31

Here We Go 'round Again

Once Paul hit Biên Hòa, he headed for the Transient Barracks, on the lookout for some "short folks." He didn't need a recon patrol to spot Weed and Hippie. They were stoned to the bone and smirking at the FNGs, standing in front of the barracks closest to the piss tubes and bunkers. There seemed to be dozens of cherries milling around a short distance away, acting like they didn't know whether to shit or go blind. The three of them grinned at each other as Paul first hove into view.

"Thought you'd be back in the world by now!"

"Two and a wake up!"

"Fucker's short!"

"Damn! He's almost invisible!"

"I'm this short!" Paul said, holding my first two fingertips a micron apart from each other.

"How'd you manage to get so short?"

"Just lucky I guess!"

"You brothers know where a tired trooper can find a bunk?"

"Welcome home, brother!" said Weed, whose real last name had become his adopted nickname.

"Come on in. We'll show you around," said Hippie, as if the fucking hooch were a grand showcase home. He wore several layers of love beads and peace symbols around his neck, and a huge Zapata moustache framed his lips.

They had taken over the Quonset hut, hanging a blanket across the middle, forcing six cherries to share three double bunks at one end and putting two double bunks at their end. A central area was cleared for a rough wooden table on which sat several ashtrays and two deck of cards. There was a small, squat refrigerator plugged into the wall.

"Don't the cherries complain?" Paul asked.

"Fuck no! We were here first! Besides that, we're," he said, shaping his hands like a megaphone and shouted toward the blanket, "SHORT!"

"This here is the community reefer" he said, opening the door and showing me a full stock of icy cold beer. "You buy your own, and I supply the electricity!"

"Let me buy one until I get to the PX."

"First one's on the house!"

"Wanna play some Hearts?"

"Does the Pope smoke dope?"

"Wooee!"

"I smell a marathon!"

"Speaking of dope, wanna smoke some?"

"Got some killer red buds from Laos!"

"Break it out!"

Weed said, "I got a package from the world just before I came down here," indicating a brown paper-wrapped package at his feet.

"I had to come down because they fucked up my Finance Records. I ain't been paid for five months! I got a month to go, and I ain't goin' back! Fuck that!"

"Amen, brother!"

He pulled a top out of his bag, and started cleaning it in a small tin lid.

"Damn! Looks killer!"

Weed reached into both pockets of his fatigue jacket and held out two closed fists toward me.

"Choose."

Paul picked the right hand and he gave him a pack of Cherry Flavored Riz-La Rolling Papers. He pulled a leaf out and rolled a joint.

"Those are yours, man. Going home present."

"Thanks, man" he said, and we dapped.

"I got chocolate, banana, mint, and pineapple too!"

"Wow! That's far out!'

"My sister sent them to me with a batch of chocolate chip cookies!"

"Wish my sister that cool!"

"Let's play some Hearts!"

"Let's roll a bunch of joints first. That way we don't have to interrupt the game!"

"Don't need much with this shit!"

"I'm ready!'

Drinking beer and shouting taunts at the cherries, the hours slipped by as they got more and more stoned. Inevitably one very straight young soul complained about the marijuana smoke.

"Fuck you, cherry! What are they gonna do to me, send me to Viet Nam?"

Followed by the three of us in a chorus, "SHORT!"

"Let's play some cards!"

"Shuffle 'em up!"

"I'll cut!"

"Pass me a mint one this time."

At some point, Paul commented on the palpable quiet.

"Where's all the cherries?"

"Probably eating chow or something."

"Anybody hungry?"

"Naw. Deal the cards."

"We can eat some of my sister's cookies later."

"Righteous!"

"Oh, shit man! The cat dumped the Queen on the first trick!"

"That's why they call it 'cut throat', man!"

"Oh man! Fucked up my shit!"

"What do you mean? I'm gonna eat big!"

"Oh shit! Look out, the fucker's running!"

"Hold a Heart!"

"I am!"

"Look at those fucking Clubs! What did you pass him?"

"Clubs! That's how I could dump The Bitch on the first trick!"

"Shit! He passed me Hearts!"

"Fuck! We're screwed!"

"I can't stop him!"

"SHORT!" Apropos of nothing else.

"How short are you?"

"I'm almost invisible!"

"How short?" asked Hippie again.

"Five and a wake up!"

"Hee-hee! Two and a wake up!"

Weed had been curiously quiet during this exchange. Hippie jerked his thumb over at him and said, "Dude here is practically a lifer!"

"How many days you got, man?"

"Thirty! But I'm gonna party down the whole time!"

"Hand me another beer, will ya'?"

The cherries had by now come back from chow, and they treated them with frequent choruses of "SHORT!" as we grew louder and rowdier. One bold soul peeked through the curtain, smiled, and flashed the peace sign, but was apparently too intimidated to invite himself in to join us.

"Fuck him if he can't take a joke!"

"Joke him if he can't take a fuck!"

The FNGs were writing letters, and making nervous conversation, only too exquisitely aware of our presence in another universe just on the other side of the blanket.

The "CRUMP!" of an incoming mortar round shattered the relative quiet as a siren began to wail, and various voices shouted "INCOMING!"

The cherries were freaking and tweaking, scurrying as they secured flak jackets and steel pots, all the while screaming.

"INCOMING! INCOMING!"

"Fucking cherries," said Hippie with a sneer.

"Shit! That was at least five hundred meters away!" said Weed.

"Deal the cards!"

"Light a joint!"

"Pass me a beer!"

"CRUMP!" Four hundred meters.

"Ole Luke the Gook is probably hitting the Administration Buildings again. He knows how important paperwork is to winning the war!"

"Shit! He's running again!"

"Pass the joint, Mr. Bogart!"

"CRUMP!" Three hundred meters.

"They're walking in!"

"Naw! They wouldn't fuck with us!"

"Yeah. We're too SHORT!"

"CRUMP!" Two hundred meters.

"They <u>are</u> getting closer!"

"Pass the joint!"

"Deal the cards!"

"Just a few H and I rounds!"

"Hand me a cookie! I'm hungry!"

"CRUMP!" One hundred meters.

"Maybe we ought to get to a bunker," Paul said nervously.

"It's right outside!"

"No sweat!"

"It's probably full of cherries!"

"We'll kick 'em out!"

"Whose deal is it?"

"CRUMPPPOWW!"

Fifty meters away, the chapel exploded into a billion tiny pieces, though it seemed like a slow-motion haze of flying wood, twisted steel and smashed sandbags. The sound cut through their substance-induced miasma, and galvanized them into action. Weed grabbed his package and three beers while Hippie stuffed the remaining joints in his pocket. Paul was the last one out, carrying his canvas bag under his arm and his weapon in the other hand. I saw Hippie get inside the bunker, Weed close on his heels. Paul turned on the run, and saw a 122-millimeter rocket headed right for them. He dived like a full back for the end zone, and hit the mouth of the bunker just as the rocket hit. It was not direct, but too damn close. Thank God for the steel-reinforcement ("liberated runway material"). The force of the blast bent some of the metal I-beam struts and split most of the sandbags on the near side. The concussion of the blast would probably have killed them all if we had not all ended up on the same end of the bunker curled up and digging for home. As it was, they were all bruised and scraped, but the next rounds walked away from us methodically, and stopped when Puff the Magic Dragon arrived on station, and started peppering the hills with six thousand rounds a minute. The all-clear siren soon sounded and we called to each other in strained whispers. Then the slow cadence of nature's chorus began, insect sounds, then birds' songs, building tentatively to crescendos.

"Wow! I am definitely <u>too</u> fucking short for this shit!"

"SHORT!"

As Paul stepped out of the bunker, he heard Hippie exclaim.

"Jesus! Will you look at that shit?"

He pulled a jagged piece of shrapnel about twelve inches in diameter out of a burst sandbag. The entire length of the bunker had effectively disappeared, and was peppered with metal fragments.

"Too fucking SHORT!"

They turned to Paul.

"Jesus man, didn't think you were gonna make it!"

"I did! And I saved the cards too!" I said holding up the deck.

Hippie smiled and said, "We got the cards, the beer and the weed. What else do we need?"

One of the cherries looked at them, and shook his head as he said to a buddy, "Jesus! I hope I don't end up like those guys!"

Stefan J. Malecek, Ph. D.

CHAPTER 32

ETS

Paul awoke, savoring the day as if it were a fresh mint lying on his tongue, feeling as invincible as a young Achilles freshly dipped in the river Styx.

He lit a joint, musing on the night before. Brothers. They really were. He would never forget it, not if he lived a thousand years.

Then it struck him.

HE WAS GOIN' HOME! TODAY!

He must be really blasted! It had taken three hits before he remembered!

HE WAS GOIN' HOME! TODAY!

Looking at this date on his calendar often enough to blur his eyesight permanently, and living with it all this time—either with great anxiety or frustration or anger, often all three simultaneously; looking at it on every set of orders he had ever had; hungering for, and fantasizing about it for more than a year—and his waiting was over! He was about to be reborn, and fuck what came next! He would be free and a civilian, with a whole new mind-set and the ability to navigate a brand-new course for himself through the stuff of Life! He absolutely knew he would be successful. Not a scintilla of doubt entered into his personal equation. It would be enough for him to have the highest rank of all—civilian.

He reviewed what to do, who to see, and how much he would have to pay in bribes. His brain was brimming, confidence rising and soaring. THIS WAS <u>THE</u> DAY, his ETS and DEROS from the bowels of the military all rolled into one! The day for which he had lived, breathed, and plotted for almost three years! No one, NO ONE, was going to take it away from him, not now, not ever!

He walked extremely slowly to the showers, feeling the weight and gravity of the day, the utter importance of each moment, fused and bonded intimately to a new NOW. He mused that it was pretty nutty to feel nostalgic, as his sensitive nose breathed the familiar scents of kerosene, rotting vegetation, unwashed human bodies, exotic spices, gun oil, truck exhaust, cooking aromas, cordite, and the ever-burning human waste. He knew he must be slipping over the edge, completely dinky dau being nostalgic over the smell of the Mess Hall!

He showered hot and long, then dried himself using three towels. He dressed carefully, arranging his ribbons on his khaki uniform shirt, totally ready to didi. He only needed those two files. He put a roll of MPC in one front pocket, and one of Greenbacks in the other, and strolled casually over to the Finance Office.

The smell of fresh money, lemon oil, and Brasso filled the air. Every one of the clerks was turned out in freshly starched fatigues with belt buckles shiny as mirrors. He got all kinds of weird looks because he refused to take off the cunt (dress uniform) soft cap holding his hair in place, and he was goddamned if he was gonna cut his fucking hair before he went home! He had earned the right—and he was gonna keep it! Fuck them!

"I'm goin' home today! I'd like my Finance Records please!"

The shorthaired Finance Clerk looked me in the eyes, and then with an impertinent motion of his chin, decided against fucking with me.

"Let's see your orders!" he said imperiously.

Paul knew this was his big test. If he could slide past this, he was almost home free. He had paid two hundred dollars for a completely bogus set of top-flight orders.

The clerk scanned the paperwork and said, "I need three copies. Didn't they give you any more than this?"

"Just one they said I should keep. They told me you could make more here if you needed them."

"I can, but I don't like it. Idiots! Don't they realize how important paperwork is?"

Paul smiled and shook his head, thinking to himself how very important that paperwork was!

The clerk pulled my file out of a deep, recessed file drawer. Then he sat down, punched numbers into his calculator, and then took the slip to one of the young Finance Officers who scribbled on it, stamped it, and signed his name.

"Lieutenant says you'll get a check when you get back to...Oakland" he said. "I made you up a bunch," he said, handing me several sets of orders. "You'll need them" he said, and signed my list.

He was due almost two thousand dollars! How fucking sweet and ironic!

Then he had a paranoid moment, startled by the fact that things were going too well! He suddenly remembered this dude who had three days left and kept having a feeling he was gonna die before he got home. He had never worn a flak jacket or steel pot the entire time he'd been there. When he got to Biên Hòa, he started wearing the shit to the fucking mess hall, the shitter, even slept in it. He got all his paperwork together, but couldn't shake the ominous feeling. He was being extra careful—didn't drink, smoke, barely played cards, just in case he stopped paying attention at a critical moment. Then early one morning, he tripped and broke his neck walking to the piss tube. They said it was due to his wearing his steel pot.

The Supply guy was so stoned that he didn't give a shit who knew it. He laughed when Paul noticed his right eye was completely red and bloodshot, while the left was completely clear and white. He found out later that he had done it purposely to freak out the lifers.

"What's so fucking funny, Specialist?"

"Oh nothing, sergeant. I just noticed your eyeballs. Wanna get loaded?"

"What time is it? Eleven hundred hours. Fuck! I haven't smoked a joint for at least an hour. Why not?" he said, and detailed his assistant to "watch the shop for a little bit." They stepped out the back door, and Paul pulled out one of his last pre-rolled numbers. They stood on the back porch and gazed at the incredible world of Biên Hòa. The supply guy coughed the first time he hit the joint.

"Shit almost blinded me! Let me have some more!"

"Hallelujah, brother!"

The man took a deep drag, and managed to keep most of it in his lungs.

"Damn good shit! You got any you want to get rid of?"

"Sin loi, man."

"Too bad" he said, holding up a considerable roach. "Mind if I keep the rest for later?"

"No. Go for it."

"I know you didn't ask me to smoke this just because you're such a nice guy."

"Why sergeant, just because I'm goin' home today doesn't mean I have ulterior motives."

Paul laughed, thinking about the thousands of interviews he had done and how good his shit detector had become. The truth was the real and only coin of the realm here.

"Now that you mention it, I could use a small favor."

"Yeah, I thought so. What is it? You want me to ship some shit home for you? Weapons? Grenades? What?"

"No! Nothing like that" Paul said laughing. "Wish I'd thought of it!"

"What is it then?"

"I lost my M-16. I was hoping we might cut through some of the paperwork."

"We might."

"A hundred?"

"Two."

"Damn, man!"

"Take it or leave it!"

"OK, OK! Get the paperwork together" I said, and handed over the money in MPC.

Out-Processing was fucking packed! Paul could not believe his eyes when he finally got there. About half of the dudes there were getting Less Than Honorable Discharges, but they were just as happy, maybe happier, than the others.

There were even a few dazed guys standing around in fatigues, fresh from the bush.

With the inimitable logic of the military, In-Processing was practically next door to Out-Processing. So, we who were leaving, the survivors, were put in almost face-to-face contact with the incoming replacements—easy targets for our angst, fear and world-weary comments. We stoned them with catcalls and sarcasm like Biblical transgressors.

"Hey cherries!"

"Stay frosty, dudes!"

"Kill a Commie for Christ!"

"Get some for me!"

"Cherry motherfuckers!"

"Remember—don't drink the water!"

"Watch out for Bouncing Betty!"

"Get some, dudes!"

"Peace, brothers!"

There was such a gulf between the homogeneously scrubbed, scared looking FNGs and them. Paul shook my head. It seemed impossible that he had looked like that just a year ago!

As the line moved again, two more guys walked out, looking dejected and angry.

"What's up, brother?" I asked.

"Some motherfucking lifer son of a bitch is making sure we all got a 'military style haircut' before we go home!"

"Jesus!"

Motherfucking lifer assholes! This was the military's last shot to fuck with them!

He was thoroughly toasted, but he had to get my records, so he drifted over to the laughing local barber to get his long mane shorn. But it didn't matter. HE WAS GOIN' HOME!

He waited with half a hundred other guys willing to ready to do anything, go to any length, to get home. The conversations were sometimes rowdy, sometimes subdued, but there was an aura of intensity and anticipation that overshadowed everything else.

Fantasies of women and food, food and women. It was all Paul could think about. Delicious images floated through his head. He almost went to the shitter several times to masturbate, but didn't want to miss his name when they finally called. He kept trying on different images of what freedom was going to feel like, an imagined imaginary freedom that he had not yet experienced, a transcendence he intuitively felt rather than knew that he knew. He played with the idea like a cat with a captive mouse, indulging in the sensations he knew would have to accompany the delightful exemptions from the "normal," whatever the fuck that was—all he knew is that he had not survived all of the shit simply to go home to become Joe Lunchbucket! He was not going to be one of the milling masses who worked daily for their meager bread and two weeks off every summer! Screw that!

He was always reminded of his father doing just that. He had busted his ass for that kind of life, even after his experiences as an Infantry First Lieutenant all the way thorough Europe in World War Two. Paul really could not, absolutely did not, understand why. The man was decidedly fucked up, the shits for a father, but come on! He went back to St. Louis, to a fucking job that would have bored the shit out of Paul in ten minutes! Paul just could not wrap his mind around it. All he wanted from the rest of his life was the finest weed and the finest women Planet Earth had to offer! It was not a lot to ask, in his considered opinion. To stay high and have sex with beautiful, loving women would be enough. There was nothing else worth doing, not discount his literary ambitions. He honestly believed he had paid his dues. He was not required to participate in the "normal" pursuits of life in the world—especially those demanded by a government that had sent him, and many of his generation, to this alien environment to die and be sacrificed in the crucible of their greed; that stole their youth and aged those who survived by a thousand years, yet admittedly gave us the opportunity to emerge from the waking dream of naïve innocence and "normality" and be initiated into a much larger and more vibrant reality—even if that awakening would cost years of tortured sleep, nightmares, violence, intrusive thoughts, broken relationships, flashbacks and substance abuse. This journey had led them to the only real home anyone has—to the heart of hearts where all must come eventually to find the essence of all that they have ever sought in the world outside—love, honor, recognition, comfort, peace, and a sense of belonging in the most cellular sense of oneness with the All That Is.

"Hey man! Wake up! You're up!"

He had been moving along as if in a waking dream. He shook his head as the man in front of him stepped to the highly polished wooden counter, handed over a stack of orders, and receiving a thick manila bound folder containing a complete list of his exploits and movements since he had entered the service—his 201 file, the most precious going-home paperwork there was, his holy grail.

"Skying up, dudes!" he said, raising his thumb in the air.

"Right on, brother!"

"Save me a spot on the Freedom Bird!"

"Get ready world! Here I come!"

This was it! His turn!

He repeated the drill and waited, standing at the highly polished counter, fidgeting anxiously shifting from foot to foot—and waited. And waited. And waited.

He started to perspire profusely, not giving a damn too much any longer about his uniform shirt. His every paranoid thought assaulted him like a colloquium of discarnate spirits released from their warding to have a holiday in his head. Something was seriously wrong.

Then the clerk returned without his file.

"What's going on, man? Where's my 201 File?"

"I'm sorry," he said in a cold and efficient voice. "Your Personnel File has been flagged!"

"WHAT??!!"

"I said your 201 File has been flagged pending administrative action. I can't release it to you. I'm sorry."

OH, MY FUCKING GOD!

Blood drained from his face. He felt his heart skip several beats, and almost shudder to a stop. He thought he might just die right there. He leaned across the counter, and whispered in a voice was so thick he could barely speak.

"I'll give you five hundred dollars! Right now!"

He watched the other man's face go from disbelief to incredulity to denial in super-fast time, quicker than the brief time it took for the thoughts to register, and be transmitted along his neural highways.

"A thousand!" He <u>had</u> to go <u>NOW</u>! Had to!

"I'm sorry, man. I'd do it for free, but your file's been sent to Phu Bai!"

OH, MY FUCKING GOD!

All the Biblical plagues of a wrathful God had suddenly been dumped on him while he was simultaneously being infused with vital nutrients to keep him alive so that he would have to be aware of his torment and unable to do anything about it. He couldn't even go comatose. Searing pain and anguish stabbed him. He was paralyzed. His whole delusional network was wrecked, in shambles. Tsunami waves of depression crashed against his chest wall, and tinnitus ran wildly echoing in his ears. He staggered away from the counter with spirals of vertigo spinning and threatening to crush him. Decades of old, moldy memories of being tortured and denigrated by his father took a dramatic rebirth as his vile words and diatribes slammed through him like a kaleidoscopic collage of razor blades—and triggered an avalanche of remorse and self-depreciation that effectively paralyzed him as effectively as a dose of curare.

BASTARDS!

Somebody was fucking with him, and somebody was gonna fucking pay! He didn't know who or how or when, but they were gonna pay! In his enormous pain, he could only entertain fleeting fantasies of slowly torturing his nameless, faceless perpetrators very, very slowly.

His previously indomitable spirit had been hit hard, but it was not in tatters from the collision with the Army's reality. Benumbed and abandoned by the Spirit of the Universe, he felt like a molested child chosen to provide sadistic pleasure for his captors. Violated for unnamed sins, as if he had walked into a black hole, the gaping vortex sucking his soul and the marrow from my body, his molecules torn apart, vaporized by the impersonal magnetic forces. He felt as if there was a small and ferocious animal trapped in his belly chewing its way out, determined to escape.

There was tremendous wheel spinning in his head, and he was trying desperately to grasp any of the vertices to stop the centrifugal progress. He had to keep moving. He had to go home! The fuckers could not keep him! His psych training told him to forgive himself for his part in the debacle. If he appeared victimized, they would fucking cut him up into little tiny ribbons., shred him without mercy! He had to go in as strong as he could, and his being so pissed off at himself was not going to help unless he could claim a psychotic break from the Romilar! Then they'd fucking bust him for drugs! Fuck! Double fuck!

He was so pissed for being mentally ill, for being him, for being so incredibly naïve, and foolish. He went in search of a bunker and some solitude. Then he collapsed and sobbed until he could almost not breathe—and then, his old friend the end, started a dialogue with him that kept growing stronger. He was visited by all the demons from Hell with his name on their dance card. He shouted and screamed.

HE WAS SO GODDAMN PISSED!

He wanted to up a whole lot of people. Fuck! He was supposed to be going home! Today! How dare those motherfuckers fuck with him! How dare they fucking keep him from his goal, from his dreams!

GODDAMN MOTHERFUCKERS!

At length, exhausted, he fell asleep against the wall of the bunker, no longer thinking, no longer caring, no longer dreaming. He was spent. The depth of his insidious shallowness had been revealed to him, and did not like what he saw—a weak, deluded individual with the thinnest veneer of awareness and sophistication; a madman most likely, wandering through the world pretending to be sane; pretending to be a grown-up—all the while harboring this quivering, shivering infant in his gut, who did not know better than to embrace a bright and shiny adventure imperiously, as if protected by the great unseen forces without coming to harm; as if he were infused by the primal innocence of the Universe that always led to paths of righteousness. There was nothing left. It was then that he fell into a dense, fog-filled dream punched up with heavy bass tones and flickering, fluttering images reflected as if on a cave wall, of amorphous, shape-shifting fiery creatures with elongated mouths emitting mournful dirges and subliminal threats in undertones. Their eerie voices were still echoing in him when he awoke in the night, feeling disoriented and disheveled. He decided to smoke the last of the weed he had saved. Fuck it! Didn't mean nothing now. He was definitely NOT goin' home!

When he looked more deeply into his inside mirror, he was able to admit, only to himself, that he had 100% well and truly fucked up! No question. He had threatened the Green Beast, and it was going to give me a royal screwing. The best he could hope for was a quick Article 15, maybe be busted a grade and given a fine before a trip home—he was already past DEROS and ETS! They could decide to give him a Court Martial, but even then, it was unlikely that he would go to LBJ, though that remained his greatest fear.

He couldn't decide what to do. He knew he had to go back to Phu Bai. Conversely, he was overwhelmed and in despair, had no energy to undertake such a journey. He had heard of a guy who had bought a fake passport and got himself home, but then had to contend with both the CID and the FBI on his trail for years until they caught up with him. He didn't have the energy for that either. Suicidal images hovered in his thoughts constantly, and he attempted to counter their intrusiveness by trying to make a decision—maybe just go AWOL in-country again. Maybe if he showed up on his own and turn himself in to Captain Browne, he might be able to avoid MPs, handcuffs, and the stockade.

At some length, he decided "Fuck it!" He had had the adventure of a lifetime; had said, and done, and been things he would never have otherwise had the opportunity; and now the bill was due. He had to stand up like a man and pay. The major impediment to that was that he had been stripped of all of his manly bravado, and exposed for being the undeveloped analog child who really ran the show!

The rage retreated and advanced in him threatening to consume him ("relapsed and remitted" they would say in psych speak). He wanted fucking revenge on whoever was fucking with him—despite the fact that, by the "rules of the game," they were "right." It didn't matter to him! Homicidal images assaulted him, demanding that he fight, that he do something, anything, rather than just lay there in a fucking sodden puddle and be swept along by whatever seemingly greater forces were at work. If he didn't do something, he would be removed from the game board like an errant pawn in a chess match.

He would not be a martyr in some juicer lifer's fantasy of fulfilling "military justice;" would not sacrifice himself on the cross of the crass, nameless and faceless bureaucracy that just did not give a fuck; that had used him and countless others throughout time for venal ends and the profit from their blood and brains; he would not be another a harvest for fat-assed corporate mass murderers in gray pin-stripe safely hiding in the boardrooms of his America—his America, the country he loved, his friend, his lover, his mother, his father. Fuck them all! He would lie, cheat, and steal to get his ass home! Fuck them! Fuck whatever bullshit they might try to pull!

This was his final arena of testing in this land that had already challenged him so severely. He had come too far, done too much, been too much hammered on the anvil of Life itself; had been too well prepared to fulfill a destiny that he as yet only sensed, still forming in days, weeks, years ahead to unfold, whose essence lay in his immediate future. The kind and quality of his being made a mighty instrument of the future was NOW! There was no excuse, no rationalization for demurral. This was undeniable, unavoidable—Fate if you will, that transcended his pitiable need to collapse and regress, only to be lost forever to himself. This was the biggest ordeal yet of his initiation, the one to which he had unwittingly chosen to submit himself for transformation. He would not, could not meekly surrender to the process of his own immolation. He would lie, cheat, steal, kill if he got the chance! Fuck them! He was goin' to go home.

CHAPTER 33

A Reluctant Return

Paul collapsed into an exhausted, dreamless sleep, and woke to greater clarity. At the flight line, he ignored the sideways looks, the taunts and jibes, the acidic diatribes, of all the jerks and assholes who took his battered emotional condition as an opportunity to dump their own shit. He just did not give a flying fuck!

He snuggled down into the cargo netting seat, and shut his eyes—more to keep a keen edge of concentration than to avoid conversation, although the maneuver successfully managed both goals quite well.

Although he was sure that the brass had been notified of his attempted end run—and honestly surprised that he had not been taken into custody for immediate return against his will—he decided to play it by ear when he got back to Phu Bai. He could undoubtedly turn himself in, but how, when, and in what situation, he had not yet determined. Contrary to Bob Dylan, he did need a weatherman to see which way the wind was blowing.

Still wearing his disheveled Class-A uniform and clutching his last set of orders, he stumbled off his flight to Phu Bai. He hadn't eaten in more than a day, but had no appetite. He was awash with the worst depression ever, a dark gray miasmic sky streaked with occasional flashing slashes of brilliant scarlet rage bolts of lightning, like the sky before a massive hurricane. He felt as twirled and twisted as if he were the eye of that catastrophic event. It was made only worse because he was the architect of it.

Everything seemed foreign, otherworldly, as if he had been transported into a doppelgänger war. He kept hoping to wake up from the bad dream. He was listless, lethargic, having no purpose, no direction. He kept seriously questioning his decision to be here, and considered over and over again the new Plan B—to just shoot myself, or swallow a grenade in a bunker. He did not have the balls or the conviction of Bồ Tát Thích Quảng Đức (*Bodhisattva Thích Quảng Đức*) who had been the abbot of the Phước Hòa pagoda who set himself on fire in 1963 to protest the Diệm government's treatment of Buddhist monks. His death did not stop the pogrom, but did serve as an outstanding example of courage and commitment.

He was plagued by volcanic surges of putrid self-repudiation and disgust. He could not resist his own negative self-talk about being less than honorable to himself, and criticizing himself harshly for all the rhetoric he had so frequently preached to others about all experience being grist for the mill for a writer. Was he fucking real or not? Where in the fuck were the guts he needed to stand up and deal with the blatant bullshit? So fucking what if he lost his precious E-goddamn-5 status? He had already milked the shit out of his quasi-Shake and Bake promotions when they were good and useful. So fucking what if I got out an E-0? So fucking what? He would then be the highest rank of all! He would be a newly minted civilian, released upon an unsuspecting world, ready to seriously rock-and-roll!

He thought he must have truly lost his mind. When he thought he saw Jed Porter jauntily walking across the compound whistling, and carrying a handful of papers. But it couldn't be! This cat was wearing Spec 5 stripes, and a Screaming Eagle on both shoulders. Paul thought he must rally be losing it!

As if attracted by a magnetic string, the man-who-couldn't-be-Jed-Porter looked over at him, gave him a cursory glance, and started to walk on before he did a double-take, shook his head, and looked again.

It was Jed fucking Porter! What the fuck?

Glancing back over his shoulder, he turned and walked swiftly toward me.

Paul didn't even have the time or energy to raise his hand to shake or dap before Jed quickly embraced him in a hug. Then he put a hand under his elbow, and very quickly moved him off the main path toward a bunker.

"Jesus Christ, motherfucker! What in the fuck are you doin' here? The fucking First Shirt is seriously fucking pissed! Captain Browne's been notified too, and he is seriously fucking concerned about your mental health! What the fuck, over?"

Paul looked at him with tears rolling down his cheeks.

"I fucked up, man! Made it all the way to my 201 File! I thought I could just slide out of this motherfucker, and get home before anybody noticed!"

"You are one crazy motherfucker!"

Paul just looked at him, a myriad of questions pouring through his enfeebled brain like a flash flood through an arroyo.

"You have taken far too many drugs!"

"I...don't...know what to do."

"That's clear as a motherfucker! You look like shit!

He tried a weak smile.

"Thanks a fuck of a lot!"

He hustled Paul toward a nearby bunker, who followed, a lank stringed puppet in the hands of the marionette, was feeling the incomprehensible weight of all that had befallen him. He felt powerless to combat the tangled skeins of victimization that had infiltrated his brain like the tangled dendrites of Alzheimer's. He felt as if he were living in a world gone mad, a brave new world without compassion, born of new rules with no guidance through the perilous passes.

He sat me down, continued his harangue, taking my inventory.

"You need some fatigues, boots and shit! Where the fuck is your M-16?

"Lost it! And my 45. I ain't got shit!"

He blew out a breath, and shook his head disgustedly.

"You are one sorry ass motherfucker, you know that?"

"Look man, just leave me here and go on about your business."

"Sure man! You're doing so fucking good on your own!"

"I got my ass here, didn't I?"

"Yeah, exactly what in the fuck <u>are</u> you doing here?"

"I...didn't know where to go. Figured the MPs would be looking for me!"

"Goddamn straight! They're every-fucking-where looking for you!"

"Shit!"

"I'm surprised they weren't waiting for you at the terminal!"

"I guess I'm just fucking lucky, huh?"

"Ya think?"

"Wait a minute! Wait a minute! What the fuck are you doing here? And when did you make E-5?"

"It was gonna be another fifteen months back in the world, so I extended."

"You what?"

"I ex-fucking-tended! Ten months! First Shirt arranged it so it comes up as a new tour, but I couldn't get the thirty days leave. So, they gave me the grade to keep me here! Official chair-borne ranger!"

"They can fuck you now! Send you to the bush!"

"Nevah hatchee, GI! They really like me. Besides, who the fuck you think does all the paperwork here?"

He started to laugh, then cry, then started hacking as if he had been smoking five packs a day.

"Wouldn't you fucking know it? You coming up roses, and I'm eating shit pie!"

"Just sit tight here. I'm gonna see if I can get you a shower and a re-supply. Nobody should bother you. If anybody does, make up some kind of story."

"Whoa! Slow down dude! You're moving really fast!"

"No, dude! You're moving really slow! Get your shit together!"

Paul managed a closed fist and we dapped.

"Righteous, man!"

Paul fell back against the wall of the bunker, and wished he could sleep some more, and wake up and find out it had all been a bad dream. Or even better, find out that he had been having a flashback and was actually at home in San Francisco, having ingested some bad drugs!

Just then this crazy-looking guy with cockeyed glasses stuck his head in.

"Wanna smoke some weed?"

I managed a crooked grin, and replied, "Hell, yes, brother!"

We dapped, and he pulled out a well-seasoned bowl. We each had two hits from his bowl that he swore had "never held anything but weed." Far more relaxed, he sat back and Paul related his forlorn tale.

"I know just what you need, brother," he said, then uncapped a small glass vial filled with a black viscous substance. Preoccupied, I drew on the pipe like a newborn at the nipple. I took another deep hit...

...and was engulfed by a tidal wave of relief, the soothing anodyne of aromatic smoke whispering to him that all would be well. He felt instantly freed of all thoughts, all fears, all feelings. He was a hollowed-out husk. The healing sacrament worked its way through his opioid peptide receptor sites leaving just a slight bittersweet aftertaste under his tongue and his bowels turned into a sloshy liquidity releasing him from all boundaries and his yearning burning heart, stripped naked, mind blanked, went on working with no needs, simply quivering for a little more.

He had another deep hit. And another. He finally drifted away. All fear had fallen as if a molted skin, as he flew away in a narcotized cloud of unconcern, enveloped in a haze, down narrow hallways and twisting defiles. He had no idea, or concern that he had been introduced to a form of salvation—black tar opium, fresh from mama-san's kettle. The euphoric sense of peace was extraordinary, beyond anything he had ever known. He had no hopes, no dreams, no aspirations, but it was not despair—it was simply the way it was.

When Jed came back, he found Paul there alone, drooling, propped up against the bunker wall, eyes glazed, adrift upon an inner sea, with the sun burning down, yet not scorching his skin. He was not hungry or thirsty, did not want anything. He was floating, listless, with no need to summon vitality—until a massive half-shark looking dinosaur breeched the water about fifty yards away; and lobtailed, sending a needle spray of water droplets toward him that penetrated his skin, and cut him into a million tiny pieces that each took flight as small carnivorous birds.

"You fucking asshole! I go away for half an hour, and you get all fucked up! It fucking figures!

"It's OK now, brother! It really is!" he said, drooling some more before he turned to the side and puked dry. There was nothing in his belly.

"Yeah, that looks really good, man!"

Paul hated puking, but the soft afterglow was analgesic. He had to have just a little more. It was magical, his lack of concern, especially when he was *in extremis*. Jed hustled him into the shower, and then gave him a worn set of set of fatigues, and even found a pair of boots that fit. Jed left to make his presence official. He told Paul to lay low, and he would manage the First Shirt and the CO. The real problem apparently was that the Command Sergeant Major (CSM) of the 101st Airborne, Maxwell "Max" Hoxley was arguing in favor of a Court Martial, claiming he wanted Paul to be an example to the rising wave of young troopers with their FTA attitudes. He did not want me to go home, and Paul could not get jail time with any lesser punishment. Meanwhile the Commanding General favored an Article 15 so Paul could just go home.

Paul immediately started having fantasies of walking into a Quonset hut to find Hoxley duct taped to a chair, blindfolded and gagged. He would only ask one question: Why him? No matter what he answered, the torture routine would be fairly basic. Paul figured he could think up some new twists to old favorites involving a blow torch, a screwdriver, pliers and a scalpel. The latter could be used to cut off his eyelids so he could not close his eyes He would also install a heparin lock so I could infuse him with either adrenaline or narcotics, depending on which way he wanted to go to keep him alive a long, long time. He was determined to get beneath the superficial answer of "making an example" of him. Paul really wanted to know. He was truly boggled by the sclerotic military viewpoint! Did the CSM actually believe that giving Paul a Court Martial would stanch the growing flow of anti-military sentiment both in the ranks and in the population at large?

Paul considered that he might be projecting his rage at his father onto yet another man who he considered abusive and arbitrarily fascist. Paul wanted Hoxley to cry through his broken teeth that his own Daddy had beat him and fucked him; and that he had become a "hard guy" to impress everybody with what a real man he was!

Jed smuggled me out some chow. Since the shower, Paul had noticed that he actually had a bit of an appetite, and a stronger sense of will, a renewed desire to live. By the time Jed joined him in the bunker for an after dinner "smoke," he was feeling pretty prime.

"So, what's the latest?"

"Muhammed Ali! He's the greatest!"

"Thanks, ass wipe! Seriously? Do they know I'm back?"

"Not yet. That's something we need to plan out so you don't end up in LBJ while you're waiting for trial."

"You think they might do that?"

"Hoxley is a motherfucker! He really wants you to go to LBJ!"

"Can they do that?"

"Depends on the Court Martial, and the panel."

"What do you mean?"

"I been studying up on this. For a Summary Court, you can ask for an NCO on the panel, a single judge, or a panel of three—unless they choose a higher level, like a Special or General Court."

"Fuck a bunch of NCOs! They'd just do whatever Hoxley wants to kiss his ass!"

"That's what I thought too."

"What else?"

"Summary Court is not much worse than an Article 15. They cannot send you to LBJ, or give you a BCD."

"That's good."

"They can decide to fine you two-thirds of one month's pay and bust you to E-4!"

"Fuck them! As long as Hoxley gets to shit in his hat about me not going to LBJ!"

"They won't convene anything as heavy as a General Court for such a piddling thing, no matter what fucking Hoxley wants. The CO got called over to Division today. They called the Battalion and the Brigade Commanders too."

"How do you know?"

"Who do you think drove the both of them?"

"No fucking shit?"

"Hell no!" he exclaimed, and we dapped.

"And?" he questioned, making the come-on sign.

"General Melda gave Hoxley permission to speak freely, and he was cursing you as being worse for morale than the NVA!"

"Fuck! No!"

"Fuck yes!"

"What did Melda have to say to that?"

"I couldn't hear it all, ya understand. I was supposed to be just waiting there—couldn't show too much interest."

"And?"

"I heard Melda telling Hoxley to back off! To give you an Article 15, and send you home. You're already past DEROS and ETS."

"Yeah, and?"

"Hoxley is so fucking pissed! Said the 101st had 'to make an example out of you, being an NCO and all!"

"What? I'm practically a civilian!"

"Tell him that!"

"Fuck! Now what?"

"Looks like you're goin' to trial, brother!"

CHAPTER 34
O-P-Yum

For the next couple of days, Paul stayed stoned, leaving the womb-like confines of the bunker only to occasionally skulk about in the earliest hours of the morning. Fortunately, they weren't getting hit too often, so he had little to disturb him in his little hideaway. He and Jed argued about the best approach to turning himself in. Paul wanted to contact the Judge Advocate General's Office to secure a lawyer. Jed countered, telling him that he wouldn't get a lawyer until he was charged, and the JAG office would just turn him in if he showed up there. They were, after all, military officers. He hadn't yet told Jed, but he had thought of turning himself in through Captain Browne.

The man with the horned-rim glasses reappeared magically at "his bunker" late, late one night. I noticed that he had a CMB above his left fatigue jacket pocket.

"Hey!"

"Hey, man!"

"How you doin'?"

"That's a hard one to answer. Better than last time I saw you, but still boo coo fucked up!"

"Sounds like you might need some medicine!"

"That shit was awesome—until I puked!"

"Totally normal."

"Normal?'"

"Your body produces opioid peptides—enkephalins and endorphins. When you use opiates, it paralyzes your gastric motility. Your belly shuts down, and it relaxes the smooth muscles. So, you get nauseated and puke—until you get strung out that is, and develop a tolerance."

"How do you know so much?"

"I always research any drug I use."

"Who in the fuck are you, dude?"

"Just call me "Tripper."

"I'm Paul."

We dapped.

"Do you want a little taste more of my magic formula?"

"Hell yes! That shit," he said, motioning to the little glass vial that had suddenly appeared in his hand, "is in-fucking-credible!

"Do you want it on your weed, or straight?"

"Why in the fuck are you being so generous? What do you want from me?"

"Nothing, brother. Just responding to a man in need."

"But why?"

"I could just say it's my job—and it is, but on a deeper level."

"What the fuck does that mean?"

"I was in the boonies for eight months. At first, I made a lot of cherry mistakes. One day I was tending to this sucking chest wound, and the whole world snapped into sharp definition. I realized that I had to do my job the very, very best I could, no matter what was expected or demanded of me by the bureaucrats! The Buddhists call it 'dharma,' sacred duty."

"Wow!"

"For me, it's more than just saving lives. I apply my healing skills wherever and whenever they are needed without any relations to arbitrary power structures!"

"What's that mean?"

"Like the other day. You were clearly in pain. But no doctor would give you opium! Fuck no! They'd put you on some kind of fucked up psych meds, and expect you to wait six weeks to feel better!"

"Fuck that!"

"I decided to listen to my intuition, and dispense you the very best medical care I could. Fuck what the system says!"

"Well, brother, 'I need some real pain killer, or I believe I will be dead!'"

"I'm a Blue Cheer fan too! You know they're all millionaire junkies, don't you?"

"No shit? I didn't!"

"God's fucking truth!"

"But why me?"

"My intuition. Simple as that."

"The smoking lamp is lit, brother!"

"Try this," he said, producing a small brass pipe with a tiny bowl.

"What the fuck?"

"It's what the locals use."

"OK."

He re-capped the liquid, and pulled out a cellophane package with a big splat of black, sticky looking stuff in it.

Following my eyes, he said, "Same same shit, just easier for the pipe."

He then rolled up a tiny ball, put it in the pipe, and handed it to me.

"Just kick back. I got this."

With that, he fired up his butane lighter (where the hell did he get that?), heated the small ball until it started to bubble, then applied the heat underneath the bowl to allow radiant heat to finish what he had started.

Paul applied his lung power to the healing smoke, and soon drifted right out of the present tense as his eyelids closed. Tripper soon took the pipe from his hand, although he would continue making frequent "home visits" to Paul's lair.

As he felt the blanketing comfort steal over him, Paul no longer felt alone. He was surrounded by invisible visitors who brought messages from other worlds, speaking to him of peace, release, quiet, surcease. Swirling pastels and neon phosphorescent splashes painted themselves against his closed eyelids—canary yellow, sea foam green, cerulean, emerald, orange, amethyst, malachite, and blazing scarlet. He flowed with the tides of fluctuating emotions that moved his mind light years from his pinpointed perspective to a vastly expanded world where he no longer cared what might come. He was safe with O-P-YUM. Joy and sorrow, all things held sacred to others, became in very short order, like a drop of water to the ocean; all human values dropped away as superficial and unnecessary, even toxic, like the rotting skin of a leper. He became a spectral figure who haunted the ancient mausoleum of his heart, a living suicide, lost in the bittersweet thrall, moment-to-moment enmeshed and inflamed, addiction flailing him with a thousand tongues of forgetfulness, transforming him in this molten crucible of his own fashioning, taking him far, far beyond the pale of normal human understanding, as if he were a demented movie projector gone berserk It did not matter. Nothing did, just him and good brother O.

As time went by, silently and without significant influence in terms of his direction in life, he found myself hearing the resonating words of one of his personal heroes, the modern American bard, Bob Dylan, playing in a loop in my mind and my life. "To dance beneath the diamond sky with one hand waving fee, silhouetted by the trees, circled by the circus sand, with all memory and fate driven deep beneath the waves—let me forget about today until tomorrow."

All time blended into a synchronous splash, and he witnessed himself and others experiencing the daily *Sturm und Drang* without really participating in it, without having to be drawn into the drama of it, or affected by all the laborious emotions and their attendant attachments. He sat in the center with whirling, swirling madness all around him. He alone was untouched by illness or injury, an arcane potentate in an abstract kingdom. It may have been days, it may have been weeks he had disappeared within his own twisting defiles, his blessed womb, the cocoon of his isolation, but Jed arrived one day to violate his insulation, invading the bunker one afternoon, shaking him heavily enough that he actually had to focus.

"What, man? What the fuck?"

"Wake up, motherfucker!"

"What? Why"

"You mumbled something about Captain Browne a few days ago."

"I did?"

"Yeah, you did."

"So?"

"He's here."

"Where?"

"Here, on the compound."

"What? Why?"

"He's here to see clients...I talked to him briefly. He wants to see you."

"When?"

"Right now. Today!"

"No can do!"

"Get your fucking ass up!"

"Aw, man, don't be a drag!"

"You been sitting here for three fucking days! The only time you've moved is to piss and light your fucking pipe!"

"So?" Three days? Felt like eons.

"Yeah!"

"Oh, my fucking God, brother! That fucking shit is a fucking miracle!"

"Miracle, my ass! The only miracle you're going to get is if they don't send you to LBJ, asshole!"

"It'll be OK. They'll just give me an Article 15, and send me home!"

"Man, are you demented? Your fucking Court Martial is just waiting for you to show up!"

"What?"

"Fucking Hoxley has the fucking MPs looking everywhere for you! He really wants you bad!"

"Shit! I forgot! What a bummer!"

"So, I talked to Captain Browne. He may be willing to help you turn yourself in."

"When?"

"I told you! Now!"

CHAPTER 35
The End?

"Well, well, Specialist Marzeky!"

Doctor Martin Browne managed to look casual and relaxed in his tailored fatigues, and a smile that expressed awareness of human nature that surpassed the ordinary and banal. He radiated empathy and compassion, even as much as he lived in this land of the ever-strange and unusual.

"Sir."

"Seems you've got a little problem."

"Sir."

"You should be home already? Is that correct?"

"Sir."

Paul could feel the walls of his isolation and cupidity breaking down even under this gentle questioning. He had a sudden flash of how horrible it might be to be interrogated by a nasty fucking lifer lawyer! Shit! He felt tears rolling down his cheeks.

He shook his head, not unsympathetically, and said, "What are we going to do with you?"

"Sir?"

"Captain Ryder always spoke highly of you."

"Sir?"

"I always thought you were an intelligent fellow."

"Sir."

"Yet you're standing here, AWOL, uniform a mess; probably no shower for what? Three days? And," he paused for what might have been dramatic effect, "You're addicted to narcotics too, aren't you?"

"Sir. Just smoking a little opium. Sir."

"As I said, 'addicted to narcotics.'"

"Sir. Yes, sir."

"I may be able to help you, but you have to cooperate with me. And you may not like how that looks."

"Sir?"

"Command Sergeant Major Hoxley wants to crucify you. You know that, right?"

"Sir."

"He has this sense that you just don't give a fuck any more about his Army! Is that correct?"

"Sir."

"Your demeanor proves that to be true. So, here's what I propose. Are you ready?"

"Sir."

"I can't stop the Court Martial, but maybe I can help blunt the effects a little."

"Sir."

"You need to start saying more than 'Sir.' OK?"

"Sir."

"I believe something significant has happened to you here in Viet Nam. I mean, starting with the death of Captain Ryder. Would I be correct?"

"Sir."

"You've got to give me more than that!"

"Sorry, sir."

"You're going to have to be completely honest with me. Do you understand?"

"Sir. Yes, sir."

"So. Tell me how you feel."

"Sir? When, sir?"

"Don't act dense! Now!"

"Sir, I've...been smoking some opium. You say it's been three days."

"That is correct."

"Well, right now, I feel OK."

"I need more than 'OK.'"

"Well, kind of spaced out, peaceful even."

"That'll all change when you stop using."

"Stop using, sir?"

"Part of the plan. Will you agree?"

"I...don't know, sir."

"Let me tell you the rest of it, and we'll see if we can't come to some sort of agreement. OK?"

"Sir."

"Sergeant Major Hoxley wants you in the stockade until your Court Martial!"

"Sir."

"So, if you are hospitalized," he said, pacing in a wide circle, "you would not be able to go to the stockade, though you might be handcuffed to the bed with an armed guard nearby."

"Sir?"

"I believe you may have suffered traumatic dissociation, or what used to be called 'Combat Neurosis' in WWII."

"Sir."

"Before I was drafted, I was working with a group of psychiatrists working on a new diagnosis based on surviving trauma. We don't have a name for it yet, but we're considering 'Post Traumatic Dissociation Disorder,' or 'Post Traumatic Combat Stress Disorder.'"

"Sir?"

"The idea is that a soldier might have had such horrible or traumatic experiences in a war that he is changed in fundamental ways, such that he is no longer able to function. He may have a psychotic break even, start using drugs for no seeming reason, maybe even go AWOL when he has, up to that point, been an upstanding soldier."

"Sir."

"Are you getting any of this, Marzeky?

"Sir. Yes, sir!"

"Do you see how this might apply to you?"

"Sir. Yes, sir!"

"So, I'm playing with an idea that might help you. But, as I said, you would have to cooperate with me."

"Sir. Yes, sir!"

"You're going to have to go to trial. No question."

"Sir."

"The greatest likelihood is that you'll not go to jail."

"Sir."

"And you will have to admit under oath exactly what has been happening to you since Captain Ryder's death."

"Sir? All of it, sir?"

"All of it, Marzeky."

"Sir, I won't give up anybody else's names, sir."

"You might not have to."

"Sir, I will not give up anybody else!"

"That will probably be OK."

"It will have to be, sir! It's a deal killer, sir!"

"OK! OK! I won't ask you for anybody else's names!"

"Not you. Not the fucking prosecutor! I won't give 'em up, sir!"

"They'll probably give you immunity to do so."

"I don't give a fuck! I'll go to fucking LBJ first!"

He looked at me for a long time, and simply said, "I see."

"God's truth, sir!"

"I understand."

"So, what the fuck am I supposed to do now, sir?"

"I'll walk you to the CO's office, and you'll turn yourself in!"

"Now, sir?"

"And then I will put you in the hospital for narcotics detoxification and Combat Neurosis!"

"But sir, there's a whole lot of guys out there who are boo coo more fucked up than me!"

"Yes, that's true. But there are very few of them who have functioned as a 91G20 in country for as long as you have—and had all the traumatic experiences you have both seen yourself, and heard from others."

"Sir."

"You not only have suffered actual and direct trauma—mortar attacks and such—but you have experienced what we call 'vicarious trauma,' witnessing the traumas of others. Captain Mieszcowitz put in a Letter of Recommendation for you."

"He did?"

"Yes. He was very impressed with the work you did at Battalion Aid with that fellow...Arrow."

"I'd feel safer if it was a done deal, sir, and I was already in the hospital when they find out about me!"

"I...am not sure I can arrange that."

"Sir, you have to! I don't trust the Sergeant Major...or any of his lifer friends!"

"I understand."

"Give me until tomorrow, sir!"

"Why?"

"There's something I need to take care of before we go any further!"

"Can I trust you to present yourself here at 1000 tomorrow morning?

"Sir. Yes, sir! My word, sir!"

CHAPTER 36

Kickin'

Paul had ten grams of black tar stashed in the hollow leg of his bunk, but he was bound and determined to keep his word. He would meet the good Captain the next morning. Between then and now he was gonna detox with a little help from his friends. He was restless and twitchy between visits to the shitter, his belly alternatively cramping and then turning liquid; his vision increasingly filled with a hostile array of dragons, serpents, gargoyles and demons, many in lurid, psychedelic colors.

He had developed the worst migraine he'd ever had, and it had started to metastasize to his inside out stomach, his wildly spasming spleen, and his madly quivering liver. It coursed through his internal highways like a sea of napalm, devastating every internal organ. Even his toenails felt ill. He was vomiting from all his pores and orifices simultaneously, as vital fluids streamed and steamed through him, as he spilled viscous gouts of tears, his fears singeing all of his cilia and villi. His throat closed, and he thought he might be experiencing total organ failure. Every muscle and tendon was completely transformed by the icy fire that infected his brain pan with the only currency his body understood—the excruciating pain that was the price of his addiction to pure Viet Namese opium—or rather the tormenting, unrelenting lack of it as he kicked, cold, cold, bitter cold turkey.

Paul felt like ten pounds of shit in a five-pound bag. Cold perspiration was copiously pouring out of him, hot urine running down his legs, and he cried "Oh sweet Jesus, help me! Make it go away!" And he prayed to just die, and found supreme empathy with William Burroughs' rhetorical question in *Naked Lunch*: "I'd kill my own mother for another shot of heroin, wouldn't you?"

He kept purging and puking. His existential madness was excoriating him. He was beyond fear. He had come to believe! Those existentially shattered moments brought him pictures of a vision beyond whatever malicious machinations might lie ahead! HE WAS GOIN' HOME! Nothing could harm him. He was beyond the pale of normal human understanding and experience, walking amongst the gods and goddesses of Mount Olympus! His exhausted sphincter let loose over and over, and he filled his pants with multiple times. He felt dirty and defiled, didn't want to be touched, could not stand to be touched! As Jed approached, he held out his hands palms out.

"It's OK, brother! It's OK!" he said and drew closer.

A whole bunch of my good brothers dragged me pissing and shitting and puking into the showers, and stripped off my clothes. HE WAS GOIN' HOME! Mother Kali was ravaging his very soul as sheets of white hot phosphorous flashed up and down his spinal column. HE WAS GOIN' HOME! He was castrated and eviscerated by syphilitic gophers; crucified and quartered; stretched on the racks of a thousand lands for unknown crimes and deprivations. He didn't care! HE WAS GOIN' HOME! Thick, black, torpid ropes of unidentifiable toxins and other viscous fluids poured out of his every pore as incandescent flames of ecstasy and exquisite agony, ate through his muscles, tendons, and nerves. HE WAS GOIN' HOME! Numinous holy flame convulsions ravaged his heart and shut down his airway. Jed jumped in to clear it, waters of initiation pouring over us both, a soul baptism, brothers forever. He WAS GOIN' HOME! Rockets and mortars slammed into the compound, shattering buildings, planes and people, but no one cared. No one left him even for a moment. His good brothers stayed with him, cared for him in the most tender and perfect ways he had ever known, as he cursed and spit, raging at them to kill him, to help him kill myself, to give him some dope, to make it stop. HE WAS GOIN' HOME! HE WAS GOIN' HOME! HE WAS GOIN' HOME!

Chapter 37
Moving Right Along

First Sergeant Moder was the first to see him, and called "Attention!" as Captain Browne stepped in beside him. Paul looked saggy, raggedy, clothes baggy, and face sallow; sunken, listless, and apathetic. He was getting clean now, his second day of living without his favorite analgesic.

We quickly worked through the preliminaries, the First Shirt trying to dismiss Captain Browne who immediately reminded him that he was there in his role as my superior officer and supervisor.

Moder looked a little nonplussed and then asked, "Where's your shit? Your weapon? Your S-2?"

"I turned it all in. I've got the slip somewhere."

"You don't have a weapon?"

"No. I lost my M-16. Gave away my SKS."

"No grenades or knives?"

"No."

"I'll have to search you."

"I understand."

I stood slowly and he frisked me, checking all my pockets, and turning them inside out.

Then he spoke to Captain Browne said, "I am under orders to take Specialist Marzeky to the stockade, sir!"

Captain Browne stood tall and spoke.

"I have already arranged a bed at the 85th Evac for the Specialist. He will be undergoing Psychiatric Evaluation and other medical procedures!"

"But Sergeant Major..."

"It does not matter what the Sergeant Major wants at this point. This man is in dire need of medical attention, and he's going to get it! That supersedes any orders for his custody! Of course, you may elect to handcuff him to his bed, and place a guard on duty 24/7. That is entirely within your purview. You may not keep me from ordering him to the hospital right now! This is a medical priority!"

Very shortly and very smartly I must admit, I was moved to the 85th Evac, showered, shaved (even my outrageous moustache, part of the deal I had cut), and handcuffed in bed. There was an armed guard posted immediately inside my room. At first, he stood at Parade Rest. Then, very shortly, he secured a chair, and was merrily reading a Richard Farina paperback. Very shortly thereafter, Hoxley sent in some of his lifer friends to intervene, or rather attempt to contravene Captain Browne's orders—all to no avail. Fortunately, Captain Martin Browne had left explicit orders that I was not to be moved, even to another bed, without his specific say so. I had no doubt that he himself would show up. Before he did, Hoxley was haranguing the doctors and nurses, trying to order them to discharge me into his custody on his own authority! Hoxley was standing by the side of my bed, harassing me, using very vile words and tones, cursing me and calling me names for which his mother would have boxed his ears—and then he got a good strong dose of my attorney's wrath.

"Danny Boy" O'Malley of "South Boston, Mass," was a very fiery fellow. He had bright red hair, and a loud voice twice as big as his diminutive size. It was my good fortune that he walked onto the ward as Hoxley was in the middle of his dramatic exposition.

"Sergeant Major! Don't you know to come to the position of attention in the presence of an officer?"

He did so, and asked, "Permission to speak, sir?"

"Certainly!"

"Sir, I don't know who you are, but this man..."

"...is my client! And I'll ask you to never again address him without my being present! Is that clear?"

Hoxley left in a palpable cloud of funk, like an octopus in a cloud of ink, muttering volubly about the Commanding General, and stormed out cursing.

"Thank you, sir. He's the miserable son of a bitch that is having me Court Martialed. He was in here spouting all kinds of bullshit about it being my 'patriotic duty' to take a jail sentence so I'll be 'an example to others!'"

"Jesus! He's worse than I thought he might be!"

"Sir."

"Rumor had it that he's a real asshole!"

"Sir." I was nonplussed by this brash man's honesty.

We shook hands and introduced ourselves.

"What about the CG, sir? I understand Hoxley has a lot of pull."

"He's one of the really old timers—WWII, Korea, second tour here, so yeah, he's got some juice!"

"So, he can fuck with me?"

"Not like that, he can't! If he shows up here again, or any of his lifer friends, make sure you get all their details. Better yet, call the guard in to witness what is being said!"

"Wow! No shit!?"

"No shit! Just because you fucked up doesn't mean we're gonna let that old lifer, or his buddies, fuck with you! You're my client now!"

"Thank you, sir! I can't wait 'til you make him eat a big pile of hot steaming shit in court!"

He held up both of his hands palms out, and said, "Whoa! Whoa! I didn't promise you that!"

"What?"

"You now have client privilege with me. Anything you tell me stays between us. I cannot be forced to divulge confidential information."

"And?" Waiting for the hammer to drop.

"And you have to 'tell me the truth, the whole truth, and nothing but the truth,'" he said, making air quotes with his fingers. "Only a total fool lies to his attorney, though God knows plenty try."

"And?"

"So, I want the full story. I don't care how bad it sounds, or how embarrassing it might be, I want the truth! Got it?"

"Sir. Yes, sir."

"Start with why you went AWOL."

Paul opened up, told him the whole story, scrolling backwards and forwards as different pieces fit together in more or less coherent ways for him. Well, almost the whole story. He left out the part about the Romilar, but that was still too weird to talk about. He couldn't find the right words to express his congealed emotions. He was still having the whirling-twirling flashbacks of neon spirals, but he was touched that "Danny Boy" had reached out. He couldn't cop to all of what had really happened, even though Perry Mason always had said you have to tell your attorney everything!

"They have the preponderance of the evidence to convict you," he said, eyeballing me as he did so.

Paul sat up in bed, rattling the frame as his metal tether caught and held.

"What the fuck? You mean I'm going to LBJ?"

"I didn't say that. They have a very strong case. They've got the paperwork."

"And what? What do we have?"

"We have me. I am one crackerjack lawyer! That's an old Nor'eastern expression!"

"And what does that do for me?"

He looked directly into my watery, pinpointed eyeballs, at my pale clammy skin, and said very calmly, "That means that I will do everything legally possible to mitigate the charges, and get you the least punishment possible under the law. Thank God you're an E-5! If you were a lesser grade, they could try to send you to LBJ. You extended your tour, you're past DEROS and ETS! It's likely you'll lose a stripe." Then almost as an aside, he said, "What a waste of time and money! They should have just given you an Article 15 and sent you home!"

"I agree, sir."

Even though Paul felt much better knowing he had a sharp lawyer, he still felt weak and monochromatically white. In his head, he was still hearing humpbacked whale songs, long, sonorous and drifting, with eerie melodic highlights and harmonic undertones. Plus, he was keeping the orderly and his guard really busy, running him back and forth to the shitter. But he had kept his word not to use narcotics. Though his detox was continuing, he was feeling better moment-by-moment, much improved. He still didn't understand the Post Traumatic Combat Dissociation thing, though he decided he would ask Captain Browne for some reading material about it.

He wasn't eating, even though he messed up the plates to make it appear that he was. He was so craving Coca-Colas and boxes of chocolate, but all he could manage was an occasional C-Rat "tropical chocolate" bar given to him in moments of compassion by various guards. He kept developing a deeper and stranger sense of kinship with the travails of William Burroughs, another expatriate St. Louisan, who wrote the stunning book *Junkie*. With little else to do but think about his past, he realized that he had probably been a drug addict all of his life. His body had always had its own needs, its own private vices, sustained and maintained like an obese sultan since the first taste of his Strontium-90 saturated mother's milk.

Mostly, he was bored. He did have the opportunity to read a bunch of novels—mostly Westerns, science fiction, and detective stories. The best that he stumbled across was

Stranger in a Strange Land by Robert Heinlein. He really identified with Michael Valentine Smith, being transplanted to a planet far, far from home—and having to make the most of a life completely foreign to him. He got tripped out on the Phillip Marlowe mysteries of Raymond Chandler from the 1930's, and '40s. And a book called *Half-Past Human* by Theodore Sturgeon really rocked him. They would not allow him access to his personal papers, though he mightily craved to start delving into the collection that he and Toad had created.

For the next three days, he had two sessions a day with Captain Browne—at the end of which time, The Boss informed him that he would be going to court soon. He himself was going to appear as a witness to support his stated position that Paul had been "combat wounded," but in a way that did not include loss of blood or limbs.

He explained to Paul, as he would later to the consternation of the Prosecutor, that traumatic adaptations had been around forever. He was going to cite Homer from *The Iliad* in 800 BCE, and Herodotus from 490 BCE, about men who had experienced combat trauma.

"But, sir, I feel so fucking guilty! All those guys who've died...even worse, the ones who've lost arms and legs and eyes! Jesus! They got a right to be boo coo fucked up! Not me!" Paul said, and started crying, crying like he was never going to stop; crying so fucking hard he thought his sternum might crack in half; crying and remembering all of the faces and names of those who come to him for comfort or simply as an administrative chore; crying and remembering all of the times when he had felt he would die, shaking and shivering in bunkers; crying and remembering his fucked up childhood, and his mean and violent father who still carried shit from his own war; crying and wondering if all of this madness of war would ever stop, or would humanity just keep passing it on to future generations, bequeathing them the legacy of their own unlived, unintegrated emotional garbage that they had collectively refused to heal; crying, sobbing, shitting, and spitting until there was nothing left, almost not even air as his airway spasmed and threatening to completely close; choking and gasping as the good Captain had me taken out of cuffs, and then called in a whole load of orderlies to carry me as gently as possible, pajamas and all, into the showers where they washed me and stopped me from slamming my head against the wall long enough for me to collapse completely into a sodden heap. There was nothing left. He knew he was done, come what may, come what might. He was done.

CHAPTER 38
Kafka Revisited

"Danny Boy" had also been visiting every day, filling him with his buoyant energy and a pugnacious spirit that lent him hope. He told me tales of growing up Catholic (now lapsed) in South Boston, and "scrappin" practically every day, often with Blacks from Roxbury—though he had a very healthy, albeit reserved, respect for Captain Browne when their paths intersected. He had told Paul to call him "Dan" when they were meeting privately, His consistent presence always infused him with strength, hope and courage. Visits from the two officers was sometimes the only thing that kept him from leaping over the edge of madness that always lingered seductively just out of reach, and threatened to engulf him.

"I'm a recovering alcoholic, Paul," Dan admitted one day. "I've been through hell with alcohol, spent years trying to stop. So, I have some small idea how difficult it must be for you right now."

Paul was afraid he was going start spouting Jesus at me, but he didn't. Thank God!

"Am I gonna have to testify?"

"Why would you want to?"

"I'd rather not."

"Then that's one less thing either of us have to worry about, isn't it?"

Paul'd started losing some of his deep angst, the sense of impending doom, of his carrying the kind of self-sealing fate that infects many. He felt that there was a certain futility of undertaking any kind of self-improvement, or rising up out of the primal ooze of his own insignificance—especially since everyone is all born just to die anyway.

Martin (privately he was Martin) and Paul had free-ranging conversations (though actually it was therapy), about the quality and nature of my experiences in the 'Nam, though he was especially interested in Paul's reactions to the men with whom he'd had close encounters fresh out of combat.

He elicited from Paul an entire laundry list of missed, suppressed, lost, displaced, or otherwise dissociated emotions and reactions that he had purposely misfiled in the deepest recesses of his internal office.

"Pretty fucked up, huh?"

"Pretty normal, I would say. If it weren't for your high intelligence, I think you might have broken down far sooner."

"Broken drown?" Paul had an eerie feeling about the way Martin said it.

"I won't present it as such, unless I really need to, but, yeah, I would say that you had a classic psychotic break, albeit drug induced—there in Taiwan."

"Sir, I would really rather you not talk about that!"

"I won't, but I need your permission to do so if I feel it's called for. I will be your main witness, attesting to your fragile mental state. Please don't handicap me with making a promise I may not feel I can keep."

"Sir, my attorney doesn't know about that!"

"I strongly suggest you tell him at your earliest opportunity. Remember what Perry Mason always used to say, "Don't lie to your attorney!"

"I loved Perry Mason! But sir, I'm not lying! I just did not tell him everything!"

"I'm quite sure he's told you about confidentiality."

"Yes, sir."

"Then tell him, in case I have to bring it up in court. He needs to know."

In our conversations, Paul kept repeating how ashamed he felt about not being "tough enough." This inevitably led to discussing his father, whose service record might prove useful for Dr. Browne's testimony.

Martin also kept expressing his belief in my potential as a mental health professional!

"Sir, I'm lying here detoxing from narcotics; and you tell me I may have some far-out psychiatric illness that isn't even official yet—and you think I might make a good psychologist?"

"I do, Marzeky. I do."

"Well thank you for that, sir! I'm still getting these blasts of icy fire running through my veins. The Darvon is helping." I'd started with sixty milligrams every four hours around the clock, and had begun a titration schedule that would have me drug-free shortly.

"Are you ready?"

"As ready as I will ever be, sir!"

"I'm glad to hear it!"

"How about you, sir?"

"Oh, I'm looking forward to this! There are only five of us who formed the core of the research team—and none of them are in Viet Nam! So, whoever they put up to rebut or repudiate my testimony will be at a distinct disadvantage—because I really know what I'm talking about!"

"I'm mighty glad to hear that, sir!"

Paul had flashing Technicolor dreams again that night, infused with what he had come to see as the usual bright lurid neon colors, and shapes that glided and swept with eerie voices both mournful and full of glee, that induced nausea and cognitive dissonance in every one of his cells even as a huge charcoal gray pall of dread hung over the battered landscape of his heart and dirges of demons played ceaselessly. In his dream, he barfed and swallowed; barfed and swallowed; needed to puke and piss and shit all at once, but had no mouth, no nose, and no anus. He awoke to cramps and a huge log of compacted shit trying to force its way out of his body through an opening far too small for the massive rock shit that was grinding its way down his intestinal track. He choked on vile acidic bile, and forced himself to swallow, as hot and cold hormones pulsed through him with total indifference to his preferences. His tremulous hands shook uncontrollably as if he had Parkinson's disease.

The guard that day was compassionate, and allowed him to shower unobserved for the first time. He luxuriated in the hot spray and washed myself thoroughly three times. He had also brought me a new set of khakis, and told him Captain O'Malley said to polish my shoes. It seemed really fucking stupid, but if "Danny Boy" said so, he would.

Pulling dignity from unknown sources, and forever rejecting his little citadel of opiated safety, Paul tore the coverings off his naked soul, and managed to walk into court with his head held high. He laughed at what he saw as the joke of "military injustice." He entered the hushed and austere surroundings, and laughed at the unfolding, inane comedy of his trial while the judges, making brief notes on yellow legal tablets as if they were Olympian jurists, glanced appreciatively at the young prosecutor. They seemed quite impressed with him, while they glared at him as if I were a Nazi war criminal in the dock at Nuremberg.

There were two Majors—one Artillery, one Infantry—and a Signal Corps Lieutenant Colonel who was the Chief. They sat behind a polished wooden table and looked on impassively as Paul stood and saluted. He took my seat next to Dan, and awaited the fireworks that were surely going to erupt. He hoped that motherfucker Hoxley would have decided to testify so Dan could rip his fucking guts! It just totally rankled him that "they," the ubiquitous "hey, had been granted the power to judge him! And by what authority?! It had been granted as if by divine fiat and then used against others as if they were, in fact, carrying heaven's blessings. He vowed to myself that he would <u>never</u> again kiss the ass of "authorities", no matter their ilk or what the cost—especially ones to whom he had not granted his authority, his ability to be the author of himself. Fuck them!

The Prosecution painted a very accurate picture of Paul as AWOL, though they had clearly interspersed flashes of the Sergeant Major's vituperative inspiration, terms like "corrupting influence," "poor role modeling for younger troopers," and "wild-eyed radical." Apparently, they were convinced of the strength of their case to the point that they only presented a batch of travel orders and other paperwork as the damning evidence against me, with no actual witnesses, eye or otherwise.

Hoxley had apparently made the wise decision not to testify, but he still found a way to contaminate the proceedings. Otherwise, Paul was quite convinced, Danny Boy would have fed him his fucking bleeding testicles right there in the witness box. Dan spared Paul the ignominy of testifying, citing it as "unnecessary." He had further agreed not to talk about Taiwan and the aftermath, though it was obviously mitigating.

The proceedings moved quickly, and soon Dan addressed the court about Paul's good service record, his many successful assignments in country, his Letters of Recommendation, voluntary extension, decorations, and then painted a vividly worded montage of the staggering consequences of the psychological horrors Paul had endured. Before the Prosecution had a chance to interrupt his eloquent flow, he called Captain Browne as his first and only to support the thrust of his explications.

The young arrogant Prosecutor must have thought he could make mincemeat of the good doctor by inferring that there was something potentially fraudulent about his credentials.

Nonetheless, his petulant attitude, and disrespectful interruptions did nothing to endear him to the Court.

"It says here, sir that you graduated from Harvard Medical School."

"That is correct."

"May I ask where in your class you graduated?"

"Second."

"I see. Out of how many?"

"Two hundred seven."

Instead of stepping out of the shit he had created with his lack of preparation, he decided to start dancing in it.

"And you entered the service immediately upon graduation?"

"That would be negatory."

"Excuse me?"

"That was 'No.'"

"I see. Exactly where did you go?"

"To Cambridge."

"I thought you were in Boston already!" he snickered as he glanced around the packed court room, looking for praise for his petty, snide attempt at humor.

"That would be Cambridge, England."

Now really aware of the extent of his gaffe, the petulant punk started thrashing around, hoping against hope to extricate himself.

"I see. And why did you go there?"

"I was a Rhodes Scholar, and had a Ford Foundation grant as well."

Paul could see the shadows of despair closing down the Prosecutor's face like window shades at dusk.

"I see. Well, thank you, Doctor."

Before the Prosecutor was even in his chair, Dan was up on his feet and gliding forward.

"And for what, specifically, were you given these singular honors, sir?"

"To study the effects of trauma on the human personality. Specifically, human reactions to war trauma. We were re-visiting the research that happened during and after World War Two on men who were diagnosed at that time as having 'Combat Neurosis.' We also reviewed the literature on what was called 'Shell Shock' from World War One. We studied the sequelae or after effects of being exposed to horrendous experiences of combat."

Dan was practically gloating now, but simply smiled. The Prosecutor's face turned an even deeper shade of crimson, as he turned to his co-counsel, desperately seeking to find a way stanch the bleeding he had initiated by not being adequately prepared, after breaking the number one rule of law: Never ask a question for which you do not have the answer!

"Thank you doctor. Is this 'syndrome' a new thing?"

"Most assuredly not! Three thousand years ago, it was documented that an Egyptian combat veteran described severe anxiety symptoms he experienced just before having to return to battle." Then after adjusting the knife-sharp crease in his khaki uniform trousers, he went on. "Herodotus, in 480 BCE, documented the case of a Spartan commander who dismissed his troops from an upcoming encounter at the battle of Thermopylae Pass because they 'had no heart for the battle,'" he said, making air quotes. "He also spoke of a case of hysterical blindness that he witnessed after the battle of Marathon in 490 BCE."

"That sounds as if it happened a long time ago!"

"Men have been creating wars for at least the last nine thousand years!"

"Still, is there any more current research?"

"We have volumes of documentation from WWI and WWII, but more recently the emphasis has been more focused and intense."

"That's quite a history! And you were part of the research group studying this at Cambridge?"

"Yes. There were five of us. I'll be returning to England to re-join the group when I leave the Army."

"Thank you, doctor. Is there anything else?

"Yes, there certainly is!"

"I am the Psychiatrist for the 101st Airborne Division. I have been Specialist Marzeky's immediate supervisor since Dr. Ryder's untimely death. He has done excellent work the whole time I have been here. In fact, I received a Letter of Commendation from Captain Mieszcowitz praising his recent work with a very seriously disturbed combat vet."

"That's all well and good, but we are more concerned here with the charges that have been brought against him."

"I understand."

"I understand that you've spent some time interviewing him vis a vis your obvious area of expertise."

"That is correct."

"And have you come to any conclusions?"

"I most certainly have."

"Would you share your conclusions with us please?"

The Prosecutor jumped up, sputtering. He was either so filled with words that he couldn't speak, or else he was having a stroke.

"Your honor...uh, sir..."

"Mr. Prosecutor?"

"Uh sir, I object!"

"To what?"

"To this...testimony!"

"Why?"

"Captain Browne...sir, he's not an expert!"

Dan jumped up, and stated with great force, "You obviously weren't listening earlier when we were discussing his credentials!"

"Well I am now!" the young Prosecutor pouted as he replied.

"Overruled!"

"But your honor..."

"Sit down, Captain!"

"As I was saying, Specialist Marzeky has been subjected to a great many mortar and rocket attacks. He has received fire during helicopter insertions and extractions undertaken while performing his duties. He has experienced what we call 'vicarious stresses' as a result of interviewing and intervening with many men coming directly from intense combat, who have poured out their turbulent emotions and their stories to him. As a result, he has experienced symptoms similar to those experienced by those who have actually been in combat."

"What is the relevance of this?"

"The charges that have been levied against Specialist Marzeky for Absent without Leave grow out of, or are a result of, his having suffered significant psychiatric injury—directly as a result of his performing his assigned duties."

"So, his are the psychiatric equivalent of a Purple Heart wound?"

"Your Honor..." the Prosecutor was up again.

"Sustained. There is no Army regulation covering psychiatric injuries and the awarding of the Purple Heart."

"Thank you, sir."

"Let me re-phrase. So, doctor, what are you saying?"

"His 'psychological wounding' was absolutely sustained in the line of duty."

"Thank you, doctor. Having unequivocally established your credentials as an expert," and here he looked at the extremely frustrated Prosecutor, "might I ask what behaviors one might expect of someone who experienced such injuries?"

"The nature of the trauma indicates, and I have research data to back me up on this, that it could potentially be life-changing."

"What specific behaviors might one expect in this good soldier's case?"

"I would submit that this type of injury could easily have been one of the precipitating factors that gave rise to an otherwise good soldier—with no previous military or civilian offenses—to act in an aberrant manner."

"Such as?"

"I submit that his behaviors might be totally consistent with his acting as if he could no longer return to any situation that had given rise to his inordinate level of stress. Acting contrary to orders that directed him to resume military duties was not at all beyond the range of what might be expected, given his injury."

"Thank you, doctor. And just to be totally clear—believing that his behaviors are consistent with his seeking to avoid further life-changing stress, in your expert opinion, what do you believe would be appropriate punishment for behaviors consistent with the aftermath of trauma and stress incurred in the line of duty?"

"The man needs to be treated as a psychiatric casualty, not punished."

"Objection, Your Honor."

"Sustained. The doctor may be highly qualified in his field, but he is not an attorney."

Hoxley's face imploded. His eyes went wild with barely-suppressed rage, and his skin turned as bright a red as a blown ammo dump. He looked like a demented three-year-old having a tantrum. Paul lowered his head, and guarding the middle digit of his left hand, raised it in his direction, and surreptitiously saluted him with it.

The Prosecutor completely lost it at this point, screaming shrilly and profaning Paul, his family, his attorney, his entire lineage—and declaiming Captain Martin Browne as "the Anti-Christ!"

CHAPTER 39

Brotherhood

Paul barely made it to the latrine. After he left, he believed that it should have been made off-limits, labeled radioactive for the next ten thousand years!

It had been a night of total celebration. He never realized whether he was popular, or just a cause célèbre. Perhaps he had become an icon for all of the young troopers who fucking hated the Army, and wanted to shove a grenade up its overfunded backside. Every time Paul turned around, somebody was offering him a joint or a bowl, a bottle or a jug. The funny thing is, after the first few hits, he no longer wanted to get blasted. He just wanted to sit and savor a little taste of quiet. He did not want to be sloppy and act without personal boundaries, without moorings, in the fleeting glory of the present. Everybody seemed to be celebrating his anticipated (though still specious) "victory" over the Army and his going home—even though there had not yet been a verdict!

Then it struck him!

HE WAS GOIN' HOME!

He could taste it with his tongue, savoring the flavor of it despite the incredibly fucked up cupric taste that seemed otherwise to pervade his whole body. If he were willing to indulge in it, despite being extremely fearful of being too presumptuous, he felt filled with the glimmerings of a great joy that shone through around the edges of the emotional weight, as if through the craquelure of a masterpiece painting. The awareness, in and of itself, was some small cause for personal celebration; and he was dedicated to not losing his mind, as he had done on countless thousands of other occasions previously, immersing himself in the great, grand flow of unconsciousness, as if it were a true escape from all the shit and grime that had otherwise surrounded him on so many occasions; as if he could really run away from all of the accumulated garbage he had experienced and endured, that he had allowed to accumulate because he had internalized it, compartmentalized it, held it as close as if it were a sacred treasure to be worshiped as a manifestation of the Divine; as if harboring all the shame that he had internalized during the course of his life was not only proper, but somehow natural or deserved; as if the entire Universe had been fashioned in such a way as to honor dysfunction, to distract newly incoming individuals taking birth, to inflict upon each and every one of them the onus of having to endure those sclerotic, contaminated boundaries.

Fuck all that! Paul said to himself, if he got out of here alive, he was going to have a brand-new life!

The vision was strong, and he was just sober enough to exult in the energy all around him, everyone ostensibly celebrating him, but, of course, ultimately using the occasion to release themselves. He could picture the possibility, even just for the tiniest fraction of a second, that such an achievement was within my grasp, the glorious, shining, luminescent possibility he had sought all of his life, pursued relentlessly as if this magnificent opportunity had been simply drifting through his galaxy like a visitor from another realm far away in both space and time.

Jed caught Paul's eye, as he sat imperturbably in the calm center like Buddha under the Bodh tree while being assaulted by all of the demons and temptations of all of his previous lives in order to absorb and integrate them, since they were ultimately all disparate and dissociated aspects of himself that he had disowned through eons of embodiment.

Paul's lifelong sensitivity loud noise had been taken a battering by his exposure to the surreal assault his ears had received there—automatic weapons, artillery, grenades, mines, jets, tanks, rockets and mortars, the screams of the dying and the eternal silence of the dead. He had developed a heightened reflex reaction to any movement that was too quick, and had come to cherish relative quiet wherever he could find it.

They drifted off and found an empty bunker on the other side of the chopper pad. Victor Charles was taking a night off, at least so far, but the collective noise of their excitement would make it easy for any errant lifer to hone in on them.

"Wow, man! Captain Browne kicked ass this morning! Did you see that asshole Prosecutor? Motherfucker blew himself up! They probably got him on a psych unit right now!"

"I thought Hoxley was going to come after me!"

"I was ready," said Jed patting the leather holster on his right side. "I had it in a shoulder harness under my fatigue jacket."

We dapped then, and Paul said, "I...don't know what to say, man!"

"Don't fucking start crying, brother!" Jed exclaimed as tears rolled down his own cheeks.

"Amen, brother!"

He laughed and punched me in the arm.

"You fucking motherfucker!"

Paul laughed, and wiped my face.

"Couldn't help myself, man! I will never forget you in the fucking shower stall! Never! Not if I live a billion fucking years! You saved my life! You cleared my airway and got me breathing again! You are my true brother forever! Any time, any time, the whole fucking rest of your life, you ever need anything, you fucking call me! You hear? Call me, and I will make it happen!"

With that, Paul started crying again, filled with love and gratitude for this man who had become a true brother to him; had sacrificed his own personal safety and comfort to help him; who had stood beside him and shared some of the highest experiences he had ever had; who had given him a connection to a larger sphere of relatedness, and been willing to share it with him. Toad had been the first to break through to him with his honesty, his willingness to communicate; to accept him as an equal even when he felt inferior and unworthy, but it was this man, "Jumpin Jed Porter, Chairborne Ranger Extraordinaire" who had shown him the greatest compassion and what he could only call love that he had ever experienced.

He was on the cusp of the next new adventure, and had absolutely no idea what might come next. Despite his debilitated condition, he felt poised, confident, and open to welcome whatever gifts and bounty Creator might send his way. He was grateful for all he had been gifted.

He and Jed hugged, then dapped.

"I'm dragging, brother! I'll see you in the morning. Thanks for everything!"

Paul awoke long before dawn rested, thinking of something Carlos Castaneda would one day say. "Each of us, whether or not we are warriors, have a quarter centimeter of chance that pops out in front of our face from time to time. The only difference between an ordinary person, and a spiritual warrior, is that the warrior has the speed, the prowess, and the training to reach out, and grab it when it appears."

He prepared myself for court as if he were meeting with a king or head of state. This was his command performance! He felt loose and fluid, as if all of his joints were well-oiled gears meshing synchronistically. His every movement was crisp and without artifice, clean and elegant. His mind felt bright, devoid of self-repudiating rhetoric, feeling as if all that had previously transpired in his life had simply been a preparation for what was still to come. Paul felt a heightened awareness of what he was beginning to think of his spirituality. It felt like an extended sense of his intuition a kind of numinous, immaculate knowing, no matter how debased his circumstances, or sullied his experience, the innate luminosity of his innate nature could never be taken from him!

Paul hit the Mess Hall when it opened at 0600, he grabbed a thick, strong cup of black coffee before the first batch had percolated through. He was tempted to eat, but his belly was still very unsettled. He settled himself comfortably in a far corner with my back to the wall when Hoxley came in, followed by two Sergeants First Class who trailed him like a pair of remoras attached to a large, ugly shark.

Hoxley glared at him, and whispered a snide aside to one of his sycophants. Paul simply smiled, and sipped his coffee. No matter what happened today, he knew he was safe and protected within himself; safe from all of the predators and shame-bearers and all of their fascist baggage. He was feeling infused with a higher energy that seemed to have been hidden deep in him, awaiting his awakening. Nascent, in embryo assuredly, but Paul had found himself, the man he'd always wanted to be alive and ready to grow, a man who was, at long last, deserving of his love.

When Paul got to the court, there was a young "butterbar" (Second Lieutenant) talking with an older Captain at the Prosecution's table. The brash, arrogant, and likely insane son of a bitch from yesterday had evidently been replaced by someone more stable. "Danny Boy" was sitting at our table, humming some kind of Celtic chant.

It did not take long for court to convene. He noticed a lot of the seats that had been filled by lifer assholes yesterday were now taken by brothers from the Medical Company, the Hospital Company, and a significant number of line troops with CMBs and CIBs.

The court came to order, and the Lieutenant Colonel asked me to stand with my attorney, then directed that the findings be read into the record.

"Specialist Five Paul Marzeky, RA 16 988 357..."

"Headquarters/Headquarters Company 326th Medical Battalion, 101st Airborne Division. It is the finding of this Summary Courts Martial Board that in the matter before it, to wit: that on or about the 14th day of April, 1968, you did willfully absent yourself without leave from duty: to wit Company C, 326th Medical Battalion, 101st Airborne Division, Camp Evans, Republic of Viet Nam, by not returning from an authorized Rest and Recuperation of five days in Taiwan, Republic of China; and did so remain absent from said duty station until on or about the 28th day of April, 1968. To all charges and specifications: Guilty as charged."

Fuuuuuuck!

Fucking Hoxley was grinning so hard Paul thought his teeth might crack!

Fuck! Did that motherfucker get to one of the panel of judges? Are these lifer motherfuckers gonna fuck him over?

"Period of time to be charged as time lost will be fourteen days..."

Paul thought, Big fucking deal! (BFD). Then he realized that it was a BFD! They were only charging him with the fourteen days!

"Reduction in rank one grade to Specialist E-4..."

Another BFD—I'd soon be a civilian!

"Pay to be charged $584..."

Clint Tyson in Finance had already assured him that he wasn't going to lose any money!

"EM will rotate to CONUS at the earliest opportunity at government expense..."

The courtroom erupted in cheers from his rowdy brothers. Paul thanked Danny profusely and soon the judge gave up hammering his gavel. No one was listening. Hoxley started freaking out, literally foaming at the mouth, cursing at the top of his lungs, before being dragged away by two of his sycophants.

Paul had just stepped outside, with a grin that ran from ear to ear, and was waiting for the back-slapping and congratulations of his fans from the court room. He had just lit a cigarette when a guy he had last met as Hamilton Burgess, CID, stepped up to him wearing tiger-stripe fatigues and a name tag that read "Oswald" above the left pocket.

"The packet was mine, asshole! Madame Wo sends her greetings!"

Before Paul had a chance to respond, the enraged man punched Paul full in the belly. All of the previous days of nausea, vomiting and caustic stomach; all of the excruciating hours and days of skin-crawling formication; all the days of smelling vile and tasting worse, immersed in his own toxins; all of the endless nights punctuated by diarrheal bursts and night sweats; all of the tortured, itchy-eyed mornings when he did not know or care whether he would live or die—all flew out of his mouth in an acidic, semi-viscous gout of projectile vomiting that hit the other man squarely in the face. He then spun and twisted, screaming and cursing, scraping and tearing at his face to get the vile excretions off. He turned back toward me readying to take another shot at me when he was immediately swallowed by fifteen or twenty of Paul's brothers who swarmed him with punches and kicks, spitting on him, reviling him as he fell to the ground in a sodden, condign heap.

They who had suffered so much fear and despair, so much shame and degradation, so much pain and frustration; who had endured the manic-depressive fluctuations of pleasure and pain that had so defined this war of attrition; who shared the bonds of muscle and thew, of vision and honor; who knew the dignity of another man's tears and the blessing in a comrade's blood; who had walked in the shadow of the valley of death, and walked out again; who were stoned to the bone and fierce of heart; whose trust in each other was a living prayer that eradicated all boundaries; who were a prophecy's fulfillment so subtle as to be overlooked like a diamond in a box full of cut glass—they knew. They would always know. They had paid with their hearts and minds, their eyes and ears and noses, buying the thousands of exotic, quixotic sights and sounds, tastes and smells, demanded of warriors throughout the ages, imprinted in their cells, an eternal, indelible bond, joining them mind-to-mind.

THEY WERE BROTHERS.

Glossary

67th Evacuation Hospital in Qui Nhon

90-day wonders officers who did a 90-day OCS

212 AR 615-212 Undesirable Discharge

AK (AK-47) Kalashnikov Assault Rifle

APC Armored Personnel Carrier

ARVN Army of (South) Viet Mam (see "Marvin")

ATC Air Traffic Controller

AWOL Absent Without Leave

Air America Airline operated by the CIA

Article 15 minor judicial punishment in the UCMJ

a wake up the last day in-country

arty artillery

BCD Bad Conduct Discharge

Binoctal Made in France, a mix of Secobarbital and Amobarbital

black ops assignments carried out without openly designated authorization

Bloods Black people

bac si medic (generic)

bangalore torpedo plastic explosive loaded into bamboo segments

berm perimeter wall

bird helicopter

boo coo   Bastardized French: beaucoup

boom boom   sex

boonies   see *bush*

bush   undeclared, often enemy-held territory (same-same boonies)

butterbar 2nd lieutenant (gold bar)

CC   Convalescent Center

CIA   Central Intelligence Agency

CIB   Combat Infantry Badge

CID   Criminal Investigation Division

CG   Commanding General

CMB   Combat Medical Badge

CO   Commanding Officer

CONUS   Continental United States

CSM   Command Sergeant Major

CYA   Cover Your Ass

C Rat   C ration: precooked individual portions of a meal in a can

Chair Borne Ranger See REMF

Clinical Specialist   91 C 20 MOS (Physician's Assistant equivalent)

Combat Stress Syndrome   old name for Posttraumatic Stress Disorder

cherry new guy (also FNG)

claymore mine   shaped charge made of plastic explosive

crispy critter   Person who has been napalmed

cunt cap   dress uniform soft cap

DEROS Date of Estimated Separation from Over Seas

DMZ   Demilitarized Zone (38th parallel dividing North & South)

didi   Go or go away (often "Didi mau, motherfucker!")

dinky dau Bastardized French: "dien cai dau" crazy; mentally ill

doufuss   incompetent

donut dolly   Red Cross volunteer

E-   Enlisted pay levels (1 to 9)

EM   Enlisted Man

ETS   Estimated Time of Separation (from the service)

early out   see *extend*

extend lengthen one's tour in country so that one has less than 5 months to serve so as to be released early from the service

FNG   Fucking New Guy

FSB   Fire Support Base

FTA   Fuck the Army

First Shirt First Sergeant

frag   fragmentation grenade; also used as a verb as in "frag the man"

G-2   company level intelligence; generic for information

HHC   Headquarters and Headquarters' Company

H & I   Harassment and Interdictment rounds to disrupt the status quo

HQ   Headquarters

ham and motherfuckers   ham and lima beans

hard hat   steel pot (helmet)

heads   drugs users, usually marijuana

hooch   housing unit

hundred-foot interrogations interrogations conducted in the doorway of a chopper, one result of which is to be expelled

Ia Drang Valley   infamous battle depicted in the film *We were Soldiers Once and Young* from the book by Hal Moore

Indian Territory   old school term for *the bush*

juicers   (primarily) alcohol users

KIA   Killed in Action

KP   Kitchen Police

K-Bar   Marine combat knife

Korsakoff's   Confabulation, memory loss, peripheral neuropathy

Syndrome   secondary to severe and chronic alcohol dependence

klick   kilometer (approximately 6/10 of a mile)

LBJ   Long Binh Jail (or Lyndon Baines Johnson)

LRP   Long Range Patrol (pronounced "lurp")

LRRP   Long Range Reconnaissance Patrol

LT   Lieutenant (also "Loot")

LZ   Landing Zone

Lurp rats LRP freeze-dried meals, just add boiling water

MAC   Military Airlift Command

MACV   Military Assistance Command Viet Nam

MOS   Military Occupation Specialty

MP   Military Police

MPC   Military Payment Certificate (in place of money); script

Marvin   see ARVN

mike mike   millimeter

Mr. Charles   Viet Cong (Victor Charles)

NCO   Non-Commissioned Officer

NCOIC   Non-Commissioned Officer in Charge

NG   No good

NVA   North Vietnamese Army

Negatory No

Newpot   Commercial cigarette wrapper filled with marijuana

Number One   The best

Number Ten   The worst

Number Ten Thousand   Unimaginably terrible

Normal   People in the box, straight people

nouc mam   fermented fish sauce

OCS   Officer Candidate School

OD   Olive Drab

OJT   On the Job Training

Oak Leaf Cluster   second award for a medal to be worn on the ribbon

PRC   Also known as Prick-25, or just 25. Field radio-telephone

PSP   Perforated Steel Planking (for runways)

PT   Physical Training

PX   Post Exchange (GI's shopping mall)

piss tube   large diameter plastic tube inserted into the ground for urination

pogie   See REMF

poop   rumors

pucker factor   How tightly your rectum puckers out of fear

REMF   Rear Echelon Motherfucker

RHIP   Rank Has Its Privileges

RPG   Rocket Propelled Grenade

RTO   Radio Telephone Operator

re-up   re-enlist

round eye White person

ruck up   literally put on your rucksack (also get moving)

S-4 Battalion level Supply

SAS Special Air Services (UK)

SOG Special Operations Group (black ops)

STAT immediately

SVAF South Vietnamese Air Force

Seabee Navy construction engineers

Shake & Bake NCOs quickly promoted without coming through the ranks

Stars & Stripes Official military newspaper in Viet Nam

safe (a weapon) assure that the safety is on

same-same nothing is different

scut menial

scuttlebutt rumors (originally a Navy term)

set group of people with whom one smokes weed

short having little time left to serve

short time brief sexual encounter

sin loi see **xin loi**

six rear or back (on the clock)

souvenir gift (used as a verb—"you souvenir me")

speed methamphetamine, though generically applied to all stimulants

strack squared away; proper

TAOR Tactical Area of Operations

TDY Temporary Duty

TNP Taiwan National Police

Tet   Lunar New Year holiday

The World   U.S. mainland (CONUS, or The Land of the Big PX)

Trilateral   a global policy-making group representing the richest and **Commission**   most   influential businessmen and politicians on the planet

tank farm clusters of armored elements

twelve   front side (on the clock)

UCMJ   Uniform Code of Military Justice

USAF   United States Air Force

USAID   United   States   Agency   for   International Development (CIA front)

unass   remove (from)

VC   Viet Cong (Victor Charles)

ville   village

WIA   Wounded in Action

Wash U   Washington University in St. Louis

White Phosphorous   used in all types of munitions. It is self-igniting, burns fiercely any combustible, including skin. producing second- and third-degree burns. It can only be smothered as it will burn the oxygen in water.

Willy Peter   White phosphorous

Winstone   Commercial cigarette wrapper filled with marijuana

xin loi Bastardized Vietnamese: pronounced "Sin Loy," meaning 'tough shit,' or 'sorry 'bout th at.' The literal translation is "excuse me."